CW00735723

The Apple Tree

JEWEL E. ANN

USA Today & Wall Street Journal
BESTSELLING AUTHOR

THE APPLE TREE

SUNDAY MORNING SERIES

JEWEL E. ANN

This book is a work of fiction. Any resemblances to actual persons, living or dead, events, or locales are purely coincidental.

Copyright © 2024 by Jewel E. Ann

ISBN 978-1-955520-56-0

Hardcover Edition

All rights reserved.

This book is a work of fiction and is created without use of AI technology. Any resemblances to actual persons, living or dead, events, or locales are purely coincidental.

Without in any way limiting the author's exclusive rights under copyright, any use of this publication to "train" generative artificial intelligence (AI) technologies to generate text is expressly prohibited. The author reserves all rights to license uses of this work for generative AI training and development of machine learning language models.

Cover Design: Boja99designs

Formatting: Jenn Beach

For rebel girls with reckless hearts, find a hero who sees your potential before you do.

Chapter One

1987
Eve

I WASN'T DEAD, but I was grounded at least six feet under. My father didn't say the word "eternity" when he took my car keys and banished me to my room "for the foreseeable future," but it was sternly implied.

He found my stash of alcohol buried by the creek that ran between our lot and the five acres that had just sold next to us on the outskirts of Devil's Head, Missouri.

"Your dad's worried," Mom said, poking her head into my bedroom as I leered out the window through binoculars at the moving van backed up to the white farmhouse past the small orchard of apple trees.

My room was the only room in the house with a full view of the farmhouse.

"Yeah? Well, what's new?" I mumbled, watching a

1

young child run up and down the ramp at the back of the truck as two guys carried a sofa into the house.

"Eve, what are you looking at? Where did you get those binoculars?"

"They were in the attic. And I'm looking at the new neighbors since I have nothing better to do."

She plucked the binoculars from my hands and brought them to her eyes, scrunching her nose. "Don't you have homework?" she asked, leaning closer to the window.

"No," I laughed and grabbed them back from her. "Duh. I graduated."

"Oh." She tried to hide her grin. "Sorry. It's just a habit to ask you that. You know who our new neighbor is, don't you?" She sat on the end of my bed.

"No," I said with a frown. "No one tells me anything except to do my homework."

"Eve, it's Fred Collins' younger brother. Do you remember Fred?"

"Dad's friend from seminary school?" I asked.

"Yes, and he was the best man at our wedding."

"And yet, you married dad. Does that mean you settled for the second-best man?"

"Ha. Ha. You're so funny. His name is Kyle, and he has a five-year-old son, but I don't know his name. We should introduce ourselves and see if they need help. Yesterday, Dad told Fred that you and Gabby would be willing to babysit Kyle's little boy."

I glanced back at my mom and offered a fake smile. "How nice of him to offer my services."

"You can't clean motel rooms forever."

"I mean,"—I shrugged—"I *could*. It's a real job. Someone has to do it," I said, demonstrating my inability to shut my mouth. My specialty was making ridiculous and often frivolous cases for things that didn't matter. And jokes. I loved a good joke.

"Also, sweetie, now that he bought that house, the apple trees belong to him. You can no longer take apples from the orchard without permission from Mr. Collins."

"As if he's going to know. Do you think he'll keep an exact count?"

Mom sighed, crossing her arms over her chest. "We taught you better, young lady. You're eighteen. Out of high school. And—"

"Grounded. Yes. I'm aware. That seems ridiculous. Adults shouldn't be grounded. I think Grandma Bonnie should ground your as—" I cleared my throat. "Your *butt* for the speeding ticket you got in Evansville last month."

"It was a warning."

I smirked. "Because you flirted with the cop."

"Eve Marie Jacobson, I did not flirt with the cop." Her cheeks turned ten shades of pink. "Listen, you live under our roof, and there are rules. If you break them, there has to be consequences," she repeated the same lines for the millionth time. "Had the cop given me a ticket, I would have had to pay it. That would have been the consequence of my action."

I brought the binoculars to my eyes again. One of the guys carried a box toward the front door. "I'm not sure treating me like a child is a fair punishment. I should get some leniency since I finished *so much* homework that they gave me a diploma. Or can't you just give me a ticket that I can pay? What about a warning? If I unbutton the top of my blouse and gasp as if I have no idea I'm breaking some law and fake a deep Southern accent with lots of 'oh mys' and 'golly gee willikers,' would you let me off with a warning?"

"I *did* not unbutton my blouse. And if your dad heard you talk to me like this, he'd tack on another week to your grounding. We'll give you leniency when you stop acting like a child."

I chuckled. "Drinking alcohol feels like something an adult would do. I was just doing grown-up things. You're always telling me I should act like an adult if I expect to be treated like one."

"I suppose we could let you suffer *adult* consequences for doing illegal things like underage drinking."

"Where's his wife? What does this Kyle guy do?" I changed the subject. "Is he a rancher?"

"I don't know what happened to his wife. Fred just told your dad that he's raising the boy alone, and your dad didn't ask any more questions. Kyle is the new high school football coach and math teacher."

"Math? Sounds like a nerd," I mumbled.

"If you mean someone with a college degree and a good job, then yes. He's a nerd." Mom shot me a smug grin when I lowered the binoculars.

"Is that another reference to my job? I bet you're glad someone cleans your room while staying at a motel. And I don't think teachers make that much money. That's probably why he's a coach too."

"Get up. Let's see if he needs help." Mom jerked her chin like yanking on a fishing pole with a big bass on the end of the line.

I wasn't a fish.

"I'm not allowed to leave my room unless it's to work, eat, or go to the bathroom," I said with an exaggerated shrug.

"Unless your dad or I give you permission."

"Gabby can help. I just started a new book, and I'm in the middle of a chapter."

"What book?" She stopped at my door and eyed me through tiny, distrustful slits.

"*The Bible.*"

Mom returned a raised eyebrow.

I shot her a cheesy grin while slipping the binoculars into their case.

"What book in *The Bible* are you reading?"

"Ezekiel."

She didn't believe me for a second. "That's a good one."

"It's not," I said, shaking my head. "It's rather apocalyptic."

She narrowed her eyes and twisted her lips. I was slightly offended that she seemed so surprised by my biblical knowledge. Preachers' daughters knew more than anyone needed to know about *The Bible*. Of course, Dad spent most of his time reciting Exodus and the Ten Commandments while I stashed alcohol by the creek and masturbated to sinful music.

"Gabby's at Erica's house. Your dad is at the church. It's just us until dinner. I'll meet you downstairs."

After a reflexive grumble, I used the bathroom and pulled my dark hair into a ponytail before heading downstairs and shoving my feet into my red and blue KangaROOS with their useless pouch that I'd had high hopes for when I bought them.

"You don't need to tell Kyle you're grounded," Mom said as I followed her outside.

I laughed. "Why? Because you know it would sound ridiculous since I'm an adult?"

"No, because telling everyone makes you sound whiny

like a child instead of an adult." The wind caught her brunette hair, which she'd recently grown out from a mullet to a layered wolf cut—very Princess Diana.

"I'm not whiny."

She laughed. "You can't even say that without whining."

I returned to my grumble instead of anything that could sound like a whine.

"Howdy, neighbor," Mom said as two men carried boxes into the house while the boy with dark, curly hair chased a dragonfly.

"Slow down," I whispered to the boy as he passed me.

He stopped, brown eyes wide as if he were in trouble.

"Hold out your hand like this and hold still." I lifted his hand out in front of him and helped him hold still. After a few seconds, the dragonfly landed on it. Then he giggled, and it flew off.

"Howdy, yourselves," one guy said.

I turned back toward my mom, and my jaw dropped when he smiled. The nerdy math teacher had a *hot* friend with golden blond hair that swept along his sweaty forehead and brilliant blue eyes with tiny creases at the corners when he smiled. He set the box in the entry and lifted his shirt to wipe his sweaty face.

I may have peeked at his abs.

My mom was happily married to a man of God (except during traffic violations), so I stared at the guy's abs long enough for both of us.

"Are you Kyle?" Mom asked because she was stupid.

Of course, he wasn't Kyle.

There was no way that guy was a math teacher with a kid. Math teachers had pocket protectors and glasses with transition lenses, not hard abs.

"I am," he said.

My gaze snapped from his abs to his face.

"I'm Janet Jacobson, Peter's wife. And this is our middle child, Eve."

"Oh, yeah. Fred told me you were my neighbors. It's nice to meet you." He offered his hand to my mom, and she shook it like a normal human.

However, I didn't notice he offered to shake mine until my mom nudged me, but it was too late. "H-hi," I stuttered, even though I wasn't one to stutter or lose my mind over a guy.

He inspected me with a slight raise of his brows, rubbing his lips together before clearing his throat. "I'm teaching Trig and Calculus at the high school. Will you be in one of my classes?" His lips twisted like he was chewing on the inside of his cheek.

Again, my mom elbowed me.

I straightened my back and smiled with a quick inhale. "No. Uh, I graduated. I'm eighteen. An adult. No longer in school."

And I had diarrhea mouth. A simple "no" would have sufficed. I didn't melt at boys' feet. But he was a man, not a boy. Still, I felt ridiculous.

"Eve wasn't the best at math." Mom tee-heed.

I shot her a scowl. "I was fine at math."

"You barely got a C in Algebra."

"It was Algebra II, and it's because everyone thought Mr. Dillon would drop the semester final, but he didn't. And I had a meet, so I didn't have enough time to study." I laced my fingers behind my back and eyed Kyle with a nervous smile.

Why did my mom insist on embarrassing me?

"Oh, this is my buddy, Adam," Kyle said as a stocky guy squeezed past him.

Adam stopped. "Hey."

"These are my neighbors, Eve and Janet Jacobson. Janet's husband and my brother are best friends."

"Nice to meet you," Adam said, smiling at my mom before gazing at me. His grin morphed into mischief as he adjusted his John Deere baseball hat. He shot a look in Kyle's direction like they had some secret. "*Eve*, I'll keep my distance." He winked at me.

Kyle pressed his lips together to hide his grin, but my mom did not try to hide her laughter. "Adam and Eve." She slapped her hand to her chest. "Oh dear. And my darling Eve loves apples. She was stealing them from the orchard before you bought the property."

Who didn't love a good Adam and Eve joke? Me. And I loved jokes, but not stupid ones.

Adam continued toward the truck.

"Daddy!" The boy ran up to Kyle and hugged him. "I want a snack."

Kyle ruffled the boy's dark, curly hair. "Okay, in a minute." He rested his hands on his shoulders and turned him to face us. "Josh, these are our neighbors, Janet and Eve. Can you say hi?"

Josh tucked his chin with a bashful smile as he mumbled, "Hi."

"Hi, Josh. It's nice to meet you." Mom playfully pinched his cheek.

He giggled and squirmed out of Kyle's hold.

"How old are you?" Mom asked.

He held up five fingers.

"Aw, the fabulous fives," Mom said.

Josh ran into the house.

"More like the ferocious fives." Kyle sighed.

"Well, our youngest, Gabby, is sixteen, and I know she'll babysit. Eve works at a motel and loiters at the nursing home to avoid chores, so she isn't as available."

"Loiters?" My jaw dropped. "I *volunteer*. And Grandma Bonnie is there. *And* I'm done between three and four every day. So, I'd be available if Kyle ever needs someone to watch Josh in the evenings."

Everyone said I was just like my mother—feisty and stubborn—and that's why we butted heads. But what kind of mother threw her child to the wolves like my mom did to me?

She rubbed my back. "Don't forget, you're always out with friends—when you're not grounded."

I wasn't supposed to mention it, but it was okay for her to call me out?

We stepped aside to make room for Adam as he carried another box into the house.

"I'll keep that in mind," Kyle said.

"What can we do to help?" Mom asked.

"I think we've got it." Kyle headed toward the moving van.

I watched his ass the whole way. He had a nice ass. Not flat like a lot of guys, but not a bubble butt either like Tom, my junior prom date. But who was I kidding? Kyle and Tom weren't even in the same league.

Boy vs man.

"Eve, grab a box," Mom said. She wasn't good at taking no for an answer when it came to helping people. My dad was the pastor at the only church in Devil's Head, so hospitality was my mom's specialty.

She excelled in potlucks and fundraisers.

Wedding receptions and funeral luncheons.

"Daddy! Snack!" Josh yelled from the front door.

"I don't have much for a snack, buddy. We have to run to the grocery store." Kyle and Adam carried a leather recliner down the truck's ramp.

"Eve can take Josh to our house for a snack if you're comfortable with that?" Mom offered.

I wanted to stay and help Kyle and Adam. If I left, who was going to keep an eye on Kyle's nice ass?

"Would you mind?" Kyle asked, glancing at me while they carried the chair to the front door.

I plastered on a smile. "Not at all."

"Josh, follow Eve. She's going to get you a snack."

"Gummy bears?" Josh looked to his dad for confirmation.

"I don't know. Just go see, and *please* be good." Kyle replied, disappearing into the house while my mom followed them.

Josh hesitated to take my proffered hand, doing his shy chin tuck before resting his little hand in mine. He didn't know we were about to be best friends because I had an instant crush on his daddy.

Chapter Two

Eurythmics, Annie Lennox, Dave Steward,
"Would I Lie to You?"

Eve

"Do you like applesauce?" I asked, leading Josh down the grassy hill and up the next to the orchard.

He replied with a slight nod.

When we reached the modest orchard, I hoisted him up. "Pick that one?" I pointed to the apple with the reddest skin.

He wrapped his tiny fingers around it.

"You have to tug at it. Pull hard."

It made a snapping sound, and Josh grinned as he held the apple. After I set him on his feet, I nodded toward the tree. "Can I pick some apples?"

He returned a blank stare for a few seconds before giving me a tiny nod. I felt proud of myself for getting permission, and I smirked while gathering at least a dozen apples, folding up the front of my shirt for a makeshift basket.

When we reached the house, I deposited the apples into a big bowl and lifted Josh onto the kitchen counter. "First, we're going to rinse off the apple," I said, quickly washing it and drying it with a towel. "Then we peel it."

He watched me with wide eyes as I peeled the apple, leaving one long ribbon to toss into the compost bin by the trash.

"Now we shred it." I retrieved the cheese grater and a bowl and pulverized the apple using the fine side of the grater. "Do you want to try it?"

Josh shifted his gaze to me and slowly nodded.

I held my hand over his and helped him move the apple along the grater until it approached the core.

"Okay," I said, wiping his hand with a damp washcloth. "Now we add some cinnamon and sugar."

He grinned. All kids grinned when they heard the word sugar.

Mom had a special shaker with the two already mixed together, so I handed it to Josh.

"Can you shake that over the bowl?"

He nodded and shook the bottle a couple of times.

"Keep going." I grinned. "These apples might be a little tart for you, so shake more onto it."

His grin doubled as he continued to shake it.

"Perfect," I said, taking the bottle from him and plucking a spoon from the silverware drawer. "Do you want to stir it?"

He shook his head.

"Okay. I'll do it." I stirred it and offered him a bite.

He hesitated before parting his full lips. At first, his nose scrunched in a sour expression, but then it softened, and his eyes widened as he smiled.

"It takes a second for the cinnamon and sugar to sweeten the tartness." I laughed. "I usually let it sit for a while, but I know you're hungry." I held the bowl in front of him and offered the spoon.

Over the next ten minutes, Josh slowly ate it, and I was dying to call Erin and tell her about my hot neighbor.

"I have to poop," Josh whispered, leaning to the side and pressing his hand to his butt.

"Poop?" I lifted my eyebrows.

He nodded.

"You need to go poop?"

Again, he nodded.

"Oh, okay. Um …" I lifted him off the counter and led him to the bathroom under the stairs. "Do you do everything by yourself?"

He looked at me like I wasn't speaking English.

"Can you get your pants down, get on the toilet, and wipe all by yourself?" I had worked many summers with kids at vacation Bible school. And not all kids his age were proficient at pooping independently.

"I'm a big boy," Josh said.

I grinned. "Of course you are." I turned on the light. "Let me know if you need help." He closed the door, and I waited for him to finish, which felt like forever.

"Are you okay in there?" I asked with my arms crossed over my chest while pacing the hallway beside the pocket door.

"Yes," he replied in a soft voice that I barely heard.

A minute later, he flushed the toilet, and a few seconds later, he mumbled, "Oh, shit!"

Did he say "shit?"

I cringed, recognizing the sound of the incomplete flush. "Josh?" I said his name while slowly opening the door.

He finished pulling up his pants as the toilet water rose to the top with a ton of toilet paper mixed with a couple of turds. "Oh, jeez!" I lifted him onto the vanity. "Uh, wash your hands while I grab the plunger."

I ran to the basement, a musky dungeon where we kept a few things like the plunger and old cans of paint. The stairway was filled with cobwebs, and I hated going down there, but I had no choice. When I returned to the bathroom, Josh had half the bottle of soap pumped onto his hands, the water running full blast, and the sink filled with bubbles. But I didn't have time to worry about that because the toilet was on the verge of overflowing. Luckily, it stopped running right as it reached the rim.

God was good.

As I dipped the plunger into the toilet, the water breached the rim and ran down the sides onto the floor, along with soggy toilet paper and a turd. "Crap, uh *crud.*" I wrinkled my nose, quickly jumping back to avoid getting my shoes wet.

"Oops," Josh mumbled, eyes wide and unblinking.

I glanced over my shoulder at his guilty face.

"It's fine. It's not your fault." It was all his fault, but I didn't want to make him cry.

Leaving the plunger in the toilet, I lifted Josh off the counter and abandoned the mess. "Let's go back to your house."

He took off running when I set him down outside our front door. I jogged after him through the orchard, down a hill, and up another.

"Hey, did you get a snack?" Kyle asked, closing the back of the moving truck.

"I pooped," Josh said.

Kyle looked at me, biting his lower lip and shaking his head.

"And the water went up up up." Josh pressed his hands to his cheeks and made an O with his lips.

Kyle's gaze flitted between us.

I found my fake smile like it was no big deal, like my dad wouldn't come home to a mess on the bathroom floor. It wasn't the first time I'd abandoned a clogged toilet. But it was just the first time it wasn't my fault.

"He clogged the toilet?" Kyle asked.

Pressing my lips together, I nodded.

Kyle pinched the bridge of his nose. "I'm so sorry. Did you get it unclogged?"

"Of course," I chirped.

"No. We ran," Josh called me out before sprinting into the house and leaving me alone with Kyle.

With a nervous laugh, I shook my head. "We didn't run. It's fine."

"I feel really bad," Kyle said, sliding his hands into the back pockets of his jeans. "You did me a favor and got way more than you bargained for. I'm—"

"It's fine." I waved it off because he was so hot, handsome, sexy, and every other word that described the man of my dreams. We didn't need to discuss runaway turds when I wanted to know if he liked younger women who had a penchant for trouble, enjoyed a few drinks, and thought nonstop about sex.

"Well, if you ever need help with math ..." He didn't finish.

I forced my gaze to his face, and he smirked. Was he making fun of me?

"Or any other favors. I owe you one." He winked.

Heat crawled up my neck, so I looked away and tightened my ponytail. I was not the butt of anyone's joke, no matter how hot they were. "What if you tell my mom you need a babysitter tomorrow night." I pulled my shoulders back and slipped my fingers into my back pockets.

"But I don't."

"Even better." I returned my version of a smirk, but I didn't go so far as to wink.

"You're grounded," he murmured, rubbing the back of his neck like he just remembered what my mom had said.

I nodded.

Kyle twisted his lips. "You want me to lie for you?"

"Lie is such an ugly word. I like your word better."

He chuckled, gazing at the ground between us. "What's my word?"

"Favor. Let's not think of it as a lie. Let's think of it as the favor you just promised me."

"Aiding and abetting?"

I laughed. "Abetting implies you're encouraging me. So just aiding."

Kyle's eyebrows peaked.

"Just because I didn't understand the inversion function of the cosine doesn't mean I don't know what abetting means." I learned the meaning of that word a few weeks earlier in a movie.

"Arccosine is the inversion function of the cosine," Kyle said.

I rolled my eyes.

"What are your plans for tomorrow night?" he asked.

I shrugged. "Does it matter?"

"Yes. It matters. I can't *aid* you if you plan on doing something your parents don't want you to do."

"My parents don't want me to leave the house, laugh, or have an original thought."

He narrowed his eyes for a few seconds and smirked. "What did you do to get grounded?"

"Does it matter?"

He slowly nodded. "Yeah, it matters."

I sighed. "I had a few drinks."

"Driving?"

I shook my head. "By the creek." I gestured to my right.

"Are you going to drink tomorrow night?"

"No."

Maybe.

"Drugs?" he asked.

I grinned. "No."

"Unprotected sex?"

All the blood in my body surged to my head until I felt my pulse in my burning cheeks. Was he making me an offer? "I'm a preacher's daughter. What do you think?"

His smile beamed. He was *so* sexy. "If you hadn't confessed to drinking by the creek, I would have assumed you were a rule-follower. A perfect angel. But I'm getting more of a rebel vibe now."

"Pfft. Angels are just rebels in disguise. I'm going to the bowling alley with friends. We bowl between memorizing Bible verses and exclusively snack on Gold Fish, Animal Crackers, and grape juice as a nod to Jesus."

Something on Kyle's face changed as he paused before responding. He rubbed his fingers over his mouth but grinned anyway. Then, his fingers curled into a fist as he laughed. "Eve ..." he said, shaking his head.

I wanted to bottle the feeling he gave me. Very few people appreciated my humor.

"So you'll say you need a babysitter?"

He cleared his throat, still grinning. "Do you have a fake ID?"

I barked a laugh. "Everyone in Devil's Head knows who I am. If I could get into a bar with a fake ID, do you think I'd drink by the creek?"

"Then where do you get your alcohol?"

"I can't reveal my source. You're a teacher, which means you can't be trusted."

"Gosh, we just met and already have trust issues?"

"I got all of your dishes and silverware unpacked," Mom announced, coming out the front door. "And Josh is looking for his monster truck."

Kyle glanced over my shoulder at my mom. "Thank you, Janet. That was very kind of you."

"You are most welcome. What else can we do to help?"

"You know, I think that's good for now. However, I was just asking Eve if she could watch Josh for me tomorrow night if that's okay with you?"

"I'm sure that would be fine. She has nothing else to do."

I frowned, and it fed Kyle's amusement.

"What time do you need her?" Mom asked, wrapping her arm around me for a side hug.

I nudged my elbow into her ribs, trying to subtly wriggle out of her embrace.

"Maybe from six to around eight thirty or nine?"

I wrinkled my nose at him. "What if your date goes better than expected? You could get home closer to ten or ten thirty, which is fine with me. Like my mom said," I shot him a toothy grin, "I have nothing better to do."

"You have a date?" Mom asked. "Wow. You just arrived. Can I ask with who? I know everyone in town."

Kyle pinned me with a look that wasn't exactly friendly. "A date. Yes. I was surprised too. After all, how could I possibly know anyone after arriving *today*?"

Oops.

I bit my thumbnail.

Kyle returned his attention to my mom. "It's a blind date. Someone at the school arranged it. They heard I was new in town and single. But if it's okay with you, I'd rather not give any more information in case it doesn't go well."

"Oh, of course." Mom nodded. "I understand. Eve will be here by six. I'll pop by, too, to ensure everything is going well."

"No," I blurted and quickly bit my lips together. "I'm eighteen. Stop treating me like a child. I don't need you to babysit me *while* I'm babysitting. Okay?"

Mom eyed Kyle while he tried to suppress his grin.

"Eve, real grown-ups don't have issues with other grown-ups helping them," she said.

I couldn't believe she was picking a fight with me in front of Kyle.

So embarrassing.

"What's that saying?" Kyle said. "It takes a village? I'm grateful to have found a village so quickly. I'm sure Josh would love spending time with both of you."

My eyes bugged out at him.

"We're just as excited to have you here," Mom said, looping her arm with mine and trying to pull me toward our house.

"I'll meet you at home," I said. "I want to run inside and say goodbye to Josh."

"Okay. Bye, Kyle."

"Later, Mrs. Jacobson."

She shot him a grin over her shoulder. "Please, call me Janet." It was the grin she used when the cop pulled her over.

After she was out of earshot, I stepped closer to Kyle and narrowed my eyes. "Traitor."

"What was I supposed to do?" He brushed past me toward the house, and I followed him.

"Uh, tell her she didn't need to check up on me. Now, I have to tell her that you no longer need a sitter."

"That's not true," he said, opening the creaky screen door. "It's been forever since I've been to the movies."

"You're stealing my night out?" I stepped inside as he held open the door.

"Stealing? Of course not. I'll pay you."

"You know what I mean."

"Is that it?" Adam asked, jogging down the stairs. "I put together your bedframe, and all your guns are locked in the safe."

"Yup. That's it. Thanks, buddy."

"No problem. I'll drive the truck back." Adam glanced at his watch. "Grab the little man, and we can get pizza after you pick me up."

"Sounds good. We'll head that way," Kyle said.

"It was nice meeting you, Eve." Adam gave me a slight nod with a smile.

"You too."

When the door shut behind him, Kyle pulled a set of keys from his pocket. "So six tomorrow night?"

I crossed my arms over my chest. "My mom said I have to stop taking apples from the orchard now that you own it, but since I've lost all respect for you, I'm taking the best ones and leaving you with the wormholes."

He narrowed his eyes briefly before the corner of his mouth curled into a tiny grin. "I feel like we've gotten off to a bad start." He fiddled with his keys while giving me a slow once-over.

Was he checking me out?

No.

Maybe.

Gah! I hoped so.

I cleared my throat. "And who's fault is that?"

Kyle shook his head. "I'll make it up to you."

"How?"

He smirked. "You'll see. Josh? Let's go, buddy. We have to pick Adam up."

"See ya, I guess," I mumbled, pushing open the screen door. When I gazed back, Kyle was looking at my ass or my legs. Maybe both.

When our eyes locked, he winked.

He. WINKED!

Chapter Three

George Michael, "Faith"

Kyle

By the time we picked up Adam from the U-Haul store and grabbed a pizza to take home, Josh was asleep.

Adam glanced in the back seat at my sleeping boy before breaching the subject that didn't need to be discussed. "Eighteen-year-old girls look twenty-five these days," he said.

I checked my review mirror to confirm that Josh hadn't woken up. "I suppose," I replied.

Through the corner of my eye, I caught Adam's Cheshire cat grin.

He scratched his neck. "Eve is uh ..."

"My brother's best friend's daughter. Barely out of high school. My neighbor. And ten years younger than me."

Adam softly chuckled. "I was going to say really hot. Miles of legs. The long dark hair. The sexy grin. Dude, she smiles like she's got a secret, and it's *hot*."

"Well, good thing you'll be flying back to Denver tomorrow. The whole Adam and Eve thing failed the first time; no need to relive the past."

He fisted his hand at his mouth and tried to suppress his laughter so he didn't wake Josh. I shot him a quick glance and a half grin. He wasn't wrong about her.

"She was practically drooling over you," he added.

"Also worth noting: I'm a math teacher at the high school and the football coach. Did I mention how small this town is? Oh, and if you look behind us, you'll see I have a son."

"I'd do her," he said with a shrug.

I didn't want to laugh, but my best friend had the most questionable morals. His favorite lines were: How are they going to find out? What are they going to do about it?

"They" meant any authority, such as teachers, police, parents, and the IRS. He was a terrible influence when we were younger, and I spent a lot of time in trouble for his bad ideas. Yet, I had no regrets.

Adam drummed his fingers on his legs. "I know you wanted to live in a small town for Josh's sake, but this seems a little extreme." He stared out the window at endless acres of land dotted with barns and farmhouses.

"Nah. It's perfect."

"You know what else is perfect? The tits on that—"

"If you mention her again, I'm going to bury your body in the orchard. It would have such a biblical symbolism of the mortality of man."

"Josh is asleep and can't hear us. You forget that I've known you since we were kids. You don't have to be a math teacher or a saint with me. So you can give me a long list of reasons why you should stay away from your neighbor girl, but nothing changes the fact that she's a wet dream. So, since

I've mentioned her again, and you're going to bury me, at least give this dying man his last wish and tell me what you really thought when you met her."

I blew out a long breath. "I thought I should have moved to Carthage."

A triumphant grin grew along his face. "Melinda's gone. You have a long road ahead of you as a single dad. Don't deny yourself a little pleasure here and there."

I shook my head. "I'll keep my subscription to *Playboy*."

"I'd just get myself a good pair of binoculars. Which room do you think is hers?"

"Shut up, man. You're such a pervert." I tried not to laugh as we pulled into the drive, but Adam was relentless. "Hey, buddy," I shut off the truck, then reached around to shake Josh's leg.

He peeled open his eyes and yawned.

"We're home. Let's eat."

THE NEXT NIGHT, the doorbell rang at six fifteen.

"You're late," I said, opening the screen door.

Eve squinted a fraction. "Sorry. Your imaginary date will be so disappointed." She stepped inside and kicked off her shoes.

"It could be a real date. You haven't seen me in twenty-four hours," I said, crossing my arms over my chest while she curled her dark brown hair behind her ears.

I told myself to keep my gaze on her face. Even though I had driven Adam to the airport earlier that day, he was still in my head, taunting me with inappropriate comments and suggestions. Unfortunately, when I opened the door, I'd caught enough of her body to know she was wearing rolled-up denim shorts and a red tank top.

"What have you done to find a date since yesterday?" Eve asked. "I don't think you made the personal ad deadline for today's paper."

"I went to the grocery store after I took Adam to the airport. Maybe I asked out one of the employees," I said.

"Charity, Susan, or Jodie? Those are the three employees at the store. Charity is sixteen, so her parents might have something to say about you asking out their daughter. Susan is married with four kids but only works evenings, so you probably didn't ask her out. However, I heard she and her husband fight a lot, so she might say yes if you did. And Jodie graduated with me, but she got pregnant on Valentine's Day, so she's about six months along. She and her boyfriend, Joe, plan to marry next year unless you asked *her* out tonight. I'd bet she'd choose you over Joe."

Eve was a handful, and even that was an understatement. She was like a cigarette, addictive and bad for me, yet oddly alluring.

"Why do you think she would choose me?" I turned toward the kitchen, and Eve followed me.

"Just for reasons."

"Such as?" I grabbed a six-pack of beer from the fridge. "Because I'm good-looking?"

"Pfft." She rolled her eyes. "I withdraw my statement, Your Honor. On second thought, you're too full of yourself for her to be interested in you. Are you taking those with you or hiding them from me?" She nodded to the cans of beer I tucked under my arm.

"Neither. Well," I thought about it, "maybe both. I probably shouldn't leave them where you can be tempted. I'm taking them with me."

"Drinking and driving is a bad thing," she said. "There have been some real tragedies around here."

"Good thing I'm not driving. Listen, Josh is upstairs playing in his room. His jammies are on his bed. Tell him to brush his teeth at seven and read him a bedtime story at seven thirty. He'll pick out the book. No water after seven. He's had dinner, so don't let him talk you into any snacks. He's sly and ornery." I grabbed an old blanket and flashlight and shoved my feet into my boots.

"Where are you going? Why do you need a flashlight and blanket?" Eve asked, crossing her arms over her chest.

I opened the back door. "I'm going down to the creek. I hear it's a great place to stare at the stars and drink."

Eve's jaw came unhinged. "You're a cruel man, Mr. Collins."

I laughed.

"By the way, I charge ten dollars an hour to babysit." She pulled her long, dark hair over one shoulder and inspected the ends as if her outrageous babysitting fee was no big deal.

I held back my response for a few seconds because she was something else. And whatever that *something* was made me want more of it.

"*I* don't make ten dollars an hour. I'll pay you four an hour, and I won't tell your parents that you were planning on sneaking out tonight."

She planted her hands on her hips as if that and a slight chin lift made her look tougher.

Damn. I had to fight my grin.

"Five an hour, and I won't tell my dad that it was Josh's poop he had to clean up off the bathroom floor yesterday."

I cocked my head to the side. "You said you unclogged it."

"I lied."

"Why?"

She lifted a shoulder. "Because I didn't want you to feel bad."

"But you're okay with me feeling bad now because you want to blackmail me into paying more?"

"No. I'm okay with making you feel bad now, *and* I'm blackmailing you because you're going to *my* creek to do *my* thing, and you're doing it just to spite me."

I slowly nodded. "Five an hour, and I'll be back in two hours."

"Perfect." Eve looked at her yellow and red banded Swatch. "I'll have my mom come over to check in around seven, so when you return at eight, I'll be in the clear to leave. Have fun, Mr. Math Teacher." She spun on her toes and sauntered toward the stairs.

Devil's Head was a terrible idea. That girl was trouble.

Chapter Four

Jody Watley, "Looking For a New Love"

Eve

"HEY, JOSH," I said, peeking my head into his bedroom as he played with his Matchbox cars on the floor. The walls were pink and white polka dot wallpaper from the previous owner, but Josh had a gray bedspread with blue race cars and a stuffed koala by his pillow.

"You can have the yellow Corvette." He held up the car.

I smiled and sat cross-legged beside him. He was adorable.

"Do you know where you lived before here?"

He made duck lips for a second. "In a house."

I laughed at myself for asking the question. Josh was five, and his answer was age appropriate.

"Was it just you and your dad, or did anyone else live with you?" I drove the car behind his, and he giggled when I drove over his car.

"Me and Dad," he said, focusing on the cars he drove up the ramp made from books.

"Will you be in kindergarten?"

He nodded.

I stopped asking questions and played cars with him for half an hour before calling my mom from the kitchen phone.

"If you want to check up on me, then you should come soon because Josh will be brushing his teeth in thirty minutes, then I'm reading him bedtime stories. If you show up later than that, you could wake him."

Or catch me getting into Erin's car at the end of the drive.

"I don't have to come over. I trust you," she said.

"You do? I mean, thanks. There's no reason not to trust me."

"Did Kyle think he'd be out past ten?" she asked.

"He said somewhere between ten and eleven. I said that's fine since it's a short walk home, and I don't have to be at work until nine tomorrow." I played it super cool.

"Okay, call me if you need anything. I think I'm going to take a hot bath. I've had a slight headache all day," she said.

"Well, I hope the bath helps."

"Me too. Bye, hun."

I hung up the phone for two seconds before picking it up again and calling Erin.

"Hello?" her mom answered.

"Hi. Is Erin there?"

"Oh, hi, Eve. Yes, I'll get her."

A few seconds later, Erin picked up. "Hey."

"Where have you been? I've been trying to call you since yesterday. You have to come get me at eight fifteen. Pick me up at the end of the Tallmans' driveway."

"I thought you were grounded."

"I am. But the guy who bought the Tallmans' house has a five-year-old son, and I'm sort of babysitting tonight, but my parents don't think I'll be home until ten or eleven, and Kyle, the dad, will be back at eight. And oh my gosh, Erin! I have so much to tell you."

"I can't go out tonight. We were visiting my grandparents yesterday and we just got home a few hours ago, but I have a sore throat and a fever, so there's no way my mom's letting me leave."

"Nooo. Are you being serious? Ugh! I'm so desperate to go out. My parents watch my every move, but tonight, I have a decoy."

"Sorry. Call Nicole."

I frowned because I didn't want to go out with Nicole. All she ever wanted to do was eat at McDonald's and shop at Claire's for earrings. And I didn't have my ears pierced.

"It's fine," I grumbled in a less-than-fine tone. "Sorry you're not feeling well. Get better, and I'll call you tomorrow to tell you *everything*."

"Tell me now."

"No. I have to get Josh ready for bed."

"Fine. Tomorrow. See ya." She hung up, and I jogged up the stairs.

"Josh, time to brush your teeth."

He made up for the clogged toilet incident by getting ready for bed without dilly-dallying or uttering a single complaint. I probably could have learned a few things from him.

By the time I got halfway through one book, he was asleep. I shut off the light and partially closed his door. Feeling extra snoopy, I tiptoed into Kyle's bedroom, but before I could find the light switch, I heard a door creak, so I hurried down the stairs, composing myself while turning the corner into the kitchen.

"Hey," I said with my hands folded behind my back, going for the most innocent pose I could find. "You know, there are brown bears here in southern Missouri. You must be careful hanging out alone at night by the creek."

"I wasn't alone." He set his blanket and flashlight on the counter and deposited his empty beer cans into the sink.

"Oh?"

"I was with my friends, Smith & Wesson." He pulled a gun out from the back of his jeans.

My eyes popped out of my head. We didn't own any guns. And while I heard Adam mention guns the previous day, I imagined a rifle, not a handgun.

"A math teacher with a gun," I mumbled.

He grinned, removing the ammunition. "What do you take when drinking by the creek and staring at the stars?"

I peeled my gaze from the gun on the counter and lifted it to his face. "I take friends."

Kyle chuckled, resting his backside against the counter and tucking his fingers into his front pockets. "And they protect you?"

After a few blinks, I overcame my shock and mustered a grin. "Yes. I'm the fastest runner."

He barked a laugh, and I felt my face flush because he had the sexiest smile, the sexiest everything, really.

I pressed a finger to my lips. "Shh. Josh is asleep."

He rubbed his mouth while his eyes gleamed with amusement. "Sorry. You're right." His gaze shifted to the clock by the fridge. "What time are you sneaking out?"

I deflated. "I'm not. My best friend is sick. Did you save me any beer?"

Kyle lifted his eyebrows. "You know those really cool teachers who give students alcohol?"

"No. I've never met a teacher who gave their students alcohol."

He shook his head. "Me neither."

I scowled. "Respectfully, you're an idiot."

"Respectfully?" He cocked his head to the side.

"I was taught to respect my elders," I said.

"Oh, so saying 'respectfully' before calling someone an idiot makes it okay?"

"Can I ask about Josh's mom?" I jumped the track to a completely different subject.

His smile faded. "What do you want to ask?"

"Does he have one?"

"No. I pushed him out of my vagina."

"Duh. You know what I mean."

"Of course, he has a mom."

"But you're not married?"

He shook his head.

"Were you ever married?"

Again, he shook his head.

"Is she alive?"

Kyle eyed me for a few seconds. "I don't know."

"Does Josh—"

"It's late," he said, cutting me off.

"It's a little past eight on a Thursday. You call that late?"

He pushed off the counter. "It's my way of *respectfully* telling you I'm done talking about this."

I stared at my feet and whispered, "Sorry." Mom was right. I was a little too nosey and had a bad habit of speaking without thinking of the consequences of my words.

"Don't be sorry. Can you walk home by yourself?"

I rolled my eyes. "Yes. But I'm not going home. Mind if I borrow your flashlight?"

"For what?"

"It's my turn to stargaze by the creek. And I wouldn't be opposed to you loaning me a can of beer too. Since I'm not your student, your silly rules shouldn't apply to me."

"I can't be your accomplice any longer. You said it yourself. There are bears."

"I'll take your gun."

He nodded slowly. "Yeah, that seems like the best idea. I don't see any ethical dilemma at all with giving an eighteen-year-old a flashlight, beer, and a gun."

"If you wouldn't mind, I could use the blanket too. By any chance, do you have a bag of Ruffles?"

When Kyle's grin swelled, my heart pulsed to a different rhythm while euphoria zinged through my body like electricity. I'd had my share of celebrity crushes—older men who made me want to be a mature woman. But Kyle was the first tangible older man who made everything inside me go haywire.

"Eve, can you imagine how much I'm second-guessing my decision to leave you in charge of Josh? I don't think you have a sound decision in that pretty little head of yours. And who eats Ruffles? Classic Lays are the only way to go."

I was fully aware it wasn't a compliment. However, my selective brain only latched on to the part where he suggested my head was pretty. "If you must know, and I think you *must*, I know the difference between right and wrong. My dad's a pastor. It's in my holy blood. I'm only reckless with myself. Never with others. When it's necessary, I'm one hundred percent trustworthy." I brought a stiff hand to my forehead and saluted him. "And thank you for the pretty head compliment." I twirled my hair around my finger. "But I think the *little* part is inaccurate. Most people would agree that my body parts are in proper proportion."

Kyle surveyed my body and quickly averted his gaze as he rubbed the back of his neck. Then he reached into his pocket, pulled a ten-dollar bill out of his wallet, and handed it to me. "Thank you for watching Josh," he said.

I shook my head and laughed. "I can't take your money. My plan failed, and it's not your fault. Besides, Josh is so good. He just played in his room, got ready for bed without a fuss, and fell asleep before I finished one book. And it's been a nice change to spend the evening outside my bedroom without watching *The 700 Club* with my parents."

Kyle snorted while returning the cash to his wallet.

I wrinkled my nose. "It's not funny. There's only so much I can do in my room. And it's embarrassing. I'm an adult who's grounded. How would you like it if you had to move back home and your parents grounded you? Can you imagine telling the other teachers that you can't go out because you're grounded?"

His grin touched the corners of his blue eyes.

"Anyway, I'll let you get ready for bed. Drink your warm milk or prune juice. Trim your ear hair. Whatever old people like you do at night."

"Let me grab my cane, and I'll walk you home." He nodded toward the front door.

I giggled, walking in front of him. "It's down a small hill, up another hill, through the orchard, and over the fence. I think I've got it."

"Yeah, but my brother and your dad are best friends, so I feel extra responsible for ensuring you get home safely."

"You can't leave Josh." I slipped my feet into my sneakers without untying them.

"He's asleep. I think we're in a low-crime neighborhood." He opened the door for me. "I'll be right back. I have to lock up my gun."

He met me on the porch less than a minute later. The humid, late August air clung to my skin as we descended the grassy hill. "So Josh said he'll be in kindergarten."

"Yes."

"Who's watching him when you're coaching?"

"After-school daycare."

"I can watch him if he doesn't want to spend every afternoon in daycare. I work days. That is if you feel my pretty little head is responsible enough to watch him."

We shared sideways glances.

"What about your volunteer loitering?"

I coughed a laugh. "My Grandma Bonnie is in the nursing home. They moved her there last year after my grandpa died. She's cool. I can tell her anything, so I keep her company way more than my mom, her own daughter. And I'm done with work in time to visit Grandma Bonnie and still be home by four."

"I'll talk to your parents about it."

"Dude! I'm eighteen. Once again, how would you like it if, when you applied for your teaching job, they wanted to talk to your parents first?"

Kyle chuckled as we trekked up the small hill. "Do you have any speeding tickets? Arrests? Recent groundings?"

"Shut up." I laughed.

"What about food prep? Can you make him a meal?"

"Are you serious? I made him homemade apple-sauce. I'm an extraordinary baker. And I have a long list of meals I can cook better than my mom. My grandma taught me everything she knows." I stopped at the orchard and grabbed an apple, plucking it from its stem.

"That will cost you," he said.

I smirked, wiping it with my shirt before taking a big bite.

Kyle reached for an apple and followed my lead. "Oh"—his face soured—"that is tart. How can you eat it plain like this?"

"My grandma says the sweetest people can eat the tartest apples. My grandpa never could eat them; she said it was because he was a grump. I guess we know what this says about you."

"That I have normal tastebuds?" He spat out the apple and chucked the rest of it behind us like a baseball.

"Josh loved my applesauce. Granted, I put a little cinnamon and sugar on it, but it was still tart, and he gobbled it up because he's *so* sweet."

"*Respectfully*," Kyle said, "your grandma's theory is flawed."

I moseyed toward the fence, savoring every bite of the apple. Then I held it with my teeth and climbed the wood rails, straddling the top one. "Nothing about my grandma is flawed."

His eyes widened as I ate the entire apple core.

"Why all the guns? Do you hunt?"

Kyle rested his arms on the rail in front of me. "Yes. But I like bow hunting best."

"What about fishing? I like to fish."

He nodded. "I have a fishing boat in the barn. Josh loves fishing."

"I asked Josh where you lived before you moved here, but he just said you lived in a house."

Kyle laughed. "He's not wrong. We lived in Crested Butte, Colorado."

"Why did you move?"

He gazed at my house. "We needed a change, but I still wanted to live in a small town, so when my brother suggested Devil's Head, and there happened to be a job opening at the school, I figured why not try here."

I nodded, but I was out of questions that didn't involve quizzing him on the whereabouts and circumstances surrounding Josh's mom. Yet, I wasn't ready to go inside and call it a night.

"I don't know if you bring your lunch to school, but the only decent meal they serve is chicken noodle soup with cinnamon rolls. Stay away from shrimp shapes. I don't think they contain actual shrimp. And don't be fooled by the beef burger. It's a rubbery patty with a funky taste. Everything else is just a version of hot dogs. The fruit is canned in heavy syrup, the cookies are concrete, and the milk is sour. But sometimes they have chocolate milk, and it's acceptable."

Kyle eyed me, trying to restrain his grin. He was *so* handsome. I couldn't believe he was my neighbor. I never wanted him to move.

"Thanks for the tip," he said.

"Oh, also, don't shake hands with Mr. Dillinger."

"The principal?" He squinted.

"Yes. He picks his nose all the time."

Kyle cringed.

When crickets were the only ones talking, I hopped off the fence. "I'm glad you moved into the Tallmans' house. We haven't had good neighbors in a while."

"What was wrong with the Tallmans?"

"They fought all the time. We could hear them from our house. Mr. Tallman threatened to cut off my hands if I took his apples. And they had a mean dog who chased me up a tree on more than one occasion."

Kyle chuckled. "So the bar for being a good neighbor has been set low."

"The lowest."

"I'll take that as a backhanded compliment."

I smirked while walking away. "You can take it however your *pretty little head* wants."

"Touché, Eve. Good night."

I waited until I felt certain he was on his way home, then I peered over my shoulder. But he wasn't walking home; he was still at the fence, watching me. When I slowed my stride, he grinned, shook his head, and turned to head home.

I was obsessed.

Chapter Five

Pretenders, "Don't Get Me Wrong"

Eve

FREEDOM WASN'T a strong enough word, but it was close enough.

The grounding ended. They returned the phone to my room. And I was permitted to hang out at the creek with the promise or *threat* that one of my parents might check up on me unannounced.

Thankfully, Erin's fever broke just in time to attend Sunday morning service, because I was desperate to tell her about Kyle.

We sat in the front of the choir. Worth noting: I was a terrible singer, and so was Erin. However, after my oldest sister Sarah (the singer in the family) left Devil's Head, my dad decided he needed one of his daughters to be in the choir like a Jacobson family mascot. My younger sister Gabby was next in line as soon as I figured out the best way to make it on my own outside of small-town Missouri. Erin was not obligated to be in the choir but joined it to keep me company or share in the misery—a true best friend.

"I have *so* much to tell you. It's been torture not having a phone in my room," I said as we watched the congregation file into the church in little groups, like ants at a picnic, deciding which crumbs to tackle first.

"What's it about?"

"Our new neighbor is a single dad. I don't know his age, but I'd guess late twenties. His older brother and my dad are best friends. And he's the new math teacher and football coach. And he is so, so, *so* hot."

Erin's brows shot up her forehead, hiding behind her big, blond bangs. "Dang it. Why couldn't he have come here a year earlier and been our math teacher?"

"I know." I covered my mouth to muffle my giggle. "I think he's going to let me babysit his five-year-old son after school."

"What happened to his wife?"

Just as I started to speak, Kyle and Josh walked up the aisle and sat next to the Smiths.

"Good morning," my dad said, resting his hands on both sides of the lectern. "Let us pray."

After prayer, the choir sang the opening hymn and I whispered in Erin's ear as we sat down, "See the blond guy and little boy next to the Smiths?"

Erin nodded.

"That's my neighbor and his son."

She squeezed my hand while pressing her other hand to her chest, confirming what I already knew. Kyle was the hottest guy in Devil's Head, maybe in all of Missouri.

Whenever he looked at me, I shifted my attention to my

dad because it was too much to handle. He and Josh wore matching navy suits, white button-downs, and robin-egg blue ties.

"I've died and gone to Heaven," Erin whispered.

I pressed my lips together so my knowing grin didn't swallow my entire face.

After the service, Erin and I hung up our choir robes in the closet next to my dad's office and joined my parents and the rest of the congregation in the churchyard.

"If you can't babysit for him ..." Erin said.

"I can do it. He's my neighbor, not yours."

She giggled. "I gotta go. It's my mom's birthday, and we're having a big family dinner."

I nodded, barely registering what she said while I focused on my parents talking with Kyle. "Bye," I mumbled to Erin.

Kyle eyed me over my dad's shoulder as I wormed through the crowd.

"You look so handsome," I said when Josh smiled at me with recognition.

"Thanks," Kyle said, straightening his tie and lifting his chin. "It's the hair gel."

My parents laughed while I rolled my eyes. Kyle's lips twitched with a restrained smirk.

"Eve, your father was just singing your praises," Mom said.

"Pastor Peter Jacobson never sings my praises," I replied, leering at my dad.

"I give credit where credit is due, young lady. And Kyle said you offered to help with Josh."

Before I could respond, Kyle said, "You've done a great job raising Eve. She's very generous, dare I say selfless, with her time. Cleary a young woman with pure motives and an abundance of selflessness."

Speaking of motives, I wasn't sure what Kyle's were with his glowing compliment meticulously wrapped in bullshit. I offered a fake smile, which seemed to please him.

"Wow, Kyle. I can't tell you how much that means. Things have been a little rocky with Eve, but I think she's come to her senses and reached a new level of maturity," Dad said, and my mom nodded.

Kyle canted his head and looked at me. "Yes. She seems to make good choices."

There wasn't a proper response to be found, so I stood there with parted lips, a dry mouth, and a narrow-eyed gaze pointed at Kyle.

"Peter, weren't you going to ask Bill Ferguson about the board meeting?" Mom grabbed my dad's hand.

"Oh, yeah." He spied Bill getting into his car. "Excuse me, Kyle."

Kyle nodded.

When my parents headed toward the parking lot, I asked, "Do you pay such high compliments to all of your babysitters?"

Kyle shrugged as Josh wiggled out of his jacket. "Only the ones who ask to borrow a flashlight, blanket, beer, and gun." He took Josh's jacket before his squirmy son ran toward a group of young kids playing chase under the oak trees.

Was he flirting with me? I couldn't imagine. My attraction toward him made it hard to interpret how he looked at me with what felt like mischief in his eyes and a flirty grin.

"Your parents invited Josh and me to your house for Sunday dinner. And your mom said you made apple pie with the apples I gave you. But I only recall you picking one apple, which you ate the night I walked you home."

"She misheard me. I told her I used apples from the ground that blew off your trees and landed in our yard."

"Hmm, I don't recall a windy day since we moved in. It's a little way from my trees to your fence."

I crossed my arms over my chest without responding.

"You have a beautiful voice. Did you sing in the high school choir as well?"

I pinched my lips together to keep from grinning. When I thought I could maintain my composure, I cleared my throat. "My father made me join his choir after my older sister, Sarah, moved out of Devil's Head. I don't like to sing."

"I figured. Your lips didn't match the words," Kyle said, flashing me a gotcha grin.

"You said I have a beautiful voice." I scowled at him.

"You do. It's rather pleasant. But I didn't say you're a talented singer. I've never heard you sing. Neither has anyone else, huh? If you're going to stand in the front row where everyone can see you, I think you should, at the very least, memorize the correct lyrics."

I *did not* like him. Sure, I wanted him to tear off my clothes and do ungodly things to me, but not because I liked him. Why did he have to be so sexy *and* call me out like an errant child?

"Mr. Collins, I don't know how my father would feel about you staring at my mouth during his sermons. Seems a little inappropriate to me."

Kyle's smile died as his Adam's apple bobbed on a hard swallow. I enjoyed having the upper hand, but never imagined having it with him. Riding a wave of confidence, I stepped closer and stared at his shiny brown shoes momentarily before dragging my gaze up his body like he had done to me on more than one occasion.

When our eyes met, I grinned. "See you at Sunday dinner, Coach."

He took a step back and adjusted his tie.

My hormones exploded like a volcano. Despite my feigned confidence, I trembled, drowning in a sea of impure thoughts about a man much older than me.

"Can I go to Ben's after we eat?" Gabby asked, setting the dining room table.

"No. Sunday is a family day," I replied, filling the water glasses from an orange Tupperware pitcher.

"Will his parents be home?" Mom asked, placing the tuna noodle casserole onto the trivet in the middle of the table.

Why did that matter? Mom did a great job of shaming Sarah and me for wanting to do anything with friends on Sundays.

"I don't know. Why?" Gabby curled her shoulder-length brown hair behind her ear on one side while scrunching her nose.

"If they have alcohol in the house, you could decide to drink," I replied.

Mom eyed me with displeasure, and Grandma Bonnie snickered from the extra dining room chair beside the oak buffet; her hands busily crocheting. She wasn't a churchgoer, but we picked her up every Sunday for dinner.

"I don't drink. That's your thing." Gabby stuck her tongue out at me.

"Then you might decide to have sex," I said.

"Eww, Ben's my friend, not my boyfriend."

"Yes. But Mom and Dad know that given the chance to have sex, their girls will have sex with anyone."

"Eve!" Mom's voice jumped an octave, and Gabby giggled.

"Amen, sister," Grandma Bonnie added, earning a scowl from Mom.

"It's true." I nodded. "Last month, when I was *volunteering* at the nursing home, I delivered some magazines to Milton Bean in his room, and I was tempted."

"Eve Marie Jacobson," Mom said slowly, but she couldn't hide her grin.

Gabby covered her mouth and snorted.

"Rumor has it, Milton was quite the Casanova in his day. You could do worse, Eve," Grandma Bonnie added with a straight face.

"Never let your father hear you talk like that," Mom said, ignoring Grandma Bonnie's commentary.

"Talk like what?" Dad asked, reaching the bottom of the stairs just as there was a knock at the door.

"I'll get it." I shot my dad an exaggerated smile as I passed him on my way to the door.

"Hey," Kyle said, handing me a paper bag of apples. "Josh wants you to make him applesauce."

I stepped aside. "Is that so?" I smiled at Josh.

They no longer wore matching suits, but I liked Kyle just as much in his jeans and white-collared shirt.

"Glad you could make it." Dad ruffled Josh's already messy hair.

"Thanks for the invitation, Peter," Kyle said as I closed the door.

"I heard you met your team the other day." Dad led them to the dining room.

"Yes. It was a preseason dinner to meet the players and their families." Kyle pulled out a chair for Josh.

"I can't see," Josh complained with his head barely peeking over the top of the table.

"Eve, get the phonebook and a few other books for him to sit on." Mom nodded to me.

I grabbed a stack of books and set them on the chair.

"Eve," Dad scolded, removing the top book before Kyle lifted Josh onto the pile.

It was an old family Bible bigger than the dictionary and phonebook beneath it.

"What? You always say God is here to lift us up no matter what we need. And Josh needs to reach his plate."

"Amen, sister," Grandma Bonnie added. She didn't believe in God, but she said "Amen" just to poke at my dad.

"Excuse our daughter. She thinks she's funny, but she's not." Dad handed Mom the Bible, and she replaced it with another book.

Kyle grinned. *He* thought I was funny.

"Kyle, this is my mom, Bonnie," Mom said. "Mom, this is Fred's younger brother and his son, Josh. They moved in next door."

"Nice to meet you, Mrs.?" Kyle's implied question hung in the air.

"My husband died. I'm no longer a Mrs. anything. I'm just the old lady for whom everyone is waiting to die."

"Mom!" My mom gasped.

Gabby and I laughed, but Kyle restrained his, just barely.

"It's true. My granddaughters are the only ones who acknowledge my existence, except on Sundays when I get invited to dinner so Peter can ask God to save my wretched soul."

"I'll never stop praying for you," Dad said, earning him an eye roll from Grandma Bonnie.

"My mother's grossly exaggerating," Mom said with no examples to back up her claim before everyone sat at the table.

I took Grandma Bonnie's bag of yarn and set it aside and then helped her to a chair at the table.

Was I the favorite? For sure. She and my mom had a strained relationship because my mom preached (lectured) Grandma Bonnie about salvation and her lost soul bound for damnation if she didn't hurry up and accept Christ as her savior before she died. Gabby was the second favorite, but she didn't regularly visit Grandma Bonnie like I did, which was her loss. Grandma Bonnie was funny. She had the most entertaining stories, and I could tell her anything because she was a vault.

After prayer, Dad dove into all things football with Kyle, leaving the rest of us with little to say.

"You know you're going to have recruiters watching Drew. He's not only the best player in Devil's Head; he's arguably the best player in all of Missouri," Dad said, wiping his mouth.

Kyle nodded. "I'm looking forward to seeing what he's got."

Gabby kicked my shin, and I narrowed my eyes at her. She needed to work on keeping my secrets without constantly reminding me that she was keeping them. Drew was a big secret.

"Well, he's lucky to have you coach him. Did you girls

know that Kyle played football at Iowa?" Dad eyed Gabby and me like it was our cue to be impressed.

I wasn't ready to give Kyle that satisfaction, but Gabby took the bait.

"Wow. Were you a quarterback?" Her brown eyes widened.

Kyle sipped his water and nodded.

"Why didn't you play in the NFL?" she asked.

"Not everyone who plays in college is good enough for the NFL." Kyle chuckled.

"He who can, does; he who cannot, teaches," I said.

"Eve, do you need to excuse yourself and spend a little time in your room, thinking about how you should behave around guests?" Dad warned.

"What?" I shrugged. "It's not my quote."

"No. It's not. And if you can tell me who that quote belongs to, I'll let you finish dinner with us. Otherwise, you can take the rest to your room." Dad smiled because he knew I didn't know the answer. "And don't you dare help her," he warned Grandma Bonnie.

With a long sigh, I tossed my napkin onto the table and mumbled, "I'm done anyway."

"We'll let you come back down for dessert," Mom said. "Since you made the apple pie and the ice cream."

"Gee, thanks."

AFTER MORE THAN a half hour in my room, staring at the ceiling, there was a knock at my door.

"What?" I said in my grumpiest tone.

The door creaked open.

"George Bernard Shaw."

I sat up as Kyle stepped into my bedroom. My father was the only other guy who had ever been there.

He smiled. "You quoted George Bernard Shaw. But for the record, some of the greatest *doers* were also outstanding teachers: Einstein, Oppenheimer, Robert Frost ..."

"I don't think you can be in my room. My dad doesn't allow it."

Kyle picked up a trophy from my desk. "Well, I told him I would talk to you because, as a teacher and someone closer to your age, I might get through to you."

"Get what through to me?" I hopped off the bed, took the trophy from him, and returned it to my desk.

"Nothing. I just said it."

I grinned. Kyle wasn't like any teacher I'd ever had.

"You ran cross country?" He eyed me.

I nodded.

"Wow."

"Don't act so surprised."

Kyle shook his head and held up his hands in surrender. "Don't be so touchy. I'm *pleasantly* surprised."

I sat in my window seat, pulling one knee to my chest. "Why?"

"Because I pictured you drinking by the creek, not running long distances."

"I'm an excellent multitasker. I did both. Who's watching Josh?"

"Gabby. She's really good with him."

"Don't be fooled. She's not reliable. I'm still your best bet. She's always got her nose in a book, writing in the margins and doodling things. She'd lose him."

"Ouch. I thought sisters were supposed to be close."

"We are close. I'm just looking out for Josh."

And I was looking out for my new part-time job.

"What's your 5k time?" he asked, resting his shoulder against my wall.

"Sub eighteen."

His eyebrows jumped up his forehead. "No kidding?"

"No kidding."

"You should have gotten scholarship offers with that."

"Maybe, but then what? I don't think they let you run cross country in college without taking actual college classes. And I don't want to sit in a classroom. I need a break from school. I don't know what I want to do for the rest of my life."

"Some people think college can help you figure out what you want to do. You take different courses and see what piques your interest."

"Is that what you did?"

Kyle nodded. "I had a football scholarship and no idea what I wanted to do, so I did what everyone who didn't have a particular interest did."

"Get a degree in education?"

He smirked. "Exactly."

"Well, I don't want to teach. I'm not good at math. Obviously, I'm not good at literature. Maybe I'm the doer who can't teach. Maybe I'll plant an orchard and sell apples or pies. Maybe I'll make apple wine so I can get paid to drink all day. Or maybe I'll clean motel rooms forever just to piss off my parents."

"Eve," he shook his head. "You don't need to have it all figured out."

I grunted. "Can you tell my parents that?"

He twisted his lips and nodded. "I can."

"Really?" I couldn't gauge his sincerity.

"Really." He nodded toward the door. "Let's have some of your apple pie and chat with your grandma. I like her."

"She's the best." I followed him to the door, and he turned before opening it, leaving me within inches of bumping into him.

"Just between us, I love your humor. It's unexpected," he said.

"Why is that?" I should have stepped back, but Kyle smelled like a good blend of fresh-cut timber and spice.

He stared at my mouth.

My mouth!

I couldn't help but wet my lips as if he would kiss me. Even though I knew the chance of that hovered around the zero mark.

"Your humor is dry like red wine, but you claim to be so sweet."

Please keep looking at my mouth.

I could hear my heart racing.

"That just makes me unpredictable," I whispered because I felt more out of breath than I did after winning a race.

Kyle's white teeth peeked through his swelling grin. "That you are. You remind me of someone."

"Who?"

He winked. "Me."

Chapter Six

The Georgia Satellites,
"Keep Your Hands to Yourself"

Kyle

AFTER I PUT Josh to bed, I carried the phone onto the deck with the cord slid under the door and sat in a wooden rocking chair.

Adam answered on the second ring. "Hello?"

"Hey. Miss me yet?"

"Hell yes. How's it going?"

"Pretty good so far."

"You haven't found a new best friend, have you?"

I laughed. "It wouldn't be that hard."

"Have you figured out the only good thing in that little town is your neighbor girl, so it's time for you and Josh to return home?"

I chuckled. "Not quite. My QB this year is the real deal. I can't miss his senior year."

"Is he better than you?"

"Maybe. I don't know yet."

"When's your first practice?"

"This week. It's supposed to cool down a bit, so conditioning might not hurt as much."

"They'll still whine like the babies they are."

I cradled the phone between my ear and shoulder and cracked open a beer. "I don't doubt that. How's Lizzy?"

"I broke up with Lizzy."

I took a swig of my beer and grinned. "You've broken up with her twelve times. I'm not sure what it says about either of you that you keep getting back together, but I know you're back together."

Adam claimed he kept getting back together with his high school sweetheart because the town was small and the pickings were slim. I didn't buy it.

"It's just sex."

Barking a laugh, I adjusted the phone and brought the beer can to my lips before mumbling, "It's always just sex to you."

"Exactly. Then she assumes it's more, so I have to tell her it's not, and she calls it a breakup when it's just a clarification."

"Well, at least you're having sex."

"Don't give me that. If I lived where you live, I'd be fucking Eve every day. Maybe twice a day."

I winced. "Man, that's my pastor's daughter—my brother's *best friend's* daughter. You can't talk about her like that."

"Like what? Fuck? Everyone knows it means **F**ornication **U**nder **C**onsent of the **K**ing."

Again, I laughed, missing my friend already. "I don't think anyone *knows* that."

"Seriously, though, can you imagine what a scandal that would be if you screwed the preacher's daughter?"

"I can, actually. And that's why we're done talking about it."

Adam sighed, releasing a hum with it. "Remember being eighteen with surging hormones? Remember wanting to screw anything that moved?"

"I remember, but I've grown up. I have a child. A job. And morals. You, however, are still that guy. So I don't know why you're acting nostalgic about something you've never given up."

"I own an accounting firm. If that's not a job, then I don't know what is."

"*Firm* feels a bit too big for your office above your dad's garage."

"Fuck you, Kyle. The garage is an auto body shop, not like my mommy and daddy's garage."

I snickered. "I miss you already. You should move here or to a real *accounting firm* in St. Louis. Then we can hunt on the weekends. You can even bring Lizzy."

"I'm missing you less and less by the second."

"Come for a game. Maybe over homecoming weekend. I'm sure they'll need extra chaperones for the dance."

"As tempting as that sounds, I think you should come back here for a Broncos game."

"Or a Chiefs game in Missouri."

"We'll draw straws. I gotta go," he said.

"Lizzy calling?"

"No."

"Baby, I'm home," *Lizzy* called.

"Shit," Adam muttered.

"I don't know why she's calling it home when you're just having sex. But I'll let you go since I'm sure the king has given his consent for you and Lizzy to fornicate."

"If I didn't love ya, I'd hate you so much right now," he grumbled.

"Aw, that's sweet. The feeling is mutual."

THE NEXT MORNING, I took Josh to the first practice, but after he had a meltdown over wanting a snack (which I forgot to bring) and endlessly smacking the players on the butt, I called the Jacobsons before the afternoon practice.

"Hello?" Janet answered.

"Hey, Janet, it's Kyle. I'm in a bind. Kindergarten doesn't start for Josh until next week, but I have two-a-day practices this week. I took him with me this morning, and we had a few issues. Would Eve or Gabby be willing to watch him this afternoon? I'll see if I can make other arrangements for the rest of the week."

"Of course. Eve isn't home from the motel yet, and Gabby's at the church with Peter, but someone will help out, even if it's me. What time do you need to leave?"

"A quarter to four."

"Someone will be there."

"Thanks, Janet. I really appreciate it."

After a late lunch, Josh mowed the lawn with me. I had never had so much to mow in my life, and I was grateful that the previous owners left the riding mower when they sold me the house. Of course, it took twice as long as it should have because letting Josh help meant we made a lot of wrong turns and sudden stops and took frequent breaks to hydrate and pee because it was hot today.

By the time we made the last pass on the north side of the barn, my long-legged neighbor girl in cut-off shorts, a pink T-shirt, and white sneakers traipsed toward the house while eating an apple with one hand and carrying a bag in her other. Eve's dark hair tangled with the wind, and she shook her head to get it out of her face just as we stopped the mower by the garage.

When she smiled, I felt it in places I didn't need to feel the effects of an eighteen-year-old girl.

Woman.

I meant it when I said she reminded me of myself, but a better version. My family never found my humor funny. And I spent a lot of days grounded in my room. I had a penchant for alcohol and other things that weren't good for me.

"You're early," I said.

Eve chewed the bite of apple and inspected her watch, which had pink and yellow straps that day. "It's three fifty-five. I figured I was a little late."

"It's what?" I looked at my watch, but it still read one fifty. The battery had died.

"Nooo. No. No. No." I lifted Josh off the mower and sprinted toward the front door. As soon as I grabbed my keys off the kitchen counter, I dashed out the front door. "I'm going to be late. And I said anyone who's late has to run an extra mile." I opened the truck door. "Sorry. Thank you. Gotta go."

Eve grinned as I started my truck. She held her hand up with the apple and waved at me with her ring and pinkie fingers. I returned a grimace because it was all I could muster before I peeled out of the driveway.

I was five minutes late to practice, and the players let me know as much.

"You said if you were late, you'd run the extra mile," one of them reminded me.

Rod Webber, my assistant coach, smirked.

I shrugged off my shirt and tossed it onto the grass before jogging to the track. "If everyone just stands around watching me, I will make *you* run two extra miles."

The team, minus Rod, jogged behind me. By the time they finished their one required mile, I was already ahead by an extra lap and a half. Rod let them grab water before they stretched and moved on to drills while I finished my extra mile.

Although I knew I would miss Adam and our other friends in Colorado, I was happy with how talented my star quarterback and the rest of the team were. We were going to have a good year.

I RETURNED HOME a little after six, and the house smelled like an Italian eatery of garlic and spices. Josh was in his booster seat, eating lasagna at the dinner table.

"Hey," I said, smiling at him before shifting my attention to Eve, who was drying the last dish. "I had ingredients for lasagna?"

"No." She laughed. "My mom sent groceries with me in case you didn't have things to eat."

"There's bologna and bread." I filled a glass with water and gulped every drop.

Eve set a clean plate on the counter. "My mom doesn't consider a bologna sandwich a proper dinner. But don't tell her I told you that. She's not one for making anyone, except her daughters, feel bad about their life choices."

I stood behind Josh and bent down to nuzzle his neck.

He giggled. "Stop, Daddy! You're sweaty."

"I know." I shrugged off my shirt and used it to wipe my face and sweaty hair. "When you're done eating, I'll shower."

"If you want to shower now, I can wait for him to finish." Eve smiled. It wasn't her usual sassy grin. It was more of a shy one that made her cheeks turn pink. And she averted her gaze when I looked at her.

"Are you sure?"

"Mm-hmm." She nodded while wiping the already clean counter with the dishtowel.

"Thanks."

Eve returned a second "Mm-hmm."

When I finished my shower, Josh was in the living room, playing with his blocks and Matchbox cars, while Eve grated an apple in the kitchen. A plate of lasagna, salad, and garlic bread was at the table, along with a folded paper napkin, fork, and a glass of ice water.

"This is beyond what I expected when I called your mom, begging for someone to help me tonight," I said, sitting at the table. "This looks and smells incredible."

Eve glanced up from the bowl of shredded apple and smiled. "Thanks."

"Are you making your special applesauce?"

She nodded.

"I might just keep you." I stabbed my fork into the lettuce.

Eve paused her hands, brown eyes wide and unblinking.

I shook my head while I chewed the salad. "That sounded wrong. I just meant Josh could get spoiled having homemade lasagna and fresh applesauce."

She cleared her throat and sprinkled cinnamon and sugar into the bowl. "Did you punish yourself for being late to practice?"

I smirked over the bite of lasagna and nodded. "It's only fair," I mumbled.

"What do you think of your quarterback?"

"Drew? He's good. Really good."

Eve put the cinnamon and sugar into the brown paper bag she brought with her.

"How was your day? Do a lot of people stay at the motel?"

"No." She laughed. "So I work slowly to get in the hours I want. I turn on the TV in the rooms while I clean. Watch a show. Clean things twice. No motel or hotel in this great state has cleaner rooms than the Devil's Head Inn."

I grinned. "By the way," I used my fork to point to the lasagna, "this is the best meal I've had in years. Have you considered culinary school?"

Her nose wrinkled. "You *just* said that's the best meal you've had in years, which felt like a compliment, but now you think I need schooling because it's not good enough?"

"No. I suggested schooling because a degree in something makes you more marketable."

"Did my parents tell you to talk to me about school?"

"No. This lasagna is amazing. Period. Forget I mentioned school."

"Is it better than my mom's tuna noodle casserole?"

"If I say yes, will you tell on me?"

"Depends." She set Josh's applesauce on the table at his seat. "What are you going to do for me?"

I nearly choked, so I drank some water and cleared my throat. "I figured I'd pay you for watching him."

"I don't want your money." She tucked her hands into her back pockets, tightening her shirt against her chest. Either she wasn't wearing a bra, or it was a thin one that didn't hide her nipples.

Fuck.

"What do you want?" I murmured, pointing my gaze at the plate of food before me.

"I want you to teach me things."

Fuck. Fuck. Fuck.

My dick wanted the same thing. But no way it would happen in hell, heaven, or anywhere between.

"Math?" I asked with a grin. "Literature?"

"I want you to teach me to shoot a gun and use a bow and arrow. And I want to learn how to drive your fishing boat and fillet fresh-caught fish."

I tapped my fork against my lips for a few seconds. "I'd have to ask your parents."

Eve frowned, canting her head to the side. "You can't be serious. I'm an adult. I can vote for the next president. Buy cigarettes. Get an abortion. Or get married. Oh, did I mention I can purchase my own gun?"

She had a good point, but it wasn't that simple for me. "I think it's better if I just pay you like I'd pay any other babysitter."

Twisting her lips, she slowly nodded. "Fine." She grabbed my plate, scraped the rest of my dinner into the trash, and set the plate and fork into the sink. Then she put the lid on the lasagna dish and gathered it and the paper sack in her arms. "Josh, your applesauce is on the table," she called on her way to the front door. "I'll see you later."

Josh ran past me as I followed Eve.

She shoved her feet into her white sneakers, but with her hands full, she couldn't get the left shoe past her heel. I squatted before her, untied her shoe, and put it on her correctly. After I finished tying it, my fingers feathered up her calf. I quickly stood the second I realized what I was doing and seemingly had no control over my unexplained impulse to touch her leg.

"You didn't have to throw my dinner in the trash," I blurted out the first thing that came to mind. Anything to dismiss what I just did.

But Eve didn't miss it. She looked like a frozen statue, not so much as a blink. After the longest seconds and most uncomfortable moment of my life, she released a slow breath, rubbing her lips together—and then she fucking smirked. "I only do nice things for people who can return a favor. You don't know how to reciprocate. You're a boring rule follower. I've never met anyone so square ... except for my parents. Good night, Mr. Collins." She turned and bent forward to push open the screen door rather than asking for help.

"I can carry those home for you," I said.

"Josh is eating. You can't leave him alone. I've got it."

"I haven't paid you."

She descended the porch stairs. "Think of it as a trial run that didn't work out. A free trial."

"Eve—"

I wanted to follow her, but she was right. Josh was eating his applesauce, and while it was unlikely that he'd choke on it, I couldn't risk it.

I touched her leg.

Could I have been a bigger creep?

Chapter Seven

Michael Jackson,
"The Way You Make Me Feel"

Eve

ERIN WAS my biggest competitor in cross country, which meant she was always willing to run with me when I needed to burn off frustration. After depositing the leftover lasagna and bag of ingredients at home, I drove straight to her house because I had a lot of steam and so much to share with my best friend.

"He touched my leg!" I said for the hundredth time after telling her the events.

We jogged our usual route in the field on the south side of town.

"Maybe he had to touch it to get your foot into your shoe."

"No. It was after my shoe was on and tied. And he just ...

teased the back of my leg with his fingers. I nearly dropped everything I was holding, and I had to bite my tongue because I almost moaned." I slowed down to let her catch her breath because she was giggling so much.

"That's so inappropriate," she said.

I didn't respond.

"Right?" she prompted.

"Yeah. Of course. I mean, it's not like I'm a minor. And he's older but not old enough to be my dad."

And I grinned after he did it.

"He has a child, Eve. And maybe this age difference later in your life wouldn't be a big deal, but I bet your parents would die. I'm serious. They. Would. Die."

"Sarah dated an older man."

"As old as Kyle?"

"I don't know. I haven't asked his age. And it doesn't matter anyway," I said, feeling winded. It had been a while since I'd felt the need to run that hard. "I totally just quit on him. I can't go back now and beg for my job back like nothing happened."

"Can you just imagine if he would have done more? Like, what if he would have kissed you? What would you have done? I would have died."

I knew what I would have done. I would have kissed him back because I had been thinking about kissing him since the day we met.

"I might have dropped the lasagna and bag of groceries. That's for sure." I laughed.

"He's lonely. He has to be lonely."

I lightly body-checked her.

"Hey!" She stumbled a few steps. "What was that for?"

"I can't believe you think the only reason he would be

interested in me is because he's lonely. Maybe he thinks I'm hot. Maybe he thinks I'm sweet with an irresistibly dry humor. Maybe he likes my cooking."

"I'm totally not saying there's anything wrong with you, Eve. Except *you're eighteen.* And we just graduated. And he's a teacher and coach at our school. What if he had come last year? Would you have made a case for having a crush on him had he been *your* math teacher?"

She had a point, but it wasn't a good one.

As soon as we finished our run, we collapsed on the field and stared at the last bit of sunlight and an orange and pink hew in the cloudless western sky.

I sighed. "I want him to kiss me."

Erin rolled her head to look at me, but I kept my gaze on the sky and grinned.

When I pulled into the drive and parked next to the propane tank, I could see a figure in my headlights just past the fence. I climbed out of my car as Kyle rested his forearms on the fence.

"I'm sorry," he said.

"Where's Josh?"

"Asleep."

"What are you sorry for?" I slid my key ring onto my finger, taking slow steps toward the fence.

"For touching your leg. It wasn't intentional." Kyle closed his eyes for a second and shook his head. "I was tired after a long day. And I was hungry, but you threw my dinner in the trash. And my mind was somewhere else after I put on your shoe. I don't know why I was touching your leg. But it was wrong, and I'm sorry."

I bowed my head, fiddling with my keys. "You know, I'm a legal adult. You didn't molest me. You're not my teacher. It was my calf, not like my boob. So, I don't know why you're apologizing for that."

"It was—" he started to speak, but I cut him off.

"If you're going to apologize for something, apologize for treating me like a child. I know I'm young, but I'm a young *adult*. You're not that old. Don't you remember what it was like to be my age? Did you want people treating you like a child? When you graduated college and got your first job, did you want people to treat you like you were unqualified even though you earned a degree?"

"I'm ten years older, by the way." A slow grin bloomed along his face.

"So. And what's that look for?" I asked.

He shook his head. "Nothing. You just always surprise me."

"Well, why don't you try a little harder to surprise me because you've been predictable so far."

He scraped his teeth along his lower lip. "You want me to be unpredictable?"

"Yes. Everything and everyone in my life is boring and predictable. Be a little more inappropriate with me."

He coughed on a laugh. "You mean unpredictable."

"Same difference."

"Uh ... it's not. But I understand what you're saying, however, not everyone will, so we need to set boundaries."

"What do you mean?"

"You babysit for me, and I'll teach you things. But we don't tell anyone that we're bartering."

"You mean my parents?"

"I mean *anyone*."

I knew I would tell Erin.

And Grandma Bonnie.

"Did you find someone to watch Josh until school starts?" I stepped up on the fence rail so we were closer to eye level.

"No." He said without backing away from me. "I'll pack snacks next time."

"What time is your morning practice done?"

"Eleven."

"I can go into the motel later and return by the time you leave for the second practice."

"Then you won't make as much money if you finish your work in less time."

I shrugged. "I don't pay rent."

He eyed me with contemplation. "Are you sure?"

I nodded. "It's just for a few days. You can buy me some beer or wine coolers, and we'll call it even."

He grinned. "I have to draw a line. And that's a hard one. I won't be providing you with any alcohol."

"You're no fun." I frowned.

"Because I had bologna for dinner instead of lasagna. You threw my fun in the trash."

I laughed. "That was your own fault. Now, when are you going to teach me something new?"

Had he not stared at my mouth, my mind would not have gone to anything sexual, but he did. And my face filled with heat.

"We can go fishing after dinner tomorrow if your sister will babysit Josh."

"I'll ask her."

"No." He pinched the bridge of his nose and laughed. "You're already failing at this. If I'm taking *you* fishing, and we're not telling anyone, then you need to have other plans tomorrow night, hence why *I* will ask Gabby if she can watch Josh."

I leaned forward until there were about six inches between our faces, and he didn't move, which thrilled me. "Or I can ask her and tell her you asked me first, and when I said I had plans, I told you I'd check with her for you." I grinned.

Gah!

Again, he stared at my mouth, and I could practically taste his lips. My heart skipped so many beats that I wasn't sure it would recover.

His gaze inched up to mine. "Can you watch Josh tomorrow night for me?"

"No." I grinned.

"Why not?"

"Because I'm going out with friends. But I can see if Gabby can watch him for you."

He smiled. "Attagirl."

"I'm going to be your best unofficial student, Mr. Collins."

"Straight A's?"

I hopped off the fence. "I've never gotten straight A's." I headed toward the house so he wouldn't see me drool over him, melt at his feet, and lose all my dignity because I had an incurable crush on my neighbor.

"You've never had me as your teacher," he said.

Oh my god …

Chapter Eight

Chaka Khan, "I Feel For You"

Eve

"Eve? You're going to be late. What are you doing?" Mom called upstairs the next morning.

Gabby was an easy sell to watch Josh. My parents didn't think twice about my plans to go out with friends. But before any of that could happen, I had motel rooms to clean and babysitting to do while Kyle coached.

However, my infatuation with Coach Collins grew exponentially overnight, and I couldn't show up to his place looking like the previous day's version of myself. I needed to curl my hair, lotion my legs (in case he wanted to touch them again), and wear something nice.

"Why is your hair down? And why are you wearing that white blouse to work?" Mom quizzed me the second I stepped into the kitchen to grab a quick bowl of cereal.

I didn't need my mom to grill me. I'd already met my quota of lies, yet she insisted I tell one more.

"I'm going to change my clothes before I go to work. Most of my work clothes have stains, and I think they smell like Pledge even though they've been washed. I'm just putting my best foot forward so Kyle trusts that I'm responsible and presentable while I babysit Josh."

I didn't believe my lie and never imagined my mom would.

But she did. "That's very mature of you." She smiled with pride.

"Thanks. I'm trying."

"Martha Wertz, Tali Rae, *and* Denise Overton have all called me about Kyle," Mom said.

"Why?" I screwed the cap back on the milk.

Mom dried her hands and grinned. "Because they are single and found out he is too."

I wrinkled my nose. "Are you serious?"

"Why the look?" She sat next to me at the table and sipped her coffee.

"He *just* moved in. Talk about vultures." I shoveled cereal into my mouth so I wouldn't be late to Kyle's.

"Eve, they're not stalking his place. And I'm sure he doesn't want to stay single for the rest of his life. Josh deserves a motherly figure in his life, and Kyle deserves a wife."

"So why did they call you? Are you supposed to be a matchmaker?"

"No. They just wanted to know if he was divorced or widowed."

"And what did you say?" I mumbled over a mouthful of cereal while milk dribbled down my chin.

Mom frowned and handed me a napkin. "I said he's neither."

"What do you mean? And how do you know?"

"Your dad talked to Fred the other day. Josh's mom wasn't ready to be a mother, but she had him anyway."

"And then what?"

Mom shrugged. "Fred said she left."

"Left? When? Recently? Or when he was a baby?"

Mom shook her head. "Your dad didn't ask. He didn't want to pry. It's nobody's business."

I couldn't imagine leaving a child at any age.

"Maybe he didn't want Josh's mom to leave. Maybe he's heartbroken. I wouldn't play matchmaker quite yet."

Mom shook her head. "I'm not. But it's a free world. If they call him and one thing leads to another, then I guess it's God's plan."

No.

God's plan was for Kyle to be my crush.

My obsession.

My favorite dream.

I didn't want to share him, even if he wasn't mine to not share.

And he didn't have time to date because he was too busy teaching me things.

"GOOD MORNING," Kyle said with an irresistible smile as I approached his house.

He was sitting on the porch swing with a steaming cup of coffee.

My gaze devoured every inch of him in his Devil's Head T-shirt, jogging shorts, and black Nikes.

"Morning. Where's Josh?"

"Still asleep. But he'll wake up soon. Do you drink coffee?"

I shook my head. "It tastes grody, even with sugar."

"Have you tried it with cream?"

"Why?" I leaned against the wooden post.

"Because it tastes better with cream."

"Better than what? If something tastes nasty, why try to make it less nasty unless it's something like broccoli or Brussels sprouts that are good for you?"

He chuckled before sipping his coffee. Then he held it out to me. "Try it."

I had no interest in trying his coffee, but I was very interested in sharing a drink with him, putting my mouth close to where his had been.

I pushed off the post and took the mug, taking a small sip.

It was still grody.

"Better, huh?"

I shook my head, handing him the mug. "No. Not better. Orange juice is better. The apples on your trees are better. Brussels sprouts are better."

"You look extra nice today. What's the occasion?"

I glanced down at my blouse and pleated khaki shorts. "They're just clothes."

"Do you clean rooms in those?"

Why did everyone have to comment on my clothes?

"Where are you taking me fishing?"

"Black Paw Lake."

"Nobody fishes there."

"Exactly. But there are fish in the lake, so two birds, one stone."

"You don't want anyone seeing us fish?"

"Bingo." He winked.

I opened my mouth to protest his need to be so secretive, but then it hit me that we would be secluded and alone, which was fine too.

He stood and sipped his coffee again before heading into the house.

"You should know that three desperate women in town are interested in you." I followed him into the kitchen. "They asked my mom about you. I said she should stay out of it. You just moved here. You have a new job. And you have Josh. So ..."

He set his mug by the sink. "You assume I don't have time to date? Or you don't think any of these women are a good match for me?"

"Yes." I returned a sharp nod.

Kyle grinned. "You don't think I have time to date, *and* you don't think any of these women are a good match for me?"

"Correct." I pressed my lips together and shrugged.

"Or is it that you don't want me dating anyone, which makes no sense."

"First, why would I care if you date someone? And you're right; it wouldn't make sense for me *not* to want you to date, but why do you think that?"

"Because if I date someone, I'll need a babysitter. And if you babysit for me, then I'll owe you which means you'll learn more things on that long list of yours. You should want me to date."

Or you could date me.

"True. But we don't have time to discuss this any longer. You have practice, and none of these women are the ones. I'll let you know if I find a good fit."

Kyle's eyebrows made a slow ascent of his forehead. "Are you my babysitter *and* my matchmaker?"

I rolled my eyes and sighed. "I hadn't planned on it, but I'm obviously the best qualified, so I'll do it."

He grabbed his keys. "Why are you best qualified?"

"Because I'm young. I know almost everyone in town. I hear all the gossip. And I have totally awesome taste in everything."

"And you're humble. So humble." He smirked, stopping beside me before continuing to the door.

I didn't turn my head at first, but when I did, he winked.

Why was he such a winker? And why did I think it meant he liked me? Like ... *liked* me.

Chapter Nine

John Parr, "Naughty Naughty"

Eve

WE MET at the lake after dinner.

Kyle was already in his fishing boat when I arrived. I walked at double speed, clenched my fists, and told myself to slow down and chill out. But I couldn't. He was taking me fishing on a lake that didn't have another boat in sight.

"What took you so long?" he asked, offering his hand to help me off the dock and into the boat.

I didn't need his help, but I liked how my hand fit into his. "You didn't tell me which dock. And there are three at this lake. I drove to the other two first."

"Oh, I thought there was only one." He gave me a half grin. "Sorry."

"Yeah, I can tell," I said before nodding to the engine. "Okay. What's the first step?"

"Oh, you're driving it today?" He narrowed his eyes.

"Yes. What did you think we were doing?"

"Fishing and filleting."

I shrugged. "Well, show me how to drive the boat, and I'll take us to the fish; then we can catch and fillet."

"Okay. First, make sure the engine is fully tilted down like this."

I nodded.

"Then you need to squeeze this priming bulb until it's full."

I squeezed it. "Now what?"

"Make sure the throttle is in neutral." He showed me that. "Key on. Choke out. Pull the cord."

I followed his steps. "Ouch!" I grabbed my shoulder after a failed attempt at pulling the cord.

Kyle chuckled. "You have to use your muscles. Do you have any?" He playfully squeezed my upper arm.

I batted his hand away. "It's not funny," I said, but I laughed anyway. "Let's skip the starting part. I just want to drive it."

"Eve, if you can't start this boat, I won't let you fire a gun. And there's no way you can pull my bow back to shoot an arrow."

I frowned. "Fine. I'll try again." I gripped it harder, and again, it didn't start, but at least it didn't hurt my arm as much.

"You'll flood it if you don't get it started soon."

"Yeah, yeah." On the third attempt, it started. "I did it!"

"Sit. You're going to fall out of the boat. Let's try less celebrating and more concentrating." He showed me how to make it go, how to steer the tiller in the opposite direction from our intended direction, and how to stop when we reached our spot to fish. Despite his repeated eye rolls and smirks, I thought I did a great job.

"Do I need to show you how to put the worm on the hook?"

"No." I wrinkled my nose. "I know how to fish. My grandpa taught me."

"But he didn't teach you how to drive a boat?"

I shook my head, putting the worm on my hook. "He just fished off the dock. Catch and release."

Kyle cast his line. "That's all we'll be doing. I don't think we'll catch anything worthy of dinner in this lake."

We reeled in our lines and cast again.

"I didn't get a chance to ask what you and Josh did this afternoon," he said.

"We picked apples, chased butterflies, and then he played in his room while I snooped around in yours," I said and bit my lip to keep from grinning while my attention stayed on my line.

I felt his gaze on me briefly before he watched his line again. "I know you're trying to get a reaction out of me, but I also don't think you're lying either. You just think I'm going to think that you're lying. So, did you find anything interesting in my room?"

"Besides your *Playboy* magazines? No."

Kyle paused his hands. "July is my favorite." Then he resumed reeling in his line.

He was right. I tried to disguise the truth as a lie or a joke. I did snoop in his room, and I did find his *Playboy* magazines.

"I didn't open any drawers. And I only looked under the mattress just to appease my ridiculous side. I honestly didn't think you'd have magazines there." I fought my smile. "I was wrong."

"The articles are really good."

I laughed. "Stop."

He grinned. "It's true. There was a recent article on AIDS that was well written and thoroughly researched."

"Is that what you read to Josh at night? Thoroughly researched articles about a deadly virus?"

"No. He just likes to look at the pictures."

"Coach Collins, you're a pervert."

"You mean a hot-blooded man."

"Oh! I got a bite!" I pulled up on my pole and reeled in the fish.

"Nice one." Kyle grabbed the fish.

"I can take it off," I said.

He eyed me with surprise and held my pole while I removed the fish and gently returned it to the lake.

"I should have brought my camera," Kyle said, handing me my pole.

"Why? So you could take a photo of me and my fish that I couldn't show anyone because, according to you, this isn't happening?"

"You're right. This is our moment. I might not remember the look on your face when it tugged at your line, but I'll *never* forget the look on your face when you tried to start the boat."

"Oh, really? My pain is more memorable to you than my joy?"

"Everything about you is memorable." As soon as he said the words, he got a look on his face that *I* would never forget.

Panic.

"I meant *entertaining*. I find your actions entertaining."

"As entertaining as the magazines under your bed?"

"Did your parents forget to teach you manners and proper etiquette for respecting other people's privacy?"

"I told you I didn't open any drawers."

"For someone with such a biblical name, you make me think Eve is just short for evil."

"Stop!" I shoved him playfully just as he leaned toward the edge.

I repeat. It was a *playful* shove.

Yet, he fell out of the boat.

"Oh shit! Kyle?"

He emerged and shook his head like a wet dog. "What the hell, Eve?"

I cupped a hand over my mouth while my other hand gripped the side of the boat as it rocked from his body rolling out of it.

"I'm so sorry. Are you okay?"

"Of course, I'm okay," he grumbled. "Now, help me back in the boat." He reached a hand toward me.

I don't know why he thought the same arm that struggled to start the boat would magically have the strength to hoist his two-hundred-pound body into it without the whole thing capsizing. However, I had no choice but to trust him. So I gave him my hand.

"Kyle—" My words died as he pulled me into the water. I surfaced and wiped my eyes while he climbed into the boat without help. "You jerk! You did that on purpose! What if I can't swim?"

He reached under the seat and tossed me a life jacket. Then he peeled off his T-shirt and rung it out over the side of the boat. "There was this article on boat safety in one of my magazines. Did you happen to read it when you were snooping?"

I didn't give him the satisfaction of carrying on like a damsel in distress. Instead, I hugged the life jacket and floated on my back, staring up at the mountains of clouds in the distance. "Do you think my dad and your brother look at *Playboy* magazines?" I asked, even though I couldn't hear his answer with my ears under the water. "I mean God probably appreciates them. Of course, He focuses on the articles, but while He's flipping from one article to the next, I bet He appreciates the titty photos. After all, it's just admiring His artwork. Don't you agree?"

When I lifted my head, Kyle was still shirtless with his back to me while he fished out of the opposite side of the boat.

"You'll be happy to know that I take much better care of your child than you take care of your brother's best friend's daughter."

"You pushed me in the water. Maybe you were trying to drown me. That's attempted murder." He set his pole aside and turned, offering me his hand.

I didn't trust him, but I was out of other options, so I swam toward the boat and flung my life jacket into it before accepting his help.

Once I was inside the boat, I held up both arms. Kyle stared at me with a wrinkled brow.

"Help me remove my shirt so I can wring it out."

He chuckled, shaking his head. "No way."

"I have on a bra. Think of it like a bikini top."

"No. Just wring it out the best you can without taking it off."

"You're shirtless. What's the big deal? No one's around here. We could skinny dip and get away with it."

"We're not skinny dipping, and you're not removing your top."

"Why? Worried you can't control yourself?"

"Eve, I haven't strangled you. I think I'm showing a lot of control."

"Don't be a square. Do you think I want to leave my clothes on after you got me wet?"

He gazed at the sky for a brief moment before tucking his chin and pinching the bridge of his nose. "Christ," he mumbled. "Don't say it like that. Just sit down. Let's head back to the dock."

I had other ideas.

Kyle stiffened, staring between his legs at my wet shirt when it landed next to his feet.

"If I were Adam, I'd remove my wet shirt, right? We'd crack open a beer, too, but you didn't bring beer, which leads me to believe you don't really think of me as that kind of friend."

"Put your shirt back on," he said, keeping his head bowed.

"No. Just look at me. My bra is on. You look at naked women in magazines. I'm not naked. Stop making this weird. You're totally freaking out over nothing."

Kyle lifted his gaze and stared at my chest like it needed to be studied. Then he peered out at the water. "What's there to look at?"

"Jerk." I wrinkled my nose.

"Snoopy perv," he said.

I bit my lip to keep from giggling, then I twisted my hair

and leaned to the side to wring out the water. "See. No big deal. We're just buddies fishing."

Little lines of distrust formed at the corners of his eyes.

"I wonder how many couples named Adam and Eve end up together. It would get exhausting dealing with the looks and snickers every time they introduced themselves. Can you imagine?" I asked, combing my fingers through my hair.

Kyle's gaze stayed firmly on the water, but he grinned.

"How did you and Adam meet?"

"I've known him since kindergarten." He squinted against the sun.

"That's how long I've known my friend Erin. You must really miss him. Erin has decided to attend a community college for her first two years, so she commutes from home. I don't know what I will do when she moves away to finish school. Maybe you'll have to fill in as my best friend. We can fish, hunt, and drink together."

Kyle kept staring at the sunset while scratching his jaw. "Think so?" He reached between his legs and grabbed my shirt, squeezing the water from it before tossing it to me.

"I'm looking at you, and you're not even wearing a bra," I said.

Kyle rolled his lips between his teeth, gazing at my feet. "This was a bad idea. You're every kind of imaginable trouble." In the next breath, he started the engine and steered us back to the dock.

He was supposed to let me drive, but I didn't make a big deal out of it, surprising myself with my new level of maturity.

"I should get back in case Gabby's having any issues with Josh," he said, climbing out of the boat.

This time, I ignored his proffered hand since he still

wouldn't look at me. "Yes. I'm sure Josh is giving her fits," I said with a heavy dose of sarcasm.

Kyle loaded his boat onto the trailer in what I imagined was record time while I sat on the edge of the dock.

"Are you going home too?" he asked, threading his arms through his wet shirt.

"I'm going to hang out here until I dry off more." With my legs dangling over the dock's edge, I leaned back, gazing at the heavens.

"I can't leave you here alone."

"Why?"

"If anything happened—"

"Bears?" I asked.

"Animals. Creepy people in the woods. Anything."

I lifted onto my elbows and caught him looking at me. "You think there are creepy people in the woods?"

After a shrug, he tucked his chin and kicked at the gravel. "Anything's possible."

"Huh." I leaned back again. "It might not look like it, but I was a late bloomer. All of my friends got curves and breasts before I did. Then, last summer, boom! I got 'em. It made me think of Creation. In her seventeenth year of life, God gave Eve boobs, and it was good. Hmm ... perhaps that's more like The Big Bang Theory."

My head lulled to the side as Kyle fought his reaction, rubbing his fingers over his lips to hide his grin. That was his thing. He did it a lot with me. Then, his body started shaking with laughter.

My new favorite thing was making him laugh and smile when he didn't want to.

"Eve," he shook his head, reeling in his reaction and regaining his composure. "You're a handful."

"You mean fun."

"I mean *evil*. And I need you to go home so I can sleep in peace, knowing you're nestled into your bed instead of alone on this dock."

"I wouldn't be alone if you'd lie next to me and trust that Gabby already has Josh in bed, and she's probably talking to a friend on the phone." I closed my eyes.

After a minute of hesitation, I felt him lie next to me.

"Attaboy." I grinned.

"I'm older. I should be the influencer, but I fear you're the bad influence on me."

"Because I'm fun?"

He hesitated, and I wanted to peek into his brain to see everything I knew he wouldn't say.

"You're ... something."

I giggled. "I'm going to pretend you think I'm something good."

He neither confirmed nor denied my assumption.

"Does Josh know his mom?" I held my breath, hoping he wouldn't up and leave me.

"No."

"Does he ask about her?"

"No."

I waited to ask another question because I didn't want to upset him by sounding overly anxious for answers. "And you weren't married?"

"No."

"Me neither."

Kyle chuckled.

"Do you have a good relationship with your family? I think my father would disown me if I had a baby out of wedlock. And since your brother is a pastor too, I bet he wasn't happy. Huh?"

"We have an older sister who has been arrested twice and to rehab more times than I can count. And she's had at least two abortions that I know of. My family loves Josh. And I have a *good enough* relationship with them. I can't be responsible for anyone's happiness but my own. Even Josh will grow up and find his own way in life, and his happiness will be out of my control."

I couldn't be with Kyle and not have my crush on him intensify. The problem was that no matter how hard I tried to convince everyone else that I was an adult, he made me feel like a young girl with hearts in my eyes and unrealistic dreams of falling for the guy who consumed my every thought. But my tenacity was bigger than all of that self-doubt. So I rolled toward him, resting my head on my outstretched arm.

His head lulled to the side, gazing at me.

"I want to live like you," I said.

Lines formed along his forehead.

"I want to feel in control of my happiness. I don't want to live my life for anyone else. And if I make mistakes, I want to find something good to take from them. I want to be fearless."

The corner of his mouth twitched. "You think I'm fearless."

"Well, I think you seem fearless. You're raising a child on your own. Maybe you're just doing a good job of acting brave and mature. I'm trying to be brave by *not* attending college because I don't want to conform. I don't want to be part of the herd. I just want to be myself and go wherever that leads me.

Maybe that means I'll spend most of my life doing odd jobs like cleaning motel rooms. I might not have a big house or a fancy car, but I don't care. I want my work to be an afterthought. Ya know? When someone thinks of Eve Jacobson, I want them to think, 'Oh, yeah. Eve loves to fish, stargaze, skip rocks along the water, pick apples and bake pies, dance to good music, go to the movies with friends, and make love in fields of wildflowers.' I don't want them thinking, 'There's Eve Jacobson; she cleans motel rooms and never went to college.' But that's what they'll think. So I want to be fearless like you and not care what they think."

He chuckled. "What makes you think I don't care what other people think?"

I smirked. "Duh. You're a math teacher."

"Which is an admirable profession."

"Mr. Collins, I'm not sure admirable is the right word. I wasn't an A student in English, but admirable implies people admire you for being a math teacher, like they think being a math teacher is cool and you make them want to be a math teacher."

He snickered. "Miss Jacobson, you're thinking of the word envy or inspiring. Admire or admirable means you regard someone with respect. It can also mean you look at someone with great pleasure. I don't want to be an astronaut, but I admire them."

I giggled. "And you probably look at those centerfolds with great pleasure, huh?"

"Well, putting yourself out there like those women do takes a lot of courage. If that's not admirable, then I don't know what is."

My side hurt from laughing so much. His gaze slid to my shoulder, and my breath hitched when his fingertips brushed my skin as he slid my bra strap up my arm and back onto my shoulder. Then he let his gaze slip to my chest.

I swallowed, lips parting to accommodate an audible breath. Either I was a total idiot, or he was attracted to me. But it scared me to assume anything because I didn't want to be wrong and feel like a fool—a naive child.

"What's next?" I whispered.

Kyle's gaze lifted to mine.

"Target shooting with a gun or a bow?" I asked.

Something akin to relief washed over his face. "This weekend, I can get out my bow."

I grinned. "Need me to find you a babysitter?"

"Nah. Josh has a bow too. Just come over early Saturday morning if you're not working. Tell your parents Josh wants to show you his archery skills."

"Should I feel guilty that you're making excuses for me?"

He looked at my chest again and mumbled a "no" before wetting his lips.

It sent goosebumps along my skin, and I tried to control my breathing, but my heart ran wildly out of my control, chasing a feeling that I wanted to be real.

"It's not an excuse. If I ask Josh if he wants to show you his bow and arrows, he'll say yes." He cleared his throat and jackknifed to sitting, running his fingers through his hair.

I sat up, too, and threaded my arms through my cold, damp shirt before standing. When he reached for me, my heart almost stopped. He gathered my long hair in his hand and pulled it out from the back of my shirt.

His gaze followed his hands like he was mesmerized by my long hair as he let it fall down my back. The way he looked at me felt intimate and sexy.

He never would have done that to a student. I don't think

he would have done that to Gabby, either. I wasn't crazy. His subtle gestures weren't simply kind; they were more.

"So I'll see you in the morning," I said before my knees buckled.

"In the morning," he echoed.

"Thanks for letting me drive your boat."

Kyle grinned. "I think I'm getting the better deal, but you're welcome."

"Because I spent more time watching Josh than you spent teaching me to drive your boat?"

"Sure." He winked. "That too."

Chapter Ten

Foreigner, "Say You Will"

Eve

"You're glowing," Grandma Bonnie said, adjusting her glasses with her arm while she crocheted from the recliner in her room.

Lillyann McDonald, a junior at the high school, played the piano in the foyer just down the hall from Grandma's room. She was trying to get volunteer hours in for college applications. I closed the door for a bit of privacy and so Grandma could hear me past the piano.

"I think I'm on the verge of doing something stupid, but I don't know how to stop," I said.

Grandma Bonnie paused her hands and eyed me over the top of her glasses. "Well, my dear, I guess the question is, do you want to stop? And if you don't, what are the consequences?"

That right there was the reason I spent so much time at

the nursing home. My parents would never have given me that response. They would have beaten the truth out of me with a big guilt trip and the threat of spending another moon cycle locked in my room.

"I don't want to stop, but I also don't know the consequences for sure."

"Is it dangerous?"

I shook my head.

"Illegal?"

Again, I shook my head.

"Does it involve a boy?"

I grinned.

She nodded slowly and returned her attention to the half-finished blanket on her lap. "Have you prayed about it?"

I giggled. Grandma didn't believe in God but supported what she called my parents' need to "imagine."

My dad always corrected her with the word "faith" or "belief."

"I know God's answer," I said.

"But?"

"But ..." I sighed, plopping onto the bed. "But what if God's answer is really just my dad's voice in my head. Maybe God would be like, 'Go for it, Eve. You only live once.'"

"Are you asking for my advice, permission, or do you just need to talk this through out loud?"

"I love you," I said with a huge grin.

Her shoulders relaxed as if my confession melted her. "Are you buttering me up?"

"No. I just wish my parents would say the things you say. I wish they'd let me figure things out on my own without feeling the need to control me and punish me for every wrong decision."

"Well, in all fairness, I've seen more than they have. Your parents feel very invested in you. When you make a poor decision, they feel responsible."

"But they're not."

She nodded. "I know. But letting go of control is hard. It's scary."

I frowned. "They just don't want me to embarrass them."

"They don't want to see you experience pain. Parents are hardwired to keep their babies safe and out of pain—no matter the age. You will forever be a part of them, meaning it will be hard for them to see where they end and you begin. So you have two choices."

"Which are?"

"You can walk the line, or you can build a fence along it so they have to stay on their side. And that's part of growing up. But it also means they can no longer be there to save you. If you want to fly, you have to be willing to fall and even crash. But if you can do that and show them that your strength is greater than your mistakes and imperfections, they will see that they raised you right."

I fiddled with the silver ring on my middle finger. "I have a huge crush on my neighbor."

"The coach?"

I nodded.

"Oh dear."

I nodded again. "Oh dear indeed. And I don't know if he could ever think of me like anyone but his brother's best friend's daughter, but I spend most of my waking hours dreaming about it."

"He's handsome." She waggled her eyebrows, and it made me laugh.

"He is. But it's more than that. He gets my humor. He *matches* it. And he thinks I remind him of himself when he was my age. His son is irresistibly cute. He loves to fish just like Grandpa did. And he thinks the apples in the orchard taste too sour to eat."

Her face lit up because she'd told me long ago that I needed someone like Grandpa. He was a tough man with a gruff attitude, except with her. Grandpa always said his Bonnie was his weakness. He said he only had one life to live, but he'd die a million deaths for her.

"I don't think that's a line you can walk," she said.

I shook my head. "No. It's definitely a fence I'd have to build."

"You're young," she murmured, tipping her chin to focus on a new row of stitches. "Are you prepared to live on the other side by yourself?"

"Sarah did. She chose love."

"Is it love that you have?"

"Can I get back to you on that?"

She smirked without looking up at me. "You know where I'll be."

I slid off the bed and squatted before her, resting my hands on hers. "Is there anything you need? Are they still being good to you here?"

She got a little teary-eyed when I asked that, and I asked it every time. Her hand pressed to my cheek. "Yes, my dear. Thank you."

During the following days, I lived for winks and smiles, extended glances, and every butterfly Kyle stirred to life in my tummy. I surprised him with apple crisp on Wednesday and muffins on Thursday.

However, on Friday, he surprised me, and I discovered I didn't like surprises.

"Do you have plans tonight?" He baited me.

Every cell in my body took on my heartbeat from anticipating his next question. I stayed calm and offered a slight headshake as I followed him to the door that morning. He only had one practice that day.

"Would you watch Josh this evening?"

It took my foolish heart a few extra seconds to register his words. "Um, sure. Why? I didn't think your first game was until next week."

"It's not," he said, opening the back door. "Your mom called last night and asked if I knew how to install a toilet. Then she asked if I'd install one for Denise Overton in exchange for dinner."

"My mom's making you dinner so you'll install a toilet for Denise?"

He returned a funny grin. "No. Denise is making me dinner."

That's what I feared.

"A date?"

"No. A toilet installation and food."

I frowned. "You're so naïve. It's a date. My mom mentioned three women on the prowl, and Denise was one of them. She probably doesn't even need a new toilet."

"It would be easier and cheaper to ask me out on a date than to pretend she needs a new toilet." He headed out the back door. "I'll see you later."

No. He wouldn't see me later; he would see Denise and her new toilet later. I followed him to his truck.

"When she answers the door in nothing but a fur coat, don't say I didn't warn you."

He turned before opening the driver's door. "It's a little hot for a fur coat."

"That's why she'll slide it off her shoulders when you step inside her house."

Kyle lifted his eyebrows.

"And I'm not saying it should matter, but she won't look like one of your centerfolds. I'm not sure you'll find the gesture *admirable*."

He coughed a laugh and opened the door. "Eve, I don't think most women look like a centerfold. I'm sure she's nice," he said, climbing into his truck.

I stepped closer so he couldn't shut the door. "Most women in Devil's Head are *nice*, but that doesn't mean you should date, envy, admire, or be inspired by them. I told you I'd find someone for you, but you haven't given me enough time."

He slowly nodded. "Well, good thing it's just a handyman job and a thank-you meal, not a date."

I deflated. Denise was nice. And pretty. She was closer to his age—twenty-seven or twenty-eight. And she worked at the animal rescue shelter one town over.

"Eve?" He woke me from my thoughts.

I glanced up at him.

"I have to go. If you can't watch Josh, that's fine. I can ask your sister or take him with me."

I perked up. Denise would have to keep her clothes on if he took Josh.

"Sorry. I have a date tonight, and Gabby's going to a movie."

It was a lie and a half. Maybe two lies. I wasn't sure if Gabby was going to a movie, but it was her usual Friday night plan.

Kyle inspected me as if he didn't trust me.

I didn't blink. That was how I made all of my lies believable. No blinking. No smiling. I just stood like a statue until he accepted it.

"Fine. I'll take him with me. Now, I have to go."

I stepped backward and mumbled a "goodbye" before he closed the door and sped down the driveway.

"Maybe I need my toilet fixed too," I said to no one except the wind as I spun on my heels and headed back into the house.

"WHERE ARE YOU GOING?" Dad asked the next morning. After I inhaled the waffle Mom had made me, I headed toward the door.

"Kyle—uh, Mr. Collins asked me to come over this morning because he and Josh are target shooting with bows, and Josh wanted me to see him hit the target."

"He's really taken a liking to you, huh?"

I glanced up, hair hanging in my face as I worked my heel into my sneaker while balancing on one leg. "It's not like that. Josh is the one who wants me to come over."

Dad narrowed his eyes. "I was talking about Josh."

"Oh, yeah. Duh. Yes, Josh likes me. He's a sweet boy. Sure, he clogged our toilet, but who hasn't?" I shot my dad a toothy grin. "See ya." I ran out the door before he could ask any follow-up questions.

I had intended on baking something to bring them that morning, but I was angry at Kyle for fixing Denise's toilet, so I showed up empty-handed.

"Let's go!" Josh yelled from the porch as soon as he saw me. "Come on, Eve! I'll show you."

I wanted a boy just like him: full of life, endless smiles, and contagious giggles.

Kyle slowly stood from the porch swing and sipped his coffee. He looked hot in his white T-shirt, faded jeans, and wet hair.

"How was your date?" I asked when Josh was already halfway to the barn.

Kyle descended the porch stairs. "Disappointing. You told me she'd be naked under a fur coat, but she was wearing scrubs and smelled like dog urine. However, dinner was good, and she let Josh finger paint, so he instantly loved her."

My face soured, so I glanced in the opposite direction as we followed Josh. "That's great," I mumbled in a tone opposite of great. "It's not like she made him homemade applesauce," I mumbled under my breath.

"What?"

I shook my head. "Nothing."

"How was your date?" he asked.

"My what?"

"Your date. You said you couldn't watch Josh last night because you had a date."

"Oh, yeah. It was fine. Good. Maybe one of the best dates I've ever been on." I should have stopped at fine, but jealousy made me reckless and a big liar.

"Sounds like it could be serious. Was it a first date?"

"Yeah." I couldn't look at him, so I watched my feet as we walked.

"A friend? Someone you graduated with?"

"Uh, no. He's not from Devil's Head. It was a blind date. He's uh ... he's a lawyer." I tugged at my lower lip after pulling that doozy out of my ass.

"Wow. You're into older men, huh? How does your dad feel about that?"

"When I go places with older men, I don't tell my dad." I felt proud of my response, so I glanced at him with a sly grin.

I couldn't read his expression. It wasn't a real smile, more like a grimace.

"Hurry up!" Josh called, jumping up and down as he pointed to an old cabinet past the far end of the fishing boat in the barn.

"Why don't you slow down?" Kyle said to him. "Hold this." He handed me his coffee mug. "But don't drink it all." He smirked.

"Har har."

He took the padlock off the cabinet and retrieved a big bow, a little one, and the arrows in a long tube.

"Do you let him shoot real arrows with sharp tips?" I asked.

"Tips? Yes. Razor tips? No."

We carried everything out back where he had targets on hay bales. Kyle handed Josh his little bow and an arrow. Josh loaded it like Robin Hood and shot it at the closest target, hitting the bullseye.

My jaw dropped.

"See, Eve?" Josh pointed to his arrow and shrugged like it was no big deal.

I nodded slowly. "Wow! That's incredible. You're five?"

I didn't know who looked more proud, Josh or his dad.

Ruffling his hair, I bent forward to nuzzle my face in his neck, making him giggle.

Kyle took the next shot with his bigger bow and hit a target much farther away, right in the bullseye as well.

"I'm outmatched. Maybe I should go back home and eat another waffle instead of embarrassing myself in front of you two."

Kyle laughed, propping his bow against an old wood barrel before taking his coffee mug from my hands. "We'll teach you."

"Eve, watch me!"

I turned back toward Josh as he loaded another arrow and shot it. Then another. And another.

"We're going to let him tire out while I finish my coffee, and then he'll play with his tractors in the dirt while I teach you a new skill. Okay?"

I glanced over at him and nodded, not wanting to smile because I was still mad that he made Denise sound like Josh's new hero. She let him play with paint. So what? It didn't compare to applesauce.

"Are you okay?" he asked.

"Yeah. Why?" I focused on Josh.

"I don't know. You seem less enthusiastic than usual."

"Long night," I mumbled, not meaning it to be anything more than a quick excuse, but when Kyle's body stiffened, I realized he thought I was talking about my date with the imaginary lawyer.

Was he jealous? I relished that idea.

"Are you seeing Denise again?"

He narrowed his eyes, watching Josh. "Depends if she says the new toilet is leaking."

"That's not what I mean."

"I know it's not." He set his coffee mug on the ground and helped Josh retrieve his arrows.

"I'm done." Josh marched toward the barn. "I have to piss." He grabbed his crotch.

I covered my mouth to muffle my laugh.

"Potty," Kyle quickly corrected.

"Adam says piss," Josh said.

"Adam's a bad influence. Can you make it to the house?"

Josh shook his head a half dozen times.

"Then go in the grass."

Josh pulled down his pants and underwear.

"Buddy, never in front of a lady. Go to the side of the barn."

I snorted as Josh waddled off, mooning me the whole way.

Kyle returned with the arrows, slowly shaking his head.

I couldn't hold my giggle in any longer.

"Don't have kids until you're ready to relinquish every last ounce of your dignity. Parenting is taking responsibility for another human's actions for roughly eighteen years."

"Bummer. That means I can no longer blame my actions on my parents." I said.

"Correct." He tried to give me a serious look, but the corners of his eyes crinkled like they were smiling.

"When he overflowed the toilet at my house, he yelled, 'Oh, shit!'"

"God damn ..." Kyle grumbled. "Of course he did." He picked up his bow. "I lowered the tension on this for you last night. Hopefully, you have enough strength to pull it back." He handed it to me, stepped behind me, and pressed his body to mine to show me how to hold it. "Don't grip it with your entire hand. It's going to rest here along the pad of your thumb. If it crosses the lifeline of your hand, your forearm will be in line with the string, and you'll hit your arm, which will hurt. And you want to keep this area as relaxed as possible while pulling back."

I wouldn't remember a single word because my brain was focused on his body heat and his fingers brushing my hand to show me where to rest the bow.

"Don't hold your breath. It will make you shake more. It's about steadying your breath."

My breath didn't stand a chance of being steady in such close proximity to him.

"Are you nervous?" he mumbled with his lips at my ear. "I can feel your heart racing. I'm not going to let you kill anyone."

With his help, I hit the first target on the edge.

"Good," he said, releasing me and helping me set another arrow on the bow, tweaking my grip. "Now you try it on your own."

I wanted to impress him, but I felt out of my league and weak like I did when I tried to start that boat engine. Of course, I missed the target by a lot.

"You held your breath, and you tensed up."

"I didn't try to."

"I know. But you did, so this time, think about the steps, relax, breathe, and know that you're not going to steady it perfectly over the target, but that's okay. The target is a lot bigger than the arrow tip."

I tried a third time. "I did it!" I turned, proud of myself for hitting the target.

Kyle's grin swelled. "Good job."

"Daddy, I'm going to get my tractors," Josh said.

"Okay, buddy. They're on the deck. Do you need help?"

"No." He ran toward the house.

I shot a dozen or so arrows before my hands and fingers hurt.

"Let's not overdo it." He winked, taking it from me as I shook out my hands and massaged them.

"Can you hit the target every time?" I asked.

He attached his quiver and shot six arrows in a matter of seconds—all within fractions of an inch from each other.

"I guess you can," I murmured.

His grin doubled as if he were trying to impress me rather than the other way around. Then, we retrieved the arrows together.

"Josh hasn't made it back, which means he's using the flower beds as a play zone. I'd better get back."

I nodded, following him into the barn.

"Does your dad hunt?" I asked.

He returned the bows and arrows to the cabinet. "Yes. My mom said they wouldn't still be married if he didn't take hunting trips."

I laughed.

"Do you eat what you kill?"

"Yes, most of the time."

"So you've eaten bear meat?"

He locked the cabinet and turned. "No. I don't hunt bears."

I tucked my thumbs in my front pockets and rocked back and forth on my heels. "Thanks for showing me how to shoot today."

Kyle eyed me, and I felt his gaze as tangible as if his hands were on my body. And I couldn't help but wonder if I was delusional. Did he look at me like a child? It didn't feel like that.

"Who set you up with an attorney from another town?"

I stopped my rocking.

"Or did you lie because you didn't want to watch Josh?"

I shook my head. "I like Josh."

"That's not what I asked. You can like Josh and not want to watch him."

"Speaking of watching Josh, we should get back to the house." I turned.

"I can pay you *and* teach you how to do things. I feel like I'm taking advantage of you," he said.

"It's not that." I walked around the boat toward the front barn door.

"Then what is it?"

I stopped, closing my eyes. "I told you I had a date last night because you were having dinner with Denise."

"That makes no sense. Is it because she's not on your list of approved dates for me?"

I was delusional. He didn't think of me as anything beyond the girl next door and maybe a friend. "No." I shook my head without turning toward him. "She's not on my list of approved dates for you. But you don't need my approval. And I don't know why I lied. I thought ... well, I don't know. Just never mind."

"What did you think?"

I rubbed my eyes. "Let's not talk about it because it's embarrassing, and I don't want things to be weird between us."

He stepped in front of me, blocking the door and forcing me to look at him in the dim light from the hanging bulb above us.

I rolled my eyes, feeling flushed from my face to my toes. "For a moment when we were on the dock the other night, I thought you were looking at me like ..." I laughed a little, fidgeting with the hem of my shirt.

"Like what?"

"Like you liked me." I pushed him out of the way and marched out the door to distance myself from his scrutinizing gaze that embarrassed me.

"I do like you." He followed me.

"You don't get it." I lengthened my strides.

"I do get it."

When I no longer heard his boots scuffing through the dirt behind me, I stopped and glanced over my shoulder.

"I do get it," he repeated, scraping his teeth along his lower lip several times. "And it's fun. *Liking* you is fun. Everything about you is fun and refreshing. Eve, women like you"—he smirked—"not that there's anyone else like you, bring men like me to our knees. But," he chuckled, shaking his head, "I have grown-up responsibilities, including a child. So my fun needs to be safer than liking my brother's best friend's eighteen-year-old daughter."

His words shot through my veins, and I felt powerful. "I can bring you to your knees?" My smile lost all control.

He veered off toward the house. "Let's not find out. I'll see you at church tomorrow, where getting on my knees is pleasing to God ... and Pastor Jacobson."

Not find out? Was he crazy? Oh, we were going to find out.

Chapter Eleven

Poison, "Talk Dirty to Me"

Eve

"WHAT IF HE'S messing with you? Being nice so you don't feel embarrassed?" Erin asked as we sat across from each other at McDonald's. She twisted her lips. "But then again, he adjusted your bra strap at the lake. That's weird if he's not attracted to you. Or maybe it was a fatherly thing." Erin shook her head. "He's totally messing with you, Eve. Don't you dare give him more. You'll feel like a fool. You need to date someone else for real, not some made-up guy. And make it a little more believable than an attorney."

I chewed on the end of my straw while processing her advice. It's not that I didn't see it that way, too, but there were so many looks and tiny moments that felt real.

Not pity.

Not a man appeasing his crush.

Not a neighbor being friendly to the babysitter.

"Take a chill pill when you're around him. Act like he's a grody old guy, and the thought of liking him is like 'gag me.'"

I slowly nodded.

"He really said Denise smelled like dog urine?" Erin grinned, wrinkling her nose.

I smirked and nodded.

"I start classes on Monday. Of course, I'll take the cutest guy I can find, but I'll look for the second cutest and set you up with him."

"Gee, thanks." I wadded my burger wrapper and stuffed it into my fry container.

"I'm serious. Don't be desperate."

"I'm not desperate."

She eyed me until I cracked.

"I'm not." I laughed. "I'm just interested."

"Obsessed."

I shook my head. "Determined."

"Delusional."

I rolled up a tiny piece of my straw wrapper, loaded it into my straw, and blew it at her.

SUNDAY MORNING, I prayed that Kyle and Josh wouldn't be at church, but God didn't grant my wish. He was probably too disappointed in my lies that week to extend me a little mercy.

Erin gave me a tight grin with wide eyes when Kyle and Josh sat behind my mom and sister. They wore their matching suits again but with different ties—yellow bowties.

Adorable.

I made it through my dad's lengthy sermon, including

communion, without looking at Kyle. After the service, I gathered in front of the church with my friends while my parents made their usual chitchat.

"Hi, Eve!" Josh hugged my waist, and my friends laughed and gushed over him.

"Hey, Josh." I ran my fingers through his dark wavy hair, and then I squatted and straightened his bowtie. "You look handsome today."

He pressed his palms to my cheeks. "You look pretty."

I melted in his tiny hands.

"Buddy, Eve's talking with her friends. Where are your manners?" Kyle said, forcing me to look at him and offer a fake smile, the smile I would have given to a grody old man.

"It's fine," I mumbled, standing straight.

"That dress looks great on you," he said.

I glanced down as if I didn't remember what dress I was wearing. It was a white dress with three-quarter-length sleeves, nothing special. He was making small talk, maybe trying to ease the tension. Heck, he probably sent Josh over to say I looked pretty.

"Thanks. Nice bowtie," I said, giving him a quick glance before looking away as if there were far more interesting people than him who deserved my attention.

"See you in a bit," he said.

That got my attention.

Kyle took Josh's hand. "Your parents invited us to lunch."

Of course, they did.

"Lovely." I plastered on a smile.

He offered my friends a courteous nod before heading to his truck.

"He's so bad. I can't wait for school to start," Lizzy said. She was getting ready to start her senior year.

"I bet he's strict with his grading system. All the *grody* guys are flawed," Erin eyed me.

"I agree," Kelly said. She was going to be a junior. "Mr. Collins is not grody, but I feel like the ugly ones are the worst teachers because they were picked on in school. And they're determined to make everyone pay and suffer like they did."

"Everyone's leaving." I nodded toward the parking lot. "See y'all next week."

Erin squeezed my arm while leaning close to my ear. "Stay strong. He's old and ugly."

He looked like every woman's dream, with a darling little boy as his sidekick. As good as I was at lying, I couldn't convince myself or anyone else that Kyle was old and ugly.

"Two weeks in a row, huh? Are we adopting them?" I asked my parents when I slid into the back seat next to Gabby before we headed to get Grandma Bonnie.

Mom glanced over her shoulder at me. "Kyle and Josh?"

"Yeah. Who else did you invite to Sunday dinner?"

"They're like family because Fred is the brother your father never had. So think of Kyle as your uncle or cousin."

It wasn't a bad idea. I had cousins, and they weren't ugly, but I didn't have a crush on them. I tried to latch on to that idea.

Kyle was my cousin with a cute little boy. We were all family. Incest was not only forbidden, it was gross.

After we picked up Grandma Bonnie and arrived home, I changed out of my white dress into a denim skirt and red blouse with tiny gold buttons. I still had to look nice for Sunday dinner, but white wasn't a good choice since we were having barbecue ribs, green beans, fingerling potatoes, and, of course, apple pie with homemade ice cream.

Gabby answered the knock at the door for our *cousin*

and his son while Mom and I finished setting the food on the table.

"Daddy got the booster," Josh said to my mom.

Kyle smiled, holding up a booster seat. No Bibles would be sacrificed during dinner that day.

"Good thinking." Mom took the booster seat and set it on the chair for Josh.

I headed to the kitchen to grab the basket of dinner rolls, but Kyle was in my way, so I gazed up at him with a platonic grin. "Excuse me."

He didn't move. "Are we okay?" he asked in a hushed tone, quickly scanning the room before returning his gaze to me.

"Of course we're good. Why wouldn't we be?" I did my best to pretend that nothing happened.

If he wanted to act like I had a crush on him, I wouldn't do anything to confirm it because it wasn't true.

Mind over matter.

It. Wasn't. True.

Liking one's cousin was gross.

I pushed past him since he wouldn't move.

"Good. Because I feel bad about yesterday," he said, following me into the kitchen.

I handed him the butter, and I grabbed the basket of rolls. "You're family." All I could muster was a cheesy smile. "Kind of like my cousin. Yesterday didn't happen because you're family. My adopted cousin."

He narrowed his eyes. "Cousins," he echoed.

I returned a firm nod. "And you teach math which makes you a nerdy cousin at that." I batted my eyelashes before carrying the rolls to the table while he followed me.

After saying grace, my dad repeated the previous week's

behavior by talking Kyle's head off about football. But Kyle didn't seem to mind. His passion was palpable.

I wanted to feel a little passion from him too.

Cousin! He's my cousin.

"Denise wasn't at church today, but I talked with her yesterday." Mom squeezed into the conversation, changing it to another topic I didn't care about. "She wanted me to thank you again for helping her out. She said she had a great evening painting with Josh and chatting with you."

Kyle finished chewing and blotted his mouth with a napkin. "I was happy to help. And Josh had a good time."

"She's great with kids," Mom added. "And she loves football. You'll see her at all the games. She even volunteers at the concession stand."

"Eve loves football too," Gabby said. "Last year, she went to all of the games." She smirked.

Mom nodded. "That's right. You did."

I shot my sister a stiff smile. She had kept my secret for a whole year, and I thought she would forget about it since it no longer mattered. Instead, she brought it up in front of Kyle, who probably thought I had told her that I liked him.

"Erin went to all of the games too," I said with a shrug, even though she went to all the games to be with me while I supported my boyfriend, whom my parents never knew about.

"Maybe you can bring Josh to some of the games. He likes football, but I can't coach and keep an eye on him," Kyle said.

"She would love that," Grandma Bonnie answered on my behalf.

I adjusted in my chair and opened my mouth to speak, but my mom interrupted.

"Oh, Denise would *love* to watch him," she said before I could speak.

I bit my tongue and shrugged as if I didn't care who took Josh to the games. When I looked at Grandma, she gave me a look. I wasn't ready to build the fence.

"It's good to know I have options," Kyle said, wiping Josh's messy face.

"I'll get the pie and ice cream." I smiled, scooting back in my chair.

"Gabby, help your sister," Mom said.

"Let me," Kyle interrupted, pushing back in his chair. "It's the least I can do after getting an invitation to dinner two weekends in a row."

I didn't wait for him because I didn't need anyone's help.

"You must have been dating a player last year," Kyle said as I retrieved the ice cream from the freezer.

I stiffened a second before turning and kicking the door closed behind me. "Why do say that?" I asked with a slight scoff.

"Because your family implied your interest in football was just last year, and you and Gabby exchanged a look." He took the ice cream from me, and I pulled the scoop from the drawer by the sink.

I shook my head, opting for no comment.

"I'm not that old. And I'm observant," he said.

"But do you have a point?" I turned, eyeing him for an answer.

He *had* to stare at my mouth, which cousins didn't do. "Today, I have sensed some hostility from you. I think you misunderstood me yesterday."

"I think *you* misunderstood *me*. So, whatever you think I meant yesterday, I didn't. Like I said earlier, we're practically family. And I'll happily take Josh to your games because that's what family does, but if you want your girlfriend to take him instead, that's fine too. I really don't care."

The harder I tried not to care, the more I wanted him. The word "cousin" left a sour taste in my mouth because I never would have considered kissing my cousin. I would not have taken my shirt off in front of a male cousin.

"You're killing me, Eve," he whispered.

"I don't know why." I handed him the scoop and turned to get the pie and wooden-handled server from the counter. "I'm just your brother's best friend's daughter. Your preacher's daughter. An eighteen-year-old. The girl next door." I stepped past him and carried the pie to the dining room.

After dinner, I washed dishes with Gabby while my mom drove Grandma Bonnie back to the nursing home. My dad and Kyle sat on the front porch and watched Josh play with the farm cats.

Dad poked his head in the kitchen as I slid the last plate into the cabinet. "Eve, can you watch Josh while I take Kyle down by the creek and show him which trees I think need to come down?"

"I suppose," I mumbled before following him outside.

Kyle looked at me. "Josh can come with us. I don't want to disrupt your day."

"Josh is the best part of my day." I scooped him up in my arms and turned in a circle while he giggled. "I prefer him to everyone else."

My dad laughed.

Kyle tried on a smile that didn't seem to fit.

"Let's go to your house," I said, setting him on the ground and taking his hand.

"Thank you," Kyle called after we headed toward the fence.

I slowed my steps and turned a fraction. If sincerity were flesh and bones, it would have looked like Kyle. My snarkiness fell away, and I mirrored his sincerity with a smile. "You're welcome."

When we reached the house, Josh wanted to play Chutes and Ladders, so we played game after game. And he kept winning.

"Josh, is your dad a happy person?" I asked, moving my girl pawn four spaces on the board.

He wrinkled his nose and flicked the spinner. "He's grumpy pants."

I snorted a laugh. "Why is he grumpy pants?"

"Because he says I'm trouble when I pee on the floor."

Joy filled me like the frosting on a gooey cinnamon roll. I wanted to be a mouse in the corner, watching Kyle and Josh talk about pee on the floor.

"My dad is grumpy pants too," I said.

Josh's bright eyes looked up at me like he was happy to have someone who understood him. "Do you pee on the floor?"

I grinned. "Not anymore. But I leave lights on and wear clothes my dad doesn't like."

The back door opened, and Kyle stepped inside, kicking off his boots.

"I won four times!" Josh beamed.

"Of course you did," Kyle said. "I bet you didn't tell Eve you have magic board game luck."

Josh giggled when I gave him a wide-eyed stare with my lips parted into an O. I put the pieces back into the box.

"Can you take this to your room while I say goodbye to

Eve and thank her for playing with you?" Kyle handed Josh the game.

"Bye," I said to Josh, giving him a little wave.

"Bye," he mumbled, skating his socked feet along the wood floor toward the stairs.

"Did my dad talk you into cutting down most of the trees by the creek? He's tired of them falling and making a dam that causes flooding."

"Not all of them. But I said I'd help him take down three dead ones when I get time this week."

"You're a good man. I'm sure my dad will be thrilled to have you around. He doesn't trust me or Gabby with a chainsaw."

Kyle chuckled, scratching the back of his head.

"Well, enjoy the rest of your Sunday." I opened the back door, and he followed me onto the deck.

"Eve?"

I stopped.

"If I didn't have the responsibility of being a father, I wouldn't think twice about being a little reckless with you," he said.

I was afraid to turn around because I was trying so hard to be his adopted family and not the girl next door with an incurable crush. What if my idea of recklessness meant the kind of intimacy that would land my soul in Hell, and he meant letting me use a chainsaw? I no longer trusted myself to read him.

"But," he continued, "very few things in my life have gone as planned, so I can't promise I'll remain steadfast in my resolve to do the right thing. This is my preemptive apology for if or when I fuck it all up." The wood beneath his feet creaked as he took a step closer.

My lips parted to accommodate my labored breathing. I liked his vulnerability. And I liked that he was unapologetic about saying "fuck" around me.

"Eve—"

"Is this a warning or a promise?" I couldn't look at him *and* act confident, so I continued down the four stairs to the yard. "Because I'm terrible at heeding warnings but relentless at making people keep their promises."

Chapter Twelve

George Michael, "I Want Your Sex"

Eve

"You said what?" Erin gasped as I stared at the ceiling from my bed with the phone cradled between my ear and shoulder.

"What was I supposed to say? I just spewed the first thing that came to mind. That's totally not true. My initial reaction was to scream and beg him to be reckless with me."

She laughed. "I would have frozen. Choked and tripped over my tongue or said something stupid and embarrassing. I'm so jealous that you had the perfect line. What did he do after you said that?"

I curled the phone cord around my finger and grinned. "I don't know. I didn't look back. I would have died. My confidence had a ten-second lifespan. So I got the heck out of there, trying so hard to walk and not run. But my heart was pounding, and I couldn't hear anything around me."

"What's next? When do you see him again? What are you going to do or say when you do? How can you not be thinking about *him* thinking about being reckless with you? Gah! And what does that mean? Like ... kissing you? Or more? Eve! Would you do more with him? Would you have sex with him?"

Erin's endless string of questions fed my nerves to the point of panic. What was I going to say and do? "Okay. We both need to get a grip. He didn't say anything was going to happen. I think he felt bad for what he said on Saturday. Maybe that's it. He said it out of pity. Maybe he rolled his eyes at my gullibility when I walked away."

"No. Don't be ridiculous. I'll admit, I thought he was leading you on, but I've changed my mind. Have you looked in the mirror? You're gorgeous. And you *are* an adult now. He's older, but not like old enough to be your dad. And he's not married. Josh likes you. Think about it. There's no reason for him not to be attracted to you except for all the reasons he already told you. So stop thinking that he's not really into you. I'm a terrible friend for making you think that. Just forget it. Okay?"

I nibbled on my thumbnail and mumbled, "Yeah, maybe. But I can't do anything. I can't make a move on him because if, by some chance, he *is* just appeasing me, I can't risk looking like a fool. I'd never be able to look at him again, and that would be difficult since he's my neighbor and goes to church every Sunday, *and* my parents have basically adopted him and Josh."

"You're right." Erin blew out a slow breath.

I loved that she was physically feeling these emotions with me.

"So play it cool. Be charming and sexy, but not desperate and awkward."

I giggled. "Charming and sexy? I'm afraid in my attempt to be charming and sexy, I'll look desperate and awkward. I think I should pretend he didn't say anything and try my best to act normal."

"Fine, go with your idea. But I think mine is better."

Erin's idea was better, and I could have pulled it off with some other guy who was closer to my age and who I didn't think about every second of every day. But Kyle wasn't that guy.

My plan worked—maybe too well.

On Monday, Kyle didn't give anything away. It was as if the moment never happened, so I had no problem acting normal. He didn't allow me a chance to act otherwise. Tuesday was a repeat of Monday. The normalcy was good yet maddening. I started to feel crazy like I made it all up in my head.

School started on Wednesday, so I didn't see Kyle in the morning. He dropped Josh off at school, and I was waiting at the end of their lane when he got off the bus in the afternoon. Two hours later, Kyle got home from practice.

"Hey," he smiled, depositing his keys on the counter.

I turned from the puzzle Josh and I were working on at the table. "Hey."

"Buddy, how was your first day of kindergarten?" Kyle asked, resting his hands on Josh's shoulder and kissing the top of his head.

"It was fun."

"Well, I'm going to start dinner, and you can tell me all about it. Macaroni and cheese?"

Josh nodded.

I stood. "See you tomorrow," I said to Josh.

Kyle followed me to the front door. "Thanks for being here for him."

"Of course." I slipped on my shoes and turned toward him.

"Are you going to the game Friday?" he asked.

"I don't know. Why?"

"Can Josh hang out with you if you are, like we talked about? Although, he won't watch much of it. You'll just have to chase him around and get snacks. But you don't have to watch him at all, if you—"

"Of course, I want to watch the game with him. Or chase him. Snacks. Whatever."

"Great. I'll be home after school and get him dinner. He can come with me to the game early. Maybe while the team warms up, he can run around and burn off a little energy so he's worn out by the time the game starts. As long as you're there by 6:40 or so."

"Sounds good."

"Thanks, I'll uh—"

"What are you doing tonight?" I blurted before he could say goodbye.

"Laundry. You?" He grinned.

"I'm thinking of walking down to the creek before it gets dark. Does Josh want to go with me?"

"You're so bored that you're willing to hang out with a five-year-old when you're not being paid?"

"Hey. He's better company than most of the guys I've dated."

"Are you sure it's not because you can run faster?"

"What?" I wrinkled my nose. "Oh!" I laughed, forgetting for a few seconds what I'd said about the bears and running faster than my friends.

"I'll guard him with my life. I'll offer myself to the bear so he can get away."

"Or I can go with you too."

Yes!

"Um, sure. I mean, if you want to. Don't feel you have to if you're busy doing laundry. I'd hate for you to wear dirty underwear to school Friday since you're supposed to look your best on game days."

"I'd just go without underwear if I didn't have clean ones."

I pressed my lips together, trying not to imagine him without underwear.

"You're not picturing me naked, are you?"

"Stop." I coughed a laugh. "No. I'm not."

"Liar," he mouthed.

I narrowed my eyes, but my flaming cheeks told the truth.

"So you'll be back over after dinner?"

"Yes." I was so giddy my voice shook.

"See you in a bit."

"Eve!" Josh called, running toward the door after I stepped outside. He had my Walkman and headphones.

"Oh, thanks. I almost forgot that," I said as he handed it to Kyle and ran back into the kitchen.

"Thought you were watching Josh, not listening to music," Kyle said.

I rolled my eyes, holding out my hand. "I can do both when he's playing with his toys."

Kyle narrowed his eyes. "What tape?"

I stepped closer to the door, keeping my hand out in a silent demand. "Just stuff I record off the radio."

"Like what?" He put the headphones on his head.

"NO!" I lunged for him, but the partially closed screen door caught my shoulder.

It was too late. He pressed *Play*.

Life as I knew it ended when his eyebrows peaked. I had stopped in the middle of a song. There were many songs on that tape, but the one he was hearing was *not* the one I was most proud of—George Michael's "I Want Your Sex."

Click.

He shut off the cassette player and slowly removed the headphones, winding the cord around my Walkman before handing it to me.

"See ya in a bit," he said with *a wink!*

AFTER DINNER, I changed from shorts to jeans and grabbed a sweatshirt before shoving my feet into my shoes at the door. "I'm taking Josh to the creek," I called.

"Is Kyle okay with that?" Dad called from the living room.

"Uh-huh."

"Okay. Be careful."

"Uh-huh." I ran out the door, hopped the fence, and ran toward his house, slowing to gain my composure as I reached the top of the hill.

It was just a song with a catchy beat. I wouldn't mention it or make direct eye contact and we'd be fine.

Josh and Kyle were playing catch with a Nerf football in the front yard.

"Heads up!" Kyle called, throwing the ball to me.

I caught it, and his grin swelled to the corners of his eyes, which I told myself not to look at. Then I threw it back to him, and that grin faded.

"Nice duck," he said, catching the wobbly ball.

"I'm out of practice."

He laughed.

"Ready to skip to the creek?" I held out my hand to Josh.

He took it, and we skipped toward the far end of the orchard and the hill that led to the creek while Kyle followed us.

"Look!" Josh pointed to the hut I built from old branches and brush near the bank. He let go of my hand and ran to it as Kyle stopped beside me.

"Your dad said that hut needs to go before spring when the creek floods."

I nodded. "Yeah. My dad is a fun spoiler."

"Or practical."

"Same difference." I shrugged.

He smirked, watching Josh peek through the branches inside the hut. "What do you do in that hut anyway?"

"Hide from bears."

Kyle shook his head. "Eve, you're ... something."

"Where's Josh? I can't find him," I said.

Josh giggled as I pressed my hand to my brow and inspected the area. "Josh?"

Again, he giggled, and I walked a few feet in one direction and then in another.

"I'm in here!"

I jumped. "Oh! I didn't see you. Can I come in?"

He pushed on the branches I tied together with rope to make a door. "Daddy, you come in too."

"Oh, I don't know, buddy. There might not be enough room for all of us in there."

"There is," he insisted as I crawled into the far corner and hugged my knees.

Kyle squeezed into the tiny hut, hugging his knees too, and the sides of our bodies touched at every point.

"Don't move. I will hunt for food," Josh said with a big smile.

"Uh, don't go too far, and stay away from the water," Kyle said.

Josh climbed over our feet and shut the door behind him. He grabbed a stick and held it like a gun. "Shh, don't scare the deer," he whispered, pointing toward an old, dead tree stump.

"Hope you're not claustrophobic," Kyle mumbled.

"No. You?"

"No." He stretched his neck right and then left to keep an eye on Josh through the hut walls. When he tried to adjust his body, it only made him rub against me more. "Seriously. What did you do in this hut? You know, as a full-grown adult over four feet tall?"

I laughed. "This is where I bring guys to make out with them." It was an obvious lie. And while turning our heads to look at each other was too close for comfort, I couldn't help it when I felt him looking at me.

"You must be attracted to tiny men."

I rolled my eyes.

Kyle's gaze dropped from my eyes to my lips, so I rubbed them together, and it was suddenly too hot to wear a sweatshirt.

"I'm sorry," he whispered.

I narrowed my eyes. "For what?"

He leaned in.

"I got it!" Josh yelled, and Kyle sat up straight.

Josh carried a handful of leaves to the hut and served us "venison" for dinner, which lasted thirty seconds before Kyle squeezed his big body through the door.

He leaned in to kiss me. *Right?* That almost happened. *RIGHT?*

I exhaled after holding my breath longer than I had ever held it before. When I crawled out and brushed off my backside, Josh grabbed my hand and pulled me toward the water.

"Not too close, buddy," Kyle said behind us.

When I glanced back at him, he smiled—not an "I almost kissed you smile." It was a normal smile.

But it happened. Didn't it?

Suddenly, my song choice seemed irrelevant.

We headed toward the house after throwing a dozen rocks into the creek. Josh alternated between walking and running, keeping ten feet ahead of us the whole way.

I said nothing.

Kyle said nothing.

Nothing was hiding the biggest something ever.

He almost kissed me!

"You need a bath," Kyle said when we reached the house.

"I want to play with my cars," Josh protested, climbing the deck stairs.

"Twenty minutes. But then you're getting a bath."

"Fine," Josh grumbled.

"Want something to drink?" Kyle asked me after he reached the top of the stairs.

I stood at the bottom, still in shock.

"Not the kind of drink you'd probably like," he smirked, "more like 7 Up or Kool-Aid."

I blinked. "Uh," I slowly nodded. "Okay."

He proceeded into the house while I moved like a sloth, which was appropriate because time was different in dreams and illusions, and that's what I was experiencing.

Right?

"I only have grape Kool-Aid, but if you mix it with 7 Up, it's pretty good. Can I interest you in Josh's favorite cocktail?"

"Sure." I didn't plan on standing directly behind him, but that's where I naturally navigated.

So when he turned with two glasses of purple Kool-Aid, I was right there.

He stiffened, eyes wide.

"You almost kissed me," I whispered.

He squinted. "I did?"

"Yes! You apologized and leaned in to kiss me right before Josh returned to the hut."

He twisted his lips with a slow nod. "Huh. Well, at least I apologized for it. Here. Tell me what you think." He handed me the drink and sidestepped to get past me. "You'll want to insist Josh try going to the bathroom by halftime or before if he grabs his crotch. And if there's a line, just go behind the bleachers or a tree and let him do his thing. I had hoped he'd be better at holding his bladder by age five, but clearly, he's not quite there."

I turned.

Kyle leaned his back against the fridge, legs casually crossed at his ankles while he sipped his drink. "Do you like it?" He nodded toward my glass.

I looked at it as if I was seeing it for the first time before bringing it to my lips for a sip. But I couldn't taste or feel anything but him.

"Well?"

I licked my lips. "It's good."

"You don't have to drink it if you don't really like it."

"I, uh"—I shook my head—"should get home." I needed to call Erin ASAP. It was an emergency.

He chewed on the inside of his cheek for a few seconds before relinquishing a nod. "Let me give you money now for the concession stand in case I forget tomorrow." He set his glass on the counter and pulled out his wallet.

I stared at the ten-dollar bill he offered me.

"Eve?"

"Hmm?" I was completely out of it.

"Are you going to take it?"

I slowly nodded without taking the money.

Kyle stepped closer, and I gulped. He slipped the ten-dollar bill into my back pocket, which meant his hand was on my butt.

I blinked heavily, staring at his chest.

After he tucked the money into my pocket, his hand drifted to mine, and the pads of his fingers teased my skin.

I closed my eyes. And just when I no longer felt his touch, he curled a few strands of hair behind my ear, letting the back of his fingers ghost down my neck. Parting my lips, I pulled in a shaky breath, and then his touch disappeared.

"Do you have any questions about Friday night?"

I opened my eyes, shooting my gaze to his as my body warred between chills and melting to the floor. Was he serious? Of course, I had questions. So many questions, but they had nothing to do with the Friday night football game.

"Daddy?" Josh called.

"So, no questions? We're good?"

My jaw dropped. "Am I good?" Of course, I found my voice when he had to tend to Josh. It was too late to ask why he almost kissed me and touched my hand and neck.

"I mean," he grinned. "I'm sure you're good, but I mean are you comfortable watching Josh at the game?"

My brain exploded. *What* did he say? Was my mind in the gutter thinking that he meant I was good at sex? Or did he mean he knew I was good, as in okay—no questions, mentally stable, capable of walking home?

WHAT DID HE MEAN BY GOOD?!

"I think I hate you," I said with a steadfast determination to keep a straight face.

"Because you're Evil Eve," he said with a wicked grin and a gleam in his eyes.

Chapter Thirteen

Def Leppard, "Hysteria"

Kyle

I MET Melinda at the beginning of my senior year of high school. She had moved to Colorado from Connecticut. Her inquisitive amber eyes, glowing brown skin, and crooked smile melted my insides like a handful of chocolate in late July. After one date, I knew I loved her. Adam called me a pathetic lovesick puppy when I had to go two days without seeing her because her family spent most weekends camping or skiing once the resorts opened. He, on the other hand, rejoiced when Lizzy had plans because he said seeing her every day was a little too much.

Melinda and I's relationship persevered long distances between us, college, two breakups, and her mother's death, only to fall apart when it seemed that we found our happily ever after. How did easy become so hard? It's like we weathered the storm only to choke to death on a piece of chewing gum while staring at a rainbow.

I lost her, but she lost everything.

At that moment, *everything* had my whistle, and he ran around the field, blowing it at my players as I scanned the area for my favorite neighbor before the Friday night game.

"Eve!" Josh pointed behind me and dropped the whistle on the ground.

I turned, breathing a sigh of relief. Her long brown hair flowed behind her, part of it tied with gold and red ribbons—the high school's colors. She wore a Devil's Head hoodie, stone-washed jeans, and white high-tops.

It took me back to my senior year when the prettiest girl in school eyed me on the football field. And I knew I'd break a new record, get the win, refuel with pizza or burgers, and strip her from the waist down in the back of my car.

Josh hugged Eve, and she ran her fingers through his hair. I was so envious. She smiled at me with her teeth trapping her bottom lip. It was as sexy as it was innocent.

"What are you doing after the game?"

I looked behind me when Drew asked Eve about her post-game plans. He wore a cocky grin as he gawked at her. I turned just as she casually shrugged.

"I have someone else who can start tonight if your head isn't in the game," I warned him.

His smirk fell off his face. "Sorry, Coach," he said, jogging in the opposite direction.

"Are you friends with my quarterback?" I asked Eve.

She watched him over my shoulder. "It's a small school. I'm friends with everyone."

"Just friends?" I asked and regretted the question before it made it all the way out of my mouth.

Josh took her hand and tried to pull her away from the field.

Her white teeth peeked out from her glossed lips. "Coach, are you jealous of your quarterback?"

It wasn't the time or the place to discuss my fucked-up feelings, so I nodded toward the bench. "Have Josh grab his backpack. Do you have the money I gave you for the concession stand?"

"It's in my back pocket. Do you want to check?" she baited me.

I'd met my match. But I never imagined she'd be eighteen.

"You have plans after the game," I said and immediately turned to approach the players as they finished warming up.

WE WON.

I didn't like how Drew looked at Eve, but the kid could light it up on the field. He threw two touchdowns, passed for one, and ran it in for another from the five-yard line.

After a post-game celebration in the locker room, I left the players to take their showers and stepped into the hallway, where their girlfriends were waiting for them.

Eve was on the floor with her back against the wall, legs outstretched, while Josh slept hugged to her with his cheek on her shoulder.

I gave her an apologetic smile and took him from her. "Sorry. That can't be comfortable."

She stood. "It's fine. I'm not an old man like you."

"Twenty-eight is old, huh?" I pushed through the door to

the parking lot and held it open with my backside while she stepped out in front of me.

"Erin and my other friends left because I said I had plans. I wish I knew what they were," she said, following me.

I unlocked my truck and lifted him into the back seat. He stirred while I fastened his seat belt, and then he collapsed onto his side, returning to sleep.

I pulled a twenty from my wallet and handed it to her. "Pick up something greasy."

She chuckled, taking the money. "Such as?"

"Surprise me."

"Anything for Josh?"

"He's down for the night. I'll be lucky to get him to go to the bathroom and wrangle him out of clothes and into pajamas."

"Okay. I'll see you in a bit. Crack open a cold one for me."

I grinned, climbing into the truck. "Root beer?"

"Minus the root," she called, walking to her car.

When I got home, Josh was as helpful as a rag doll, but he peed, mainly in the toilet and a little on the floor for me to clean up. Pajamas weren't worth the effort, so I tucked him in with just his Micky Mouse underwear.

By the time I drank half a beer and turned on the news, Eve came through the front door with a Taco John's bag.

"I was totally expecting pizza," I said, taking the bag from her.

She dug the change out of her pocket and deposited it on the kitchen table before joining me on the sofa. I pulled the tacos and Potato Olés out of the bag and set them on the coffee table.

"If you wanted pizza, then you should have said pizza," she wrinkled her nose at me.

"I'm kidding. You did good."

She grabbed my beer, and before I could stop her or protest, she took several big gulps.

I frowned, reclaiming the can. It was easy to compare her to Melinda, but she reminded me more of myself at her age. Fred was the perfect child, always following God's and our parents' rules. I, on the other hand, had a knack for finding trouble. I wasn't a leader or a follower, but I rarely passed up the opportunity to have a good time, even when Melinda tried to talk sense into me.

"Good game, by the way," she said, unwrapping a taco. "Your quarterback friend lived up to the hype."

Eve stared at the TV and nodded while slowly chewing. "He's good," she mumbled.

"Did Josh give you any trouble?" I popped a Potato Olé into my mouth before unwrapping a taco.

"No. He's adorable. All the girls were totally going crazy over him. He should be the team's mascot."

I chuckled.

"By the game's last two minutes, he leaned his head onto my lap and fell asleep. Even when the crowd cheered, he didn't flinch."

"He's a sound sleeper like his dad."

"I'll get us another beer," she said, standing.

I grabbed her wrist and shook my head when she peered back at me. "I don't want another beer." I lied. There were too many lines I wanted to cross with Eve, but giving her alcohol felt most wrong because it wasn't legal for her to drink.

However, it was technically legal for her to do other things I wanted to do with her, but not drink.

"You're no fun," she said with a pouty face.

"I'm a little fun."

She stared at my fingers around her wrist, then glanced back at my face. With a nervous laugh, she pulled away and cleared her throat. "So you said you have root beer?"

"Not in the fridge." I followed her into the kitchen and grabbed a Dad's Root Beer bottle by the back door.

She watched me with wide, cautious eyes as I filled a glass with ice and poured the root beer over it. While I capped the bottle, she took a sip. When she licked the froth from her top lip, my dick stirred to life.

Our tacos were getting cold. Josh was upstairs, although dead to the world. There were ten years of life between us. And all of that was above and beyond the family connection and her father being the town's preacher.

Still, I pushed the hair off her shoulder, and she swallowed hard before her lips parted. I took the glass from her and set it on the counter with my other hand.

"Why do you have to be eighteen, Eve?" I said, gazing at my hand as my knuckles brushed her neck.

"Because my parents had unprotected sex in 1968." She bit her lip.

This. Girl. Was. Me!

I was a wise guy at her age. Trouble found me, and I welcomed it. Conforming felt like a crime, and rebellion flowed through my veins. Had I been dead, I would have said Eve was my reincarnation.

When I looked into her eyes, she rolled her lips together to suppress her grin, but I made no effort to control mine.

"They had it in 1966 too, but my twenty-year-old sister is taken."

She made my face hurt from grinning nonstop. "Why do I want to kiss you so badly?" I murmured.

Her chest rose and fell faster and faster, and her lips parted to accommodate each quickening breath. "Um ..." Again, she swallowed, and her face tensed with concentration.

"It's a rhetorical question," I whispered.

Eve bobbed her head several times.

"We should finish eating. I'm terrible at *just* kissing." I handed the drink back to her.

Eve inhaled a shaky breath and took the root beer, but she didn't look at me.

There was no logical reason to kiss her. The math didn't add up. But I loved the sparkle in her eyes when she looked at Josh, and the way she bit her lips to hide her smile when she gazed at me.

The fire in her belly ignited something inside of me.

For a stolen moment, I wasn't a single dad; she wasn't ten years younger. I was a man who wanted to kiss a woman.

Because she was beautiful.

And funny. God, I loved her humor.

Her insatiable curiosity and rebellious desire.

The way my little boy squealed with joy in her presence.

Her shy grin.

Long, fluttering eyelashes.

Tart apples.

Sweet cinnamon and sugar.

Stargazing on the dock.

Defiant chin lifts.

And the sheer euphoria I felt when she walked into any room because she was so unpredictable.

Eve stared at her drink for several seconds before returning it to the counter. Then she rested her hands on my chest (a really bad idea) and lifted her gaze to mine. "I'm not that great at *just* kissing either," she murmured.

I gave her credit for feigning confidence, but her voice trembled. Her whole body shook.

I couldn't uncross the line, so I idly stared at it. "This is a terrible idea," I whispered more to myself than her.

She shrugged a shoulder. "How do you know? You haven't kissed me yet."

Take a bite of the apple.

"I hate cold tacos," I said, stepping backward and turning to lead the way back to the sofa.

"You can't do that to me." She followed on my heels.

I sat on the sofa and resumed eating my taco. "Do what?" I mumbled, slowly chewing.

Eve parked her hands on her hips. "Tease me. I will not be toyed with like a cat. You can't say that and not kiss me."

God, she was even more beautiful when she was mad. Her pink cheeks and the determination in her dark brown eyes tried to unravel me.

"It was just an idea," I said, watching the TV. "Talking out loud. Like should I go fishing or hunting? Then I think over the pros and cons of each and make a decision."

"You didn't give *me* a say in the matter."

I swallowed and licked my lips, shifting my attention to her. "Sorry. What say you?"

She crossed her arms over her chest but didn't speak.

My heart raced because whether or not it was a good idea, I knew she'd let me do just about anything to her. And that made my mind go in directions it didn't need to go. It was a war between my fleeting rational thoughts and my dick that wanted me to let things happen, fuck the consequences.

"You're getting in over your head," I said, shifting the blame to her. I was fine, completely in control.

Liar.

I was the wolf, the hunter.

Eve was my prey, and I was giving her time to run.

But she didn't have a bone of self-preservation in her body. Eve didn't just gravitate toward trouble, she was trouble.

For three full seconds, I felt like my self-control was winning because her hands fell to her sides as she deflated. But in the next breath, she shrugged off her hoodie and then her T-shirt.

Fuuuck ...

Her tan skin flushed, but she kept going despite her visible nerves. And I didn't stop her.

Not when she removed her jeans.

Not when she stepped closer to me, so close that I had to spread my knees to let her stand between them. The women in the magazines under my mattress didn't hold a candle to Eve.

My hands remained at my sides on the sofa's edge while hers threaded through my hair. I curled my fingers into the sofa to keep them from touching her. But I wanted to unhook her bra and slide her thin, white cotton underwear down her long, toned legs.

Eve's nearly naked body shredded my common sense. My nose brushed the hollowed space between her cleavage. She smelled like flowers and sweet spice. Responsibility lurked over my shoulder like a good little angel.

I slid my hands up the back of her legs, pausing when she drew in a sharp inhale. But then her fingers curled, tugging my hair, bringing my face closer so that my lips grazed her breast over her bra.

Teetering on a razor's edge of control, I slid my right hand into her panties and palmed her butt.

She buried her face into my hair, kissing my head.

There was only one problem. Well, there were many problems, but my waning sense of responsibility focused on the most immediate one: I didn't have a condom.

Not a single, fucking condom in the entire house.

But my dick was so hard that my irrational mind played the bartering game. Maybe I didn't need a condom.

You need a fucking condom!

We could just kiss. Yeah, that's what we would do.

I leaned back and guided her to straddle my lap. That seemed like the smartest position to *just kiss*.

"I won't be anyone's regret," Eve said, teasing her fingers down my neck.

"Not kissing you is the only thing I would ever regret," I whispered, ghosting my lips over her cheek, dancing around the point of no return.

"What are you waiting for?" she murmured.

"Just taking my time. We only get *one* first kiss." I teased her earlobe with my teeth while both of my hands breached her underwear, gripping her perfect ass— a bad idea.

She rubbed herself along my erection—the worst idea.

I rested my forehead on her shoulder and watched as she worked her pelvis back and forth over the bulge in my jeans. I was so damn mesmerized, tightening my grip on her ass to guide her. Her fingers dug into my upper back.

We needed to stop.

I couldn't stop. I was *dying*. So, I tortured myself by keeping my left hand on her bare ass while my right moved between us. I teased my fingertips along her inner thigh before snagging the crotch of her panties, pushing it to the side so her flesh rubbed along my denim. I wanted to see how wet she was for me, and I was hellbent on killing myself.

Eve paused her motions and leaned back, lust-filled eyes finding mine. As she wet her lips, her delicate fingers unbuttoned my jeans.

Stop her.

She eyed me the whole time as if she were silently asking permission.

Stop her.

As she started to pull down my zipper, I framed her face in my hands. She froze as we stared at each other, our lips a mere breath from touching.

"Eve," I whispered while grinning.

Her smile mimicked mine, face flushed, wayward strands of hair teasing her eyelashes that fluttered shut as I kissed her for the first time.

I felt ten years younger. The hottest girl in school was straddling my lap with her tongue teasing mine and ribbons in her hair. The perfect mix of naughty and nice.

Everything inside me buzzed with need. I wanted to kiss her harder and deeper, but I didn't. She deserved my patience, after all, I had no clue what I was doing or where things were going between us. But I liked kissing her, and I liked pretending that it was okay to touch her. Before it ended, she reached behind her to unhook her bra.

I broke the kiss. "We can't," I said, taking a deep breath while running my hands through my hair.

"I'm not," she quickly said. "I'm, uh … not a virgin."

She was so fucking irresistible.

At the same time, where the hell was my head? I hadn't thought about the possibility of her being a virgin.

"I've just never had someone look at me like you're doing," she said, blowing her hair out of her face. "That's why I'm a little shaky."

"How am I looking at you?"

She slowly shook her head. "I don't know because I've never seen that look before," she murmured, leaking more vulnerability.

I suddenly felt a wave of responsibility—but not necessarily to do the right thing in someone else's eyes. She deserved to be acknowledged as a beautiful, desirable woman who held a lot of power over the man looking at her.

"Eve, you're happiness personified and fucking gorgeous. *That's* how I'm looking at you."

A tiny smile broke through her nervous expression. "Like the centerfolds in your magazines?"

I felt like a pervert. She would never forget about those magazines.

"No one compares to you. But that's not—"

She kissed me while her hands made another attempt at unzipping my jeans.

"No." I lifted her off my lap and scooted to the sofa's edge, rubbing my eyes while trying to settle my breathing. "Dammit. I'm sorry."

Eve quickly righted her bunched-up underwear. Her hair covered her face, and she kept her chin tucked.

I leaned back to button my jeans, then reached for her wrist as she stepped away to get the rest of her clothes.

"I don't want to hear it," she said, yanking her arm out of

my hold and wrestling with her jeans to right the legs that were inside out.

I sighed. "Eve—"

"No. Don't say a word. I told you I wouldn't be anyone's regret, and you—"

"And I *don't* have a fucking condom."

She stilled with her back to me, jeans on but not zipped, hair covering her shirtless torso. The buzz of cicadas through the screen door was the only sound between us while I waited for her to process what I said—while I waited for my stupid brain to process the possibility that Josh could have woken up to see Eve straddling me half-naked.

I'm an idiot.

After a long pause, she turned. God, she was beautiful. Eve made me want to burn every magazine under my mattress. I stood, sliding past her to retrieve her shirt. Then I pulled it over her head.

She didn't help me. Instead, she stood there, staring at my chest with a blank expression and rosy cheeks. So I guided her arms through the holes like dressing Josh.

Finally, she lifted her gaze to mine. "What if you had a condom?" she murmured.

"I'd be deep inside you, probably with a hand over your mouth to keep you from waking Josh."

A grin bloomed along her face. "You think I'm a screamer?"

I smirked. "I think I'm that good." It wasn't *not* true, but I only said it to get a reaction.

"Will I be graded on a curve, Mr. Collins?"

I stepped back and laced my fingers behind my neck. Worth noting (on record) that I *never* had inappropriate thoughts about a student or anyone who had ever called me "Mr. Collins."

Until Eve Jacobson. It had to be in the name. Eves were evil temptresses. Period.

God must have smacked his hand against his forehead, laughing at me.

Her name is Eve, and she loves apples.

"It's just a metaphor," I whispered to myself. There was nothing in the Bible specifically stating it was an apple.

"What did you say?" Eve asked.

"Nothing." I pressed my lips together and looked at her while swallowing hard. "You can't call me Mr. Collins. Got it?"

Her tongue made a lazy and torturous swipe along her lower lip before she grinned. "Not into roleplaying?"

"Not unless it's with Josh and we're playing with toys. And we call it pretend play, not roleplaying."

"What do your students call you?" She cocked her head to the side.

"You're not my student."

"You've been teaching me things. And I'm eager to learn more from you."

I was going to hell despite having been baptized. The "once saved, always saved" only applied to guys who didn't kiss preachers' daughters named Eve.

"Kyle," I said. "You can and should call me Kyle. Or Handsome. Even Awesome works. But not Mr. Collins."

"Coach?" She stepped closer.

I shook my head.

She grabbed my shirt, head tipped back. "Boss? After all, I work for you."

"Call me Kyle," I whispered.

That adoring gleam in her eyes seemed less innocent and more evil. Eve made me grateful that I had a boy to raise instead of a little girl who might someday use her body and flirty smile to drive men wild.

She glanced at her watch.

"Do you have a curfew?" I asked.

She shook her head. Then she laughed and nodded, covering her face with her hands. "It's so embarrassing. I'm an adult and no longer in school." She dropped her hands. "But since I still live at home, I have to be back by eleven during the week and midnight on the weekend."

It was almost twelve.

"I'll walk you to your car." I nodded toward the door, stopping while she put on her shoes. "Thanks for getting the tacos."

She pulled her keys out of her pocket and descended the porch steps. "Thanks for buying them."

"What are you doing tomorrow? Want to target shoot?"

She turned at her car door. "I'd love to, but I offered to fill in at the motel since Rose is on vacation."

"Another day then." I fixed one of her untied ribbons and pulled a few stray hairs from around her eyes.

She nodded. "Another day."

"Good night," I said, ducking my head to kiss her.

She wrapped her arms around my neck, pressing her chest against mine. Her tongue teased my lips, and the kiss intensified when mine darted out to meet hers. I couldn't remember the last time I enjoyed kissing a woman so much. Every time it slowed, and I thought I should end it, she leaned into my body a little more and it fed the fire.

Finally, I ended the kiss, adjusting my erection.

Her gaze followed my hand, making her grin stretch to

her ears, but she didn't say anything about my uncomfortable situation. "I have to go so I can talk to my parents about us before they're in bed," she said, opening her door and plopping into the driver's seat.

"You can what? Wait!" I held open the door.

"What can they say? We're consenting adults." She shrugged, putting the key into the ignition.

"Eve ..." I narrowed my eyes.

Her gaze washed across my face before she relinquished a shit-eating grin. "Are you panicking?" She smirked. "Of course you are because *I'm that good.*"

"Evil."

She laughed while I shut her door.

Chapter Fourteen

John Cougar Mellencamp, "Paper in Fire"

Eve

I ALMOST CALLED in sick to work the following day, but since I was filling in for another employee, I couldn't bring myself to leave the owner without someone to work. I wasn't all evil.

It was the longest day of my life because I needed to talk to Erin so badly that by the time I reached her house after work, I was ready to explode.

"Eve, how are you?" her mom asked, answering the door after I rang the bell twice and knocked a dozen times.

"Great. Uh, is Erin home?"

"Yeah, she's in her—"

"Thanks!" I called, already halfway up the stairs toward Erin's bedroom.

She had music blaring from her boombox, and I opened her door without warning.

"Hey," she said, glancing up from the edge of her bed where her foot was propped up while she painted her toenails red. "How was working on a Saturday?"

I turned down the volume on her boombox just enough to talk without yelling.

"I almost had sex last night," I said so quickly it sounded like one long, indecipherable word, like I was trying to talk while being electrocuted.

"What?" Her face scrunched, keeping her head bowed to paint her toenails.

I kneeled before her, taking the nail polish from her hands and setting it on her nightstand.

"I'm not done," she whined.

"I. Almost. Had. Sex. Last. Night."

Her eyes shot open, along with her mouth.

I covered mine to muffle my scream while nodding repeatedly.

She grabbed my shoulders and shook me. "Oh my gosh! Oh my gosh! Oh my gosh! Tell me everything."

I hopped onto her bed and gave her every tiny detail.

"So have you talked to him today? Is he getting condoms? Are you having it tonight? What about Josh?"

I shook my head and giggled at her vomiting endless questions without taking a breath. But I couldn't blame her because I told the whole story in one breath without pauses for punctuation. "I don't know. I had to work, so I haven't talked to him. What am I supposed to do? It's Saturday night. Do I call him? Just go over there uninvited?"

"Eve! He had his hands on your bare butt! He slid the crotch of your underwear out of the way so he could see your private parts, and he nearly made you orgasm. YES! You go over there tonight and finish the job."

I gnawed the heck out of my lip for a few seconds. "What if he didn't get condoms? Do you really think he took Josh with him to get them today?"

Erin hopped off the bed and dug through her purse, pulling out a condom. "Take it." She handed it to me.

I stared at it.

"Take it." She shook it in front of me.

I slid it into my pocket.

"Why do you look so nervous?" she asked, sitting beside me to resume painting her nails.

"Because last night we were in the moment. You know how after a football game, especially a big win, everyone is excited and celebrating and …"

"Horny."

I giggled. "Yes. Tonight will feel different. Like, what if I go to his house, and he's like, 'Hey. What's up? Why'd you come over?'" I bled insecurity in the safety of my best friend's company.

"Stop. He's not going to say that. He'll be like, 'Josh! Time for bed. NOW!'" Erin said in her deepest man's voice.

I snorted.

"Whatever you do, you *have* to call me as soon as it's over and tell me everything."

"Good idea. I'll ask to use his phone while he discards the condom." I rolled my eyes.

Erin capped the nail polish and shook it before switching feet. "You know what I mean. I just don't want you doing it tonight and telling me about it at church tomorrow when I'll have to control my reaction. Besides, I know Hazel Johnson always has her hearing aids in and turned up to hear the sermon and every word anyone says."

"Why do you say that?"

"Because she's always scowling at us."

"Huh. I hadn't noticed."

"Go have sex and call me." She jerked her head toward her bedroom door.

I stood, feeling like the condom in my pocket was a gun that everyone could see. "It might not happen."

"Or it might. But if you don't go, we'll never know."

"Okay. Wish me luck."

"Good luck. And *call* me!"

"Are all your friends busy tonight?" Mom asked, passing me the creamed peas. "It's rare to have you or Gabby join us for dinner on a Saturday night."

I shrugged. Gabby was with Ben, and it was weird being home tonight. "I didn't feel like McDonald's tonight, but I'm meeting everyone at the bowling alley after I'm done eating."

"Kyle called," Dad said.

I dropped the serving spoon, and it clanked against the bowl. Mom frowned at me while I cringed.

"He said he'd help me take down that last tree after dinner tonight if someone can watch Josh."

"I'll do it!" I blurted.

"You just said you're going out with friends," Mom said.

"Yeah, but I don't have to."

"You worked all day. I'll watch him. I watched him earlier while they took down the other trees." Mom smiled at my dad.

"Do you need help with the tree?" I asked.

My dad gave me the hairy eyeball.

"What?" I shrugged, taking a bite of my steak. "I'm eighteen now. Only a few of my friends are still in town, and Erin's in school, so she has to study most nights."

My parents exchanged a look.

"I like this adult version of you," Dad said, offering me a rare, sincere smile. "You can help pile up the branches."

I controlled my excitement and returned a smile and nod.

After dinner, I walked with my parents to Kyle's house. As soon as he opened the door, his smile vanished.

It hit me: He probably thought I told my parents, and they'd dragged me over to talk with us about our sinful behavior and to tell Kyle he wasn't allowed to get anywhere near me ever again.

"Hi," he said cautiously.

"Eve's going to pile up branches for us," Dad said in a rare moment of fatherly pride.

It took Kyle an extra second to return a nod, and his smile was barely believable as my mom stepped inside.

"Is Josh in his room?" she asked.

"Uh, yeah." Kyle continued to trip over his words.

It was weird, as if the previous night didn't happen. I stared at his hands that had been in my underwear, and his lips that had kissed mine.

Dad jabbed his thumb over his shoulder. "I'm going to head that way. I need to run back home first because I forgot my gloves. I'll meet you two at the creek."

"I'll grab my handsaw and be there soon," Kyle said to my dad while staring at me with an unreadable expression as he stepped outside and squatted to tie his brown work boots. "No plans tonight?" he asked.

"Nope," I said, watching my dad trek back toward our house.

He stood and headed toward the barn, so I followed him, staying a few steps behind.

"Did you think I told my parents about last night?"

He shook his head, opening the barn door. "I don't know what I thought."

I stepped inside as he held it open.

"Why would I tell them?" I laughed, following him toward a wall of tools hanging from rusty nails beside the cabinet where he kept his bow.

"I don't know. I thought maybe Jesus made you do it," he said.

"Jesus died so we can sin."

He laughed, plucking a handsaw from the wall before facing me. "I love your interpretation of the Bible. Your father would be proud of your vast knowledge."

"Thank you." I grinned. "Nothing makes me happier than making my dad proud. Now, are you going to kiss me?"

Kyle eyed me for a second before shaking his head. "Your dad will be waiting for us."

I shrugged. "It's just a kiss."

"It's never just a kiss," he said without looking directly at me.

I stepped closer until my boots tapped his. "Just one."

He grunted a laugh and pointed his attention past me as if someone was there. "Evil."

I pried his fingers from the saw handle, and it fell to the ground. When his attention returned to me, he grabbed my head and kissed me.

It was one *long,* hard kiss.

It's how I imagined a man should kiss a woman—passionately, confidently, unforgettably.

And boy, was it *ever* unforgettable.

He had strong hands that cradled my jaw like he owned me as his fingers splayed along my neck. All I wanted was to experience how he would touch and manipulate the rest of my body if given the chance.

When he released me, his mouth bent into a sexy smile. He knew what he did to me. After he retrieved the saw from the ground and took several steps toward the door, I dropped to my knees. He peered over his shoulder, halting his steps.

"You're slowly torturing me." I pressed a fist to my chest, gesturing a dagger to the heart.

Kyle wasn't five, but his blue eyes sparkled with an innocent wonder when he gave me a once-over. It's how Josh looked at him.

That wonder morphed into something else, but I couldn't read the emotion behind it.

"I'm in uncharted territory. You have to be patient with me," he said.

I climbed to my feet and hurried after him. "I'm not a patient person, but I'm working on it."

"I wasn't patient at your age either." He opened the door, and we headed toward the creek. "Eve, you must be careful, falling to your knees like that."

"I've spent many hours praying. My knees are used to it," I said.

He chuckled. "That's not what I meant. I'm not worried about your knees."

"Then what's your point?" I glanced over at him.

"When a guy kisses you as I did, and you fall to your knees, he doesn't think your knees are weak; he thinks you're suggesting something else. It's false advertising, Eve. You need to be more careful."

"Something—" The light bulb went on in my *pretty little*

head. "You thought I was going to ..." I bit my lip and looked at him again.

He kept his focus on the grassy path, trying to control his grin while he shrugged.

"I haven't. I mean, I would. I think. I'll look into it." I tapped a finger on my chin.

He lost control and snorted, pressing a fist to his mouth.

"What? Stop laughing at me." I bumped into him, and he stumbled a few steps to the side.

"Sorry. I wasn't expecting that reaction," he said.

"What reaction? You assumed I would be more experienced?"

Kyle playfully nudged me back. "No. I don't assume you're experienced. I'd like to think you've been *selective.*"

"A virgin?"

"Judicious."

I laughed. "You're such a nerd."

"Let's get this done before it gets dark," my dad said as we stepped into the clearing just beyond the bend in the path.

"My hut!" I gasped at the pile of sticks.

"Darling, I told you it was going to come down."

"No, Dad. You said it *should* come down. And I said it shouldn't. Period. We weren't done discussing it."

When I looked to Kyle for help, he rolled his lips together and shrugged.

"Did you help him tear it apart?" I pressed.

"Eve, we don't have time to discuss it. What's done is done," Dad snapped.

I kept my expectant gaze on Kyle.

He returned the tiniest headshake as if he didn't want

my dad to know that he was absolving himself of wrongdoing.

While they took down the last dead tree, I dragged limbs and branches to the burn pile. My thoughts were all over the place. One minute, I was composing a long spiel I planned on giving my dad about the hut, the next, I was thinking about my lack of experience with blow jobs. It made my head hurt because thoughts of my dad didn't belong anywhere near blow job contemplation.

"That's good, Eve. I'll finish up with the rest tomorrow," Dad said, gesturing toward the path back home.

On the way up the hill, he and Kyle discussed widening the path between our two properties so Gabby and I didn't tear up his grass when riding the four-wheeler or Anikan, the horse we inherited from Sarah's boyfriend.

I hung back a few feet for a bit of privacy while I pouted.

"I'm going to say good night to Josh," I told my dad so he didn't question why I was heading toward Kyle's house instead of ours.

"Thanks again, Kyle. See you at church in the morning." My dad veered to the right as I followed Kyle toward the orchard.

"See you in the morning," Kyle replied.

After my dad was out of earshot, Kyle slowed down and waited for me to catch up. "I told him the hut didn't need to be torn down, but he didn't want a storm to blow it into the creek," he said.

"And you told him that was highly unlikely, right? Then you told him that Josh loves the hut. Right?"

"Sure."

"Liar."

He laughed. "It's not the end of the earth."

"It's not the end of the earth," I parroted mockingly.

"I miss the *woman* from last night." He shot me a look with one eyebrow raised.

I was being a woman. An irritated, pissed-off woman.

"I miss the man who stands up for me, protecting me and my things at all cost. My knight in shining armor. Oh," I smacked my forehead, "that's right. I've never met that man."

"Ouch. You haven't given me a chance."

"I did! You had the chance to save my hut but tucked your tail between your legs and bit your tongue."

Kyle turned one-eighty to face me, and I bumped into him and frowned. "Eve, last night I let the preacher's daughter grind against my cock in nothing but her bra and panties. *Patience.* A hunter waits for his shot. A knight doesn't storm the castle until he knows he can take the rook and the king. One move at a time. Okay?"

I stared up at him and rolled my eyes. "I don't play chess. So what move did you make today?"

"When you were at work, and I was helping your dad take down the trees—"

"And my hut."

He sighed. "When I *was helping your dad take down the trees*, he thanked me for trusting you with Josh. And I sang your praises."

"You sing?"

He smirked. "Probably better than you."

"Jerk."

"Evil."

It shouldn't have thrilled me to be called Evil, but it did when Kyle said it.

"I got a condom," I informed him with pride.

He narrowed his eyes. "You *got a condom?*"

I nodded.

"Why?"

I was crestfallen by his reply. "Last night, you didn't have—"

"No. I'm aware of what I didn't have last night. I'm just really confused as to why *you* got a condom. And just to be clear, it's 'a' condom?"

"Do you double up? You're not supposed to."

He closed his eyes and shook his head. "Where did you get a single condom?"

"Erin." As soon as I said her name, I cringed.

He widened his eyes. "Erin? As in your friend Erin?"

I wrinkled my nose and nodded.

"So you told your friend about us, even though I told you to tell no one?"

"She's my best friend."

"I said no one."

"She's not going to say anything."

"Eve, *you* weren't supposed to say anything, but you did. So why do you believe she won't?"

"Dude, we're not doing anything wrong. What's the big deal?"

He pinched the bridge of his nose. "If it's no big deal, we should tell your dad, right? And I'm sure he'll be happy for us."

"Well, I think we should wait to tell my dad."

His hand flopped to his side. "Oh, you do, huh? And why is that?"

I twisted my lips for a few seconds. "Since I'm still living at home, he has a tendency to treat me like a child. So I don't think he'd be okay with us yet."

Ever.

My dad was never going to be okay with me dating a man ten years older than me.

"So we agree that things are murky, a little gray. And perhaps telling anyone, and I mean *anyone,* isn't a good idea right now."

I frowned. "What do you expect me to do? I can't exactly un-tell Erin."

He turned and marched toward the house, seemingly a little miffed at me. "I'm twenty-eight, Eve. I have a son, a house, and a job. I don't need you getting condoms for me. I'm a big boy. I can walk into a store and buy them myself. No shame. No big deal."

"You're mad," I said, following him.

"Yes. I'm mad. I don't need my colleagues finding out that I've been messing around with one of their recent graduates. I don't need my brother discovering that I tried to screw his best friend's daughter less than a month after moving next door."

"So we're just going to be secret lovers?"

Kyle's stride died, and I stopped to keep a safe distance.

He shook his head and chuckled. "Listen, I'm attracted to you. You elevate the mood of every room you walk into because you have a *lively* personality. I feel ten years younger when I'm with you. But I just bought a house and started a new job. I'm responsible for another life. I don't want to get shamed out of town right now. So I don't know if we're *lovers* or what we are. I just know it's way too early to put a label on it, which means it's also too early to risk telling *anyone.* So no, let's not be secret lovers. Let's be adults with a little discretion."

I opened my mouth to argue but quickly clamped it shut, fearing my reaction might sound too childish.

He waited with his back to me for a long moment before continuing to the house. "I'm impressed," he said.

"Why?"

"I expected you to go off about something."

"Well, I'm impressive, not childish."

He chuckled.

The cat was out of the bag with Erin, and Grandma Bonnie, but that was neither here nor there. So it had to be okay to talk to them since they knew. If I'd had it to do over ... yeah, who was I kidding? I totally would have told Erin and Grandma.

Guys came and went. They inflated hearts and broke them. Best friends and awesome grandmas picked up the pieces and mended them. Guys were givers and takers, but best friends shared everything. They made everything real.

"I'm going to head into your house instead of following you to the barn," I said, stopping by the front porch stairs.

Kyle turned. "Why?"

"I think you should work a little harder for it."

His tongue made a lazy swipe along his lower lip, and he nodded. "And by *it,* you mean you?"

"Yes."

He beamed with amusement. "Okay." After several steps, he looked back at me. In the next breath, he continued toward the barn.

My heart felt tortured. Self-torture, of course. But I needed to stop dropping to my knees, even if everything he did made them weak.

Chapter Fifteen

Berlin, "Take My Breath Away"

Eve

APPARENTLY, Kyle was too busy doing his job and raising his son to work for my affection.

After that Saturday, he was nice to me. Nice, like someone would be to their babysitter.

Two weeks.

He went *two weeks* without acknowledging he'd seen me nearly naked.

Two Sunday dinners at our house, acting like a cousin.

Two weeks of cordially thanking me for watching Josh during football practice.

Two away football games where I gave up my Friday night to watch Josh and put him to bed on time. And again, Kyle thanked me with a smile and cash.

No greasy food runs.

No kissing.

Not even a wink.

"To be fair, he is busy," Erin said while we jogged on Saturday morning.

"To be fair? Uh, no. It's not fair. He's had plenty of opportunities to be alone with me. Josh goes to bed at eight, and I don't have to be home until eleven—or twelve on the weekends. Today, he could be taking me hunting with him. Instead, he asked *Gabby* to watch Josh while he went by himself. How did standing up for myself turn into ending everything?"

"Why don't you just ask him?"

"Nooo ..." I could hear my mom's voice in my head, telling me to stop whining. "If I ask him, then he wins."

Erin laughed. "It doesn't have to be a game."

"It's not. But you know what I mean."

"Maybe you need to show up uninvited and seduce him after Josh is in bed."

I giggled. "Like, trench coat with no clothes under it? I don't own a trench coat, do you?"

"No. Why would I own one?" She laughed. "Do something else. Just jump on him and start kissing him."

My steps faltered from laughing so much. "Throw myself at him? What if he does that head-turn thing like in the movies and rejects me? What if he says, 'It's not you; it's me.' I would be totally mortified."

"Then just ask him!"

"Then I sound whiny and desperate."

"Not if you don't ask him in a whiny and desperate way. You have to chill. You freak out too easily. Be cool."

Cool.

I could do that.

Nothing said cool like stalking him from my bedroom window with binoculars. He arrived close to dinner time and parked his truck by the barn. Josh ran down the porch stairs, and Gabby followed him. I bolted into the bathroom to curl my hair before changing into black jeans that were too tight for my father's approval, a white T-shirt, a fake leather jacket, and black boots.

"Where are you off to?" Mom asked when I reached the bottom of the stairs. She was tying her apron to make dinner.

"I'm not sure what we're doing yet." I smiled.

Erin was going to a movie with Nicole. So *we* was me. And it wasn't a total lie. I didn't know my plan. I just knew I'd drive around until after Josh's bedtime. DQ sounded good. A burger and sundae.

"Have fun."

"I will." Just as I opened the door, Gabby walked up the porch stairs. "Oh, hey. How was watching Josh? Did Kyle get a deer?"

She sighed. "I think I'm in love with our neighbor."

"Josh is so sweet," I said, sliding my purse strap onto my shoulder.

"No. Well, yes. But I'm talking about Kyle."

I closed the door behind me before she could walk inside the house. "He's dad's best friend's brother. And twelve years older than you." I wrinkled my nose. "Gross."

"Gross? Are you blind? He's not gross. He's like ..." She fanned herself. "He's dreamy. I sit in the front row of his class. We have assigned seats, but I told him I couldn't see the blackboard, so if he says anything to you, just tell him that Mom hasn't taken me to the eye doctor yet. Oh, and he's wearing camouflage pants and a tight, long-sleeved shirt. And I could see every muscle. Also, he needs to shave. Normally, facial hair is grody, but everything about him is," she looked around and lowered her voice, "sexy."

I didn't move and forbade any part of my body to give anything away. "You need to say an extra prayer tonight."

"Pfft. You're one to talk. You just have poor taste in guys, just like Sarah."

"Sarah has poor taste in guys?" I narrowed my eyes.

"Yes. She let the good one go." She shouldered past me into the house, shutting the door without a goodbye.

"I have flawless taste in men," I mumbled with a grin on my way to the car.

I drove around town listening to music, pulled into the gas station to chat with a few friends, and grabbed dinner at DQ. By eight, I made my way to Kyle's, parking at the end of the drive behind a patch of trees so my parents couldn't see my car from our house.

After messing with my hair in the rearview mirror, applying ChapStick, and checking my teeth for food, I popped a Mentos in my mouth and nervously walked toward his house, stopping when I saw something moving.

He was sitting on the porch swing, drinking a beer. "Eve," he said, drawing out my name for at least three seconds.

I gulped. Why was I so on edge? We'd almost had sex.

"My sister has a crush on you," I said.

Why did I say it?

No clue.

He paused the can of beer an inch from his mouth. "She's in my Trig class. I really have to draw a line, and sixteen is nonnegotiable."

Don't laugh!

My boots clicked on the wooden stairs, and I pressed my lips together, sucking on the mint. "Is Josh in bed?"

He nodded before drinking the last of his beer.

"When I said I wanted you to work for it, I thought that might involve some effort."

"It has." He stood, eyeing me with an unreadable expression as he opened the screen door.

I followed him inside.

"Are you saying it takes a lot of work to ignore me?"

"Ignore you?" He tossed the can into a bin by the back door. "I haven't ignored you. I see you and talk to you almost every day."

"You talk to me like I'm ..." I drew in a long breath.

Stay chill.

"Like you're what?" He crossed his arms over his chest and cocked his head.

My fake, calm smile felt psychotic. "You haven't kissed me, touched me, said anything that's the least bit suggestive, or even winked at me in two weeks."

Kyle made duck lips and returned an easy (infuriating) nod. "Because I've been focused on working for *it*."

I pumped my fists. He was too chill.

Too dismissive.

Too everything except making any sense.

I rubbed my hands over my face and then ran my fingers through my hair, and he had the audacity to let his lips twitch into a tiny grin.

"Ugh! You're such a jerk." I turned and stomped my feet toward the door.

"What are you doing here?" Josh asked in his blue jammies from the top of the stairs, rubbing his tired eyes.

"Hey, sorry. Did I wake you?"

"Go back to bed, buddy," Kyle said, climbing the stairs. He framed Josh's face in his big hands and kissed his forehead. "Bad dream?"

Josh nodded.

No. I couldn't let him make me weak in the knees again, not just from being a good dad.

"Did you show Eve the hut without me?" Josh asked in a soft voice.

"That was a secret," Kyle whispered, but I heard him.

"What hut?" I said.

Kyle deflated, hanging his head.

"Me and Daddy built you a new hut."

"Go to bed, buddy."

"Show me," I said.

Kyle looked at me. "Not now. It's getting dark."

"Bring a flashlight."

"I can't leave Josh."

"I'll come too." Josh perked up.

"You should be asleep."

Josh clasped his hands together in a prayer pose at his face. "Let's show her. *Please.*"

Kyle frowned.

"I'll get my boots on." Josh slid past him and hopped down the stairs, sticking his jammie-covered feet into his little cowboy boots.

Kyle rolled his eyes, taking his time descending the stairs. He disappeared into the kitchen and returned with a flashlight.

We didn't head in the direction of my old hut. Instead, Kyle guided us further north, away from my family's land, to where the creek snaked between a long grove of trees at the bottom of a hill.

Kyle pointed the light to the right, and there was a hut, but it was more like a treehouse on the ground, made from wood and much larger than my hut.

"Come inside," Josh said excitedly, waving me toward the door.

I stepped inside as Kyle shined the light behind me.

There was a log bench along one side and a window on the opposite side, which had hinges for opening and closing.

"Do you like it?" Josh asked.

I was speechless, my heart free-falling, taking every ounce of air from my lungs, so I nodded.

I sat on the log bench and gazed up at Kyle. He offered a shy grin.

"Okay. We showed her, now you need to get to bed." Kyle stepped out of the hut, and Josh followed.

"Coming, Eve?" Josh asked.

I smiled. "In a minute. I'll catch up." I wiped my eyes before either one of them saw me getting emotional over a hut. Then, I brought up the rear as Kyle gave Josh a piggy-back ride back to the house.

"Bed. Do not pass go. Do not collect two hundred dollars," Kyle said.

"What?" Josh giggled as he rode Kyle's back up the stairs.

I followed them and stood in the hallway while Kyle tucked him back into bed.

"Love you, buddy," he said, closing the door most of the way. Then he lifted his gaze to mine as if surprised to see me waiting for him.

I grinned, stepping past him, teasing the palm of his hand, and threading our fingers together while wordlessly leading him to his bedroom. Releasing his hand, I quietly closed and locked the door behind me.

"You built me a hut," I whispered, closing my eyes briefly before turning to face him.

He didn't speak.

I stepped closer, resting my hands on his chest. We gazed at each other in the dim moonlight that snuck past the partially closed curtains. I clutched his shirt, working it up his body and over his head. Then I did the same to mine.

Kyle's hands rested at his sides. His patience only fueled my desire.

I was wind and fire—destructive and out of control. He was earth and water—a grounding, calm force.

But when we kissed, it felt like waves crashing, flames spreading, and the earth quaking beneath us. It felt like his arms were made to hold me. He dragged his lips down my neck while unhooking my bra.

I couldn't breathe, and my lungs didn't care. Kyle became the only thing that mattered to my body. If he filled me, I could live in that moment forever.

I undid his jeans and pushed them past his butt, sliding my hands into the back of his underwear, curling my fingers into his firm muscles.

Warmth flowed across my skin. It felt like a dream, like Gabby sitting in the front row of her math class, imagining Mr. Collins finding her irresistible.

He groaned, grabbing my face and kissing me. One hand dropped to my breast, squeezing it before his finger and thumb playfully tugged at my nipple. I turned my head to break the kiss and bit my lower lip to avoid making noise, unsure how quickly Josh would fall back asleep or how well sound traveled in the old farmhouse.

"If you don't have condoms, I'm going to cry," I whispered past the dizzying marriage of euphoria and desperation while he kissed down my chest and slowly removed my jeans.

"Me too," he murmured over my skin, teasing it with butterfly kisses.

I tugged at his hair, and he grinned. "I have condoms."

He guided me to the bed and gazed at me with a sparkle of appreciation in his eyes as I lay back, hands over my breasts. A pang of vulnerability arrested my confidence because Kyle was only the second guy I'd had sex with. At least, I assumed (hoped) we were going all the way.

"Eve, you're so fucking beautiful I can't think straight."

I trapped my lower lip between my teeth.

He kissed the inside of my knee while dragging my underwear down my legs. My heart raced from every nerve firing at the same time. Kyle rested both hands on my inner thighs and spread my legs.

I swallowed hard, closing my eyes while my heart thrashed in my chest. I couldn't look at him with his gaze affixed down *there*. My skin burned under his touch. Another man had taken my virginity, but Kyle made it feel like the first time.

"Oh god," I said in a harsh whisper. My hips jerked when he kissed me right between my legs. "K-Kyle," I stuttered through my labored breaths as my knees tried to snap together because the tip of his tongue touched my clit before sinking deeper between my legs.

It was a first. A good first.

"Eve, do you want me to make you come like this?" he asked with a thick voice.

Just because I wasn't a virgin didn't mean I knew what I

wanted. No one (and by no one, I meant the one person who took my virginity) didn't give me options.

"Uh ..." I fumbled my answer.

His tongue made another slow swipe between my spread legs, his stubbly jaw brushing my inner thighs.

My back arched, one hand clenching his hair, my other squeezing my breast, pinching my nipple like I did when I touched myself alone in my bedroom—when I only dreamed of Kyle doing that to me.

He chuckled, kissing my inner thigh. "I take that as a yes."

Pressing my lips together to avoid making noise, I quickly nodded several times.

It was unlike anything I had ever experienced, as if his tongue was made to do that to me. Every muscle slowly tightened like one big knot, an overload of need, like my mind disconnected from the rest of my body.

My breath caught in my chest, and a blinding sensation spread along my skin, hot and tingly, as I released in tiny waves.

Heart pounding.

Tiny pants falling past my parted lips.

Incoherent thoughts collided until I barely knew where I was.

He continued his journey up my body, sliding his fingers between my legs when he kissed my breasts, flicking his tongue over my nipple and teasing it with his teeth.

And then he was gone.

No fingers.

No tongue.

No teeth.

He'd climbed off the bed and pulled a condom from the

nightstand drawer, rolling it on with steady hands. Those same hands rested on my inner thighs again to spread my legs.

Our gazes locked when he pushed two fingers into me. On a heavy blink, I released a soft moan, feeling the tight fit of his fingers. He seemed mesmerized by my reaction, pulsing into me several times before pulling out and settling his hips between my legs. His face hovered over mine while he watched my reaction to his erection penetrating me as he hooked his hand behind my knee and guided it to his hip.

My jaw relaxed in a silent cry, and he paused inside me, kissing me a long moment before he began to move. My young heart exploded into fireworks when our gazes met again, and he grinned—sexy but vulnerable.

He gave me everything I imagined that kind of intimacy would be.

Happy and playful.

All-consuming and explosive.

The passion.

The unharnessed desire.

There was no comparison, yet I couldn't keep my mind from making casual observations about Kyle's patience. He was steady like the act mattered just as much as the result. We rolled in the sheets as his mouth and hands explored my body. He made me feel beautiful and perfect, like a woman in every way.

Every smile.

Every time he called me "beautiful."

Every kiss that made my toes curl.

When he guided me onto my stomach, I rested my cheek against the mattress and whispered, "You built me a hut."

Kyle lifted my hips a fraction and entered me from behind.

He planted his hands next to mine by my head and kissed my shoulder. "I built you a hut. You make me want to do all kinds of crazy things."

I bit my lip as my body tingled and tensed, preparing with each thrust for another wave of pleasure.

"Don't stop making me want to do crazy things," he said with his breaths chasing one another, each one a little more ragged. "You make everything so fucking good." His hand snaked under my chest, claiming my breast as the bed swayed with a few creaks every time he pistoned his hips against me, his rhythm becoming more erratic.

Then he stilled. "Eve ..." His hand drifted lower between my legs, and he rubbed me until I orgasmed. He jerked his hips a few more times like my pleasure became his again.

I *loved* sex with Kyle.

But I also loved my parents and Jesus, and I needed those things not to be mutually exclusive.

Chapter Sixteen

Tina Turner, "What's Love Got to Do with It"

Kyle

"I DIDN'T BUILD a hut so you'd have sex with me," I said with one arm behind my head and Eve tucked under my other arm.

"Now you tell me," she said, drawing random patterns on my chest with her delicate fingers.

I chuckled because her humor landed with me.

I was a twenty-eight-year-old father with a naked woman in my bed—who had a curfew. The math didn't add up, but emotions rarely did because there were no rules or formulas, and everything was a variable.

I liked Eve—a lot—and had since the day we met. One plus one equaled a hundred. Everything felt magnified with her. Perhaps we were chemistry more than math.

"Are you going to tell Erin?"

"Yes," she said.

"Jeez, at least try to lie to me."

She sat up, leaned to the side to turn on the lamp, and held the sheet to her chest. "Do you have chips? They don't have to be Ruffles, but that would be a bonus. I had DQ for dinner with a sundae, and now I'm craving something salty."

I wasn't done with her, not even close, so I tugged at the sheet. She tried to keep hold of it, but I won. Dear god, did I ever win. Her perky nipples poked through her long, messy hair. She looked like a goddess. My hand traced the soft curve of her hip, up the side of her body to her breast, and I brushed the pad of my thumb over her nipple.

Her cheeks pinked as her lips curled into a tiny grin. My gaze flitted between her nipple and her deep brown eyes, drinking in every ounce of her sexy vulnerability.

She cleared her throat as if my affection was too much to handle. "If you want to look at naked women," she leaned over me and pulled a *Playboy* magazine out from under my mattress, "there are plenty in these pages." She lay beside me and opened the magazine.

"Stop." I laughed, throwing an arm over my face.

"Do you prefer blondes or brunettes?" she asked, flipping through the pages. "And there *is* a correct answer to this question."

I groaned. "I'm burning all of those magazines first thing tomorrow."

"Before church? God will like that. Or you can wait for my dad to invite you to the bonfire he'll have with all those branches and my hut's remains. He often needs a little paper to get it started anyway. Kill two birds with one stone."

"Are you done?" I peeked at her.

She continued her page-flipping, stopping for an extended inspection of the centerfold. "I'm thinking about shaving my pubic hair. What do you think?"

I thought I wanted to die.

"Erin shaves hers down to about nothing. I trim mine during the summer. A buzz cut. Not like a bald eagle."

"Eve," I shook with laughter, trying to control myself so Josh didn't wake up.

"Speaking of hair, now that I'm eighteen, I'm thinking of cutting mine. Getting bangs and maybe a perm. My boring hair makes me look like a seventies flower child. Surely, my parents won't evict me if I no longer look 'wholesome.' I want to look eighteen. Modern. Chic. And I want to pierce my ears. Maybe get a tattoo. What do you think?"

I thought she was perfect. She didn't need big hair or any sort of embellishments. "I think you're stunning."

She sat up, no longer caring about covering herself with the sheet. "But you would be more attracted to me if I looked like one of these girls with modern hair. Right?"

I rubbed my hands over my face. "Where were you twenty minutes ago when I was worshipping your body, coming undone from every tiny moan that vibrated up your chest to your lips? Eve, you're fucking *perfect*."

Her lips twisted, and she gazed at the magazine in her hands. "What about bigger boobs? Would you like that?" She held up the centerfold over her torso so I could see it.

I snatched the magazine and tossed it aside. "I'm going to buy you a dictionary so you can look up the words 'stunning' and 'perfect.' Let's go. I have Ruffles downstairs."

Her eyes widened, and she covered her mouth to muffle her squeal. I pulled on my jeans and T-shirt while she pieced herself back together.

"You said you were a Lays guy."

"I am. But the babysitter likes Ruffles."

She zipped her jeans and glanced up at me, blowing her hair away from her face. "The babysitter? Is that all I am?"

"What do you want to be?" I wasn't trying to set her up. And I regretted asking the question the moment it left my mouth.

"It's too soon to be your girlfriend," she said, but it sounded more like a question—and maybe a trap.

"I told you before that we don't have to label anything," I said.

She combed her fingers through her hair while I tucked the magazine under my mattress. "But you just asked me what I want to be." Her lips twisted, and it made my stomach twist as well.

What had I gotten myself into? I couldn't imagine it ending well.

"I think our only option right now is lovers." Her nose wrinkled. "Not cheesy lovers like that 'Friends and Lovers' song. I totally mean something like Billy Ocean's 'Loverboy.'" She bit her lips and gave me the sexiest once-over.

I wanted to throw her onto the bed and tear off her clothes all over again.

"Do you wanna be my loverboy?" She snaked her arms around my neck and smirked. "If you give me a beer with the chips, I'll get on my knees."

Fuck me.

"And pray?" I asked. "To quote you: God would like that."

"Come on, Loverboy." She eased open the door and tiptoed past Josh's room and down the stairs.

"You have to be home in ninety minutes," I said, looking

at my watch while she opened every cabinet in the kitchen, hunting for Ruffles.

"Are you suggesting we have sex again? Or are you trying to remind me that my life sucks because I'm an adult living with my parents *and* a curfew?"

"I'm implying we need to keep an eye on the time so you don't get grounded again."

"So you don't get in trouble for screwing the preacher's daughter? Bingo!" She pulled the chips out of the cabinet to the right of the fridge.

"I feel cheap. Is that all I am to you? A quick screw?" I said timidly, crossing my arms over my chest so my hands covered my pecs, and I curled my shoulders inward while frowning.

She giggled, opening the bag of chips and popping one into her mouth. "Why would you feel cheap?" she mumbled, sending a few crumbs flying out of her mouth. "I'm the one who babysits for nothing more than your attention."

"I've paid you."

"Not every time."

"Well," I shrugged. "After tonight, I think we're even."

"What makes you think you're that good in bed?"

I rolled my eyes. "I was talking about the hut I built for you. Pervert."

Eve snorted. "Sorry. Yeah, we're even then." She brought a chip to my lips.

"Evil." I grinned, grabbing her wrist and guiding the whole chip into my mouth along with two of her fingers. I ate the chip *and* the tiny gasp she released.

She cleared her throat, taking a step backward. "Erin is my Adam. If you tell me you haven't talked to Adam about me, I'll call you a liar."

"Guys don't gossip like teenage girls."

Teenage girls.

Who was I kidding? I was the pervert.

"If I tell Erin we had sex, it won't be gossip. And if you *don't* tell Adam, then he's not really your best friend."

"I'm fine with that. I'm not telling him."

He would drag it out of me, but I had a point to make with Eve, even if I quickly lost sight of it.

"Because you're ashamed of me?" She shoved two more chips into her mouth.

"We've been over this."

"Well, let's go over it again."

I rubbed the back of my neck. "Keeping things between two people is okay until you figure it out. Telling everyone, feeling the need to label it or make a grand commitment, is just messy. Keeping something private doesn't have to mean you're embarrassed; it might just mean *it's private.*"

She frowned, setting the bag of chips on the counter. "You're treating me like a child."

"I'm having a discussion with you. If you can't discuss things, then you're acting like a child."

She deflated. "So it's just sex."

I rested my hands on my hips and dropped my head. "How do I explain this? When I was recruited to play football in college, the scouts didn't look at me and think I was ready to join the team and be their starter. They saw potential and knew I would get better with time. So they took a chance on me, knowing I would make many mistakes, but those mistakes would only make me better. And they wanted me to be with them when I reached that point."

Eve returned a blank stare.

"It's not just the sex, Eve. I like being with you. And I

can imagine—envision—that as you mature and spread your wings, you'll shine even brighter. So I don't know anything for sure. I can't predict the future, but I can *imagine*. And that's all we can be right now. A possibility."

Most of the time, Eve surprised me with her maturity, especially with Josh. I never would have acted on the physical attraction had she not been mature in other ways first. But I never imagined having sex would make her more insecure and immature.

"Just ..." She shook her head. "Don't treat me like a child."

"Then don't act like one," I said. Perhaps I had my own maturity issues. I needed to brush up on my verbal restraint.

The muscles in her jaw flexed. Then she glanced at her watch and shrugged. "I have to get home before my curfew because I'm a child. Good night, *Mr. Collins*." She brushed past me.

I had to restrain my grin. Eve was a fiery individual, and I loved that about her because I was pretty fiery at her age, too. Had we been the same age and met ten years earlier, we would have burned down the town and ourselves with it.

Our age difference wasn't unfortunate or inconvenient. It was necessary.

She hopped on one foot, then the other, pulling on her boots before she walked out the door without looking back.

Again, I tried to keep from grinning or chuckling as I followed her. She stomped along the gravel drive to where she parked by the mailbox.

I grabbed the back of her jeans, hooking my fingers into the waist to stop her.

"Hey!" Eve whipped around, and before she could say another word, I grabbed her face, grinned, and kissed her.

She resisted for less than a second.

After making my point, I released her. "*Now* you can go home and be mad," I said before returning to the house.

Chapter Seventeen

Bob Seger, "Shakedown"

Eve

"WHAT HAPPENED?" Gabby asked, poking her head out of her room just as I stepped into the bathroom.

Our parents were in bed, but I knew my mom had her alarm clock set for midnight to see if I was home. It was only eleven.

I narrowed my eyes and whispered, "What are you talking about?"

With a sly grin, she slid into the bathroom with me and shut the door. "Where were you tonight?"

"Why?"

She sat on the toilet seat. "Michelle and Vicky came over, and they missed our drive, so they turned around at the end of Mr. Collins' drive, and they saw your car parked there. Were you babysitting? Mom and Dad said you were with your friends at the movies. Why was your car there? What movie did you see?"

Kyle's drive was the second to the last on our dead-end gravel road. My parents always turned right when leaving our house. They never had a reason to turn left, which meant they turned into our drive on their way home before reaching Kyle's. That's why my car was safe by the trees at the end of his drive.

I never thought my sister's idiot friends would miss our drive and have to turn around in his.

"Well?" she prodded.

I had nothing. No good excuse. Lies usually came easy to me, but that was because I anticipated needing to lie and planned accordingly.

When I was Gabby's age, my older sister, Sarah, confided in me about personal things that could have landed her in trouble. Eventually, everything did blow up on her, but not because of me. I kept her secret. And it made us closer than we had ever been before that.

Could Gabby be my friend and not just my sister? Having someone on the inside, helping me cover my tracks, seemed like a good thing. But I didn't know if Gabby could keep a secret of that magnitude. She struggled to keep my last boyfriend a secret, and it wasn't a big deal in comparison.

"Can you keep a secret?" I asked.

"Duh."

"No. Not *duh*. This isn't about me hiding alcohol by the creek or going steady with someone and not telling Mom and Dad. This is much bigger. Sarah level of big."

Gabby's eyes grew into saucers.

"You can't tell *anyone*."

Yes, I understood the irony in saying that to her after Kyle lectured me over telling Erin.

"You can't tell Ben. You can't tell Michelle or Vicky or Erica. You can't squirm at the dinner table or make funny faces like it's killing you to keep a secret. You have to guard this with your life. Can you do that?"

She gulped and nodded.

Just hours earlier, I made fun of her for having a crush on her math teacher. Oh the irony.

"I've met someone who I really like. And I was with him tonight. But he's older, and as we know, Mom and Dad don't like when their daughters fall for older guys."

Had I fallen for Kyle? Yes. A thousand times yes.

Was a month long enough to fall in love? I didn't know. I hadn't been in love before.

Yet, he was determined to keep me at arm's length while he decided if I was more than a casual date, a one-night stand. But dang, when he kissed me and told me to go be mad, I lost a part of my heart, left it on the ground by his boots. No one had ever let me be myself without fearing punishment, harsh judgment, or disappointment, until Kyle.

"How old?" Gabby asked.

"Twenty-eight."

"What?!"

"Shh!"

She slapped her hand over her mouth.

I frowned. She was already proving to be too young to handle my secret.

"You made fun of me for calling Mr. Collins sexy, and you're seeing someone his age?"

Oh, Gabby ...

"I'm sorry." I wrinkled my nose. "That was wrong of me. You were right."

"What do you mean I was right?"

"Mr. Collins is hot."

"Pfft. Duh." And then the lightbulb came on. It started with her whole body freezing for several seconds.

The wheels were turning to keep the light on.

Then her eyes swelled to saucers again as her jaw dropped.

A blush crawled up my neck to my face, and I bit back my grin.

She shot off the toilet seat and grabbed my shoulders, shaking me. "You are totally joking. Right? Right? *Right?*"

I slowly shook my head.

Something in my sister died. She released a breath that seemed reminiscent of someone being stabbed in the gut. Even her torso buckled a fraction as she stepped away from me. "Why does this keep happening?" she whispered.

"What do you mean?"

"You and Sarah take the best ones. I liked him first."

"Oh, Gabby." I hugged her. "You're his student."

"But now I can't dream about him because he's yours. And Mom and Dad are going to be so mad, and I'll have to live through the Sarah incident all over again."

"Oh, no, Gabbs ..." I rubbed her back. "Sarah had something much more tragic happen; I hope you don't have to go through that with me. And"—I released her and grabbed her hand, squeezing it—"I don't know if he's truly mine or ever will be. But even if that happens, you can still dream about him because he *is* dreamy."

And stubborn.

Infuriating.

Sexy.

Overly analytical.

And I was mad at him for saying so many nice things to me and making me feel like a beautiful woman without needing to change a thing, and in the next breath, reminding me that we might not ever be anything more than temporary.

Gabby laughed a little. "Have you kissed him?"

My younger sister was a lover and dreamer. She wrote poems in her Bible during church and knew the words to every 80s ballad. Gabby would lose her virginity on her wedding night, not just because that's how she was raised. She'd do it because she liked things to follow a specific order.

A flirty look.

Holding hands.

A chaste kiss.

Months of wooing with flowers and love notes.

A grand proposal after asking our father for her hand in marriage.

Church wedding.

Wedding night jitters.

Baby nine months later.

Sarah and I were nothing like her. We rode the reckless high of raging hormones and the adrenaline rush of rolling in the sheets with bad boys who felt *so good*.

I wasn't sure Kyle was a bad boy—until he got into the preacher's daughter's pants.

"We've kissed." I smiled.

Gabby sucked in a breath and smiled. "How was it?"

"Amazing."

"Was there tongue?" She blushed.

I nodded with a tight smile.

She narrowed her eyes. "Why do you have that look?"

"What look?"

"It's the look you give me when you think I'm young and stupid."

"What? No. I don't think that, and I don't have a look either."

"You do. It's your uncomfortable look. You think I don't have a poker face, but neither do you."

"Shh ... it's late. You need to go to bed. And I need to shower." I removed my shirt and jeans, so she'd give up and leave.

"Um, Eve?"

I turned on the shower. "Huh?"

"Your underwear is inside out."

I looked down. "Oh. Oops."

"Oops? You didn't know you put your underwear on—" She slapped her hand over her mouth again and then slid it to her waist. "You did it, you did it, you did IT," she hissed. Her jaw dropped like a brick from a ten-story building.

"I didn't."

"Nobody puts their underwear on inside out unless they're doing it quickly and in the dark!"

"Shh!" I put one hand on the back of her head and my other over her mouth. "Why don't you wake up the whole town? I knew I shouldn't have told you."

She wriggled out of my hold. "I hope you get pregnant." She scowled at me before jerking open the door.

Chapter Eighteen

Rod Stewart, "Love Touch"

Eve

"TELL ME EVERYTHING," Erin said as we put on our choir robes before church the next morning. "And you should have called me last night!"

"Let's go, ladies," my dad said, peeking around the corner.

Erin frowned.

I shrugged. "It's not my fault you were late this morning."

"It was my brother's stupid fault," she grumbled.

We quickly got to our seats just as my dad welcomed everyone and bowed his head to pray.

"Just tell me if you did it?" Erin whispered.

I folded my hands and closed my eyes as if I didn't hear her.

She elbowed me.

I elbowed her back.

Dad cleared his throat in the middle of his prayer, which meant he saw Erin and I misbehaving.

"Amen," everyone echoed my dad.

As the choir sang, my gaze navigated to Kyle, and he smirked. I was sure he thought I was lip-syncing—and I was. However, I wasn't in the mood for his smugness because I was still mad at him. So I didn't give him another glance for the rest of the service.

"Call me immediately!" Erin said after the congregation filed out of the church before I joined my parents and Gabby.

I nodded.

"Eve," Drew called my name as I descended the steps in front of the church.

"And the plot thickens," Gabby mumbled, hugging her Bible.

I shot her a scowl before facing Drew.

"Wanna go to homecoming with me?" Drew asked. "I got your dad's permission."

"Uh ..." I surveyed the churchyard and found Kyle and Josh talking to the Vanderleests, but his attention was laser-focused on me. "I graduated."

"No duh. So what?" Drew said.

"I broke up with you," I whispered.

He chuckled. "I'm not asking you to go steady with me again. I'm asking you to homecoming because I don't care to take anyone in my class. But I'll probably be homecoming king, so I think I should have a date. You know?"

I barely registered what he said because Kyle and Josh headed toward us.

"Ask Erin," I quickly said with a stiff smile.

"No offense, but I'm not that into Erin."

"Drew," Kyle said, putting his hand on Drew's shoulder and giving it a firm squeeze. "Did you ice your arm after Friday's game?"

Drew nodded. "Yes, Coach."

"Hey, Drew?" Marcus, Drew's friend, yelled from a small huddle of guys, all seniors like Drew. "What did she say?"

They all snickered.

"Your friends are laughing at you." Kyle gave Drew's shoulder another squeeze.

Drew rolled his eyes. "Uh ..."

"He asked me to homecoming, *Coach*," I said, batting my eyelashes.

Drew blushed, shifting his weight from one foot to the other. *Coach Collins* intimidated him with nothing more than a shoulder squeeze. But he no longer intimidated me.

"And what did she say?" Kyle looked only at Drew for the answer.

"Uh, nothing yet. But she was about to say yes." He smiled so wide it made the corners of his eyes crinkle like he was giving his coach a wink, like he thought his coach would be proud of him.

"Is that so?" Kyle eyed me with peaked brows.

"I'm hungry, Daddy," Josh said, pulling on Kyle's leg.

I held open my arms to Josh, and he let go of Kyle's leg so I could pick him up. "Are you coming to my house for dinner?" I asked Josh in my sweetest voice, before turning my back to both arrogant *boys* and carrying him toward my parents.

Hugging me with his arms and legs, he mumbled a "yes."

My mom smiled while we approached her. "He's like the little brother you never had," she said.

I bit my tongue and returned a smile.

"Buddy, you're going to get Eve's dress dirty from your shoes," Kyle said. I knew he'd be right behind us.

Josh's tiny fingers dug into my neck for a quick second. Then his body jerked. I felt something warm and wet pool around my neck, oozing into my dress and sliding down my back.

"Oh no!" my mom said.

"Oh, jeez, Josh." Kyle quickly took him from me as I stood unmoving like a board.

Josh wiped the back of his hand across his mouth, smearing *the vomit*.

"Oh!" Gabby turned green and cupped her hand over her mouth and nose.

"Poor thing. Was your tummy hurting?" Mom handed Josh a wad of tissues because he had a little vomit on his face.

Kyle grimaced at me. "Eve, I'm so sorry."

"It's nobody's fault," my dad reassured Kyle. "Eve, let's take you around back. There's a spigot. We can get you rinsed off before you get in the car. Gabby, grab some paper towels from the bathroom and a choir robe your sister can wear home."

Everyone was staring at me.

"I'm sorry, Eve," Josh murmured in a weak voice.

I started to shake my head, but it only made more of the vomit slide into my dress. "It's fine," I said, trying to sound genuine, but I knew my smile was as stiff as the rest of my body. And the sour stench was making *me* nauseous.

Mom jerked her head, gesturing for me to follow her to

the back of the church where she and Gabby hosed me off like a muddy pig.

"COLD!" I jumped and tried to get out of the direct stream, but Gabby kept the stream on me while grinning.

"Hold still, Eve, so she can get you cleaned off," Mom said.

After the vomit was rinsed from my body, Gabby checked both sides of the church to make sure no one was coming while mom unzipped my dress, blotted me with paper towels and covered me with a choir robe.

Erin was going to be bummed her family left so quickly and she missed the big event.

"GUESS WHAT?" Gabby startled me when I opened the bathroom door after my shower.

I dried my hair with a towel. "What?"

She followed me into my bedroom. "Mom wants you to take dinner to Kyle and Josh so you can let Josh know that you're not mad. Kyle called to apologize while you were in the shower. He said Josh was crying on the way home because he felt so bad."

"It wasn't his fault," I said, putting on my bra and underwear.

"Check them well so you don't put them on inside out."

I glanced up at Gabby. "I need to know right now if you can keep this secret or if I need to tell Mom and Dad and risk getting kicked out. But I won't let you hold this over my head. And let's be clear; if you can't be more mature about this, then don't *ever* expect me to be there for you or take your side on anything."

She narrowed her eyes and tipped up her chin before spinning the other way and exiting my room while slamming my door shut. I overreacted, and I knew it the second she shut the door. Fear made me nervous and irrational.

After eating a partial chicken leg and two bites of scalloped potatoes, I took the food my mom had packed to Kyle's.

He opened the door, and a regretful smile marred his face. "I'm so sorry," he said, taking the bag of food from me while I slipped off my shoes. My hair was still damp from my shower, but my jeans and red button-down blouse were clean, and that's all that mattered.

"Stop apologizing. He didn't get sick on purpose. Where is he?" I poked my head into the living room, but he wasn't there. Kyle had a football game on the TV.

"I gave him a little ginger ale when we got home, and now he's upstairs taking a nap. I told him you were coming over with dinner, but he couldn't stay awake." Kyle removed the foil-wrapped plates. "Did you eat?"

I nodded, sliding my hands into my back pockets. "Aren't you going to ask me if I'm going to homecoming with Drew?"

He kept his chin down while removing the foil. "No."

"Why not?"

"Because I know the answer."

"How can you possibly know the answer? Because you built me a hut?"

"No, Eve." He rested his hands on the counter's edge and glanced over at me. "If you're emotionally still in high school, that's fine. Embrace your youth and enjoy your last two years as a teenager. But I'm out. You can be my babysitter, and I'll pay you a fair wage, but that's it."

"Is that an ultimatum?"

"It's a fact." He pulled open the drawer in front of him and grabbed a fork.

"Why are you being such a jerk to me?"

Like I'd been to Gabby.

He set his fork on the counter next to the plate, and it seemed to take everything inside of him to control his response. I had that effect on people.

"*Why* are you so angry and confrontational with me?" he asked.

"Because I feel like ..." My face scrunched as I shook my head. I didn't know how to explain it, and that frustrated me. His insisting I try to explain my feelings bothered me even more.

"You feel like what?"

I shook my head. "I-I don't know. Just ... just like you're waiting to see if I'm worth your time. I feel like I'm being judged, like you know I'm going to mess up, so you can say I'm too young for you." My words came out faster and louder on a wave of panic. "And that's a lot of pressure. I always feel like everyone around me is waiting for me to screw up because that's what I do."

"Just chill."

"I CAN'T CHILL!"

He winced, and our gazes shot toward the stairs as we listened for Josh.

"I'm not a chill person," I said. "I'm sorry. It's not in my genes to chill. If you must know, I'm needy and sometimes whiny. I nag until I get what I want. You're on my mind twenty-four-seven." I pointed in the direction of my house. "I look for you through my bedroom window—with binoculars. Every song I hear is about you. I can't shower without touching myself and thinking of you. When I go for a run, I imagine I'm chasing you. My life went from boring to *amazing* because you moved into this house with the world's cutest little boy. I watch Josh and make dinner or an apple dessert, and I pretend that this is my house too, and he's my son.

"So, if you need to know why I asked about home-coming with Drew, it's because I like you *so* much, and when you changed Denise's toilet, I went crazy jealous. And I wanted you to show me a teeny-tiny fraction of jealousy."

I felt fairly certain that I had ended us.

Whiny? Check.

Jealous? Check.

Needy? Check.

Immature? Check.

Desperate? Double check.

Psycho? Absolutely.

We weren't "going together," but had I been in his shoes, I would have sent me home, changed the locks, and filed for a restraining order.

I showed him the worst version of myself because I had *no chill.* Which was worse? Being oblivious to my least desirable traits or seeing them flashing like a neon sign without feeling control over them?

"Eve—"

I covered my ears because some childish behavior remained in me. "Don't. I know you're going to lecture me. You're going to be an adult. And we are over. I know. I really do. You're too mature to say or do anything as stupid as I just did. So save me the embarrassment of you being perfect. I'll just go." I turned, closing my eyes for a second and berating myself on the way to the door.

Before I slid on my shoes, I heard his footsteps behind me.

"Eve," he said. "Follow me, please."

I turned as he headed up the stairs.

"Now," he said, halfway up.

I bowed my head like an errant child and followed him. He peeked into Josh's room and softly shut the door the rest of the way. Then he continued to his room. That's when I noticed he had something in his hand.

I stared at that something as I stopped at his door.

He jerked his head for me to keep walking. As soon as I passed the threshold, he closed and locked the door.

The can of beer in his hand hissed when he opened it and handed it to me. I hesitated, gaze flitting between the beer and him. Then I took it.

Kyle tugged the button to his jeans and pulled down the zipper. "I don't care which you swallow first. Your choice."

Chapter Nineteen

Def Leppard, "Pour Some Sugar on Me"

Kyle

MELINDA THOUGHT she was always right.

Caring.

Giving.

Independent.

Confident.

Perfect.

The list of self-declared characteristics went to infinity.

Then she left me with our newborn baby and a letter filled with lies and excuses.

Eve unloaded everything all at once. Maybe any other guy would have run, but I focused on what mattered: She thought of me when she masturbated, and she liked imagining Josh was hers. Sure, some questionable things were mixed between those, but I stayed focused on the important ones.

In the end, I knew she needed me to be human and flawed, to see my impulsive and irrational side.

So I gave her a beer and told her to get on her knees.

A+

Eve was a quick study.

I told her to spit on it, and once she got past her initial embarrassment and apprehension, she gave me the best damn blow job I'd ever had.

"Oh fuuuck ..." I groaned as quietly as possible, tipping my head back.

She gazed up at me and grinned. Then she picked her beer off the floor and stood. "How'd I do, Coach?" She took several gulps of the beer while I tucked myself back into my underwear and jeans.

"I'm not proud of that," I said because I wasn't.

She sat on the end of my bed, taking another swig of beer. "No? Why not?"

I shook my head, unable to entirely hide my grin. "I'm capable of being a much better man. But I wanted you to know that I'm not perfect, not even close. I make poor decisions that lead to questionable behavior. I don't think bad decisions are a flaw; it's one's inability for self-reflection and willingness to be humbled by our mistakes that makes us insufferable humans."

Eve drained the rest of the beer and stood. "Your problem is you think everything has to be a lesson. I suppose it's an occupational hazard." She handed me the empty can. "Just admit you've thought about me doing that to you since the day we met." With a flat hand, she patted my chest. "They say you're already halfway there if you can visualize something. So way to go."

She eased open the door, and I stepped into the bathroom. By the time I made it downstairs, she was gone.

I headed downstairs to eat the lunch she brought, but as soon as I turned the corner at the bottom of the stairs, I heard a shrill, bloody-murder scream coming from outside. So I pulled on my boots and ran out the front door toward the barn where the screaming was coming from. Just as I reached the door, Eve hysterically fled the barn.

I caught her, and she buried her face in my chest.

"Ohmygodohmygodohmygod!" Her body shook.

"What are you doing? Is there a bear in there?"

She shook her head, but it was more like a violent shiver, teeth chattering, breaths short and fast. "It l-looked at m-me ... its e-eyes are ... ohmygodohmygodohmygod!"

I released her and slowly opened the barn door. There wasn't anything except ... I chuckled. "Eve, are you talking about my deer hanging from the rafters?"

She stared at me with wide eyes, both hands covering her mouth as she slowly nodded.

"I'm draining the rest of the blood. I plan on taking him down later today. What are you doing in the barn?"

Her hands slowly dropped to her side. "Snooping," she whispered, wrinkling her nose.

I closed the door.

"Snooping for what?"

She shook her head. "Nothing. Just snooping. Haven't you ever just snooped?"

I couldn't help my grin. She was stubborn and childish, yet sexy as hell, and I ate up her attitude like a bowl of hot buttered popcorn.

"Do you feel bad when you kill animals?" she asked.

I closed the door and leaned against it, sliding my hand into my pockets. "No. I feel grateful for the sacrifice."

"Do you think I could kill a deer?"

I chuckled. "Baby, I think you can do anything you put your mind to."

"Will you take me hunting with you?" Eve was full of surprises.

I shrugged. "Eventually."

Her face lit up. "Really?"

"Really."

She squealed and threw herself at me, arms around my neck, mouth fused to mine. Opposites were supposed to attract, but I had the female version of myself and felt damn happy about it.

"DID EVE SAY YES?"

"Coach interrupted," Drew said, warming up on the field the next day with Terrell, his wide receiver.

I turned. Drew's back was to me, but Terrell saw me.

"I'll see if she wants to go to a movie tomorrow night. Remind her what she's missing." He threw the ball to Terrell and made a dick-stroking gesture. "She'll say yes by the end of the night."

Terrell cleared his throat, eyeing me over Drew's shoulder. Drew turned.

I widened my stance and crossed my arms. "What's *the preacher's* daughter missing, Drew?"

Did I see the hypocrisy in my question? Of course. I'd self-reflect later.

"Nothing. I was asking her to homecoming yesterday,

but you interrupted. Totally cool, though, Coach. She seems to like your kid. Think he can put in a good word for me?" He caught the ball when Terrell threw it back to him.

"Why would someone who's graduated want to return to a high school dance?" I asked.

"Can ya keep a secret, Coach?" Drew asked as though we were friends.

I didn't have to answer because he was dying to tell me anyway.

"Eve and I were a thing last year, but only a few people knew. We kept it private because she didn't want to deal with her dad—"

"Pastor Jacobson," I corrected.

"Yeah, Pastor Jacobson finding out. She was really into me. And I've heard she's not with anyone at the moment."

"She's a runner, Drew. You'll stand a better chance of her saying yes if you can prove you're a runner too. Everyone to the track!" I hollered.

"They already ran," Rod, my assistant coach, said.

"I'm aware." I took the ball from Drew. "Go," I nodded for him to run while I passed him the ball.

He hesitated for a moment before jogging fifteen yards away. I threw the ball so hard that the second it hit his hands, he dropped it and winced, rubbing them together while shooting me a look.

I smiled.

I ARRIVED home to surprise company. My brother's car was parked in the drive.

"Daddy! Eve got me a puppy, and we made caramel

apples!" Josh barreled toward me the second I stepped into the back door, and right behind him was the puppy.

"Don't worry," Peter said. "I'm making Eve take the dog back. The Wilsons had a litter and were giving them away. I don't know what Eve was thinking. Sorry."

The aroma of chicken noodle soup hung thick in the air. My brother Fred, his wife Anne, and Pastor and Mrs. Jacobson were gathered in the kitchen, sipping apple cider while Eve stood at the stove, stirring a stock pot of soup.

She turned, resting her chin on her shoulder while offering a tiny grin and wrinkled nose.

"Surprise." Fred held up his cup of cider as though their unannounced visit warranted a toast.

Family and a puppy. It was a lot.

"Surprise indeed," I said, slipping off my shoes then squatting to pet the yellow Labrador puppy.

"His name is Clifford," Josh said, hugging him.

"He's not red," I replied.

And he wasn't staying.

When I stood, Fred and Anne took turns hugging me.

"We decided to get away for our anniversary, a little road trip. Thought we'd stay a few days with you and Josh," Fred said. "Hope you don't mind."

"Not at all," I said. Josh loved his aunt and uncle, so I wasn't about to spoil his fun. They'd be a good distraction when Clifford got sent back.

"Eve offered to make everyone dinner. I told your dad that Austin could use a nice girl like Eve." Anne shared a look with Eve's mom as though they were in cahoots to fix Eve up with my twenty-one-year-old nephew.

Austin was painfully shy. Smart, but more nerdy than a math teacher. Eve would eat him for lunch.

"Dad, look!" Josh pulled my hand to show me the rows of caramel apples on the cookie sheet.

"Did you help make them?" I asked.

He nodded with a big smile. Eve curled her hair behind her ear and snuck a peek at us, locking gazes with me for a second.

"When we arrived," her mom said, "they were eating one of the caramel apples before dinner. I fear Eve needs to be a better influence on Josh."

"Eve took a *big* bite!" Josh opened his mouth like a shark.

"Yeah, she can fit a lot into her mouth," I said.

Eve stiffened, eyes bulging as she looked at me and then glanced at her mom.

I smirked. "I've seen her stuff huge handfuls of Ruffles into it."

Her mom laughed, but Eve scowled.

She had no right to scowl. There was a fucking dog in my kitchen.

"Let me run upstairs and take a quick shower." I ruffled Josh's hair and headed down the hall and up the stairs.

After a quick shower, I stepped into my bedroom, rubbing the towel through my hair, but my motions stopped when I saw Eve sitting cross-legged on my bed, holding a ladle. I glanced toward the stairs before closing the door.

"What are you doing?"

"Running to my house to get a ladle because you didn't have one."

"I have one."

Her gaze drifted to my bare chest and jeans that I hadn't yet zipped and buttoned. "I know." She held up *my ladle.* "But they don't. So you're up here, but I'm at my house." She winked before setting the ladle aside and leaning forward on her hands and knees.

"Take the ladle downstairs. I'll be down in a minute. And that dog is not staying. You *do not* buy pets for kids that aren't yours." I pulled a shirt out of my dresser drawer.

She wrinkled her nose and sat back on her heels. "He needed a home. He'll be an excellent hunting dog. And all young kids should have a dog. Also, what's up with your attitude?"

"My quarterback let it slip that you were sneaking around with him last year." I turned toward her, tucking in my shirt and buttoning my jeans.

She rolled her lips between her teeth, brown eyes extra wide.

"I don't care, Eve. But if you screwed my QB, I'd like to know since I have to listen to him and his friends talk about you. If I punish them for being disrespectful, I need to know if it's justified."

After a few seconds, she nodded slowly. "We messed around, but we didn't have sex. My older sister told me to lose my virginity to someone who knew what they were doing. Drew was sixteen when we were first a thing. If you want to know what we did—"

"I don't." I ran my hands through my hair.

"Are you mad?"

"No. Get downstairs before they start asking questions, and make sure that dog doesn't pee everywhere."

"You sound upset." She slid off the bed. "If you must know, I was with Drew because his dad owns a distillery outside of town." She shrugged. "He never noticed when a few bottles of alcohol went missing from his bar."

I rested a hand on my hip and stared at the ceiling. "You let a guy touch you because you wanted booze?"

"When you say it like that, it sounds bad. Drew is nice. And he's fun." She pulled my hand from my hip and guided it around her, placing it on her ass while she pressed her chest to mine and stared up at me.

I didn't want to look at her because she was a massive weakness of mine, but I did anyway.

"Kiss me," she whispered.

It was a bad idea since my emotions teetered somewhere between brooding and insanity, but I kissed her, squeezing her ass. She moaned into my mouth, so I released her because I was getting an erection.

"Go," I said.

She frowned and turned, but something in my brain short-circuited. I slid my hand around her waist to bring her back to my chest. My other hand pulled her hair away from her neck, and I kissed below her ear. She smelled sweet like apples and sugar.

Her head lulled to the side as I unbuttoned her jeans and dragged down the zipper.

I thought of Drew talking about her.

I thought of Fred and Anne suggesting she date Austin.

I thought of the no-name who took her virginity.

I thought about taming the rebel child in her.

Then I slid one hand down the front of her underwear, and my other snaked up her shirt and into the cup of her bra. She embodied everything that made men weak and impulsive.

"You're fucking with my head, Eve," I said, and it came out as a growl like I was upset. And maybe I was.

She made me reckless, and it felt like a high I had to chase.

The ladle dropped to the carpet, and she arched her back while one of her hands covered mine between her legs, her nails digging into my skin as she widened her stance. Her other teased my damp hair.

Once again, I was engaging in a not-so-proud moment with two ministers in my kitchen, my son unpredictably running around the house, and Eve's mom giddy over the idea of Eve meeting a nice boy.

Who was I kidding? No one would tame Eve, least of all me.

Her breath caught in tiny staccatos as I fingered her.

A long "ohhh" fell from her lips.

I was so aroused, torturing myself, so I did the math. Did I have time to slide her jeans and panties just past her perfect ass and take her quickly from behind? And could I grab a condom and get it rolled on without prolonging things to the point where someone would have to send Josh to check on me?

Eve started to make a loud sound, so my hand on her breast made a fast track to her mouth. Her body buckled in my hold as she orgasmed.

So much for my math calculations; I didn't factor in her responsiveness.

I pulled her closer to me. Her hands pressed flat to the door as I rocked my pelvis against her ass and kissed her neck. I was in a bad way, painfully desperate to release.

Eve was the dealer who just kept dealing, the temptress. She left one hand on the door to steady herself as her other hand tried to push her jeans down a little farther. I was so out of my mind there wasn't a coherent thought in a five-mile radius. My hand disappeared from between her legs, and I unbuttoned my jeans and yanked down the zipper.

Get a condom.

My brain made an effort to show a little responsibility, but my dick wanted nothing to do with reasoning. The condom was on the other side of the room.

Eve's bare ass was pressed to my erection, shielded only by my cotton briefs.

Don't be stupid!

My heart pounded, and I was uncomfortably hard. And that made me stupid. I sucked her earlobe into my mouth and teased it with my teeth, and she moaned.

That was the final straw, my complete undoing. I pushed my jeans and briefs down just enough to release my erection. I wanted to be inside of her more than anything.

Josh squealed with delight, and the puppy barked from downstairs. We froze, our labored breaths the only sound for several seconds until we heard laughter and more barking. That was just enough to let reality and some goddamn common sense slide into the forefront of my mind.

I stepped back several steps and quickly zipped and buttoned my jeans. That almost happened.

Shit.

Had Josh not screamed, I would have mindlessly thrust my dick into her without a condom or another thought. I wanted her *that* much.

After she pulled up her jeans and fixed her bra, she lifted her unblinking gaze to mine. The truth was in her expression. She, too, knew what nearly happened.

And instead of apologizing or making some excuse, I chose not to acknowledge it. I was too rattled by the close call. So I cleared my throat. "Thanks for making everyone dinner," I murmured.

She nodded a half-dozen times, seemingly content not to talk about it either, as she squatted to retrieve the ladle.

"When they ask why you're flushed and out of breath, tell them a bear chased you on your return trip with the ladle."

She continued to nod her head before she caught my subtle humor. I was cracking a joke as if I hadn't just dodged a bullet.

Eve smirked, cheeks red. "Shut up." She started to open the door and then stopped. "Can you be vulnerable with me again for like five seconds?" she asked. "Tell me you were a little jealous when you heard Drew talking about me."

Was she serious? I was on the verge of potentially changing our lives forever because a cocky seventeen-year-old punk made me see red when he talked about Eve. And I couldn't wait to prove that I was the only one who was allowed to touch her body.

Her unexpected vulnerability flabbergasted me, but I gave her what she needed. It was the least I could do. "I wanted to break all ten fingers and bust out his teeth."

Chapter Twenty

Eric Carmen, "Hungry Eyes"

Eve

WHILE EVERYONE SIPPED SOUP, laughed, and talked over each other, I stared at Kyle's hands as he gripped the spoon, held the napkin to blot his mouth, and clutched his water glass. His rugged, masculine hands had calluses, and those hands had touched me intimately.

We were a tinderbox, and every touch and look sparked an uncontrollable flame. He was desperate to have sex with me, and that made me feel so powerful.

"Are you okay?" Mom rested her hand on my lap. "You're not eating."

I returned a slight headshake and sat up straight, bringing Kyle's attention in my direction.

"Your face has been flushed since you got back from our house. Are you feeling okay?"

A bear chased me.

I started to giggle but disguised it by clearing my throat. "Yes. No. Actually, I'm a little tired. Would it be okay if I went home to lie down?"

"Of course," she said.

I pushed my chair back.

"Feel better," Anne said. "Maybe we'll see you tomorrow."

I bobbed my head several times and found a fake smile to give everyone as I stood.

"Can you walk home?" Mom asked.

"Yeah, I should be fine. I'll take Clifford."

"No!" Josh protested.

"The dog can stay for the night," Kyle said. "And I'll drive you home real quick. Just get in my truck." His words were slow and calm, like an afterthought. He did a much better job of pretending I wasn't anything or anyone more than the girl next door who babysat for him.

"Thanks, Kyle," my dad said as if God offered to escort me home.

I set my bowl in the sink and headed straight outside. It took Kyle a little longer than expected to meet me and climb into the driver's seat.

He started the truck and shoved it into *Reverse*. "Are you feeling okay?"

I smirked. "Of course."

"Then take off your jeans and underwear."

"W-what?" I laughed.

"Just do it." He didn't look at me. Instead, he stayed focused on driving down his lane, leaving a plume of dust behind us as we fishtailed onto the gravel road to drive a hundred or so yards to my lane. He took a sharp right while I wriggled out of my jeans and underwear.

The second he stopped and killed the engine, he undid his jeans and plucked a condom from his front pocket.

That's what took him so long. He didn't have to say another word. As soon as he had the condom rolled on, and the seat was adjusted as far back as it would go, I straddled his lap. Despite the urgency of our time restraint, Kyle smiled at me like he had done in his bed. Sexy and vulnerable, as if he knew it was wrong, but it didn't feel wrong.

I thought about it for a moment. He always smiled right before he kissed me.

Our lips sealed, and we moved together.

I thought it was just me—a boy-crazy freak who started thinking about sex years earlier and spent the better part of my high school days and nights dreaming of being the woman I was with Kyle. But it wasn't just me; it was him too. It was us.

It was hell-bound, lustful sex. Screwing like rabbits.

An undeniable attraction.

An unavoidable scandal.

By the time we finished, the windows were foggy from the cool evening temperature.

"I'm not even a little sorry," he murmured in a winded whisper while he nuzzled his face in my neck, both hands still up my shirt, cupping my breasts.

I grinned, climbed off him, and pulled on my underwear and jeans. Then I leaned over to kiss him, leaving a breath between our lips. "One: Clifford is a hunting breed. I got him for you as well. Two: I'm gonna love ya, and if you don't like it, that's just too bad. I'm not even a little sorry."

"AHH!" I jumped. "You scared the life out of me," I snapped at Gabby, who was in my face the second I closed the front door.

"S. L. U. T," she said, crossing her arms over her chest.

I couldn't look at her. "What are you even doing home? Mom said you were supposed to be studying with friends." I jogged up the stairs.

"I got home fifteen minutes ago. And I heard something out front. So I looked out the window, and *guess* what I saw?" She chased me.

"You saw nothing because it's late, and there's barely any sunlight left, so whatever you thought you saw, you did not."

Before I could lock my bedroom door, she turned the handle and rammed her shoulder into it.

"Get out!" I yelled, putting my body weight into it in the opposite direction.

"Let me in, or I'm telling Mom and Dad."

I didn't *hate* her, but I really, *really* didn't like her. Without warning, I stopped pushing and stepped aside. The door flung open, hitting the door stop as Gabby tumbled onto my floor.

"His truck was moving!" she yelled, jumping to her feet and brushing her hair away from her face. "Like someone was shaking it. And you were on his lap, bouncing up and down." She parked both fists on her hips. "Was he giving you a pony ride on his knee like Dad used to do to us?"

It was none of her business, and I was furious that she felt she had the right to scold me. But, oh my god, I couldn't believe she said that. Both of my hands covered my mouth.

Her eyes were squinted; mine were bugged out. And the room was silent.

I broke first with a loud snort and then a fit of laughter that made my eyes water.

"Stop—" She clamped her jaw shut, but her lips still quivered. "Stop laughing," she cried, falling apart into a fit of giggles.

We collapsed onto my bed, bodies curled into tiny balls of laughter.

After several failed attempts to gain our composure, we finally relaxed with hard sighs while we stared at the ceiling.

"I love him," I said.

She didn't respond right away.

"It's too weird. You can't love Dad's best friend's brother. You can't love my Trig teacher. Do you know how hard it will be for me to sit in class tomorrow and not think of him giving you a pony ride?"

Again, we started giggling.

"Gabbs, you've ruined pony rides. They can never be innocent bounce play again."

Her body shook with more laughter.

"And don't you *ever* talk about my sex life and Dad in the same breath."

She rolled toward me, propping her head onto her arm, and I did the same, facing her. "This is bad, Eve. Maybe not Sarah level of bad, but Dad will be *so* mad. And what are you going to do if you get pregnant?"

"We're using protection."

"It's not a hundred percent."

I wrinkled my nose for a beat. "I don't know. If it were to happen, then I guess we'd have a baby. And I'd have to tell Mom and Dad."

"You're totally going to have to tell them eventually,

right? Or do you think it won't last like with Drew, so there's no need to cause a stir?"

It pained me to think of us not lasting, but Kyle wasn't exactly proclaiming his love to me, so she had a point.

"Did he say he loves you?" Gabby asked as if she had read my mind.

"Not yet."

"If you got married, would Josh call you 'Mom'?" She was jumping too far ahead.

"It's not that I don't want to get married someday, but I don't dream of it like you do, Gabbs. But ..."

"But?"

I grinned. "Sometimes, I imagine what it would be like to live with him and feel like Josh was mine."

Gabby's face lit up. "That's so romantic."

I restrained from rolling my eyes. But it was shocking how she went from wanting to kill me, threatening to tattle to our parents, and wishing for me to get pregnant, like it was a curse, to thinking my living with Kyle and Josh would be romantic.

But she was finally on my side, the way I was on Sarah's, and that's all that mattered.

"Don't worry, Gabbs, we'll find you a good man someday." I squeezed her hand.

Chapter Twenty-one

The Beatles, "Let It Be"

Kyle

"FRED AND ANNE ARE HERE. A surprise visit, *and* Eve got Josh a fucking dog," I said to Adam when he called me after everyone was in bed. I was sitting on the deck with said dog curled up on my lap. He knew he needed to bond with me to stand a chance of staying.

As soon as I could have a coherent thought around Eve that didn't involve planning the easiest and quickest way to put my dick inside her, we were going to have a serious conversation about the dog.

Adam chuckled. "Who buys someone else's kid a dog?"

"Precisely."

"Josh must love having your brother and Anne there. They spoil him."

"Yeah," I said, staring into the night sky filled with stars. "They said a few days, but I bet they stay until next week because Fred will want to listen to Peter preach this Sunday."

"Sounds like you'll have a babysitter then while you hunt on Saturday."

"I have two sitters living next door."

"Yeah, how's that going? Are you still being a better man than me?"

I didn't answer. Was Eve right? Did friends tell each other everything?

"Kyle Marcus Collins," Adam mimicked my mom's voice. "You haven't put your filthy hands on the preacher's daughter, have you?"

I chuckled. "You'd make a terrible woman, which is surprising because you're such a pussy sometimes."

"You're dodging my question."

The shit-eating grin on my face felt so good. I couldn't think of Eve and not feel euphoric, despite the dog. "I put my hands on the preacher's daughter."

"YES! I knew you would, you lucky bastard. Was it everything I imagined it would be? Shit, was she a virgin? Is she a freak in bed?"

"You dumbass. You mean, was it everything *I* imagined it would be?"

"Sure, buddy. Whatever. Just answer my questions."

I sighed, dragging a hand through my hair. "I don't know what I'm doing."

"That's understandable," he said. "It's been a while. But when that thing between your legs gets hard, you put it in the hole between her legs. The front one unless she's adventurous."

"Shut the hell up," I said with a laugh. "I'm acting like a horny teenager instead of a father and grown man with a job and real responsibilities. I'm on the verge of letting my world implode. It can't last. And then what? Her family and mine will hate me. All for what? A good lay?" It was more than a good lay.

Eve got me. And I got her. The explanation was far more simplistic than the possible ramifications.

"Kyle, dude, you can't do this again. It's a repeat of Melinda. It's okay to have sex, fucking amazing sex, with a woman and not marry her or impregnate her. It's called casual sex."

"What if she thinks it's more than casual sex?"

"She's eighteen. Of course, she'll think that. But you're the grown-up. Set boundaries."

"This is rich coming from you."

He laughed. "I know. But I'm not robbing the preacher's cradle."

I pinched the bridge of my nose. "You're not helping."

"You're a teacher who deals with teens all the time. Be diplomatic with her. If she can't handle it, then tell her it's over. Do you really think she'll rat you out to her parents?"

I didn't say anything.

"Unless," Adam said slowly, "it's more than casual sex to you. Tell me it's not. This won't end well. Get a grip on the situation. Don't blow up family relationships over some girl. Think of Josh. Don't put him in the middle."

"What if I just talk with Peter? I'm his best friend's brother. You know, just be honest with him."

Adam chuckled. "What are you going tell him? That you think Eve is pretty, and you want to ask her out on a date? Read the Bible together? Maybe hold hands? Or are you going to tell him you've had your dick in her, and now you can't imagine not putting it in her again and again?"

"I was thinking less is more. Wait to see if he asks questions."

"And if he asks if you've had sex with his daughter, what will you say?"

"I'd tell him I can't believe he's asking me that."

"Kyle," Adam laughed, "I taught you well. Fucking perfect. But no. That won't work with him because he's known you your whole life, and he knows you weren't the guy any father would trust with his daughter. Did you forget he knows you have a child out of wedlock? He knows you used to drink like a fish. Sex was your favorite pastime—still is, I bet. He's heard your foul mouth. At best, you've grown up since having a child and becoming a teacher, so he's okay with you being his neighbor. He's okay with Eve babysitting Josh, but I will give you a money-back guarantee there is *no* way in hell he will ever think of you as a worthy man for his precious little girl, regardless of the ten-year age difference."

"I didn't take her virginity."

"Yeah, lead with that. So if he thinks she's a virgin, you'll basically be letting him know his daughter sleeps around."

"You're an awful friend. First, you tell me to go for it with my neighbor; now you're saying it's pointless."

"Pointless? Was it bad sex? If not, I'd hardly call it pointless."

"I like her," I said more to myself than to Adam, because something inside of me refused to let her be casual sex and nothing more.

"This isn't good, man."

I rubbed my jaw as the deck boards creaked beneath my wooden rocker. The dog readjusted on my lap, resting his snout on my knee.

"I like the world through her eyes. I like her young, wild

heart, and I think it would be tragic if she ever conformed to anything but staring at the stars, picking apples, and ..." I trailed off, slowly shaking my head.

Making love in wildflower fields.

"She doesn't take herself too seriously. She's perfectly content cleaning rooms at a motel like it never occurred to her that everyone else her age is falling in line to get an education so they can live the American dream—whatever that is. Sometimes, I think she's not the best role model for Josh because her standards are so low, but other times, I think the world might be a better place if more people like Eve were content with being themselves. Let living be the dream and work be an afterthought."

I quoted the young woman who refused to think math teachers were admirable because she wasn't thinking clearly about what the word meant. That made me smile because Eve was brave and *admirable*; she just didn't see that in herself yet.

"How much have you had to drink tonight?"

I laughed. "Not enough."

"Just don't do anything stupid. Don't think with your dick; that's my MO, and don't fool yourself into thinking there's even a tiny chance that her dad will give the two of you his blessing. Are we clear?"

"We're clear," I sighed as something moved to my left.

Eve sauntered toward the stairs in baggy gray sweats, a pink hoodie, and a bottle of booze in her hand.

"I gotta go," I said.

"Alright. Later, man," Adam said.

I stood, eyeing Eve as she stopped at the bottom of the stairs, taking a drink of clear liquid from a glass bottle. I set the dog on his feet to go to her before I quietly opened the back door, set the phone on the counter, and returned to the deck.

"It's past your curfew," I said.

"I know. That's why I had to sneak out." She wasn't slurring her words, so she was only one or two sheets to the wind.

"Where did you get this?" I sat on the steps and leaned forward, taking her bottle of tequila as the dog jumped to sniff it.

"In the old milk box by the garage." She grinned, picking up Clifford. "In plain sight. It's where my mom keeps a planter, but no one ever looks inside."

"Is this leftover from Drew's dad's place?"

Her lips pursed into duck lips. "No. I have a new supplier."

"Who?"

She shook her head. "Nope. Can't tell you, Mr. Collins. You can't be trusted."

I narrowed my eyes and tried not to laugh. "*I* can't be trusted?"

"You're a mandatory reporter."

I laughed. "I'm not sure that applies. And you're not my student or a minor."

She let the squirmy dog down and reached for the bottle as I held it just out of reach.

"Can I ask why?" I stared at the bottle, wondering how often she drank.

"Why what?"

"Why do you drink this shit?" I took a swig. It was cheap tequila. Horse piss.

"Because it's free."

"So are STDs. I mean, why do you drink cheap alcohol all by yourself at eleven at night?"

She shrugged. "I like the buzz."

"Do you like the headache in the morning?"

"Nothing two ibuprofen can't handle."

"You're awfully small to drink hard liquor. A few ounces of this adds up to several cans of beer."

"Must we do math tonight?" She stepped onto the bottom stair and reached for the bottle again.

I pulled it away.

"Hey!" She lunged at me as I emptied the bottle over the side of the railing.

"Shh!" I let the bottle fall to the ground so I could catch her.

"That was—"

I pressed my hand over her mouth so she didn't wake anyone.

"I need you to be quiet so you don't wake anyone who might tell your parents about your jailbreak tonight. Do you want to be grounded again?"

Kneeling on the step between my legs, eyes wide, she shook her head.

I removed my hand from her mouth and brushed the hair away from her eyes. "You can't be here," I whispered, not wanting her to leave, but I knew someone could wake up and open the door behind me without warning.

She frowned. "You don't want me here."

"Baby, I want you everywhere I am." I stroked her cheek with the pad of my thumb. "But that's not a good idea right now."

She turned into my touch, kissing my palm. "You can't call me 'baby' and send me home." She closed her eyes as my hand slid down her neck. "You can't touch me like you did today and send me home."

"I'm sending you home because I'm scared of never getting to touch you like that again if we get caught."

Eve opened her eyes. "Let's be brave together and not care what anyone thinks."

I smiled. "I'll walk you home."

She stuck out her bottom lip.

"I'm going to bite that lip if you insist on tempting me with it." I stood, taking her hand and whistling at Clifford, who was eager to follow us toward the hill.

Eve hugged my arm while we meandered toward her property, taking unhurried steps.

"I had fun making caramel apples with Josh today. When he giggles, I feel it in my belly like someone's tickling me, and I can't help but laugh too. But nothing will ever compare to the look on his face when I gave him Clifford. I know everyone is upset that I got him a dog, but A, he was free. C, Josh is so in love with him. And D. Well, I don't know what D is, but you can't make me regret it."

"A. No dog is *free*. I will have vet and food bills. You skipped B because you're drunk. And, of course, Josh is in love with him. He doesn't have any responsibility for the dog."

She dropped her head, moping along beside me.

I squeezed her hand. "I'm not happy about the dog. But the way you care about Josh and see the innocence and pure joy in his laughter means a lot. I used to think the same about him cooing as a baby. And the soup was amazing. I bet your grandma is proud of you for taking everything she has to pass along to you and gracing your friends and family with culinary love."

"Culinary love?" She giggled. "I like that. And yeah, I think I'm her favorite, which says a lot because I know I'm not my parents' favorite."

"I don't think parents have favorites," I said as we reached the bottom of the hill and started up the last hill before the orchard.

"That's because you only have one child. If you have another, you'll have a favorite."

I laughed. "Think so?"

"Yes. And don't fool yourself. Fred is your parents' favorite."

"Nah. You know what I think?"

"Huh?"

"I think parents take the weakest one and make them the favorite because they know they need a little extra love if they're struggling. So my sister is hands down the favorite."

"Hmm ..." She stared at the ground as we headed up the hill. "Then I might be the favorite. Or Sarah. Definitely not Gabby. She's too sly. A conformist on the outside but a rebel on the inside. In their eyes, she can do no wrong."

"Maybe you should consider not drinking so much. I bet that would go a long way to earn their trust."

"Maybe. But now that I know I might be the favorite, I can't risk being too good and losing that *extra* love. Can you just imagine how hard they will love me if they find out about us?"

I laughed. She always made me laugh, even when I tried to be serious. Eve was quickly becoming dangerously irresistible.

Clifford ran ahead of us and peed on the first apple tree he came to.

"How do you feel about a movie Friday night after the

homecoming game? Not in Devil's Head. Either Filmore or Raven. Fred and Anne will be thrilled to watch Josh. If you can figure out how to sneak away with me."

She stopped and stepped in front of me between the rows of apple trees. "A date? Are you asking me to homecoming? Do I get to wear a dress?"

"A date." I snaked my hands around her waist. "Minus the homecoming."

She frowned.

"I'll wear my Sunday best, and you wow me with your sexiest dress."

She giggled. "I'm a preacher's daughter. I don't own anything sexy."

"*You* make the dress sexy." I dipped my head and kissed her neck below her ear. "The dress doesn't make you sexy."

Her fingers weaved through my hair. "Why do I love when you say the word sexy?"

"Because you love sex," I murmured in her ear. "I know what's on that tape in your Walkman."

She giggled, pushing me away. "Will we have popcorn and sodas?"

I grinned. "Popcorn and sodas."

"Mike and Ikes?"

I shook my head. "Junior Mints."

"What movie?" Eve reached for an apple and plucked it off the tree.

"Your choice."

She wiped the apple with her sweatshirt and took a bite. My face soured just thinking about the tartness, but she didn't flinch.

"Dirty Dancing. I've seen the previews. I think it's about my life."

"Is that so?" I was wasting time. We were a few yards from the fence along the property line, but I didn't want to say good night.

"Well, we'll see. But I'm going to be pissed if they made a movie about me without my permission."

I no longer tried to hide my amusement with Eve. She made me laugh, and it felt good. And something about the smile on her face said I made her feel good, too.

"Meet me at our favorite lake after the game. Okay?" I said.

"Black Paw Lake is not our favorite lake. You said it your-self: Nobody's there, the fish are not great, I flubbed up starting the boat there, and ..." She snapped her fingers.

I tried not to laugh at her sluggish brain.

"Oh, yeah, it's where you first rejected me."

"Rejected you?"

She took another bite of the apple and nodded while chewing.

"How did I reject you?"

"You avoided looking at me for the looongest time, and when my bra strap slid off my arm, you put it back in place instead of going in the opposite direction."

I shook my head, snickering. "Shut up. We were friends."

Her head jutted backward. "Uh, speak for yourself. I've been heavily stalking you since you moved in. I don't know what took you so long. You're so dense, Mr. Collins. You've spent too much time looking at women in magazines, not having to do any work to see their titties, that you've become lazy with your efforts to woo women."

I leered at her.

She rolled her eyes and pivoted, traipsing toward the fence in a crooked line. "I can read your mind. Just say it."

I chuckled. "I promise, there's no way you're reading my mind."

Eve popped the apple core into her mouth and climbed over the fence. "You love me, too. And you love Clifford."

I opened my mouth to protest, but my heart climbed up my throat to block the words as it whispered *let it be*.

Chapter Twenty-Two

Chris de Burgh, "The Lady in Red"

Eve

WITH FRED AND ANNE VISITING, I did not need to watch Josh for the rest of the week, which left lots of time to distract Erin from studying.

"This can't go on forever. If you love him, you have to tell your parents," Erin said, looking up from her textbook as I spun in circles in her desk chair while she sat on her bed with Clifford.

My dad insisted I find a new home for the puppy, so I took him with me to work and pretended I was doing my best, but the look on Josh's face when Clifford ran to him after school prevented me from being serious about my rehoming promise.

"I don't think 'Daddy, I love him' will work. I think Kyle should tell Fred, get him on our side, and then Fred can tell my dad."

"Do you think Kyle can get Fred on your side?"

"Absolutely not." I laughed.

"You know how this story goes, don't you?"

I stopped spinning and gave her the hairy eyeball. "How does it go?"

"Your parents find out. They disown you, like they did with Sarah. But you don't care because you love him. And then Josh's mom returns and takes what you risked everything to have."

I wrinkled my nose. "You are a terrible friend. Why would you say that?"

She shrugged, returning her attention to her textbook while rubbing Clifford's tummy. "Friends are honest with each other. You have to be prepared for anything, including his past coming back. Have you talked to him about her? What do you know? Was he madly in love, or was it some one-night stand who popped out a kid and dumped him on his doorstep with a note?"

I rocked back in the chair and stared at the ceiling. "I don't know. He doesn't like to talk about it."

"I think you should run off and get married and *then* tell your parents. Don't risk everything until Kyle's willing to be your new everything."

"We've known each other for less than two months. I'm not sure he's ready to propose."

"But he's taking you to a movie after the game tonight. That's a step. Right?"

I nodded.

"What movie?"

"*Dirty Dancing.*"

"What? NO! You can't see that movie without me. We agreed we'd go together."

"I'll see *Fatal Attraction* with you."

"I heard it's a stalker movie. I want to see a real love story."

"I'm giving you a moment-by-moment account of *my* love story. What more could you possibly want?"

She slammed her book closed and grinned. "I want to know about the sex. You're too vague. What position do you do it in? Do you orgasm? Does he go down on you? Does he kiss you after he does? That freaks me out. Like, do you really want to taste yourself?"

I giggled. "I didn't think about it. He did. It was *amazing*, and then we kissed, but I was focused on how he looked at me and how he felt inside of me, not how I tasted in his mouth. I must taste pretty good." I smirked.

Erin covered her mouth to suppress her laughter. "That's ..."

I sighed. "Doesn't matter. I *love* having sex with him. I feel like such a perv with a one-track mind. It's all I think about when we're together. He'll talk to my dad about football, and I think about *his* balls and how they sound slapping against me when we're doing it."

"Oh my god!" Erin cackled, falling onto her back.

Clifford jumped on her and started licking her face.

"I have it bad for him. If he dumps me, I will not survive. And it's not just the sex. It's the way he smiles. It's like he gets me. Whenever we look at each other it's like we're sharing a secret."

"Well, you are," Erin said.

I shook my head. "Yes, but not that one. It's been this way since the first day we met. It was one look, and this instant feeling like ..." I bit my bottom lip.

"Like what?"

I shrugged. "I know it sounds stupid, but it felt like recognition."

Her nose wrinkled. "Like you'd met?"

"No, like finding something you were looking for. Like, 'Oh! There you are.'"

Erin gave me a blank stare.

"Doesn't matter. I'm just saying I love everything about him. He's playful and such a good dad. I swear I fall harder in love every time I see him just being a dad to Josh. Ugh!" I growled, hugging my fists to my chest. "He's so manly and rugged, yet smart and caring. He's just ..."

"Perfect?"

I sighed. "Yeah."

"Oh, Eve, it just feels that way because he's your first love."

"I don't know. I've liked other guys, and I've wondered if my feelings were love. But this is different. My heart skips so many beats just thinking about him. I may never know what I want to *do* in life, but I know I want to *be* with him."

I CURLED my hair at home and tucked my dress, shoes, and illegal makeup (not mom-approved) into a bag and headed to the game.

With a few minutes left on the game clock, I left the school and headed to the lake. My car light wasn't ideal for applying makeup, but I made it work. Then I changed into my red dress. My mom always called it raspberry red. It was one of the outfits I wore for my senior pictures.

Sleeveless.

Long and flowing.

I felt like a woman in the dress, not a girl.

That ache in my heart and the fluttering in my tummy, which could only be described as love, never seemed to ease. It didn't matter that Kyle had seen me soaking wet, naked, tipsy, and everything in between. I still wanted to look my best for him. I wanted to make his heart skip and dance like mine. If he could love me even a little, that was enough.

Just a seed.

I would nurture that seed and wait for it to grow. And maybe, just maybe, he might find a way for us to be together without destroying everything we had between our families. If Josh's mom came back, Kyle would still choose me.

When headlights shined in my rearview mirror, I stepped out, adjusting my dress and primping my hair one last time.

Kyle hopped out of his truck wearing his navy suit and Robin's egg blue tie, which he probably wore to school that day since everyone was dressed up for game day.

"Hi." I grinned.

"Eve," he drew out my name, gaze slowly taking me in. When he pressed a hand to his chest, a kaleidoscope of butterflies took flight in my tummy.

I lifted my dress, holding it out to the side and turning in a slow circle so he could see the back.

"I'm speechless," he said.

I blushed. "Thank you," I whispered.

His hand ghosted along my jaw and cupped the nape of my neck while he kissed me. I gripped his jacket lapels.

"How can I love this dress on you so much yet want nothing more than to take it off?" he asked, kissing down my neck as I closed my eyes and grinned.

"We're overdressed for a movie," I said.

"Not yet." He reached into his truck and came out with a plastic container.

"You got me a corsage?" I beamed.

He pulled the white rose corsage from the container and slid it onto my wrist. "*Now* we're overdressed for a movie."

"If you're trying to make me not love you, you're doing a terrible job."

Kyle smirked, hooking my arm around his as he walked me to the other side of his truck and opened the door. He helped gather my dress, so it didn't brush along the bottom of his truck as I climbed inside.

"This is the most unforgettable night of my life," I said.

He eyed me for a few seconds before a slow grin slid up his face, along with a tiny blush. "How can you say that already?"

"No one has ever looked at me like you are now."

He winked and closed my door.

I picked up the corsage box as we pulled out of the parking lot. "Why does this have Drew's name on it?"

"In the locker room after the game, he was complaining to his friends that his homecoming date wasn't as hot as you. And while that's a no-brainer, I thought he was being an asshole for saying it. So I took the corsage he had next to his suit in his locker. If he's going to be an asshole, he might as well look like one too."

As we cruised down the highway, I rolled down my window just enough to toss out the corsage.

"What are you doing?" Kyle whipped his head in my direction.

"You can't give me someone else's flowers. I don't accept it."

"You steal alcohol, but when it comes to flowers, you're a purist? I thought we had a Bonnie and Clyde thing going."

I kept my gaze on the road and fought to keep a straight face, but I liked the idea of being the Bonnie to his Clyde.

After my silence convinced him to give up on the corsage discussion, I flipped through the radio stations.

"Stop," Kyle said. "Go back."

I turned the dial.

"There." He grinned and started singing the song. Of course, he was a better singer than me.

But I focused more on the words.

It was Chris De Burgh's "The Lady in Red."

I knew the lyrics, but I let him sing them. No one had ever serenaded me. And I wanted to know if he would sing the entire song because the last line would mean everything to me if he whispered it the way Chris did. As the end approached, I held my breath.

He sang the second to the last line.

My heart flipped and flopped in my chest.

And then he sang the last line, whispering it like in the song.

"I love you."

I didn't look at him because I was afraid he might roll his eyes or smile in a way that made it clear he was just singing lyrics. My heart latched on to hope, and I refused to let my mind ruin it.

When we arrived at the theater, I felt like a princess with my prince at my side, opening doors, resting his hand on my lower back, and something in his expression that felt like pride.

He was proud to have me on his arm.

His lady in red.

We caught plenty of looks being so overdressed for a movie, but it didn't matter because his gaze was the only one that mattered to me.

"Butter?" he asked, ordering our popcorn.

I nodded, finding it impossible to control my grin, and he gave me an extended glance as if my excitement was contagious.

"Come on, gorgeous." He handed me the popcorn while he stuck the candy boxes in his jacket pocket and carried our drinks.

No one had ever called me gorgeous.

When we found seats in the middle of the theater, an older couple behind us smiled as we sat down.

"Your dress is beautiful," the lady said.

"Thank you." I smiled.

She glanced at Kyle. "You're a lucky man."

It was too much for my young heart. We were secret lovers in Devil's Head, but at the movie theater in Filmore we were a couple. I never wanted to go home.

"Thank you," Kyle said. "I agree." As soon as we sat in our seats, he leaned toward me, lips at my ear. "The luckiest," he whispered.

We ate our popcorn and candy and watched the movie. Had I not met Kyle Collins, I would have envied Frances Houseman's character. I would have watched the movie with Erin, and we would have left with our hearts stolen by Johnny Castle.

The movie was good.

My love story was better.

The man who set our popcorn bucket and candy boxes on the floor midway through the movie so he could hold my

228

hand was a million times better than any man I had seen on the big screen.

And that was a tall order because *Top Gun* released the previous year, and Tom Cruise had starred in most of my dreams.

"I knew it was my story. Older man. Forbidden love," I said on the way back to Devil's Head.

Kyle laughed. "But I teach math instead of dance."

"Exactly." I looked at my watch.

"Are you going to miss your curfew?"

"Depends."

"On?" He shot me a sideways glance.

"If I go straight home when we get back to my car."

"Then that's what you'll do."

"What? No." I unfastened my seat belt to scoot across the bench seat next to him, angling my body to kiss his neck. "You can't take me to a romantic movie and not give me some romance before I go home."

"I'll kiss you good night." He grinned.

I loosened his tie and undid the top buttons of his shirt so I could kiss his chest.

"Eve," he warned.

"I don't want just a kiss good night." I kissed along his collarbone and slid my hand up his leg until I felt the hard bulge in his pants. "Even though I love the way you kiss me like you do."

"Eve," his warning came out a little harsher, a little more desperate as he pulled into the parking lot at the lake. "How do I kiss you?"

"Like you want me to know that no other man will ever kiss me again."

A tiny smirk pulled at his lips.

"By the way, I have *nothing* on under this dress," I whispered in his ear.

"What's your punishment for being late?" His question thrilled me because it meant he was considering it.

"I'm grounded for a week from going out with friends."

He shoved it into *Park* and unbuckled. "Good thing we're not friends." His fingers dove into my hair and he paused—of course he paused—a breath away from my lips.

"Then what are we?" I asked.

"You know what we are." He grinned.

"We're lovers."

"Lovers," he echoed as our lips touched.

Chapter Twenty-Three

Cyndi Lauper, "Time After Time"

Eve

"You're late," my mom said, startling me as I turned on the light in my room a little before one in the morning.

She was sitting on my bed, hugging my pillow.

"Sorry," I said quietly, easing my bag to the floor, hoping she didn't question what was in it.

The dress.

The heels.

The makeup.

Memories from the best night of my life.

"Where were you?"

"I went to a movie." I kept my head bowed as I pulled a nightshirt from my dresser drawer.

"Look at me," she said.

I gave her a quick glance before heading to the bathroom.

She followed me, closing the door behind us. With a firm grip, she grabbed my chin and made me look at her.

"Have you been drinking?"

I shook my head.

"Why do you have so much gaudy makeup on your face?"

I pulled away, turned on the water, and grabbed the bar of soap to remove the *gaudy* makeup from my face. "Because sometimes I like to wear makeup."

"You said you were with friends. Which friends?"

"I said I was going out. You assumed it was with friends. I had a date." I worked the soap along my cheeks with tiny circles.

"With whom?"

"Someone who goes to the community college with Erin."

"What movie?"

I splashed water onto my face and then dried it before sighing. "*Dirty Dancing.*"

Her nose wrinkled. "What on earth kind of movie is that?"

I laughed, rolling my eyes. "It's rated PG-13. Don't freak out over the title. It was a romance about forbidden love, star-crossed lovers, and strict, unsympathetic parents. Things like that." I started to remove my shirt but remembered I wasn't wearing a bra or underwear.

Mom frowned. "What did you do after the movie?"

"Talked. I lost track of time. And that's why I'm late. Sorry."

"I wasn't born yesterday, Eve. I don't believe you just talked."

"What did you and Dad do on dates?"

She narrowed her eyes. "Why?"

"Because. I want you to think of what you did with Dad on dates and imagine that's what I'm doing on dates." I grinned while squeezing toothpaste onto my toothbrush.

Her nose wrinkled, looking at my reflection in the mirror.

"What's that look for?" I mumbled past the suds in my mouth. "Were you and Dad naughty?"

She gave me her usual eye roll while tightening her robe's sash.

After I spat and wiped my mouth, she grabbed my shoulders, forcing me to face her. "I'm going to ask you something, and I need you to be truthful with me."

I blinked several times, waiting for her to continue.

"Do you still have your virginity?"

I pressed my lips together and mirrored her narrow-eyed gaze. "Like ... on me right now? It might be in my purse. I'd have to check. If it's not there, I could check the back seat of my car. You know I tend to lose things. I've lost my car keys twice, and I still haven't found my lower retainer."

"Eve Marie Jacobson, stop it. This is nothing to joke about."

"Even if I tell you I'm still a virgin, will you believe me? No. Of course you won't because no one ever believes me." I reached past her to open the door. "Now, can I have a little privacy to pee?"

She gave me an evil stare for a few more seconds. "You're grounded for a week."

I shut the door behind her and mumbled, "Of course I am."

"Where's Dad?" I asked at breakfast on Saturday morning.

I assumed he'd be waiting for me with a new lecture scripted in my blood.

Mom set a pitcher of orange juice on the table while Gabby had her nose in a book between bites of French toast. "Well, you're probably not going to believe it."

"Why wouldn't I believe it? Is he still at the strip club?"

Gabby whipped her head out of the book, eyes wide.

Mom scowled at me. "What am I going to do with you?"

"Love me. That's your job," I said, pouring juice into my glass.

She hummed as if she needed to think about it. "He went hunting with Kyle and Fred."

I choked on my juice. "W-what?" I fisted my hand at my mouth.

Kyle didn't say anything about hunting.

Mom gently laughed. "I know. I can't imagine it either. Can you see your dad in camouflage?"

We giggled.

"Is he really going to kill a deer?" Gabby asked.

"I highly doubt it," Mom said, buttering her French toast. "Fred talked him into going."

"Does Fred hunt?" Gabby asked.

Mom shrugged. "I guess."

"Kyle's a good hunter. And he's really cute in his camouflage," my ornery, instigating sister said, eyeing me while smirking.

"Kyle's like family," Mom said, giving Gabby a funny look. "Don't talk about family that way."

"You're right." Gabby pressed her lips together and nodded. "It would be really weird to think of Kyle as anything but family."

Unless he had put his face between your legs and teased you with his tongue, then it would have been really weird to think of him as anything but the hot dad next door. But to each their own.

"When will they be back?" I asked.

"I'm not sure. They left before four this morning. I imagine they'll be home by dinner." Mom sipped her coffee.

"Why? You miss Dad?" Gabby asked without glancing up from her book.

I didn't respond, but I did the math. Mr. Collins would have been proud. Even if he went to sleep the second he got home, he had less than three hours of sleep. And he knew he was giving up sleep to be with me.

"Where are you going?" Gabby asked, nudging me aside as I curled my hair after we finished washing the breakfast dishes. She squeezed toothpaste onto her toothbrush.

"Nowhere. Just doing my hair."

"For Kyle?"

I shrugged.

"Do you two have more pony rides planned?"

"Shut up." I grinned just as the phone rang.

"I got it!" Gabby bolted toward her bedroom as I sprinted toward mine. It was probably Erin. I had *so* much to tell her.

We both answered at the same time.

"Hello?"

"Gabby? Eve?" Dad said.

"Yes," again, we answered at the same time.

"Hang up, Gabbs," I said.

"You hang up."

"Girls! I need to talk to your mom. And I need one of you to go to Kyle's house and watch Josh."

"Why?" I asked.

"Because Kyle fell out of the tree stand, and we're at the hospital."

"What? Is he okay?" I tried not to sound panicked, but I was beside myself.

"They're taking him in for surgery. It's not life-threatening. We'll know more later. Now, please put your mom on the phone, and one of you go over to Kyle's so Anne can come to the hospital."

"Mom!" Gabby yelled.

I was torn between hanging up and heading to Kyle's house. But I chose Josh. For some reason, I wanted to be close to him, and I thought Anne might have heard from Fred and know more. So I hurried down the stairs, shoved my feet into my sneakers, and ran to Kyle's house.

Anne was sitting on the porch swing when I got there, reading a book to Josh as Clifford played with a toy at their feet.

"There she is," Anne said, and Josh looked up at me, hopped down, and ran to hug me.

"Daddy got hurt," he said.

I held on to him as if I were hugging Kyle. "I heard, buddy." I kissed the side of his head.

"But we've already said a prayer, and God will take care of him," Anne said. "In the meantime, Josh, Eve will stay with you." She stood, setting the book on the bench. "There's a casserole in the oven. If you could pull it out when the timer goes off and ensure he gets fed, I'd appreciate it. I don't know when I'll be back, but—"

"It's fine," I said, shaking my head and acting brave despite every part of my body trembling with fear. "Um," I swallowed hard. "I'll take care of him. I know the routine. But would you mind calling me when you know more?"

Josh grabbed his book and went into the house.

"Of course," Anne said, resting her hand on my shoulder.

"Did Fred give you any details? My dad was vague."

Anne snagged her purse up off the railing and slid the strap over her shoulder before tucking her short blond curls behind her ear. "He just said he broke his arm." She glanced past me to see if Josh was near the screen door. "The bone was sticking out from the skin. Fred got nauseous looking at it, so he offered to run and call for help while your dad stayed with Kyle."

I was nauseous, too, but hid it with a clenched jaw and a tiny nod.

She started down the stairs.

"Can he walk?" I asked.

Anne turned, brow tense.

I shrugged. "My friend's uncle fell from a tree while hunting, and he's in a wheelchair for the rest of his life. It was a spinal cord injury."

Worry claimed her brow in tiny lines. "I think so, but I didn't ask. I'll call you."

"Thanks," I murmured.

I stared at the phone while Josh ate dinner, and after we played with Clifford and took him outside to go potty, we read a bedtime story.

"When's Daddy coming home?" Josh interrupted in the

middle of the book. He was tucked under my arm, so I kissed the top of his head.

"When he's feeling a little better. The doctors are working to get him better. But it won't be tonight."

"Are you staying with me?"

"I'm staying until your aunt and uncle get home."

"I want you to stay until Daddy comes home. So does Clifford."

The puppy raised his head at the end of the bed as if he recognized his name.

It didn't take much to melt my already fragile heart. "Okay," I whispered before resuming the story.

When he fell asleep, I returned to the kitchen with Clifford and stared at the phone again. I wanted to call Erin but couldn't be on the line if Anne or my mom tried to call with an update. The waiting gutted me.

Two soft taps brought my attention to the back door. I jumped out of the kitchen chair to open it.

"Hey," Erin said, wrapping her arms around me while Clifford jumped up on her legs. "I didn't want to knock at the front door and wake Josh."

I stepped back. "How did you find out?"

"Gabby called me." Erin squatted to pet the excited puppy. "She didn't know if you'd told me, but she thought you could use a friend."

Gabby came through for me. It made me feel a little guilty for stealing her crush.

I blinked back my tears for two seconds.

"Oh, Eve." She stood and hugged me again as I fell to pieces.

"No-nobody has c-called. I d-don't know if he's okay."

"My mom's friend Charity works at the hospital, and the

last she heard, he was still in surgery. But he'll be fine. Charity said his arm took the brunt of the fall."

I released her and sniffled while nodding. "His sister-in-law said the bone was sticking out of his skin."

Erin grimaced. "Well, that's probably why it's a long surgery."

The phone rang, and I stiffened.

"Breathe," Erin said.

I took a long breath and wiped my tears before picking up the phone. "Hello?"

"Hi, Eve. It's Anne. Sorry it took so long. Kyle is out of surgery. It went well. All of his other injuries are minor. He'll be here for a couple of days, but then they anticipate releasing him. Your dad just headed home. And I'll leave soon too. Fred is staying the night with Kyle. How's Josh?"

The tension released from my body, and it sagged in relief. "That's really great news. Josh is asleep. He asked me to stay here tonight. So if it's okay with you—"

"Of course. That would be great. If you're going to stay, I might hang out here a little longer. Fred hasn't eaten anything, and I want to get him some food."

"Take your time," I said.

"We don't want to wake you, so you can sleep in Kyle's bed if you don't want to sleep on the sofa. I don't know if there are clean sheets in the upstairs linen closet, but you could check."

I didn't need clean sheets; I wanted them to smell like him.

"Thanks. If he wakes up, tell him ..." I paused.

Tell him I love him.

"Tell him I'm taking good care of Josh, and we can't wait to see him."

"I will. Thank you, Eve."

After she disconnected the call, I slowly hung up the phone. "He's out of surgery, and he's going to be okay."

Erin nodded. "That's a relief. Are you going to go see him at the hospital?"

"Would that be weird?"

"No. It wouldn't be weird even if you weren't in love with him. You babysit for him, and he's a good family friend."

I nodded. "Maybe I'll go after church tomorrow."

"Good idea."

It was a good idea if my heart could survive seeing him in a hospital bed without wanting to hug him and expose all of my feelings in front of his family.

Chapter Twenty-Four

Paul Young, "Every Time You Go Away"

Eve

"Wake up, Eve," a soft voice whispered above my face.

I was tangled in Kyle's sheets, hugging his pillow, and I peeled open my eyes.

"Good morning," I murmured to the smiling face before me.

Josh pulled the pillow away from me and slid under the covers so I'd hug him instead. It was the perfect trade. My poor heart was so invested in Josh and his daddy.

Clifford jumped onto the bed and licked my face.

"Aunt Anne is making breakfast," Josh said.

"That's nice of her. Think we should go help?"

He nodded and began to wiggle out of my embrace, but I didn't let go.

"I need to hug you for ten more seconds."

"Daddy says I'm his favorite teddy bear."

I hummed. "I can see why. You're so cute and cuddly."

Josh let me steal an extra thirty seconds instead of ten before breaking free and running down the stairs.

After using the bathroom, I shrugged off Kyle's T-shirt and dressed in the previous day's clothes.

"Good morning," Anne said. "Thank you so much for staying."

I smiled.

"There's my girl," Mom said, sipping coffee at the table while Anne pulled cinnamon rolls out of the oven.

"Hey, where's Dad?" I yawned.

Mom slid Josh's cup of juice closer to him as he climbed into his booster seat. "He and Gabby headed to church. I thought I'd watch Josh and the dog this morning if you want to go to the hospital with Anne. I figured you'd want to see him."

"You did?" I said slowly while sitting next to Josh.

"Of course. You've been watching Josh for almost two months. I know you've become good friends with Kyle."

Good friends.

With a tight smile, I poured a glass of orange juice and took a sip.

"When do you think you'll be ready to leave?" Anne asked me, setting the plate of rolls on the table.

I gulped down my orange juice. "I need a quick shower." I stood. "These look amazing, Anne. I'll eat one on my way home and be back in less than an hour if that works."

"No rush, honey," she said.

There was an enormous rush. I needed to see my guy. *My lover.*

As we walked through the hallway toward Kyle's hospital room, nerves quaked throughout my body, and my heart raced. When we walked inside the room, Fred was talking on the phone. He nodded at Anne and smiled.

"How are you doing this morning?" Anne stood beside Kyle's bed, and rested her hand on his right arm, the good one.

I remained a few feet behind her, wishing I'd stayed home because it hurt too much to see his bandaged arm—scrapes and cuts on one side of his face—and not be able to hug and kiss him and tell him how scared I was yesterday.

"I'm in a little pain," Kyle whispered with a forced smile. His groggy gaze shifted to me as if he just noticed I was in the room. "Hey," he said, and his smile changed.

It felt real.

"Hey." I swallowed my emotions.

"Mom and Dad said they can come stay with you after we leave if you need help," Fred said, hanging up the phone.

"They don't need to come. It's just a broken arm," Kyle said in a voice that sounded as groggy as his eyes looked.

"You don't have to decide now. See how you're feeling when you go home." Fred tucked in his wrinkled shirt.

"Eve stayed at your place last night because Josh asked her to stay." Anne glanced back at me and smiled. "Kyle, we're so glad you decided to buy the place next to the Jacobsons. It's like living next to family and having nieces to babysit for you and another brother and sister-in-law looking out for you and Josh."

Kyle hummed, gaze finding me. "A niece. That's ..."

Disturbing.

I cleared my throat. "I'm glad you're okay."

Kyle silently gazed at me.

Every. Single. Inch.

I was *dying* to touch him. "I slept in your bed. I hope that was okay. I'll wash your sheets before you get home. Who wants their sheets smelling like their niece?"

Kyle's lips twitched.

My nose wrinkled. "And I have a terrible habit of needing to hug something at night, so I hugged one of your pillows. Your whole bed probably smells like my floral perfume and shampoo. Sorry."

He burned me to the ground with a look. I was so relieved that he would be okay, but I needed to get my greedy hands on him.

"So, no cast?" Anne asked.

"No," Fred answered for Kyle. "It was an open humerus fracture. They repaired it with a plate and screws. It will stay wrapped and bandaged in the sling while it heals. No cast."

"You look tired." Anne said.

"It's the pain meds," again, Fred answered for Kyle.

"Have you had breakfast?" Anne narrowed her eyes at Fred.

He shook his head.

"I could use another cup of coffee if you want to go to the cafeteria," she suggested.

"Okay."

"Do you want to come with us?" Anne turned, eyeing me.

"I'm uh, good. Thanks."

"Okay. We won't be too long. I'm sure you don't want to spend your day at the hospital." She smiled while stepping past me to the door.

And then it was just the two of us. We didn't say a word for a long moment. Maybe he was waiting to make sure they were out the door. I was waiting to find my voice past the lump in my throat.

"Hey, beautiful," he said. "You can come closer. I won't break any more than I already have."

It wasn't funny, but I smiled as I hesitantly stepped closer to the bed while quickly rubbing my teary eyes. "I was so scared," I whispered, taking his good hand in mine. "You could have ended up in a wheelchair."

"But I didn't." He pulled my hand to his mouth and pressed his lips to my wrist.

I rested my palm on his stubbly cheek. "I'm glad you're okay."

"Me too," he whispered against my wrist. "And don't you dare wash my sheets."

Again, I laughed despite the tears in my eyes.

"How did you fall out of the tree?"

"Your dad—" He paused. "You don't know?"

I shook my head, running my fingers through his messy hair.

His eyes drifted shut. "It doesn't matter," he whispered.

"My dad, what?"

His head rolled side to side. "Nothing," he mumbled.

"I want to tell everyone, and I want it to be okay."

"Tell what?" His words slurred, and his hand relaxed.

"Kyle?"

He was asleep.

I slowly peppered kisses over his face and whispered, "I want to tell our families that I love you, and I want it to be okay with them. I want them to be happy for us."

Chapter Twenty-Five

UB40, "Red Red Wine"

Eve

TUESDAY AFTER WORK, I raced home, nearly running two stop signs. Gabby was still in school, my dad's car was gone, and my mom was nowhere in sight. So I ran to Kyle's house, knowing Josh would get off the school bus in less than an hour, and my lover was supposed to be home.

I entered the house after two quick taps on the screen doorframe. "Hello?"

"In here," Mom called from the living room as Clifford barked and barreled toward me.

I leaned down to pet him while poking my head around the corner. She was on the far end of the sofa with Anne in the middle and Fred on the opposite end. Kyle gazed at me from his recliner, feet up, covered in a blanket.

"Hey, um ..." I tried not to stare at him too long. My emotions were hard to hide. "I was just seeing if you needed me to wait at the end of the drive for Josh in a bit?"

"That's sweet of you," Anne said. "We were just discussing who will help out while Kyle's recovering. He's being stubborn about it."

Kyle rolled his eyes. "I don't need anyone's help. My right arm is fine. I'm very capable of doing things."

"As I was saying," Anne frowned, "we want to stay or have his parents come be with him, but he's being *grumpy* about it."

I bit back my grin.

"I assured them we can help take care of him," Mom said. "Between the four of us, someone should always be able to be here."

"That's overstepping," Anne said. "But we really appreciate all that you've done."

"It's the least we can do given the circumstances in which it happened," Mom said dismissively.

"What does that mean?" I asked.

"Has no one told you?" Mom narrowed her eyes.

"Apparently not. Told me what?"

"Nothing," Kyle mumbled.

"Your dad wanted to check out the tree stand with Kyle, and while they were up there, your dad started to fall. Kyle grabbed him, but while your dad grappled to find leverage, he pulled Kyle out of the stand."

I winced. "But Dad didn't fall?"

"Kyle saved your dad from falling," Fred said.

"Your dad is indebted to him forever," Mom said, smiling at Kyle.

"Yeah," I said slowly. "My dad owes you a lot."

Some might have said my dad owed Kyle his first-born,

but Sarah was taken, so Kyle would have to settle for the second-born.

Kyle eyed me with an unreadable expression.

"Well," I clasped my hands before me, "I can get Josh breakfast every morning and on the school bus. Then I can work at the motel. But I can be home before he gets off the bus. Make dinner. Get him ready for bed. Laundry. Whatever needs to be done."

"That's a lot to ask of an eighteen-year-old." Fred shook his head. "Our parents will come stay whether he likes it or not."

"Stop. I'm not a child. This is my house. I'm not in a wheelchair. I'm capable of doing things, and if I need help, I'll ask. Okay?" Kyle sighed, lips resting into a scowl.

Fred and Anne exchanged a look.

"You have a child. Don't let your stubbornness get in the way of doing what's best for him," Fred replied, thickening the tension in the room.

"Listen. Our family has this." Mom jumped in to save the day. She could organize anything. That's what preacher's wives did.

Fundraisers.

Community volunteer days.

Bridal showers.

Funeral luncheons.

Vacation Bible School.

Nothing was too big for her.

"Let's take Clifford and wait for Josh," Anne said, squeezing Fred's hand.

I was planning on doing that, but I didn't argue. Fred needed some fresh air.

With a nervous smile, Mom stood too. "I'm going to head

home for a bit. I'll get dinner started soon and bring it over around five thirty."

"Thank you so much," Anne said.

My feet remained rooted to the floor as all three passed me and exited through the front door.

"Are you mad?" I asked Kyle.

"I hate being treated like a fucking child," he grumbled.

"On the upside, I bet you'll need a sponge bath several times a week. I could help with that."

He eyed me, jaw muscles clenched despite his lips wanting to curl into a grin.

"My dad *owes* you. I say we tell him about us and let him deal with it."

"Eve," he mumbled, pinching the bridge of his nose, "yeah, that's a great idea. Before my brother and Anne leave, let's drop that bomb on everyone. That's just what I need—everyone judging my poor decisions when I'm already at my lowest."

My back stiffened.

Poor decisions?

"You're right. How stupid of me."

"Eve—"

"I gotta go." I turned.

"Eve, stop."

"I'd better help my mom with dinner."

"Eve—"

"Feel better, *Mister* Collins." I fought to keep my emotions in check. I ran out the door and straight home as soon as I got my shoes on.

Before I reached the front door, I stopped and stared at the milk box. Then I removed the planter, grabbed a bottle of vodka, hid it in my sweatshirt, and headed inside.

"Eve?" Mom called my name from the kitchen.

"Huh?" I said, halfway up the stairs.

"Want to help me with dinner?"

"Uh, I'm feeling a little unwell. Menstrual cramps. I want to lie down," I said.

"Okay, honey. We'll be taking the food to Kyle's house. Are you going to join us?"

"I'm not hungry."

"If you change your mind, you know where we'll be."

I continued to my room and locked the door behind me before screwing off the cap to the bottle and taking several big gulps.

I told him I wouldn't be anyone's regret.

"Eve, wake up." Gabby patted my cheek a half dozen times.

I grumbled, rolling to my side and curling into a ball.

"Wake up before Mom and Dad come home. Why are you drinking tonight?"

"I was a bad"—I rolled onto my stomach and mumbled with my face in the pillow—"not bad. Poor. I was a poor decision."

"I can't hear you." She shoved my shoulder to roll me onto my back. "Josh wants you to stay the night. He's been asking for you. But you can't go over there now. What's your problem?"

Peeling my eyes open, I tried to focus on Gabby's grumpy face. "He called me a poor decision."

She frowned. "Well, you probably are. If you were a

good decision, you wouldn't have to keep your relationship a secret. And you wouldn't be drunk."

My face soured. "That's ... you're just jealous and mean."

"I won't be jealous when Dad kicks you out of the house." She wedged herself next to me on the bed.

We stared at the ceiling.

"They're going to find out you got plastered."

"Pfft. I'm not plastered. I'm just really, really very," I giggled, "a lot relaxed. And I think," I waggled my finger at the ceiling, "it will take more than one beer to get me on my knees. Ya know?"

"What are you talking about?"

"Nothing." I dropped my hand to my stomach and closed my eyes. "I just thought he liked me. And he'd fight for my honor like Peter Cetera."

Gabby snorted. "What are you talking about?"

"'Glory of Love.' The song. Remember? In the second *Karate Kid*?" I sighed. "Why can't Kyle fight for my honor like Daniel LaRusso?" I cackled. "*Daniel-san!*"

We laughed.

"Grandma Bonnie said I have to stay on my side of the line or cross it and build a fence. But what if I build a fence and Kyle tosses me over it because I'm just his poor decision? Then, I'll have to stay at the cleanest motel in Missouri and masturbate to *Playgirl* magazines."

"Eve!" Gabby slapped a hand over her mouth. "Stop!" She hugged her belly and laughed. "W-what are you talking about?"

"Kyle has naked girls under his mattress. Well, not the actual girls." I laughed. "That would be totally weird. Just the magazines. Sexy centerfolds with perfect titties." I pinched my nipples through my shirt.

"Stop!" Gabby rolled to her side and lifted onto her elbow. "Are you serious?"

My head fell to the side, and I tried again to focus through the alcohol fog. "We looked at them together. I wasn't jealous of their titties. I have good titties. But they have big hair, pretty makeup, and pierced ears. Screw it!" I sat up, and the room spun a little. "I'm gonna do it. I'm eighteen. I'm getting my ears pierced, and there's nothing Mom or Dad can do to stop me." I crawled over Gabby and fell onto the floor.

"Well, I'm going to stop you," she said. "At least until you sober up. I guess I'll have to stay with Josh tonight." She swung her legs off the side of the bed. Her dirty-socked feet hovered just over my face. "And if Kyle needs anything and doesn't want to bother Fred or Anne, I'll be there for him too. Maybe he'll need someone to sleep next to him in case he needs help going to the bathroom."

"Shut up, you bimbette." I batted my hand at her feet.

Gabby sighed. "Take me to bed, or lose me—"

"Stop it!" I scrambled to my feet, reaching for my desk chair to steady myself. "He's not your Maverick. He's mine. My Pete Mitchell. My Daniel LaRusso. My Johnny Castle. I'm going to talk to him." I ran my fingers through my hair.

"Not tonight," Gabby said. "Mom already told them you were having menstrual cycle issues."

I winced. "She did *not*!"

Gabby's nose wrinkled as she nodded.

"Gah!" I covered my face. "Why is she so mean? I'm not having my period."

"Then you should have told her you were going to drink

away your anger instead of telling her you were having cramps."

I squinted at my alarm clock. "It's seven. I'll shower, eat something, take a couple ibuprofen, and be fine to tuck Josh in at eight."

"You're not—"

"Just go. I'll be ..." I headed toward the bathroom. "Good and fine and ... just go."

Chapter Twenty-Six

U2, "With or Without You"

Eve

I PARTIALLY DRIED MY HAIR, put on a pink sweat suit, and grabbed a peanut butter and jelly sandwich to eat on my way to Kyle's. Just as I opened the door, my parents and Gabby were opening the screen door.

"Oh. Are you sure you're feeling better?" Mom asked.

I didn't make eye contact with her. I just nodded, squeezing past them.

Gabby cleared her throat, and I shot her a scowl.

"Anne said you don't need to spend the night. Once Josh is asleep, you can come home."

"Yeah, I'll see," I said.

"There's no place for you to sleep except for the sofa," she added as I walked toward the fence.

When I arrived, Josh was in his jammies, running around the kitchen as Clifford chased him.

"Eve!" Josh ran to me with Clifford right behind him.

"Oof!" I grunted. He nearly knocked me over, hugging my waist. I picked him up and avoided eye contact with Anne and Fred. "Ready to read a book?" I asked, kissing his pink cheek.

"Thanks for doing this," Fred said. "He's taken quite the liking to you."

"Yeah, well, I spend a lot of time with Mr. Munchkin." I quickly headed toward the stairs.

"Shh!" Josh held his little finger to his lips when I set him down. "Daddy's sleeping."

I couldn't safely carry him up the stairs. I needed to hold the handrail just for good measure. Giving him a smile, I nodded before following his lead.

"You need to go potty before we read a book," I whispered.

Josh hurried into the bathroom, partially shutting the door, but not before Clifford squeezed in behind him.

That dog was his shadow. And I was grateful that my dad had stopped pestering me to find him a different home.

I listened for Anne and Fred before cracking open Kyle's door. The lights were out, and he was on his back with his injured arm in the sling, hugged to his stomach. He didn't speak or move, so I assumed he was asleep. When the toilet flushed, I closed the door.

Josh bolted toward his bedroom.

"Wash your—" I gave up, not caring if he washed his hands.

"This one," Josh said, holding up a book.

I nodded toward his bed and tucked him in before sitting beside him. He hugged my waist and stared at each page. Halfway through, he fell asleep. I set the book on the nightstand and shut off the light. As I slid out of bed, Josh stirred and reached for me, so I squeezed into his single bed along with Clifford at our feet, hugged him to me, and fell asleep.

EARLY THE NEXT MORNING, I slipped out of Josh's room and tiptoed down the stairs with Clifford. "Oh!" I startled, walking into the kitchen and letting Clifford out back to go potty. "Good morning." I quickly combed my fingers through my hair. "I didn't think anyone else was up."

"Good morning. We weren't sure you'd stay. Sleeping in a single bed with Josh couldn't have been comfortable," Anne said, sipping a cup of coffee. "Kyle made it clear last night that he doesn't want us to stay *or* his parents to come help him. So ..." She wrinkled her nose and shrugged. "We're leaving after Josh gets up. Your parents promised to keep an eye on things. Kyle shouldn't be driving, but since it's his left arm that's injured, he thinks he'll be fine. That man is stubborn to a fault."

I couldn't say much. Everyone thought the same thing about me.

"We really can't thank you enough for all you've done for Kyle and Josh. You're very mature for your age," Fred said, glancing up from the newspaper.

With a tight smile, I nodded. "Josh is irresistible. I adore him." I twisted my lips. "Kyle is nice too. He taught me how to shoot a bow and arrow."

And he built me a new hut.

Too bad I was his bad decision.

"He won't be shooting that bow anytime soon," Fred mumbled.

Anne eyed him with a frown. "Because he saved your friend."

"Morning," Kyle's gravelly voice sounded behind me.

I swallowed before glancing over my shoulder. His jogging shorts hung low on his waist, and he wasn't wearing a shirt. His gaze flitted between me and his brother.

"How are you feeling?" Anne asked.

Kyle winced while reaching for a glass.

"Let me help—" Anne started to say.

"I got it," he mumbled, setting it in the sink and then turning on the faucet.

Anne and Fred exchanged tiny eye rolls, and I let Clifford inside.

"Might be time to take something for the pain," Fred suggested.

"Makes me too drowsy," Kyle said before drinking the entire glass of water.

"I think resting is a good idea," Fred replied, narrowing his eyes.

"I have a child. Sleeping during the day isn't a good idea. I don't need to close my eyes to rest."

"Well, as soon as Josh wakes, we're taking off." Anne put her coffee mug into the dishwasher.

I wanted to slowly back away and run out the front door. The tension was thick.

"Thanks for visiting. He's enjoyed having you here," Kyle said.

"I fear our visit is what caused your accident," Fred said. "Had we not visited, I wouldn't have suggested Peter and I go hunting with you."

"Bones heal." Kyle set his glass on the counter.

"Let's finish packing, honey." Fred pushed back in his chair. "Josh should be up soon."

Anne followed him to the stairs.

I waited a few seconds before risking a glance in Kyle's direction.

"Eve," he said.

That was it. Just my name accompanied by an indistinguishable look.

Was he angry that I was there?

Waiting for me to explain myself?

Expecting an apology for being his poor decision?

"Mr. Collins," I said, keeping a neutral expression.

His head slowly cocked to the side. "Are you done pouting?"

"You're an asshole."

"Maybe."

"You think I act like a child, but let's remember that I'm eighteen. You're stubbornly refusing help from your family. You're twenty-eight. You have a son. You should know better. So what's your excuse?"

"I'm not stubbornly refusing anything. I simply don't need their help."

"Are you sure? Because last I heard, you've been making *poor decisions*."

"I was referencing the past. You took it personally and ran off before I could explain."

"Oh, that's right. I'm not a poor decision. I'm the woman you're testing—trying to decide if I'm worth the trouble that our relationship will cause."

"It's not just me, Eve."

I shrugged. "Josh loves me. Anne and Fred thought he loved

them, but last night, it was me who he wanted when you couldn't put him to bed. You don't have an issue with kicking your family out. So what is it? My family? The teachers at the school? Are you secretly embarrassed to be with me? I get it. I'm ten years younger. Devil's Head thrives on gossip. Just stop lying to me."

"Fine. Tell them about us when they come back downstairs," he said.

"Me?" I narrowed my eyes. "Why me?"

"Because you want everyone to know. So tell them."

I crossed my arms over my chest and tipped my chin up. "Fine. I will."

"Okay," he said, turning to fill a mug with coffee.

My confidence felt overinflated, like at any moment, it could pop and vanish into nothing.

"Eve!" Josh ran toward me in his dinosaur jammies.

"Morning, cutie." I hugged him just as Fred and Anne reached the bottom of the stairs with their bags.

Gulp.

"Well, we're taking off," Fred announced.

My gaze shot to Kyle. He sipped his coffee with his backside leaning against the counter.

"Bye, honey. Take care of yourself, and don't be too prideful to call if you need anything," Anne said, giving Kyle a side hug.

"Thanks," he said.

"Love you, brother." Fred gave him the same awkward one-arm hug.

"Love you too," Kyle replied. "Oh, Eve has something she wants to tell you."

My heart slammed against my rib cage, and my mouth dried up like a late July drought.

Fred and Anne looked at me expectantly while Josh hugged Kyle.

It was a test. He didn't think I'd tell them. But what if I did? Would he admit that he loved me too?

I had the chance to build the fence. Be brave. Risk everything for love like my sister Sarah did. But she knew she had someone's love. Kyle hadn't given me that. So I stood among his family with my heart on the verge of being exposed, open for anyone to step on it.

And that pissed me off.

He needed to love me more.

More than his need to avoid a scandal.

More than his need to appease my father.

More than I loved him.

Grandma Bonnie told me to find a man who I loved with my whole heart but who loved me just a little bit more.

He had my entire heart, but I didn't know if I had a single beat of his.

I cleared my throat. "I wanted to thank you for the kind things you've said about me, for trusting me with Josh, and for keeping me in the loop after Kyle's accident."

They smiled. Kyle dropped his gaze to the floor, lips twisted, as Josh rummaged through the cabinet for a cereal box.

"You're welcome. We'll call to check in when we get to our next stop," Fred said, and they headed to the front door.

Kyle gently pushed off the counter to follow them.

Tears filled my eyes, and I quickly blinked them back. I was so scared of loving him too much and losing my heart to someone who didn't know if he wanted it.

He stopped on his way to the door and inspected me while I curled my lips between my teeth to keep them from quivering, but I kept my gaze on him, wishing he could see and *feel* everything I wanted to say.

"Baby," he whispered. "I only have one good arm, but I'll carry you."

Emotions beyond anything I had ever experienced bubbled over, and I blinked an endless stream of tears.

He stepped past me as I frantically wiped my face before Josh saw me crying.

"I love her," Kyle said.

I couldn't turn around because the tears wouldn't stop. My heart swelled into my throat, making it impossible to breathe.

"Sorry, what?" Anne said casually, as though she really didn't hear him.

"I'm in love with Eve."

Josh, bless his heart, padded into the living room, turned on cartoons, and sat on the sofa with an open cereal box. He was oblivious to the epic confession ten feet behind me at the front door.

Fred released a nervous chuckle. "What are you talking about? Eve ... as in Eve behind you? Is this a joke?"

"It's not a joke. It just happened. Chemistry. Kismet. Fate. God's will. Whatever. Eve is generous. Funny and nurturing. She has a young and wild heart with an old soul. To know her *really* is to love her. And the joy she brings to both Josh and me is immeasurable. Maybe I don't know where this is going, and I haven't said anything to her family yet, but she deserves a bold, selfless love. And if I'm honest, my feelings for her can't be contained any longer. So if you have a problem with this, then you don't know me, and you certainly don't know Eve. But I know she's worthy of the very best in life, and I think I'm at least worthy of a little luck."

I gave up on controlling my tears, so I turned.

Anne's eyes instantly filled with emotion when she saw me. But Fred kept his focus on Kyle.

"Have you been," Fred cleared his throat, "*respectful* toward her."

Sex.

Fred wanted to know if we'd had sex.

"I'm afraid that's personal," Kyle said.

Fred clenched his teeth. "It's not right," he whispered, slowly shaking his head.

"Yeah, well, it doesn't feel wrong either," Kyle replied.

My heart dripped from my chest into a messy pool of liquid at my feet. Kyle melted it with his words. He put Daniel LaRusso and Pete "Maverick" Mitchell to shame.

"May God forgive you both," Fred said, opening the door.

Anne eyed me a little longer, as if she needed to know if I was all right.

I shuffled my feet to Kyle and wrapped my arms around his waist, resting my cheek on his bare back. Seconds later, the door clicked shut. Turning my head, I pressed my lips to his spine, dotting slow kisses along his skin.

"I'm sorry. I—"

"Don't," he said, turning and wrapping his good arm around me and kissing the top of my head. "Don't apologize."

"You love me," I whispered.

"So much."

Josh giggled at his cartoons.

"I have to go," I said, pulling away and looking for my shoes. I found them by the door and slid my feet into them.

"Where are you going? If you're telling your parents, I want to be—"

"I'm not telling them. Not yet." I opened the door.

"Eve?"

"Huh?" I glanced back at him.

He stood idle and expressionless.

"What?" I asked.

Still, nothing.

I smiled, stepping back into the house and lifting onto my toes to kiss him. He grinned in the middle of the kiss.

"I'm going to give you a sponge bath after Josh is in bed later," I murmured over his mouth.

"Damn right you are." He beamed.

Chapter Twenty-Seven

REO Speedwagon, "Keep On Loving You"

Eve

I WENT TO WORK.

If I was going to prove to everyone that I was worthy of Kyle's style of epic love, then I needed to be a grown-up. And since that didn't involve college, I had to go to work.

But as soon as I clocked out, I headed to the nursing home.

"There's my sweet Eve." Grandma Bonnie glanced up from her yarn and crochet needle. "How was your day, dear? Your mom told me about Mr. Collins. Is he home?"

"He's home," I said, closing the door to her room, kicking off my sneakers, and sitting cross-legged on her bed. "And he loves me." I laced my fingers together, squeezing tightly to control my excitement.

Grandma's thinning eyebrows lifted.

I nodded a half-dozen times at her unspoken questions.

Then I spilled every detail, every word that was exchanged that morning. I knew my parents would be furious.

Sarah and Gabby would be happy for me in a reserved way, knowing I'd be in trouble.

Erin would share my joy, but she'd share it as an eighteen-year-old with her questionable behavior and choices too.

But Grandma Bonnie loved me through and through. She knew all about love and life. She championed my desire to choose my path. Her opinion mattered the most. And when she smiled, it was genuine—it was everything.

"He's a keeper," she said with a soft smile and easy nod.

I beamed. "I think so too. Would you mind telling Mom and Dad for me?"

She barked a laugh. "Oh dear. No. I'm sorry. That is a very important experience you need to have in life. It's necessary for personal growth. You want to be a strong woman, don't you?"

I wrinkled my nose. "Well, it's not a big deal to me. I had a terrible time starting Kyle's boat. I'm a runner. My upper body strength isn't the best."

Grandma laughed. My mom would have rolled her eyes and told me to be serious.

With a slow sigh, my smile faded. "I know I need to tell them. I just have never forgotten listening to Sarah and my dad yelling at each other when he kicked her out of the house. My mom was crying, and it was awful. And I think Dad loves her more than he loves me. Sarah was always the golden girl. She could do no wrong. So imagine what he'll do to me—the daughter who has been the biggest disappointment."

"Love is a funny word, Eve. We use it indiscriminately. It

can mean everything, like what you felt when Kyle said it this morning, or it can be very little when we try to use it as a measurement for favoritism. I promise your parents don't love one of you girls more than the other. It's just that you're all three very different. And your parents' tolerance for certain things feels like a measure of love, but it's not." She shook her head. "Your Uncle Andrew used to try my patience like no one else, but I've never loved him a single ounce less than I love your mom." She held up a finger. "But if you ask either of them, they'll say your mom was my favorite."

I smiled. "Okay. I believe you. But I still think my dad is looking for any reason to kick me out."

"Wherever would you go?" she asked, focusing on her needle and yarn.

"I'd stay at the hotel or live in sin if Kyle lets me move in with him."

"It's better to live in sin than die in sin."

I giggled. "You think?"

"Oh yes. When you die, that's when you do all that confession stuff, begging for forgiveness, requesting permission to cross the golden arches."

"Grandma, I think it's a golden gate, not an arch. McDonald's has golden arches."

"Potato potahto."

"I'll tell them this Sunday after church."

"During dinner?" she asked.

An idea hit me, and I grinned. "Yes. That. Definitely that."

"Where have you been?" Mom asked when I peeked into the kitchen.

"After work I went to the nursing home, then I stopped to talk to Erin. Need help?"

"No. It's just chili. It's simmering, and the cornbread is on the cooling racks. Do you want to take some over to Kyle and Josh? Or do you want me to run over there? Your dad said we needed to give Kyle a little space. Last night, Kyle and Fred had quite an argument over everything. Kyle thinks he can do it all alone, but I know he'll feed Josh TV dinners every night if we don't send over some food."

"I'll take it over there and eat with them. Then I can make sure Josh gets tucked into bed. He might want me to stay again. If he wakes in the middle of the night, he could try to jump in bed with Kyle and hurt his arm."

Mom cringed. "I didn't think of that."

"Yup, it could be bad. I'm going to run upstairs and take a quick shower."

"Okay, hun. I'll wrap up some bread and ladle the chili into a smaller pot."

I took a quick shower and fully dried my hair. Even though Kyle was in a sling with a broken arm and plenty of pain, I wanted to look nice for him.

Since I had so much to carry, I packed it in my car and drove to his house.

"Eve's here!" Josh and Clifford ran down the porch steps as Kyle slowly stood from the swing.

"Hey, Mister. How was school?"

"Good," Josh said, taking the bread while I carried the soup.

Kyle held open the door with his good arm.

I stopped while Josh continued toward the kitchen. "Hi," I whispered.

Kyle's grin mirrored mine as he ducked his head to kiss me. "Hi," he said after a slow kiss.

"How are you feeling?" I headed toward the kitchen.

"Better now."

I shot him a flirty look over my shoulder. And he winked. God, I loved that wink.

The three of us ate dinner together, and it felt so natural. Afterward, I ensured Josh bathed, put on his jammies, and brushed his teeth. While Kyle read him a story, I tidied up the kitchen, took Clifford outside, and put a load of laundry into the washing machine.

"You don't have to do our laundry," Kyle said.

I turned on the washer and pivoted to face him. "I know. You don't have to love me, but you do it anyway. So laundry seems pretty simple in comparison."

With his good shoulder leaned against the doorframe, the corner of his mouth twitched. "Where did you go earlier?"

"To work." I stepped closer.

"Is that it?"

"Doesn't matter. Just kiss me," I whispered.

He gazed down at me with what I'd come to recognize as love in his eyes. "I need a shower."

"You mean a sponge bath since you can't get your incision wet."

"Yes. I need help bathing. And it's a little degrading."

"Are you in pain?"

"Not when I'm looking at you."

I slowly shook my head. "That's code for you're hiding

your pain from me. Let's go." We shut off the lights on the main level, and I locked the doors. Then we headed upstairs.

I ran water in the bathtub and helped him out of his clothes. The water hit just above his waist when he eased into the tub. I grabbed his soap bar and started washing what I could without getting his injured arm wet.

"Ignore my erection," he said.

I grinned, kissing his ear. "I can't ignore it, but I won't acknowledge it if it makes you feel better."

We stared at each other while I washed him. It wasn't sexual, despite said erection. But it was intimate. Sometimes, he let his eyes drift shut like my touch took away some of his pain, especially when I guided his head back and washed his hair, massaging his scalp.

Our flirty glances continued as I helped him out of the tub and dried him off.

"I could get used to this," he said as I pulled his boxer shorts up his legs.

"Says the guy who kicked his family out because he wanted to do everything himself." I hung up his towel and then squirted toothpaste onto his toothbrush.

He took the toothbrush from me. "Did it ever occur to you that I kicked them out so you could bathe me?"

I rolled my eyes.

After he finished brushing his teeth, he eased into bed. I stole one of his T-shirts and returned to the bathroom. A few minutes later, I opened the door, and he eyed me in his shirt as I made my way to the other side of the bed, reaching for the lamp to turn it off.

"Wait," he said, eyeing me. "Let me look at you in my shirt."

I glanced down. It was just a gray T-shirt with a Nike swoosh.

"I'm scared," he said.

My gaze shot up to his.

Tiny lines formed along his forehead. "My life felt perfect." His gaze affixed to the shirt, but it looked like he was seeing something that wasn't in the room or the present. "Maybe not perfect by other people's standards, but it felt perfect to me. I was in love. We were having a baby. House. Jobs. 401(k). It all seemed logical. The dream was there. We just had to take it. But she didn't want it." His brow tensed more, eyes narrowed. "How do you carry a life inside of you for nine months, push it out of your body, hold him in your arms, and then just walk away?"

Kyle looked at me. "How did I fall in love with someone who would do that?"

I swallowed, but there was no right response. I felt *only* eighteen under the weight of his question.

"When Josh was born, my heart exploded. It was like everything I had done up until that point was frivolous and inconsequential. When they let me hold him, I didn't want to let him go. He's just ..." Kyle's eyes reddened. "He's the best part of every day. Everything in my life is better because of him. *I* am better because of him."

I used his shirt sleeve to wipe my eyes and snotty nose.

"So I'm scared, Eve. I'm scared because I don't trust my heart. And that little boy trusts everyone."

"You don't trust me," I whispered.

"I love you."

I nodded slowly. "But you're scared to love me."

He stared at the ceiling.

I waited.

And I waited.

"Eve, I'm terrified to love you. And I knew it the second I saw the look in my brother's eyes. It was the look he gave me when I said I was going to be a dad and ask Melinda to marry me. He's always thought I make rash decisions."

"I don't want to be your regret."

"I would never regret you."

"But if we don't work—"

"I would *never* regret you." He stretched out his good arm. "Come here."

After a slight hesitation, I turned off the light and crawled into his bed, hugging his arm and holding his hand.

"Regret isn't the right word. It's the pain that terrifies me. It's the loss. The self-doubt. The responsibility I feel for Josh's well-being. Telling my brother and Anne felt like the point of no return. That's a lot of pressure to put on you at your age."

"Why does everything come back to my age?"

"Because it matters, Eve. You're trying to figure out where you fit in the world now that you're out of school. You have a job, but you live at home. You're impulsive, and you have a need to push boundaries, which is—"

"Why does everyone say I'm impulsive?" I released his arm and rolled to my back with a harsh sigh.

He chuckled, and it infuriated me. It felt condescending.

"You're making my point by not letting me finish. It's natural to be this way at your age. And it's one of the things I love about you. But it's also really fucking scary because it makes you unpredictable. So, yeah, I'm glad you're here in my bed. I'm beyond grateful for what you've done for Josh and me. And I want things to work out between us, but I don't see it happening without a lot of battles, blood, sweat, and tears."

He reached for my hand. "But I'm in. I wouldn't have told my brother and Anne unless I was fully committed. But I won't lie to you and say I'm not terrified. Every day won't be fishing and hiding in a hut by the creek."

"I know that," I grumbled.

Again, he chuckled.

"Stop laughing at me."

"It's joy. You bring me joy, even when showing your stubborn side."

I rolled again to turn my back to him. I wasn't being stubborn. I was pissed off that there was no way to expedite my way into being a "mature" adult. I was still a fucking teenager.

He hooked several fingers into my underwear's waistband and pulled me closer to him, giving me a wedgie.

"Stop," I said, wriggling to fix my underwear.

"You stop." He tucked me under his good arm. "Sweet dreams, my love."

My love ...

Chapter Twenty-Eight

Whitesnake, "Is This Love"

Kyle

I woke with a pain radiating from my shoulder to my fingertips, and my whole body tensed.

"Good morning," Josh said, jumping on the empty side of the bed where Eve had been.

"Buddy," I said firmly, reaching for his ankle to stop him. "My arm *really* hurts when you do that."

He stopped and frowned. "Sorry."

"Can you gently lie next to me?"

He not-so-gently plopped down onto the bed.

"Where's Eve?" I asked with a grimace as the pain lingered. "What time is it?"

"It's nine thirteen o'clock," he said, peering at my alarm clock as I stared at the ceiling and fought the nausea that the pain instigated.

"Not o'clock," I said, breathing slowly and deeply. "Just

nine thirteen. Buddy, you're late for school. You missed the bus. Why didn't you or Eve wake me?"

"Don't know."

"Are you ready for school? Did you have breakfast?"

"Oh man eggs with cheese and vegetables. Toast with butter and strawberry jam. And my teeth are brushed. Eve said you'd walk me to the bus."

I slowly turned my head to look at him. "Oh man eggs?"

He nodded. "They were melty."

I narrowed my eyes. "An omelet?"

He nodded, and I tried not to laugh. "Why didn't you or Eve wake me?" I narrowed my eyes and listened. There was a buzzing noise. "What's buzzing?"

Josh held still, then he smacked his hand against his forehead. "Eve said wake you up when it buzzed."

"Didn't you hear it?"

"I was watching Sesame Street."

"And you didn't hear the buzzer?"

He held out his hands, shoulders at his ears. "I forgot."

I closed my eyes and slowly shook my head. "I can drive you to school or you can play hooky."

"What's hooky?" He giggled.

"It's when you're not sick, but you pretend that you are so you don't have to go to school."

"But school is fun."

"For now." I chuckled. Josh caused a lot of pain, but he also made everything better.

"Whoa ..." Eve's voice woke me from my nap.

I didn't mean to fall asleep. As I sat up in my recliner, she was surveying the mess.

Josh had all of his toys strewn throughout the living room. A chip bag and a spilled cup of milk were on the coffee table, and Clifford was working to lick it all up. The TV was on PBS. And Josh was asleep on the sofa with a Matchbox car clutched in his hand.

"He didn't go to school," I explained.

She nodded slowly before sliding the chips into the bag and picking up the tipped cup. "I can see that. Why not?"

"You didn't wake me before you left, and he didn't wake me in time to get him to the bus. And it's not a good idea to leave a five-year-old and a puppy unattended."

"I set a timer for him to wake you. He was watching TV. And Clifford had already done his business. He shouldn't have been *unattended* any longer than he's been when you've walked me home," she said on her way to the kitchen.

Josh stirred, rubbing his eyes before opening them.

"We're in trouble, buddy," I whispered. "You need to pick up your toys or Eve won't make us dinner."

His eyes widened.

I nodded toward the mess. "Get going."

Josh slid off the sofa and started depositing his cars into one of my old shoe boxes.

"I set the timer, Mister," Eve said, standing over him with her hands on her hips.

"I forgot." He shrugged, putting on the lid to the box and carrying it toward the stairs.

"When he hears that timer," I said, "*if* he hears it, I think his brain is trained to assume someone (not him) needs to take something out of the oven. But it was a good try, and I appreciate you letting me sleep in."

She wiped up the spilled milk. "What you said last night, it upset me. I *hate* the constant reminders that I'm so young."

"Eve—"

"But ..." she turned, folding the milk-soaked rag, "What you said to your brother and Anne ..." She took a moment as if to keep her composure.

"It was so much more than I ever expected. There was this moment where I wondered who you were talking about. *She* seemed like an amazing person, but that person didn't feel like me." Eve pointed her gaze at the floor.

"I meant it."

"I know. I just feel unworthy of it. Like you said those things in an effort to set the bar high. And now I have expectations to live up to."

"Which part wasn't true?"

She peeked up at me. "Do you really think I have an old soul?"

"I think anyone who gleans so much information from their grandmother must have an old soul. You have respect for her wisdom and willingly learn everything she has to teach you. And you're empathetic."

Eve chewed on the inside of her cheek. "Is your brother going to tell my dad about us?"

"No. He knows it's something I need to do. Trust me, he wants it to be me who tells your dad."

"When are you telling my dad?"

"Whenever you want."

She frowned. "Why the change of heart? You wanted us to keep things a secret."

"And you needed the world to know. I want to give you what you need."

Eve remained idle in deep thought, still gnawing away at the inside of her cheek. "Will you hate me if I don't want to tell my parents yet?" she murmured.

I squinted for a few seconds before slowly shaking my head. Eve felt like a seedling I'd been given to transplant, not like Josh who had been rooted in my life since the beginning of his. Despite her strong will and determination, Eve was fragile. I knew I could lose her if the conditions weren't just right. And it reaffirmed why I felt so terrified.

Chapter Twenty-Nine

Prince & The Revolution, "Purple Rain"

Eve

I LOVED HIM. It was unlike any love I imagined—too good to be true. There was a one hundred percent chance I would ruin everything.

If we told my parents and I messed things up with Kyle, I would have no one and no place to live. The fact that Kyle was terrified to love me made me even more scared of screwing up.

I put the brakes on my heart and focused on work, visiting Grandma Bonnie, and taking care of Josh, Clifford, and Kyle before and after school. My parents didn't question my staying at his house all night. They assumed I was sleeping in the spare bedroom. After all, Josh and Kyle were "family." I knew it was only a matter of time before I blew up their world and mine.

"Where did you get that?" Kyle asked as I helped Josh into his Cookie Monster costume.

The last football game was that night, followed by a scavenger hunt around the church for good Christians who knew that Halloween was Satan's holiday. The church-going kids in Devil's Head waited almost two weeks after October 31st to don their costumes.

"I made it," I said, buttoning the back of it.

"Like made it with a sewing machine?" Kyle eyed me while he stepped into his boots. He was back to work and coaching.

I laughed. "Yes, with a sewing machine."

"Look, Dad! Mmm ... me Cookie Monster. Num num num ..."

Kyle's face lit up, which made me feel warm all over.

"I go look in the mirror," Josh said, running toward the stairs.

"Damn, I love you, baby." Kyle kept his beaming smile for me.

I tried to return the same sentiment, to act as though I wasn't feeling the pressure not to screw up. So far, I'd been playing the part of a responsible adult. Occasionally, I snuck a few drinks to take the edge off, but no one noticed. For the first time, I felt nothing but pride from my parents.

"I love you too," I said.

He stepped closer, giving me a look I hadn't seen in a while. It was a hungry look, sexy and sensual. Besides a few kisses, we'd acted more like roommates than lovers, which felt normal, given his injury. But this look was different, and a wave of nerves hit me.

He ducked his head to kiss me but quickly stood straight when Josh raced down the stairs.

"Mmm ... me need cookies," Josh said in a gruff voice.

I curled my hair behind my ears and tucked my hands into my back jeans pockets. "There will be lots of cookies at the fall festival," I said. "Let's get going to the game." I snagged Kyle's car keys just as he reached for them.

"You don't have to keep chauffeuring me around."

I winked like he did to me. "I do. Let's go."

DURING THE FOOTBALL GAME, Josh ran around with the other kids in their non-satanic costumes. Kyle barked at his players because it was the closest they'd come to losing that season, but Drew threw for a twenty-five-yard touchdown to win the game with less than fifteen seconds left on the clock.

When we arrived at the church after the game, Kyle's jaw dropped. "Did you help with this?" There was a maze of angel-carved pumpkins lighting up the churchyard, a dunk tank (that my dad was going to sit in), food, and lots of games.

"I made the caramel apples. But my mom, Gabby, and some other ladies did the rest. I've been busy playing Nurse Jacobson to Mr. Collins."

He smirked at me as we opened the truck doors, and Cookie Monster hopped out.

A half hour later, most of the football team, along with half the town filled the churchyard to play games in honor of "fall" instead of Satan's holiday.

It was all a little weird, but I was used to Jesus being infused into everything, often in a peculiar way.

"Want to be my partner in the three-legged race?" Drew asked, playfully draping his arm around me.

"Um ..." I nervously smiled while looking for Kyle.

He was pitching baseballs at the dunk tank with his good arm, and on his second attempt, he hit the target, and my dad fell into the water.

I laughed.

"Coming, Eve?" Drew pulled me toward the starting line.

"Uh ... sure." I stood next to him while he tied our legs together.

When Kelley Ross yelled, "GO!" Drew and I took off running.

It wasn't our first three-legged race. We were town champions. A well-oiled machine. However, after crossing the finish line way ahead of everyone else, Drew tripped, or he seemed to because the next thing I knew, he was on the ground with me on top of him.

"I miss you," he said with a huge grin, our faces a few inches apart.

"I don't know how I feel about my star player trying to run with his leg tied to someone else. Reckless behavior like this could end your football career before it starts."

I rolled off Drew when I heard Kyle's voice, my hands quickly untying our legs.

"Jeez, Coach, we were having a moment," Drew said jokingly.

But when I jumped to my feet and looked at Kyle, his scowl didn't convey humor.

"Eve Jacobson, you should see if your mom needs help, check on Cookie Monster, say a prayer ..." A little evil resided in Kyle's eyes.

I held his gaze for a long moment, a silent standoff.

He jerked his head. "Run along."

Run along?

That was something one said to a child. I wasn't a child. I was the *woman* who had been making his meals, bathing him, taking care of his son, sewing a costume, and working a full-time job. How dare he tell me to *run along*.

"Trouble in paradise?" Erin asked as I pulled a container of apples out from under the food table to refill the tray while she rinsed out paintbrushes at the table next to me. Since she was artsy, she volunteered to do face paintings.

"Coach Collins likes to treat me like a child when he's jealous of a seventeen-year-old."

"I have to pee!" Josh ran up to me and pulled on my hand. "I'm stuck." He reached for his buttons.

"Oh, dear. Let me—"

"Nooo ..." he grabbed his crotch.

I pulled the costume down his body, but he'd already wet himself.

"My costume," he said with a quivering lower lip and big tears.

"Oh, buddy. I'm sorry. Let's get you cleaned up." I looked around for Kyle.

He was talking to some of the players' parents, so I led Josh into the church. It was dimly lit because Dad only had it open for people to use the restrooms.

"Now w-we have to g-go," Josh said, sniffling.

"Yes, but we'll do something fun to make up for it. Okay?"

"What? I wanted t-to play g-games."

I closed the restroom door, helped him out of his soiled clothes, washed him off, and then pulled off my hoodie and put it on him. It nearly reached his ankles.

"Listen, sweet boy." I lowered before him and cradled his face, wiping his tears with my thumbs. "I'm going to wash your costume tonight. Then tomorrow, we'll do something extra special. Okay?"

He sniffled. "Will I get to wear my costume?"

"Absolutely." I kissed his forehead. "Now"—I pulled the hood over his head—"Let's sneak out. No one will know it's you." I took his hand and led him out of the church.

As we headed toward the truck, Kyle spotted us and made his way toward it too. "What are you—" he started to ask before he eyed the wadded costume in my other hand.

"Sorry, Dad," Josh mumbled with his head down.

I wrinkled my nose. "It was my fault. I put the buttons in the back."

Kyle shook his head. "It was an accident. Nobody's fault." He opened the door, and I helped Josh into the back seat. "You should have told me. I would have dealt with him."

"Why? You think I'm not capable?" I walked around to the driver's door.

"No," he said when I climbed into his truck and started it. "Is everything okay?"

"Why wouldn't it be?" I put the truck into reverse.

"Watch out for—"

Thunk!

"Oh my gosh!" I covered my mouth.

Kyle closed his eyes for a second.

"What happened?" Josh asked.

"We hit a utility pole," Kyle said slowly while I put the truck in *Park* and jumped out.

"Eve Marie Jacobson!" Mom cried, running toward the truck.

It wasn't just her. Everyone gathered as though I had run

his truck through the front door of the church. I was so embarrassed.

"Darling, what on earth were you doing?" Dad asked as we surveyed the dented bumper.

Worth noting: It was *barely* a dent.

Still, I wanted to cry, but I didn't. There were too many people. And grown-ups didn't cry when they ran their vehicle into something. But it wasn't my vehicle. It was Kyle's truck.

"We'll get it handled, Kyle. I'm so sorry about that. Eve won't see her paycheck for quite some time," Dad said.

Barely. A. Dent!

"It's fine. It was an accident," Kyle murmured, rubbing the back of his neck while staring at the bumper.

I hung my head.

"You broke his arm, and now Eve dented his bumper," Mom said to my dad. "I bet he regrets moving here."

"Maybe it's best if someone else drives you," Dad said.

"Eve's got it," Kyle replied, opening the passenger's door.

Keeping my head bowed, I sulked to the door and climbed into the truck. "I'm *so* sorry," I muttered, starting the truck and putting it in *Drive*.

Kyle sighed. "It was an accident."

That was all he said the rest of the way to his house.

Josh and I headed straight upstairs and Kyle let the dog out. I made sure Josh took a shower before putting on his jammies and brushing his teeth.

"What story do you want tonight, buddy?" Kyle asked as I straightened the covers on Josh's bed.

"This one!" Josh held up a book and Clifford jumped onto the bed.

"I'm going to make a grocery list," I said without looking at Kyle.

"You can go home if you want," he said.

My heart cracked, each chamber barely holding together. And I swallowed past the rush of emotions.

"I just mean, you've been living out of a backpack. Tomorrow is Saturday. Josh will sleep in a bit, and so will I."

I returned a slight nod, heading toward the stairs.

"Eve?"

I continued down the stairs.

"Eve, don't leave until I'm done reading to Josh."

I wasn't going to stay. Everything inside of me wanted to run home, even if it meant getting a lecture from my parents on my driving. But I stared at the refrigerator when I grabbed my purse from the kitchen counter and decided to look for something to take the edge off.

When Kyle found me on his deck, I had already downed one-and-a-half cans of beer to soothe my nerves, and his little radio by the door played U2's "I Still Haven't Found What I'm Looking For."

"Think that's a good idea?" he asked, sitting in the rocker beside me.

I stared out at the clear autumn sky with a glitter of stars. "Does it matter if my ideas are good?"

"It's a small dent, Eve. I don't expect you to hand over your paycheck."

"I know it was a small dent, and I might not have hit the pole had you not treated me like a child in front of Drew and everyone else. I have been doing my very best to prove that I'm not a child. I didn't mean to fall on him, but our legs were tied together. And ..." I leaned my head back and closed my eyes with a giggle that stole my thunder. "I don't remember where I was going with that."

He reached for my beer, and my eyes snapped open as I tightened my grip.

"It's my beer." He smirked.

"I earned it."

His gaze shifted to the hoodie I borrowed from his closet since Josh had mine, which needed washing. "And the hoodie?"

"I earned it too," I said, trying to keep from grinning. "But I'll let you have the rest of my beer if *you* earn it back." I wasn't fully drunk, but my inhibitions were lower. After setting the beer on the floor, I stood and removed my jeans and underwear, but his long sweatshirt hung mid-thigh keeping me covered.

As luck or Satan would have it, the next song that came on the radio was George Michael's "I Want Your Sex."

One of Kyle's brows quirked up his forehead, and I knew what he was thinking.

I nodded to the beer before sitting down. "I don't care which one you have first." I rested one foot on the rocker's edge, and then the other, as I leaned back.

Kyle didn't jump out of his seat right away. He took his time, arching his back for a stretch before standing.

Without that liquid courage, I wouldn't have been able to hold his gaze as his lust-filled eyes flitted along my body. My nerves would have eaten me alive knowing my legs were spread, everything on display for him to see.

I felt confident, sexy, and deserving of what he was lowering to his knees to do.

The music.

The lyrics.

It was all so perfect.

He gripped my ankle with his good hand and lifted my leg, resting it on the chair's arm.

The cool evening air found my sensitive flesh, and I sucked in a tiny breath and trapped my lip between my teeth. George Michael and one and a half beers were the perfect combination to keep me from comparing myself to the centerfolds under Kyle's mattress or any of the women in town who were pining for him. One and a half beers made me feel powerful.

He picked up the beer, and I waited for him to drink it or do something kinky, like pour it between my legs and lick it off.

"Baby," he tipped the beer, letting the rest spill over the railing, "the only thing I need in my veins is you."

The can clinked, and his head bowed. He held the inside of my thigh as he kissed me, teased me with his tongue, and stole my breath.

"God ..." I whispered, closing my eyes while my other heel pressed harder into the chair. My fingernails scraped along the wood arms.

The song lyrics seduced me. He seduced me.

Thoughts collided with feelings and mind-blowing sensations. I couldn't tell if I was thinking the words "don't ever stop" or if I was chanting them aloud.

I'd spent weeks trying to please everyone else. It was my turn. I wanted someone to care for me, even for only a few *amazing* minutes.

Chapter Thirty

Phil Collins, "In the Air Tonight"

Eve

AFTER WHAT I fondly dubbed "the best beer and a half of my life," I accepted Kyle's suggestion to sleep at home because I wanted to take Grandma Bonnie breakfast, and she was an early riser. Just as I took the apple strudel out of the oven to cool a few minutes before seven, my mom pulled up to shit on my day.

"I'm glad you came home last night," she said, tightening her robe's sash.

"Yeah, well, I didn't want to wake Josh or Kyle by leaving their house this morning." I pulled the hot pads off my hands and shut off the oven.

"There's been some chattering around town, specifically among our church family."

"About?" I poured myself a glass of orange juice while I waited for the strudel to cool.

Mom filled the coffee pot with water. "It's silly, really. But we can't have people jumping to conclusions no matter how ridiculous they are."

"Jumping to conclusions about what?"

"You and Kyle." She rolled her eyes and measured the coffee grounds.

I paused my juice glass an inch from my lips. "Me and Kyle?"

"I know. I know. It's so disappointing that people's minds jump to such impure and, frankly, offensive ideas. You're helping Kyle and Josh out. You've been *so* amazing. And we couldn't be more proud of you." She waved her hand in the air. "Sure, there was the mishap last night, but your dad thinks Arnold Wells will fix it in exchange for a couple of your pies. My point is, as nonsensical as the rumors are, your dad and I have decided you need to sleep at home, and if there's a concern about Josh needing help, then he can sleep here in Sarah's room until Kyle's arm is better."

"Um ..." I cleared my throat, "what specifically are they saying?"

"He's not married, and you're a beautiful *young* woman. They don't see you two as family the way we do. But your father is the pastor, so appearances matter."

"And yet, you still wear reinforced pantyhose with open-toed shoes."

"Stop it, Eve." She laughed. "I'm not talking about that kind of appearance."

I tore off a piece of foil to cover the strudel. "Well, the rumors are correct. Kyle and I are having hot sex, a torrid, scandalous affair. We can't keep our hands off each other. I've never felt more like a woman than I do with him." I shot her a toothy grin.

Mom rolled her eyes. "Can you be serious for two seconds?"

"I am being serious. Do you have any idea how good it feels to get this off my chest?" I dramatically placed my hand over my heart and sighed.

"Eve Marie Jacobson, don't even joke about something like that. You know how hard it was on me when your father found out about Sarah's secret relationship. I cried myself to sleep for weeks. Your dad and I were at each other's throats. I didn't know if we'd survive it. So before you do something stupid like that, let me know. I'll slit my wrists or drive my car off a bridge first, so I don't have to deal with the fallout again."

I kept it together on the outside but fell apart on the inside. I opened my mouth to remind her that suicide was a sin but quickly clamped my jaw shut. When my father kicked Sarah out of the house, I spent most evenings drinking by the creek or locked in my room. It was the best way to drown out my parents fighting. And they never fought in the house (with my sisters and I in earshot) *until* the Sarah incident.

I laughed nervously. "You wouldn't really take your own life, would you?"

She sipped her coffee. "I pray not. But nobody thought Debbie Rice would take her life when she found out about her husband's affair." She slowly shook her head. "We're all human. We're all sinners. And sometimes life feels unbearable no matter how many prayers one says." She gave me a sad smile. "I never imagined feeling like I did after your dad made Sarah leave. Maybe God gave me that trial so I would have greater compassion for others."

"You know Sarah is happy now. And Dad has forgiven

her. Maybe God gave him that experience to have more compassion for his other two daughters."

She took another sip before nodding. "Hmm … perhaps. Your father is a Godly man. Loving and forgiving. But he's also a father with raw emotions. So let's just play it safe and not test him like Sarah did." She set her mug on the counter. "Anyway, I'm glad you came home last night. If anyone says something, I'll make sure they know you're not staying at Kyle's place anymore because he doesn't need you during the night."

I offered a reluctant smile and a tiny nod.

"HAVE you ever thought about taking your own life?" I asked Grandma Bonnie as she ate her apple strudel while I wound the yarn from the partially crocheted scarf that she decided to abandon.

She stopped eating mid-chew. "Eve," she mumbled before swallowing. "What is going on?"

I shook my head. "I'm not suicidal."

"But you know someone who is?"

"No. Well, it was something Mom said this morning. She made me think that if I made Dad upset in the way Sarah did, she'd slit her wrists or drive off a bridge. At first, I thought she was kidding, but I'm not so sure."

Grandma frowned. "She's taken the role of wife too far. The 'love, honor, and *obey*' is too much. She feels responsible for your father's success and happiness—and you girls' too. When Sarah fell in love, your mom felt it was her fault that Sarah didn't choose a man your father approved of. She takes the blame for everything that's perceived as wrong. But she never takes credit for your successes. Being a wife and mother is a hard balance between unimaginable joy and complete insanity. You get stretched so thin some days, it feels like there's nothing left to hold yourself together. But that's not your problem. I'll talk with her."

"Don't tell her I said anything."

"I won't. I'll just check in on her. That's what mothers do."

"I want to tell my parents about Kyle and me, but if Dad reacts badly, which he will, and my mom cries herself to sleep every night like she did with Sarah, and she decides to take her life ..." I swallowed hard and blinked back my emotions. "It would be—"

"Her own fault."

I shook my head. "It doesn't matter. I don't want her ever to be that sad again. It's not about blame; it's just that I love her. And I know that—" I stopped. It was easy to forget that I was talking to my mom's mother.

"You know what?"

I shook my head. "Nothing."

"I love her too, dear. That's why I'm going to talk to her. It's not fair for her to feel responsible for anyone's happiness but her own. And that's what you need to remember too. Understood?"

"Yeah," I whispered.

ON MY WAY HOME, I pulled into the gas station and used the phone booth to make a collect call.

Sarah accepted the charges.

"Why are you calling me collect?" She laughed.

"Because if Dad sees it on our phone bill, he'll ask why I called you."

"What's going on that couldn't wait until Thanksgiving?" she asked.

"I'm in love with a man who's twenty-eight."

Silence.

"Sarah?"

"Um, yeah. I'm here. That's ten years."

I rolled my eyes. "I'm aware."

"Do Mom and Dad know?"

"What do you think?"

"Are you still living at home?"

"Yes," I said.

"Then I think you haven't told them."

I leaned against the side of the phone booth. "Did you know Mom was so upset over Dad kicking you out that she felt suicidal?"

"What?"

"She didn't say those exact words, but it was implied."

"Oh my gosh," she whispered.

"Ask me who I love."

"Do I want to know?"

"Did Mom tell you about the new neighbor?"

"Fred's brother?"

"Yeah."

"Well, it's him."

"Nooo ..."

I pinched the bridge of my nose. "Yup."

"And he likes you?"

"He loves me."

"Oh, Eve."

"Don't act like it's okay for you to fall for someone who everyone else thinks is the wrong person, but I—"

"Eve, I wasn't going to say that. I just feel bad for you because it sucks to have to choose between your family and the man you love. And don't get upset with me for asking, but are you sure it's love? Have you done *stuff* with him?"

"Sex?" I chuckled because Sarah didn't talk about sex as much as I did. "Yes. Amazing sex."

"Are you being smart?"

"As smart as a B-average girl can be."

"You've always excelled at being a smart *ass*," she said.

"We use condoms."

"I don't know what to tell you. There was a lot involved with Dad finding out about us, but when he finds out you're sleeping with Fred's brother, I think it could be worse because he's *ten* years older, not six. And he has a child, right?"

"A son. Josh. He's five. I love Josh so much."

"Who are you?" She laughed.

"I know I'm eighteen, but since Kyle and Josh moved in, I've grown up a lot."

"No longer sneaking alcohol?"

"Listen, *grown-ups* drink alcohol."

"Alcoholics drink alcohol like you."

"I'm not an alcoholic."

"Are you sure?"

"*Anyway,* as I was saying. I'm not just scared of Mom and Dad finding out because I'll get kicked out of the house. I'm scared that Mom will get really low again, but this time what if she tries to kill herself?"

"Eve, I think you're overreacting. Mom is not the type of person to do that."

I frowned. It was easy for her to say. She didn't know what I knew. I opened my mouth to tell her because I'd carried the burden alone for too long, but the words clogged in my throat.

"Eve?"

I quickly wiped my tears. "I'm here. Um, I should go so you don't have a big phone bill."

"It's fine. You can call collect anytime. And I think you need to tell them. Keeping secrets is painful, and covering them up only sets you up for more trouble and more lies. Learn from my experience. Okay?"

"Yeah," I whispered.

"Are you okay?"

"Mm-hmm."

"Are you sure?"

"Yeah," I managed without my voice cracking.

"Tell everyone 'hi' and we'll see them at Thanksgiving."

I cleared my throat. "I can't, stupid. I'm calling you collect from a phone booth so that nobody knows about our call."

"Oh." She giggled. "True. Sorry. See you in a few weeks then."

"Bye."

I wasn't that girl. The one who carried hidden scars from my past. As I hung up the phone and opened the door, I pulled in a long breath and let it out while heading to my car and repeating it again.

I wasn't that girl.

Chapter Thirty-One

Pat Benatar, "Love is a Battlefield"

Eve

"Hey, we thought you might be taking the night off. So I've managed to make a frozen pizza with one arm," Kyle said when I stepped inside the back door. "As long as I can take it out of the oven with one hand."

"I'll help!" Josh ran toward the oven with a hot pad in his hands.

"Stand back, buddy," Kyle said, opening the oven. "And keep Clifford back too."

"I've got it." I set my Gatorade bottle on the counter and took the cookie sheet from Kyle. Then I used the spatula to scoot the pizza onto it. "Oh!"

"Josh!" Kyle yelled as I bumped into him, and the pizza slid off the cookie sheet.

A blood-curdling scream filled the room.

"Dammit!" Kyle pulled Josh toward the sink and lifted him up.

"Eve, turn on the cold water."

I stood stunned, staring at the hot pizza sauce and cheese burning Josh's arm.

"EVE!" Kyle yelled.

I jumped and turned on the water.

Josh screamed.

"I'm so sorry," I said, but it was barely a whisper because I couldn't believe what had happened.

"We have to go to the hospital. It'll be okay, buddy," Kyle said.

"Eve, grab a clean towel."

I stared at the burned skin along Josh's arm.

"Eve!"

My gaze snapped from Josh's arm to Kyle's face.

That's when we made eye contact.

Kyle frowned. "Give me the goddamn towel, Eve!"

I handed him the towel as Josh cried uncontrollably.

"Look at me," Kyle said, wrapping Josh's arm in the towel.

Everything felt like a bad dream. His cries pierced my ears.

"Look. At. Me!" Kyle demanded. It took him less than two seconds to get his answer. "Go home."

"But he needs to go to the emergency room," I said.

"Are you going to drive him?"

I winced at his sharp tone and slowly shook my head. "I'll ride in the back seat with him."

"Hold on to my neck, Josh," Kyle instructed Josh to put his good arm around his neck.

"I'll carry him."

"You won't," he said, lifting Josh with his one good arm. "Shut off the oven and grab my keys."

I turned in a slow circle, looking for the keys.

"On the counter, Eve."

I found his keys and opened the door. Then I climbed into the back of the truck with Josh while Kyle drove to the ER.

"Shh ... you'll be okay," I said, trying to soothe Josh on the way.

When we arrived, I helped Josh out of the truck and Kyle held him with his good arm and a grimace on his face. It was clearly hurting his injured arm.

"You can't go inside. Just stay in the truck," he said.

"But—"

"Eve! Just do as I say."

After they disappeared into the entrance, I closed the truck door and wiped my tear-stained cheeks.

What had I done?

Two hours later, Josh had his arm wrapped, a sticker, and a pack of wafer cookies for being a good little patient, and Kyle was tucking him in bed. I stepped back into the hallway.

Kyle closed his door halfway and nodded toward the stairs. When we reached the kitchen, I turned and rested my hands on the counter's edge behind me. Kyle picked up the bottle of Gatorade and held it between his legs to open it. My gaze dropped to the floor as he took a sip.

"Booze," he mumbled. "You can't be drunk around my son. What the hell is wrong with you? You dropped a fucking hot pizza onto him. He has second-degree burns that might leave scars all along his arm. What the hell were you thinking?"

I winced. The first tear landed between my feet, and then the next few hit my socks, disappearing into the white cotton. "I'm sorry," I whispered.

"I'm not asking for an apology. I know you're sorry. It's been on your face all night. I'm asking what you were thinking?"

"I was just taking the edge off."

"Christ," he grumbled. "The edge off what? You're eighteen. You have a home and food on the table. You have a family who loves you. A job. Friends. You have me and Josh. Please, *please* tell me what fucking edge you're taking off?"

I wiped my tears and sniffled. "It's us. I'm tired of keeping us a secret."

"I can't do this tonight. You're all over the goddamn place. One minute, you're dying to tell everyone, the next you're not. Just fucking tell them." He rubbed his temples.

"I can't," I whispered.

"Whatever. Then I'll tell them. Just not tonight. I need you to just go."

I shook my head. "You can't."

"Why not?"

My head continued to shake. "It's too much."

"Too much what?"

I lifted my gaze, eyes narrowed. "You don't understand. But it's just more than they can deal with."

He studied me for several seconds before sighing. "Fine. But you can't come to my house intoxicated. Do you understand me?"

I nodded.

"In fact, just stop drinking. You're eighteen, and—"

"Gah!" I clenched my hands into tight fists. "I know! I'm eighteen. I know my age. Everyone knows my age. Would you stop starting every sentence with my age? If it's such a big deal to you then break up with me. Go be with someone whose age you're not embarrassed about."

"I'm bringing up your age because it's relevant to our conversation about your drinking."

"Welp," I said, holding my hands out to the side, "I'm done drinking. I'm not smoking. No drugs. I won't even vote in the presidential election next year if it makes you happy and takes the burden off bringing up my age in every single conversation. Happy?"

Kyle frowned. "My son's upstairs with burns all down his arm. Do you think I'm happy?"

Everything hurt, and everything was my fault.

I pushed off the counter and marched to the door, shoving my feet into my sneakers.

"Eve ..."

I hurried out the door, pounding my feet along the wood planks, down the stairs and toward the hill.

"Eve?" He followed me.

I picked up my pace.

"Stop, Eve! My fucking arm hurts. I'm not running after you."

I didn't want him to run after me. I just wanted to go home and be alone with my feelings and as many sad songs as I could find on the radio.

"Dammit!" he grumbled.

I could hear his footsteps getting closer. He was running.

"Stop!" I yelled when he hooked his fingers into the

waist of my jeans. I swung around, arms flailing to get him to let go of me.

"Ouch! Fuck!" He hugged his slinged arm and buckled at the waist after I accidentally hit it.

"I'm sorry," I mumbled behind the hand I cupped at my mouth. "I'm so sorry."

"You're so stubborn and infuriating," he seethed while standing straight.

Just as I opened my mouth to protest what was probably the truth, he grabbed the back of my head with his right hand, my hair gripped in his fist, and he smashed his mouth to mine.

It was a long kiss. Hard and punishing.

Considering everyone called me stubborn, I melted at his feet every time. I loved his hand in my hair, his tongue in my mouth, and the way he stepped so close to me that his leg wedged between mine.

He ended the kiss as abruptly as it started. "Now you can go home and be mad," he said, turning one-eighty and making his way up the hill to his house.

After I caught my breath, I sprinted home to call Erin and tell her everything.

Chapter Thirty-Two

Patrick Swayze, "She's Like the Wind"

Eve

I WASN'T SHOCKED when Kyle and Josh weren't at church the following morning, but Erin wasn't there either. I needed her more than I had ever needed my best friend. After church, Gabby and I picked up Grandma Bonnie for dinner, and I couldn't tell her, either, because I wasn't ready for Gabby to know about Josh's burns.

"Hey," I said to Kyle and Josh sitting on the sofa while Mom and Gabby set the table for dinner. I didn't expect to see them since they hadn't been at church.

They were quite the pair: Kyle with his sling (because of my dad) and Josh with his arm bandaged (because of me). Did they tell my parents that I was responsible for Josh's injury?

Kyle smiled.

"Eve, you didn't mention the pizza accident," Mom said, placing the pot roast in the center of the table.

"Uh ..." My eyes ping-ponged between Kyle and my mom.

"I told her how I accidentally bumped you, which made you bump into Josh, and it was all just an unfortunate accident," Kyle said.

Josh was too busy playing with one of his Matchbox cars, running it along his leg, to dispute the false story.

"Yeah," I murmured, giving Kyle a thank-you smile.

"Let's eat, everyone. I just need to grab the bowl of green beans," Mom said as my family gathered around the table.

I lifted Josh onto his booster seat, then squatted in front of him before pushing his chair in. "I'm so sorry," I said, getting choked up.

What if the pizza had landed on his face? What if it did leave a permanent scar and he'd always look at it and think of what I did to him.

"I wish I could make your owie all better with a kiss." I gently pressed my lips to the bandaged area on his arm.

Kyle smiled at me as everyone sat around the table.

Mom held the bowl of green beans, waiting for me to move so she could set them on the table. "Aw, kisses make boo-boos better, don't they, Josh?" Mom asked as I stood.

Josh nodded. "Like Daddy made Eve's boo-boo better with a kiss."

I laughed a little. "What are you talking about, silly?" I stood to scoot in his chair without making eye contact. "I don't have any boo-boos." I was a little uneasy, and I felt everyone else's unease, too, but I brushed it off with a little chuckle and no eye contact.

Then a five-year-old imploded my entire world in ways I

could never have imagined in my wildest dreams. It was the most unintentional revenge.

"Daddy kissed your boo-boo right here," he pointed between his legs, "on the deck."

Crash!

Mom dropped the ceramic bowl of green beans onto the wood floor.

"Uh, oh," Josh said, leaning over the side of his booster seat to see the mess.

No one said anything or even moved a muscle.

I laughed to break the silence. Laughter was good. It was my friend. Why wasn't anyone else laughing at Josh's nonsense.

He saw us! Did he know what we were doing?

"That's uh ... silly." I said, staring at the beans on the floor while scratching the back of my neck. "I'll grab a broom and dust pan." I risked a quick glance at the faces around me.

Gabby's lips pressed together, eyes wide.

Grandma Bonnie's expression bled sympathy.

Dad squinted at me and then Kyle as if the math wasn't adding up. I hoped Kyle could help him with that since math wasn't my thing.

But it was my mom's livid expression, clenched jaw, and tears in her red eyes that slayed me.

I hurried into the kitchen and knocked over a few bottles of cleaner under the sink to reach the dust pan and small hand broom. When I stood, Mom was in my space.

She grabbed my wrist.

I winced as she dug her nails into my skin, and I could feel her whole body shaking.

"What have you done?" she asked, voice quivering.

I quickly shook my head. "I—"

"Don't you dare lie to me," she seethed.

As she blinked, releasing angry tears, my eyes burned with some impending grief and guilt, but mostly fear. I wasn't worried about my fate, but I was terrified of hers.

The back door slammed shut, and my gaze shot in that direction. It had to be my dad and Kyle. Out of the corner of my eye, I caught Gabby carrying Josh to the front door, probably taking him home to protect him from the fallout. When that door clicked shut behind them, Grandma stepped into the kitchen.

"Eve, give me a moment with your mom," she said.

"Mother, this is none of your business," my mom said, with her claws still planted into my wrist.

Grandma gently rested her hand on my mom's until she released me.

"Eve, I've got this," Grandma said to me.

I wanted to tell my mom it was my fault.

Confess my sins.

I wanted to beg her not to slit her wrists or drive the car off a bridge.

Or take a whole bottle of pills.

Instead, I headed to the front door. My vision blurred behind my tears as I held up my dress and slid my feet into my old cowboy boots. By the time I ran down the front porch stairs, Gabby and Josh were way past the orchard. I could hear my dad and Kyle arguing out back, but I couldn't make out the exact words. I kicked the planter off the milk box and grabbed a bottle of vodka. Then I headed to the creek, where I followed it past our property to the hut Kyle built for me.

I loved Kyle and Josh beyond anything my young heart could have ever imagined, but as I took drink after drink of the liquid that burned my throat, all I wanted was for it all to be a bad dream.

I wished Kyle and Josh never moved to Devil's Head.

And then I wished I was never born.

Mom should have taken that bottle of pills when she was pregnant with me instead of the pregnancy she ended after Gabby.

Feeling responsible for someone else's will to live was the worst fucking thing in the world.

I WOKE up in the hospital with my mom in a chair next to my bed, bent over, her cheek resting on my hand. There was an IV in my other arm and an oxygen mask on my face. Dad was staring out the window with his hands in his pockets. I gingerly lifted my arm with the IV in it to pull the oxygen mask off my face.

Mom quickly lifted her head. "Eve," she said with a breath of relief.

Dad turned.

"What happened?" I whispered.

Mom batted away her tears before they made it down her face. "You—" she choked and had to clear her throat.

"You poisoned yourself with alcohol," Dad said with less emotion, resting his hand on my mom's shoulder as she gently sobbed. "You could have died." He narrowed his eyes, displaying a hint of pain. "That dog— that you were supposed to get rid of—led Kyle to you. He carried you to his house, and an ambulance brought you here."

Kyle carried me? I tried to imagine it. He must have hoisted me over his shoulder with only one arm to steady me.

Then he had to carry me up a long hill to get back to his house.

I was an awful person.

"We're taking you to St. Louis tomorrow," Dad said.

"For what?" I whispered, and it made my mom break down with a new round of tears.

"For thirty days of treatment at a rehab facility," Dad replied.

"What?" My head rolled side to side. "No. I don't need that. I was upset. I'm fine. I don't have a problem. Please. No. Just—"

Dad rested his hand on my leg. "If you go, you'll have a home to return to. If you don't, then you're on your own."

It was happening again—another Jacobson girl being kicked out of the house for falling in love with the wrong guy.

"I'll stay with Kyle," I said.

"Kyle's moving back to Colorado at the end of the semester," Dad said.

All the oxygen left my lungs; it felt like it left the room.

"What? No. I love him."

"Eve, you are the most indecisive young woman. You have no idea what you want to do with your life. You have a substance addiction. And you're eighteen. I'm not sure you know what love is," Dad said. "Kyle is an infatuation. He misled you. And I hold him just as accountable, if not more than you, for everything that's happened."

I started to say something but stopped before the words escaped because I looked at my mom's exhausted face and red, lifeless eyes. Was I next in line to sacrifice my happiness for the well-being of others?

"Okay," I whispered.

Chapter Thirty-Three

White Lion, "When the Children Cry"

Eve

"WHAT'S THIS?" I asked the next day after getting discharged from the hospital. There was a bag in the back seat.

Dad started the car. "A few things to get you by for the next thirty days."

Mom shot me a sad smile over her shoulder.

"Uh ..." I chuckled. "We're not going home first? What about Thanksgiving? This is happening *now*?"

"Addiction doesn't care about holidays, Eve. This way you'll be home by Christmas."

I didn't have an addiction. What was happening? I thought it was a threat, a test to see how I'd react. I kept my mouth shut the previous day. It wasn't fair.

"I didn't get to talk to Erin or Grandma. I didn't get to say goodbye to ... Josh."

"It's for the best, honey," Mom said.

"How is not saying goodbye for the best? Does Erin even know I was in the hospital?"

My parents shared a look.

"To help you save face, we're telling anyone who asks, that you are on a mission trip." Dad glanced at me in the rearview mirror.

"You're lying to people?"

"We're protecting you," Mom said.

"From what or who?"

I looked out my window and quickly batted away my tears. The longest I'd been away from home was two weeks, and that was with friends and adults from the church who I knew. I wasn't ripped away from my life and everyone I knew for a month over Thanksgiving.

They were protecting themselves.

Erin would know it was a lie. The truth would come out. And what about Kyle? He was okay with letting me leave? Of course he was. After all, he was taking Josh back to Colorado.

I envied Sarah for getting the hell out of Devil's Head. I envied her for falling for someone who put her first above everything and everyone else in the world.

For the rest of the trip to St. Louis, no one said a word. My heart ached a little more with each passing mile, and my eyes never stopped leaking painful tears.

"We'll get you checked in, and be back to visit before Thanksgiving," Dad said, opening his door.

I grabbed my bag and climbed out. "Don't bother. I don't want to see you." I headed toward the entrance.

"Eve," Mom said, following me.

I whipped around right before reaching the door. "I'm

doing this for you. Only you. So don't forget it. And don't do anything stupid and selfish like slitting your wrists or driving off a bridge."

"Eve," Dad said in a sharp tone.

Mom swallowed hard and blinked back her tears.

I ignored my dad.

"Eve," Mom whispered.

"Just answer me. Do we have a deal?"

She slowly nodded.

"Great. Let the fun begin." I opened the door and headed for the front desk.

"Can I help you?" A smiley blonde asked.

"Eve Jacobson," my dad said.

I didn't make eye contact with anyone. The lady took me through a long list of questions. I had to consent to being admitted because I was eighteen. *And* I could leave whenever I wanted to leave.

But the look on my dad's face was a reminder that if I left early, I wouldn't be welcomed home.

My parents left me with hugs and whispered "I love yous." Then I was escorted to another room where they went through all of my belongings.

I fucking hated my life.

DESPITE CRYING myself to sleep every night, the people at the rehab facility were friendly. It was the kind of prison I imagined convicted celebrities went to. I got outdoor time every day and three square meals.

The surprising bonus was the therapy sessions, group

and individual. There were some really messed up people in the group sessions.

"Eve, would you like to add anything today?" the therapist asked after I stayed silent for the first week.

On one hand, it felt weird sharing intimate family details with strangers, but I also thought it might feel freeing to bounce my woes off people who wouldn't take sides because they didn't know me or my family.

"My name is Eve, but you already know that." I wrinkled my nose while tugging at the arms of my sweatshirt. "I guess I'm one week sober." I shrugged because I had gone much longer than a week without alcohol.

I wasn't an addict. But celebrating sobriety seemed to be the theme, so I went with it.

"I started drinking when I was fourteen. I came home early from a friend's house, and I overheard my mom and dad arguing in their bedroom. My mom was crying. My dad was like, 'What have you done?' And my mom said she couldn't do it. He said, 'Do what?' And the next thing I heard was him whispering, 'You're pregnant?' She said it was too much. She didn't want four kids, and she knew it was awful and sinful, but raising three girls, two years apart, and being a pastor's wife who took care of the congregation like an extension of our own family was too much. Dad asked if she took the whole bottle of pills and said she could die. She said ..." I fought the unexpected rush of emotions.

Their argument had played in my head too many times to count. It usually made me angry. But this was the first time I tried to say the words out loud.

I cleared my throat, offering a sheepish smile as I blotted the corners of my eyes. The group of eight offered nothing but sympathetic looks.

"She said she'd rather die than start all over again." Scraping my teeth over my bottom lip, I stared at my lap. "And I wondered, why? Then I thought of all the times she told me I was going to be the death of her. And I couldn't remember her ever saying that to my sisters. So I've always felt it was me. I was the child who made her think that death would be preferable to having a fourth child. And had she waited any longer to get pregnant with my younger sister, she might have tried to end that pregnancy too. But I was two when my younger sister was born, so I must not have been awful yet."

I laughed, scratching my head and glancing around the windowless room. "Sorry. That was a lot, and I still haven't explained the alcohol part."

"It's fine, Eve," the therapist said. "And if you don't want to share everything today, you don't have to."

"I feel like I'm almost there, so why quit now?"

She nodded and smiled.

"My mom spent several days in the hospital or somewhere. I don't know. We weren't allowed to see her. Dad said she was having 'routine testing.' But that's all the information he gave us. When mom returned home, she was herself. They didn't mention the pills or a baby. And after a few months, I realized there was no baby. Not anymore. Then I overheard some older kids from school talking about their hangout spot in the woods not too far from my house. I knew they were drinking, and one of them, who had recently lost his dad, said life didn't suck after a few drinks. The next weekend, I had my first drink. And he was right, life didn't suck as much after a few drinks."

"It's not your fault," one of the other patients said. She was an older lady with weary eyes but a kind smile. "I have four kids. Great kids. But by the fourth I was past the point in my life where I felt like I wanted to change diapers or chase a toddler. My third child was already sixteen. The idea of starting the eighteen-year process all over again was unimaginable. But I did it. However, I don't blame any woman who doesn't feel like she can. And I'm sure your mom wasn't thinking of you when she took those pills."

She didn't know my mom, but I wanted to believe her.

"Thank you," I whispered.

"Do you have family coming for Thanksgiving?" A guy who looked close to my dad's age asked as I sat on a park bench in the courtyard and watched two squirrels.

"I doubt it."

He gestured to the bench.

I nodded and scooted over to make room for him. He sat next to me and lit a cigarette.

"Can you have that here?" I asked.

"Yeah." He took a puff and blew out the smoke. "They want me to get better, not kill myself." He laughed.

I grinned.

"I'm Raymond," he said, offering me the cigarette.

I shook my head. "I don't smoke."

He wiggled it closer to my hand. "But you could."

I stared at it. "I have getting my ears pierced, bangs cut, and a perm on my list before smoking." I took the cigarette. "But I bet there's not a salon in this place."

He laughed.

I took a puff and instantly coughed, handing the cigarette back to him.

"It's glorious, isn't it?" he asked.

"It's not really." I wrinkled my nose.

"It'll grow on you."

"But what does it do for me?"

"Keeps you from being hungry."

I shrugged. "I'm not fat. Who cares? I like food. I'm an excellent cook and baker."

"No shit?" He gazed at me.

"No shit," I chuckled.

His lips pursed as he took another long puff.

"How long have you been here?" I asked.

Raymond twisted his lips and turned his head to blow the smoke away from me. "Seventy-two days. But who's counting?"

"I thought this was a thirty-day program?"

"I suppose it depends on what you're here for."

I brought a knee to my chest and hugged it. "What are you here for?"

"You name it. I took it. There's not much I haven't swallowed, snorted, or shot up my veins. What about you? Wait, let me guess. I'm pretty good at this." He angled his body toward mine, eyes narrowed. "You look like a coke girl."

"Cocaine?" My head jutted backward. "No." I laughed. "Supposedly alcohol, but I think I'm here as a punishment for having sex with my dad's best friend's younger brother."

"How old are you?" He took another drag.

"Eighteen."

"So how can you be punished for sex if you're a legal adult?"

I frowned. "I live at home, and my father is the preacher of a small town."

"What town?"

"Devil's Head."

"Never heard of it."

I laughed. "No one has."

"Ya get knocked up?"

I shook my head.

"Then what's the problem? Premarital sex?"

"Well, yes, but mostly the ten-year age difference."

"Pfft ... that ain't nothin'. I was with a woman who was fifteen years younger than me. Of course, I was thirty. Did a little time for statutory rape, but when I got out five years later, we got married."

"But you're no longer married?"

He gazed off into the distance, puffing his cigarette. "She died."

"I'm sorry."

"Me too. We had a kid together. That's why I'm here getting my shit together because I just found out I'm going to be a grandpa in five months. It's amazing what you'll do for family."

"Amen," I said.

He looked over at me and smirked. "You're here for your family?"

"I'm here so my mom won't kill herself," I mumbled.

Chapter Thirty-Four

Kim Carnes,
"I'll Be There Where the Heart Is"

Eve

"What brought you here?" My therapist asked in our one-on-one session. He asked me the same question every time.

Every time, I said, "My parents."

And every time, he said, "That's *who*, not what."

"They want me to stop drinking, but really, they want me to stop sleeping with the neighbor. I'm an embarrassment."

That led to the story about my mother swallowing a whole bottle of pills. I always thought we were making progress, but he never stopped asking me what brought me there.

This went on until the week of Thanksgiving. I had ten days before I could check out and be welcomed home.

"What brought you here?" he asked again.

I was feeling down that day. My heart ached for Kyle and Josh. I missed my sisters and Erin. It was a hard week. And I so badly wanted to check myself out and stay at the motel where I probably no longer had a job. When my parents said I couldn't work at that motel for the rest of my life, I never imagined it would be because I'd lose my job.

"Eve?" He brought my attention back to him.

I ran my fingers through my hair and stared out the window at the nearly naked trees. A few dried-up leaves clung to branches. I empathized with them. I was still hanging on, too, but just barely.

Twenty days, and nobody came to visit me. Granted, I told them not to.

"What brought me here ..." I whispered. My parents drove, but I had to check myself into the clinic.

I told myself it was for my mom because I was scared she'd take her life. And that wasn't untrue, but I used it as an excuse for being there. I pretended I didn't need to be there for me—that I didn't have a problem.

Then I thought of Josh.

And I heard his screams.

I saw the look in Kyle's eyes when he realized I'd been drinking.

My lip began to shake, and tears filled my eyes. "I showed up at Kyle's house with a Gatorade bottle of vodka. And I took a hot pizza out of the oven and dropped it on his son." I covered my mouth and shook in silent sobs.

He handed me a tissue, and I wiped my eyes and pressed it to my nose. "H-he was b-burned s-so badly." I sniffled repeatedly, fighting for composure to go on. "And Kyle's arm was still in a sling. So he had to carry Josh to the truck and drive him to the hospital because I couldn't."

"And that's why you're here?" he asked.

The fact that he posed it as a question instead of a statement made me think I had yet to give him the correct response. It was frustrating. If he knew the answer, why didn't he tell me?

My mind only focused on my broken heart.

Twenty days and no one came to visit me.

How could Kyle have carried me in his condition and rescued me but not visited me at the hospital or the rehab center?

"Eve, if this is too much for you today, we don't have to go the whole—"

"I'm here because I almost died." I lifted my gaze to his, no longer attempting to keep up with the tears. "That's what brought me here."

Self-reflection hurt. I looked to everyone else to explain my behavior.

"I'm not addicted to alcohol, but I abuse it. And it's hurting me and others. It robs me of my life, my happiness. *I* did this. It was *my* choice."

He relaxed, removing his glasses and offering me a sad smile as he leaned forward, resting his elbows on his knees. "Yes," he whispered.

More tears escaped as I sat with my thoughts.

Drinking didn't make me feel like an adult. Sobriety did.

THE DAY BEFORE THANKSGIVING, I had my first visitors. When I reached the common area, my girls were waiting for me.

Sarah, Gabby, and Erin stood from the old brown sofa, smiles on their beautiful faces.

I walked toward them and stopped with six feet between us while I looked at the ceiling. "I'm not going to cry. Don't you dare make me cry," I said.

But my words made all three of them laugh ... and then cry.

Sarah hugged me first. "You've got this. Eight more days."

I couldn't speak past my emotions, so I just nodded, not wanting to let her go.

She released me and pressed her hands to my cheeks. "I love you."

I nodded.

Gabby hugged me next. "At least you're not pregnant."

I laughed through my tears.

"Has he said anything to you about me?" I asked.

Gabby stepped back, knowing exactly who I meant by "he." Her smile faded as she shook her head.

I smiled to hide my pain, and I shrugged as if it wasn't a big deal.

"I knew you weren't on a mission trip," Erin said, wrapping me in her arms.

"Of course you did."

She released me and frowned. "I should have known. I knew you drank sometimes, but not—"

I shook my head. "It's not your fault. It's not anyone's fault but my own." I looked around. "Where are Mom and Dad?"

Gabby nodded at Sarah.

"I told them you needed nothing but happiness and good vibes. Let's be honest; they are pretty much the opposite of that," Sarah said, sliding her blond hair over her shoulder.

"True." I chuckled. "Let's go outside." I untied my sweater from my waist and pulled it over my head.

We sat at a picnic table, and it was a little breezy, but the sun was out, and the temperature was close to sixty.

"Will you get served Thanksgiving dinner tomorrow?" Gabby asked.

"Gabbs!" Sarah elbowed her. "We agreed we wouldn't make her feel bad."

"What? I'm just making small talk."

I laughed. "It's fine. I'm sure they'll serve dry turkey, soggy stuffing, and flaked mashed potatoes. But I'm okay. I had a breakthrough in therapy on Monday, and for the first time since I got here, I feel like I need this time away from home. I discovered I have more healing to do than I thought when I arrived."

They couldn't hide their crestfallen faces, and I didn't blame them for not trying harder. I would have had the same reaction had I been in their shoes.

"Smile." I teasingly leaned into Erin before reaching my hands across the table to squeeze my sisters' hands. "I'm making progress. It's a good thing."

"Do you want to tell us anything? We're here for you," Sarah said.

I smiled, squeezing their hands again. "No. But thank you." Early on, I couldn't wait to tell my sisters about our mom and the baby she lost from overdosing. I'd kept it for so many years that I thought the only way to get past it would be to share the burden with them. But I didn't need to share the burden anymore. I needed to let it go. No one deserved that guilt.

"You seem different," Gabby said.

I chuckled. "I hope so. Leaving here the same as I was when I got here will be a huge waste of money for Mom and Dad. As it is, I don't know how they're affording this. Did they ask you for help?" I looked at Sarah.

She shrugged and shook her head.

"Did they have a fundraiser at church?" I asked.

Erin laughed. "That would have required them to tell people."

"True." I rolled my eyes.

Gabby chewed her nails, but she only did it when she was nervous.

"Gabbs?"

She shook her head, but she wouldn't look at me.

"Gabriella," I said again, reaching across the table to pull her hand away from her mouth.

She huffed. "Fine, but you can't tell anyone that you know."

"Know what?" Sarah asked.

"Kyle took money from his savings and gave it to Mom and Dad to pay for it."

"Why didn't they ask me? We would have helped," Sarah said.

Gabby shook her head. "I don't know. I'm just the nosey one at the top of the stairs, eavesdropping on everyone's conversations."

"That's so romantic," Erin said with a dreamy sigh.

"He's moving back to Colorado at the end of the semester. That doesn't feel romantic," I said.

Sarah shot me a sad smile.

"It's an epic kind of love," Erin insisted. "His love for you is unconditional. He doesn't need to be with you to love you and want what's best for you. I think that's *so* romantic."

"It's tragic," Sarah said, wrinkling her nose.

"Why is he leaving?" I asked Gabby.

"How am I supposed to know?"

"Because you're an eavesdropper."

She stared at her non-existent fingernails. "He knows your relationship will get out, and he doesn't want Josh living in a small town where his dad is the center of gossip." Her nose wrinkled. "And Dad threatened to tell the school board."

"What can the school board do?" Sarah asked. "You're not in high school anymore."

"They'd find another reason to fire him." Erin frowned.

"How's Mom?" I asked Gabby.

"Fine. I guess."

"Does she seem depressed? Down? Anything like that?" Sarah eyed me.

"I don't think so. Grandma's been at the house a lot. I think Dad's tired of her being there, but she and Mom have long talks. I don't eavesdrop on them because Grandma talks too slowly. I don't have the patience for it."

Erin snorted.

I was relieved to hear that Grandma Bonnie had been with Mom.

"Well, if she seems depressed or stressed or anything like that, give her a big hug. Okay?"

Gabby squinted for a second before nodding, but Sarah blinked away her tears, and she didn't even know the full story.

"I heard Dad say he talked to the motel manager, and

your job will be waiting for you when you get home," Gabby said.

That surprised me, so I smiled. "That's a relief. But enough about me. Are you a star yet?" I asked Sarah.

And for the next two hours, my girls caught me up on their lives. And I lived vicariously through them until it was time to say goodbye.

Eight days. I could make it.

Chapter Thirty-Five

Journey, "Open Arms"

Eve

As EXPECTED, the turkey was dry, the stuffing was soggy, and the potatoes were instant. But the pumpkin pie was surprisingly delicious.

And the six people gathered around my table were exactly who I needed—sinners with a desire to do better, and a need for other non-judgmental sinners to hold their hand, share space, and let them know they're not alone.

Raymond said the Serenity Prayer before we ate.

After the meal, some of us gathered in the common area to play board games and work on puzzles. I thought I'd spend the day in my room crying and feeling sorry for myself. Instead, I (appropriately) gave thanks for Kyle loving me unconditionally. My parents for doing what they felt was best. And, of course, to God for granting me this new perspective.

For surrounding me with people who care.

And for saving my life.

"My family is here, if you'll excuse me," Raymond said, pushing back in his chair.

I continued to work on the autumn tree puzzle with two other people until they left me to visit with family as well. Finding another piece of the puzzle, I leaned over the table to place it next to an edge piece.

"I colored this for you."

I froze, except for my heart. It lurched into my throat at the sound of Josh's voice. When I inched my head in his direction, he grinned, handing me a picture of an apple orchard and a bouquet of red roses.

"Thank you," I whispered because I could barely speak past the lump of emotion in my throat.

He hugged me, and I closed my eyes while running my hands through his hair. I knew Kyle was standing behind him, but I couldn't look at him.

Not yet.

There weren't enough boxes of tissues in the entire rehab clinic to handle the tears I knew I'd cry when that moment came.

And it came all too quickly because Josh released me, and my gaze lifted.

"Hey, beautiful," Kyle said, unzipping his Carhartt jacket. He no longer had his arm in a sling.

"Hey," I said, but my voice immediately broke, and I cupped a hand at my mouth. I refused to blink, but it didn't matter. The tears freely flowed down my face.

Kyle didn't hesitate for a second before his good hand cupped the side of my face, his thumb smearing my tears before he cradled the back of my head, and his injured arm hooked my waist. I threw my arms around him and buried my face in his neck.

"Oh, baby," he whispered, kissing the top of my head.

Everything at that stupid rehab center peeled away a layer of my skin—the scars and stubborn calluses—until I felt exposed and raw. My time there changed me forever. I had to experience all the emotions from the previous four years without the numbing effect of alcohol. And I wondered what else I robbed myself of feeling completely.

Joy?

Peace?

Love?

"Are you feeling better?" Josh asked.

I released Kyle and wiped my tears while sniffling. Then I turned toward Josh, sitting at the table and looking at the puzzle while he wriggled out of his coat.

"I am," I said with a smile, just above a whisper.

A new round of tears hit hard and fast when I saw Josh's arm and the pink raised scars.

"Are you coming home today?" Josh asked.

My gaze shifted from his arm to him, and I quickly wiped my tears again while shaking my head. "Not yet. But soon. How is your arm?" I sat next to him.

He looked at it. "It's getting better."

"That's good," I said past the lump in my throat.

"The doctor said he'll have minimal to no long-term scars," Kyle said as we sat at the table with Josh.

Was he saying that to make me feel better? It didn't. The sound of Josh screaming would stay in my head forever.

I combed my hair with my fingers. "I wasn't expecting visitors."

Josh rested his elbows on the table and his face in his hands. "You look pretty."

My heart twisted, wringing more tears from my eyes because he was so sweet, and I couldn't stop looking at his arm.

Those scars could have been on his face.

Kyle mimicked Josh's pose and grinned. "I second that opinion."

I blushed and laughed. "Thank you. How's your arm?"

"Better. I'm doing my exercises for it."

My smile faded. "You shouldn't have carried me. That was too much."

Kyle twisted his lips and bobbed his head. "Perhaps it was too much, but it's exactly what I should have done, and that's why I did it. The alternative wasn't an option."

Letting me die.

When Josh shifted his attention to the puzzle again, I curled my hair behind my ears and stared at my hands folded on my lap. "I've been rehearsing so many apologies in my head." I squinted and shook my head. "But you caught me off guard today, and I want to get it right when I say it—"

"Eve, you don't owe anyone an apology for anything."

"I do." I lifted my gaze to his. "I really do. I let my past, my ego, and a million other things lead me down the wrong road. And I blamed everyone except myself. So I need to take responsibility for what I did wrong and the people I hurt." I glanced out the window at the gray, overcast sky. "I fell so hard for you," I whispered.

"You fell?" Josh asked without looking up.

We chuckled. There was too much to say that wasn't for Josh's ears. And I didn't know if I'd ever get to say it. He was leaving, and I was ... well, I didn't know anything beyond that moment. My time at rehab taught me to slow down, be grateful for tiny accomplishments, and not buy tomorrow's problems.

Still, I wanted to ask him what my dad said, if he'd talked to his brother, and if he would miss me.

"Did you have turkey today?" I asked.

"Your mom snuck us two plates filled with turkey and trimmings," Kyle said.

I told myself to be happy for them and not feel slighted by my parents not visiting me with a plate of home-cooked food. I told them not to, but I no longer meant it.

"However, she only brought one piece of pie," he continued. "And she made it abundantly clear the pie was for Josh."

I grinned.

"It was yummy," Josh said, finding a piece to the puzzle.

I nodded. "My mom makes good pie."

"As good as yours?" Kyle lifted an eyebrow.

"Pfft. Of course not." I held a serious face for a few seconds before cracking a grin.

Kyle and I stared at each other for a while without saying anything. I would have given all of my tomorrows to have known what he was thinking.

"Have you made friends?" he asked, breaking the silence.

"Sure. But they can't be lifelong friends. I think it's a bad idea for addicts to be friends. We're all a bunch of bad influences."

He nodded, brow furrowed. "I was a bad influence."

The can of beer in exchange for a blow job.

I didn't mention that in counseling when we discussed people in my life who were enablers of my addiction.

"I hid it well," I said because I didn't blame him, and I didn't want him to blame himself.

"You didn't," he replied.

I didn't argue. What was the point?

"I hear you're moving home." It took *everything* inside of me to bring that up. It was the equivalent of tearing my heart out of my chest and asking Kyle to crush it with his boot.

But it was one of several elephants in the room. Therapy had done a lot for me in three weeks, but my self-preservation instinct still needed some honing.

He focused on Josh and slowly nodded.

"Do you have a new job?" I asked, but I didn't care.

There were more important questions like, were we just a short fling? Was it not really love? Would he ever really forgive me for burning Josh? Were they visiting me because he wanted to see me or because Josh wanted to? Would we keep in touch? Did he regret what we had? Was I worth the chaos of moving to Devil's Head for a few months?

"I'll substitute teach for the rest of the school year and see what comes available for next year."

"We visited Colorado Springs when I was like ten or something," I said. "We rode up to Pikes Peak."

He offered a melancholy smile and a tiny nod. "The Cog Railway. It's pretty fun. I haven't taken Josh yet. Maybe next summer." He leaned forward and helped Josh fit another piece into the puzzle.

"How's my dog? Are you leaving him or taking him?"

Josh giggled. "Clifford is my dog."

Kyle squinted at Josh. "But where does he sleep?"

Josh sighed. "With you." He did the cutest shrug, lifting his hands. "But I don't know why?"

"Josh and I took him pheasant hunting last weekend. I think he's a hunting dog."

I grinned, and it felt good. "Told you."

Kyle's grin mirrored mine. "You did."

I joined in again on the puzzle, and we worked on it for the next half hour, keeping our conversation Josh-friendly.

"When are we going?" Josh said when he was bored with the puzzle.

Kyle looked at his watch. "We can go anytime, buddy. Let's have you use a restroom on the way out."

I stood. "Give me a hug, munchkin."

Josh hugged me, and the small lump in my throat that had been there for their whole visit began to swell. When he released me, I feathered my fingertips over his arm. Josh's gaze followed my touch. Then he looked up at me and smiled while whispering, "I forgive you."

In the next breath, he put on his jacket and turned toward Kyle.

I remained frozen in place, with his dagger of forgiveness lodged into the center of my heart.

"A week to go," Kyle said as I stood straight. "I'm proud of you, Eve."

I nodded since that lump was so thick that words couldn't squeeze past it. I glanced away and pressed the pads of my fingers to the corners of my burning eyes.

No one was keeping me there. I checked myself in, and I could check myself out. And if Kyle would have asked me to leave with him, I would have.

But he didn't.

"Come on, Dad." Josh pulled Kyle's arm.

"Okay, buddy."

I swallowed hard, but I still couldn't breathe. With a

brave smile, I hugged him, but I kept it brief and quickly stepped back, staring at my feet while sliding my hands into my back pockets.

"Let's go, Dad."

Don't move.

Not a blink.

Not a single breath.

Kyle let Josh pull him a few feet closer to the door.

Don't move.

Not a blink.

Not a single breath.

A tear escaped.

And then another. But I kept my head down so he wouldn't see them.

Just as holding it in became unbearable, I slowly lifted my head, hoping they were gone, but I was met with Kyle taking several long strides back to me. He took my face in his hands and kissed me.

I released a sob, gripping his jacket. When the kiss ended, he dragged his lips along my cheek to my ear and whispered, "I fell hard too."

Chapter Thirty-Six

Peter Gabriel, "In Your Eyes"

Kyle

I MADE sure Josh got fastened in the back before I climbed into the driver's seat of my truck and closed the door. Then I started the engine to pull out of the rehab center's visitor parking. My hand wrapped around the gearshift, and I clenched my teeth, every muscle in my body tensing to hold it together. But all I saw was her face covered in tears, her pleading bloodshot eyes, and her quivering lower lip. And I wanted to scoop her up in my arms and take her away from all the pain.

Releasing the gearshift, I fisted my hand at my mouth as my eyes pinched shut, and my body shook with emotion. Everything ached bone-deep, and my heart didn't beat right. It had been the worst three weeks of my life. And that said a lot, considering the mother of my child abandoned us.

But I felt like I had abandoned Eve and didn't know how

to make it right. As much as I wanted to be everything she needed, I wasn't. I failed her, like I had failed Josh. And when we walked into the rehab center, and I saw her for the first time since carrying her unconscious body back to the house, her light didn't shine as bright.

I let that happen.

And for that, I felt undeserving of her and her love.

Had I been her father, I would have wanted me as far away from her as possible too.

"Daddy?" Josh whispered as I tried to make it stop.

The pain.

The tears.

The waves of body-racking agony.

His seat belt clicked when he released it, and he climbed over the seat to get to me, wrapping his arms around my neck. "Don't cry," he said.

And fuck ... if that didn't make me cry even harder.

"Do you have a boo-boo?" he asked.

I found a smile for him as I wiped my eyes. "Yeah," I whispered. "Right here." I pressed the heel of my hand to my chest and rubbed it.

Josh rested one hand on my arm and his other on the steering wheel to bend forward and kiss the spot I just rubbed. "There. All better." He hugged me again.

I wrapped him in my arms and closed my eyes. "Yeah. All better."

Chapter Thirty-Seven

Chicago, "Hard to Say I'm Sorry"

Eve

I DIDN'T WANT my parents to visit me because I was mad at them, but I had the emotional capacity to be equally mad at them for not visiting me.

It was complicated.

And not giving Kyle a piece of pumpkin pie was petty, and not what Jesus would have done.

But they were my transportation back to Devil's Head on the day I walked out the front door of the rehabilitation clinic, so I was about as happy to see them as a cab driver.

"How are you, darling?" Dad asked before hugging me.

"Cured like a ham. Let's go," I said, giving my mom a brief hug as well.

My therapist said it didn't serve me to hold grudges when I left rehab. I needed to think of my relationships starting with a clean slate. While I did owe my parents an apology for my wrongdoings, they weren't innocent in the fallout either. But I knew they would never admit any wrongdoing, making it a little harder for me to be the bigger person and offer an unconditional apology.

"It seemed like a nice place," Mom said, making small talk on the way home.

I stared out the window with the side of my head resting against it. "Yeah. A real resort. I'll have to keep it in mind for a honeymoon destination when I get married."

"I see you didn't lose your sense of humor," she replied.

"I just got it back. When I checked in thirty days ago, I had to leave all prescription meds and sharp objects in a bag, along with all funny business. Just got it back thirty minutes ago."

My parents exchanged a glance. I couldn't see my mom's face, but my dad had a tiny smirk.

I sighed and kept my head to the window. I didn't physically need a drink. No jitters, cold sweats, or racing pulse. But emotionally, the pre-rehab version of me would have been anxious to get home and have a couple drinks to take my mind off Kyle moving.

Leaving me.

Since there was no quick escape for my emotions, I used the ride home as an opportunity to cross an apology off my list.

But the wrong thing came out when I opened my mouth to speak. "I'm sorry if I'm the reason you didn't want that fourth child."

That fourth child left no room for anything but the truth.

Dad slowed the car and pulled off at the first available exit. When the car was in *Park*, he reached over and squeezed my mom's hand.

She cleared her throat. "How do you know about that?"

"Erin's mom dropped me off early, and I overhead Dad losing his mind over the bottle of pills you swallowed. I heard that discussion, and I don't think I'll ever forget it."

"Eve ..." Mom started.

"For the record, I'm not fishing for an apology. My therapist explained something called postpartum depression to me. If you had that, I understand why you didn't want to have another baby. I'm just saying that *if* it was me specifically, I'm sorry. I wish I would have known better. And maybe I wish I would have told you I knew about the pills. Maybe I wouldn't have taken that first drink. As frustrating as some of the things you've done or said to me have been—the rules I disagree with and the lack of power I feel over making decisions for my own body—the mistakes are mine and mine alone. I made poor choices when I knew better. I made the mess that forced you to send me away for a month of rehab. I accept the blame and responsibility, and I hope you can forgive me in time. But I'm not saying all of this for your forgiveness. I'm saying it for my journey that I hope involves wiser decisions."

My dad stared at me without blinking, and my mom slowly turned to face me. They were speechless, and just as well because I needed to get out my apologies, but I wasn't in the mood to discuss anything. And I was done crying.

No more tears.

I'd given all of them to Kyle.

With nothing more than a sincere, whispered thank-you from them, my dad pulled back onto the main road and drove us the rest of the way home. When we arrived, he carried my bag inside, but my mom reached for my hand to keep me on the front porch.

I lifted my shoulders toward my ears because the wind was strong, and the cold nipped at my skin.

"Eve"—she shook her head—"I'm beside myself. I wish I would have known that you knew."

"Knowing wouldn't have changed the fact that you wanted to ..."

Gah!

I didn't want to cry, but it was hard to say the words to her. It made them feel more real.

I cleared my throat and swallowed. "Feeling like you're one bad situation away from ending your life is unbearable." I shook my head.

Mom wiped her eyes.

"It's one thing to feel the privilege of contributing to a person's happiness, but it's torture to feel like my actions could lead to you taking your life. Don't you get that?"

She continued wiping her tears while nodding. "I'm *so* sorry. And I do understand this. Grandma and I talked. I'm okay." She squeezed my hand. "You don't have to walk around on eggshells. I can handle whatever happens. I promise."

I returned a slight nod, and she hugged me.

"Eve, all this time ... I can't believe you've lived with this secret, feeling like it was your fault. I will never be able to make this up to you. I'm so, *so* very sorry, my sweet girl."

I hugged her until I could speak past my emotions. "It's cold. Can we go inside?" I asked.

She laughed. "Of course. Let's make hot chocolate."

AFTER A SHOWER TO wash the rehab clinic from my skin, I dried my hair and joined Mom in the kitchen. "Where's Dad?" I asked.

"He had some things to do at the church." She set a mug of hot chocolate in front of me when I sat at the table. "We're having a family dinner tonight. Gabby knows you're coming home, so she'll be here. And your dad is picking Grandma up on his way home."

I nodded, blowing at the steam as she sat across from me and held her mug cupped in her hands.

"Eve, I need to know if Kyle did anything to you that wasn't consensual."

My gaze snapped up to hers. "What? No!" I shook my head a half dozen times.

She returned a sad smile. "I had to ask."

"I love him. And maybe I'll never get to be with him, but I love him with my whole heart. And that means that through this process, losing him has destroyed my heart. So don't do this. Don't blame him or me for falling in love. It was mutual and *consensual*. Everyone is so focused on the ten years between us, but that's just a stupid number. We fall in love with our hearts, not with our brains. This wasn't me trying to rebel and upset you and Dad. Do you think feeling like we couldn't tell anyone about our relationship was easy or fun?"

"Eve, we only want what's best for you."

"But why do you get to choose? Why do you even get a say in it? I'm going to spend my whole life making mistakes. That's part of being human. Isn't it exhausting to feel responsible for everyone's choices? You have to let me do this. My decisions are mine now. I don't need you to make them for me. I need you to love me. You and Dad have always preached about unconditional love. A Godly kind of love. Let me live. Let me stumble. Let me figure things out as I go. Just *love* me. That's it."

"We do love you."

I shook my head. "Dad kicked Sarah out of the house. That's not love. That's control. You have to love us even when you can't control us, or else it's not unconditional love."

"That wasn't about love, Eve. That was about respect. That was about following rules. Sometimes, there's tough love, and that's how you learn valuable lessons in life. It wasn't easy to leave you at the rehab center, but we did it out of love. Not control. Not anything else. It was tough love. Tough for you and tough for us."

I started to speak but swallowed my words. Instead, I sipped my hot chocolate and let her words replay in my mind. Perhaps she had a point, too.

Chapter Thirty-Eight

Lionel Richie, "Say You, Say Me"

Kyle

"Is she home?" Adam asked as I carried the phone onto the deck to watch the first snow after tucking Josh into bed.

Clifford jumped into one of the rockers.

"I think so, but I don't know for certain." I brushed the light dusting of snow off the chair and sat down.

"She's an adult. Bring her back here with you when you come home."

I chuckled. "Just like that, huh?"

"Yeah, man, just like that."

"She just got out of rehab. I don't want to fuck it up. I don't want to fuck *her* up." I rubbed the back of my neck. "I was an enabler. She's going to need a good support system."

"You and Josh. I'll be here to help too."

"You drink like a fish," I said.

"I don't have to drink around her."

"It would feel selfish, like I'm thinking of myself more than her. I can't love her like that."

"Can you really love her if you're not with her?"

"Yeah, I can let her go. It might be the best way to love her."

"Do you think she'll see it that way?"

I brushed a little snow off my leg. "Not at first, but eventually."

"I bet Josh's mom thought the same thing. She knew you'd eventually be okay and that you'd discover that her leaving you was for the best. Right? How many days have you thought that?"

Zero days. Until I met Eve.

"We're okay," I said.

"What if Melinda showed up on your doorstep tomorrow? Would you take her back?"

"No."

He laughed. "Why?"

"Because ..."

"Because you love Eve? But that makes no sense if you're leaving her. You might as well give Josh one woman who loves him."

"Melinda doesn't love him."

"I bet Eve does."

I didn't reply.

"Kyle, you've said it so many times. That boy thinks Eve hung the moon just for him. Don't lie to him. Let him see that she loves him but also that she needs both of you to take care of her, too."

"I don't know," I said. "Do you give an eighteen-year-old with an alcohol addiction an instant family? Take her away from the only home she's ever known? Hope that she finds a job? Hope that she continues to love me and my son the way I love her? Would I be setting her up to fail? If so, that would feel really fucking unforgivable."

Adam slowly hummed. "When you put it like that, I start to reconsider my recommendation. What happened to us? We used to seize every moment and deal with the consequences after the fallout. Are we ... old?"

I laughed. "Not old. More mature. We, well, *I* have real responsibilities."

"I take offense to that."

"Take all the offense you want. I stand by my comment." I grinned, and it felt good to joke with my friend because the gravity of my emotions surrounding Eve had been suffocating.

After the laughter died, Adam blew out a long breath. "You're going to take a hit on buying a house and turning around and selling it so quickly."

"I might keep it and rent it out for now."

"Then you won't have a down payment for another house unless you drain your savings."

He didn't know my savings was already partially drained from Eve's rehab.

"Josh and I don't need a lot of space. We'll rent something small for a few years. I'll sell my fishing boat and a few other things."

"So that's it, huh?"

"What do you mean?" I asked.

"You sound pretty set on your plans. No Eve? Just you and Josh?"

I stared in the direction of her house, but through the dark mixed with flurries, all I could see was a single light that had to be coming from her bedroom window.

"I thought Melinda and I were on the same page. For nine months, she made me think we were on the verge of living the dream. I was so wrong. So I don't trust my judgment anymore."

"That doesn't mean you should stop taking chances."

"It's not just me," I murmured. "I'm risking Josh's heart too."

Chapter Thirty-Nine

Kenny Loggins, "Meet Me Halfway"

Eve

I RETURNED TO WORK.

Dad told everyone at church that I'd been on a mission trip in Guatemala.

Christmas was just around the corner, but I didn't feel the holiday cheer.

"Tell him you want to move to Colorado with him," Erin said as we watered the poinsettias in the church before Sunday's service.

"I haven't seen or talked to him since Thanksgiving. That was two weeks ago. He hasn't been at church. And I'm scared to go to his house because I don't want to stir up trouble with my parents right before Christmas."

"Since when have you been afraid of stirring up trouble?" Erin smirked. "I feel like you left my best friend at that rehab clinic."

"The day he left the rehab clinic, it felt like a last good-bye. And if he wanted to see me, he would. Right? And honestly, what I did to Josh is unforgivable."

"How can you say that? You said Josh forgave you. And I don't think Kyle will call and risk one of your parents answering the phone. And he's not going to knock on the door and ask if you can come play."

"Stop." I giggled. "You know what I mean."

"You should get Josh a Christmas present, so at least you have an excuse to see him one more time before they leave."

"I already got him a Christmas present, but I was going to have Gabby take it to him. Nothing will ever make up for that burn on his arm and the awful pain he went through."

"Stop." She groaned. "No. *You* have to give it to him. What did you get him? A cat? A hamster?"

I led the way to my dad's office to drop off the watering cans. "Not funny."

"It is and you know it."

I laughed.

"I got him a Matchbox race car track."

"Oh, he'll love that."

"I hope so." I opened my dad's office door, but he was still outside shoveling snow.

Church started in an hour.

"Are you getting something for Kyle?"

I set the watering can by my dad's desk. "Do you think I should?"

"Totally."

"What if he doesn't have something for me, and then I make him feel bad?"

"Well, that's his problem." She smirked. "It doesn't have to be expensive. But do something. Then tell your parents that you're driving to my house to give me a gift, and they won't suspect a thing."

I sat in my dad's desk chair. "They will because we don't buy each other gifts."

"Fine." She frowned. "Then I'll call your house mid-afternoon and tell you about something I got for Christmas, and you'll say you're going to my house to see it."

"You said you're leaving town for Christmas. My parents will know if your family is out of town." I swiveled back and forth in his chair.

"Ugh! Why are you making this so difficult?"

I laughed. "I'm not trying to. I just don't want a Christmas Day fiasco."

"Okay." She clapped her hands together in front of her at her lips. "How about this? You just tell them the truth. You have gifts and want to give them to them. It's not like you're going to have sex on Christmas in the middle of the day with Josh awake. In fact, invite your parents and Gabby to join you."

I wrinkled my nose. "I don't think I need to go that far. But yeah, I could try the truth. That would be a nice change." I bit back my grin, but we started laughing simulta-neously.

I GOT KYLE A GIFT, but I wasn't sure if it was the right gift.

With a week until Christmas, I was dying to see him. I told myself I needed to get used to that feeling because he was moving. Before long, I would sit in my window seat and gaze through my binoculars, but I would no longer have a chance to see him coming or going because he wouldn't be in Devil's Head anymore.

After everyone else went to bed that night, I gazed out the window, hoping to see the exact moment the lights went out at his house. I liked to crawl in bed at the same time and pretend that he was lying beside me, arms wrapped around my waist, face in my hair, lips depositing the occasional kiss.

I waited.

And waited.

But the lights in his main level never turned off. When I lowered the binoculars from my eyes, my gaze dropped to the fence between our house and the orchard.

"Oh my gosh," I whispered.

He was there, resting his back against the rails, boots half-buried in the snow, Carhartt jacket zipped to his chin, and a stocking cap. What was he doing?

I didn't know the answer, but I couldn't wait to find out. So I threw on my jeans and a sweater, then tiptoed downstairs and shoved my feet into my snow boots while putting on my jacket and hat.

I prayed for the door not to squeak too loudly, and God seemed to answer that prayer. It took all the control I could muster not to run to him as I hopped through the snow.

He turned as I approached the fence.

"Are you lost?" I asked, adjusting my hat.

"Something like that." He rubbed his lips together.

I grinned because my heart needed to feel the joy he brought to me just with one look.

"How are you?"

I shrugged. "Still sober."

His smile died. "That's not what I meant, but I suppose that's good too."

"How do you want me to be?" I asked, stuffing my hands into my jacket pockets.

"I want the best for you."

"Is that why you paid for my rehab?"

He narrowed his eyes, and I waited for him to deny it, but he didn't. Instead, he relinquished a tiny nod.

"Thank you."

Again, he paused before nodding again.

"How's your arm?"

"Better. I'm still doing my prescribed exercises."

"That's good. How's Josh's arm?" That was a much harder question to ask, but I couldn't avoid it.

"He's fine. I told you the doctor said his scars could completely fade over time."

I swallowed past the painful lump in my throat because I knew what he said at the rehab center, but I didn't know if it was true or if he said it to make me feel less awful. "Is he excited for Christmas?"

"Of course." Kyle stared at his feet.

"Why are you here at eleven o'clock at night?"

He kicked at the snow, taking his time to answer. "To be near you," he whispered.

"It's cold."

"That's because you're there, and I'm here."

I grinned, high-stepping the last few feet in the snow to reach the fence. "Better?"

He slowly shook his head.

I wormed my way between the wood rails and stood before him. "Better?"

The familiar look in his eyes made me melt, even if he didn't feel the heat yet. He shook his head again.

I grabbed his jacket and lifted to my toes to kiss him, then I whispered, "Better?"

"Not yet." He grinned, resting his hands on my hips while he turned and pressed his back against the fence post. He lowered to his butt, bringing me with him, straddling his legs.

"Your backside will be wet."

"So," he murmured before kissing me.

I unzipped his jacket and then mine, pulling my arms out. He held my jacket to me like a blanket while I hugged him, cocooning myself next to him, sharing body heat and long kisses.

"Baby, you're so beautiful," he whispered in my ear, sliding his hand along my neck beneath my hair.

I closed my eyes, memorizing the feel of his touch, his breath at my ear, and the soothing vibration of his voice.

My fingers curled into his back. "Take me with you," I pleaded.

He teased my earlobe with his teeth, then murmured, "It's not our time."

"Why not?" I turned my head and kissed a trail from his cheek to his lips, and again, we kissed like it could be the last kiss we ever shared.

Then he rested his forehead against mine. "Because I need to get a new job, find a place to live so Josh feels settled again. And you need to find your feet again. You need to stand on your own."

I pressed my palms to his cheeks. "I found my feet, and I'm standing on my own." Desperation wrapped around my words, making a case for my aching heart.

"Maybe," he whispered with tension in his brow as I traced his lower lip with the pad of my thumb. "But I don't know if I've found mine. When I carried you up that hill"—he closed his eyes briefly—"you were just so fucking lifeless, and I lost something in that moment. And I won't give you anything unless I can give you everything. So maybe right now I'm the one who's a little unsteady."

"I made a mistake. How many times do I have to apologize?" I buried my face into his neck and snaked my arms around his body again. "How can you just walk away from me like everything that happened before that night no longer matters?"

He didn't answer, but he held me a little longer before dropping his hands to his sides. "I have to get home," he said.

It was my fault. Despite my desperate pleas, I knew he'd never be able to forgive me. And even though I didn't blame him, it still hurt. I pulled back, searching his eyes, but he wouldn't look at me, so I stood, threading my arms through my jacket. "I know you paid for my therapy so I wouldn't hate you when you left me, but—"

"But you hate me," he said, standing and wiping off his backside. "And I paid for your therapy because I love you."

I looked away to keep from crying. "You're such an asshole," I mumbled. "If this is love, then you're a terrible lover. When you love someone, you stay. You fight for them. You forgive them. You—"

"Eve!" he said, making me jump. "I have a child. And I love you *so* much that I can't fucking stay away from you. But I love him more." He slowly shook his head. "I'm not perfect. I don't know if this is the right decision, but it is an excruciatingly hard one. And I may regret it for the rest of my life. And maybe you'll hate me for the rest of yours. But I ..." He swallowed hard. "I gave you alcohol. And I ignored all the signs because you reminded me of myself. And I reasoned that I didn't have a problem, so you didn't either. I saw what I wanted to see."

I turned my back to him, gazing up at the dark sky. "I'm *so* very sorry. Josh experienced unimaginable pain because of me. Then you saved my life, and it's unfair of me to ask you for more, but I'm doing it anyway. Take me with you." I faced him again. "I'll get a job and pay my part. I'll make all the meals and do laundry. I'll sew Halloween costumes and stay with Josh while you hunt. I'll read George Bernard Shaw and learn about the inversion function of cosine. Just ... take me with you."

A painful laugh bubbled from his chest to accompany his sad smile. "Oh, baby." He framed my face. "I would never forgive myself if I said yes and you, in fact, didn't learn arccosine."

I laughed through the pain. "*Please*, Kyle," I whispered, holding my emotions inside as best as possible.

He kissed me and murmured, "I won't leave without saying goodbye." And then he walked away.

"Don't say goodbye!" I yelled.

He stopped.

"Don't say goodbye. I don't want your goodbye. I want you. And I want Josh. But you don't want me. You have no horse. No armor. No honor. You don't know how to play chess. You don't know how to love me. You stand at this fence because you want to be near me. Well, fuck you. It's not all about you. If you walk away, don't come back. Don't look back. Don't say my name. Don't even think about me. I told you I wouldn't be anyone's regret."

He tucked his hands into his pockets and continued to walk away.

I squeezed through the fence and ran inside. Then I

kicked off my boots while holding my hand cupped over my mouth to muffle my sobs.

Someone touched my shoulder, and I jumped. Gabby had a glass of water in her hand, hair messy, nightshirt hanging off one shoulder. When she saw my tears, she set the glass on the floor and hugged me.

"He-he's l-leaving without m-me ..." I whispered between soft sobs.

She stroked my hair. "I'm sorry, Eve."

Chapter Forty

Billy Ocean, "There'll Be Sad Songs"

Eve

"CHEER UP, MY BEAUTIFUL GIRL," Grandma Bonnie said, wrapping her arm around me as I flipped the gingerbread pancakes on the griddle Christmas morning.

I tried to smile.

"What's keeping you here?" she asked, removing the cranberry muffins from the pans and arranging them into a basket.

My mom and sisters were setting the table, and my dad and Sarah's boyfriend were huddled by the wood-burning stove, drinking coffee.

"He doesn't want me," I said.

"Oh, I don't believe that."

"He said it's not our time. That means he doesn't want me."

"When did he say that?" she asked.

"A couple weeks ago."

"He's scared."

I shrugged. "Well, I want to be with someone who's not afraid, so his loss."

She chuckled. "Indeed."

I didn't mean it. I wanted to be with him whether he wanted me or not. I wanted to be with Josh. I wanted Clifford.

A messy life.

New adventures.

Fights that ended in passionate kisses where he called me out on my stubbornness.

I wanted the teasing and flirting.

Winks and whispered song lyrics.

"Let's eat," Mom said, taking the plate of pancakes as soon as I slid the last few onto it.

Dad said the Christmas morning prayer, thanking God for bringing his family together, for taking care of me in my troubled times, and for His unconditional love. I smiled on cue, barely registering the conversation about Sarah's life or Grandma's griefs with the nursing home.

"Have you talked to Fred?" Gabby asked. And she never asked about Fred, nobody did except Mom.

Dad blotted his mouth with the napkin and cleared his throat. "I talked to him yesterday and wished their family a Merry Christmas."

"They're not visiting Kyle and Josh for Christmas?" Gabby kept quizzing him.

Mom eyed Dad. Sarah eyed me. And I shot my gaze to Grandma who seemed more interested folding her bacon before taking a bite than paying any attention to us.

"No. They're with his parents for Christmas. But everyone will be together for New Year's after they move back to Colorado," Dad said without actually saying Kyle's name. "Sarah, are you still attending the same church in Nashville?" He changed the subject.

Sarah bowed her head and murmured a quick, "Mm-hmm," while cutting her pancake.

She wasn't going to church. I almost felt sorry for my father for believing her. The only prayer Sarah did on Sundays involved screaming God's name with an orgasm.

I wanted to go to that church too.

"Didn't you get Josh a Christmas present?" Gabby asked me.

I was ready to throttle her. We'd been on good terms. She was on my team. What was happening?

I cleared my throat and offered everyone's expectant gazes a stiff smile. "Yeah, I did. I'll probably run it over later." And by run it over, I meant I was going to set it on the porch step and run away so I didn't have to see Kyle.

"I'll take it over. I think one of our pie plates got left there, and I want to get it before they move," Mom said, smiling at Dad.

He studied me as if getting Josh a present was a sin. Maybe Gabby thought she was helping me by easing into the topic of the gifts I planned on taking next door. But there was no easing with my father. I felt his shame in front of everyone on Christmas morning, and it was embarrassing.

I pushed back in my chair and rested my hands on the edge of the table, releasing a slow breath. I didn't want to see Kyle, but I also didn't want anyone telling me that I couldn't see him. "I want a drink right now." I murmured. "Because it's how I dealt with this overwhelming feeling of judgment.

And it's how I escaped emotions that were too much to bear. So, while it might be easy for everyone to ignore that I fell in love with Kyle, it's not easy for me."

My vision blurred behind my tears as I focused on my plate of half-eaten food. "And the only thing worse than feeling like my heart doesn't matter or I'm wrong for feeling the way I do is the soul-crushing reality that he's leaving soon. And I have nothing to ease the pain." I slowly stood.

Sarah reached for my wrist. "Go with him," she said.

"Sarah," Dad warned.

I gave her a sad smile, pulling my hand from her hold to wipe the tears that broke free. "I can't," my voice broke. "He doesn't want me."

Sarah's eyes instantly reddened. We had always shared each other's pain.

I sniffed and looked at my parents. "Happy? He doesn't want me to go with him. Do you feel redemption? Are you dying to say you told me so? Should we go around the table and let everyone share something stupid Eve has done to show how immature and naive I am?"

"Eve," Mom said, pushing back in her chair.

"Don't." I shook my head. "I should have stayed in rehab. Nobody judged me there. They just"—I wiped more tears—"listened. Like God—He just listens. And He lets me live my life, love who I want, and learn lessons in my own way. All the while just ... silently listening." I sniffled and released a tiny laugh. "I see why you like to talk about Him so much. He's pretty awesome. If only all fathers could love like that." I headed toward the stairs, pressing the back of my hand to my nose and holding my breath to keep from letting them hear the sobs that were clawing to escape.

THE TEARS SUBSIDED, and I fell asleep. I woke sandwiched between my sisters, Gabby at my back, and Sarah's big blue eyes staring at me too close for comfort.

"Come to Nashville with us," Sarah said. "The only way not to spend the rest of your life hating our parents is to leave and give everyone room to breathe."

"You can't leave me," Gabby said, hugging my waist.

Sarah smirked at Gabby. "The world feels so small in Devil's Head. Everything is magnified and suffocating. And freedom is magical. It's nature's drug."

"And I'll forget all about him?" I asked.

She frowned. "No. But if you stay here, all you'll do is stare out that window and think of him, even when he's no longer there. And you'll feel guilty for missing him because our parents will never let you feel anything but guilty. They love us. They just have a painful way of showing it."

"It's like I'm not here," Gabby said. "You can't leave me."

"Pfft. You're the baby. Eve and I have paved the way through blood, sweat, and tears. As long as Dad never sees that you've been defacing your Bible, you'll be fine. Stay a virgin until you marry the man of Dad's dreams, and you'll be golden."

"Shut up." Gabby laughed, and so did I.

"Do you have room for me?" I asked.

"Of course. We have a spare bedroom. We'll help you find a job. You're going to love Nashville."

"Mom and Dad won't be happy," Gabby said.

"They're never happy," Sarah said.

"When?" I asked.

"We're going to stay with Isaac's parents over New

Year's, but after that, we can come back here and help you get packed and moved."

I twisted my lips.

"You're supposed to squeal and jump up and down. You're moving out of Devil's Head. Isn't it your dream?"

My dream wasn't a place. It was a person.

Chapter
Forty-One

Orchestral Manoeuvres in the Dark
- Pretty in Pink, "If You Leave"

Kyle

THERE WAS a knock at the door, and Clifford barked as Josh ran to open it.

"It's Eve!"

I felt that familiar pain in my chest—an intense longing for her.

Melinda broke my ability to trust in love. She crippled my intuition.

I was willing to risk my heart, but I wasn't sure I was ready to risk Josh's. One day, he would know that Melinda didn't stay, and what if I took a chance on Eve, and she didn't stay?

"Merry Christmas, my little munchkin."

Just the sound of her voice made everything bleed. I

stayed in the living room, taking a few extra seconds to find a breath and a smile that didn't look as painful as it felt.

"This is my big sister, Sarah," she said as I stood and ran a hand through my hair.

"Where's your dad?" Gabby asked.

"In here." Josh ran into the living room.

"Clifford, you've already gotten bigger on me." Eve's voice got closer.

My heart pounded a little harder.

"Hey, Mr. Collins." Gabby smiled.

I grinned. "You can call me Kyle. I'm not teaching math today."

"This is our sister, Sarah," she said.

"Nice to meet you." I offered my hand to the blonde with big blue eyes and a kind smile.

"You too."

Eve and Clifford came around the corner, and my heart forgot for a few seconds that we were leaving, and Eve wouldn't be in our lives anymore. All my heart knew was Eve made it beat stronger, and the room always got a little brighter with her in it.

She smiled, curling her hair behind one ear. "Merry Christmas."

I tucked my hands in my back pockets to keep them from reaching for her as they liked to do on instinct. "Merry Christmas."

"Dad, look!" Josh yelled, ripping open his present from Eve. "It's a race track." He climbed to his feet and hugged Eve. "Thank you."

"You're welcome." Eve kissed his head.

"Uh, have a seat." I nodded to the sofa. "Can I offer anyone something to eat or drink?"

"We're good," Gabby said. "Eve and Grandma made a huge breakfast."

"Of course they did." I chuckled.

Eve glanced up from the edge of the sofa where she sat to pet Clifford. Her cheeks turned pink when she smiled.

"We're going to Colorado." Josh beamed.

"I heard," Eve said to him.

"You want to come too? *Please* come too!"

I. Fucking. Died.

She exchanged a look with her sisters before returning her attention to Josh. "I can't. I'm moving to Nashville with my sister Sarah. She plays music, and there's really fun stuff to do there. But thanks for inviting me."

Eve didn't look at me because I was the asshole who didn't ask her to come with us. But she was moving to Nashville. So maybe I wasn't an asshole after all.

You are.

Josh frowned. "Don't go. I'm going to miss you."

The knife dug a little deeper into my chest.

Eve pressed her hands to his cheeks. "I'm going to ..." She swallowed hard and cleared her throat. "I'm going to miss you too."

"Are you sure I can't get you something to drink?" I looked at Gabby and Sarah, feeling desperate for any reason to leave the room.

"We're fine. Thank you," Sarah smiled.

"This is for you." Eve leaned forward and handed me a small present.

"You shouldn't have gotten me anything."

"Open it, Dad."

I untied the gold ribbon and unwrapped the green and red striped paper. It was a recipe box.

"They're all of Josh's favorite recipes," Eve said as I opened it. "Hope you live near an apple orchard at your new home."

I slowly nodded, giving my emotions a chance to settle so I could speak past the lump in my throat. "Thank you," I managed.

"Well, we said this was going to be a quick trip," Sarah said, standing from the sofa.

Gabby jumped up. "Yup. That's right. Come on, Eve."

Eve ignored them, staring at me with an unreadable expression.

"Josh, Sarah and I will help you carry your race track to your room before we go," Gabby said, picking up the pieces he'd taken out of the box.

They headed up the stairs, and Eve dropped her gaze to the floor and stood, adjusting her sweater. Without a word, she turned, taking steps toward the door.

"Eve, wait. Give me a minute."

She stopped, but she didn't turn. "I can't wait. I have nothing to wait for. And I can't give you a minute because I've already given you everything. Months. Days. And so many minutes. I've given you every part of me, even the ugly parts. And I've given you my heart. Yet you don't want it. But someone will."

"Eve," I said with a thick voice, the pain in my chest intensifying as if she had a fishing hook lodged into it, and the tension compounded as she walked away.

Stretching.

Tearing.

I couldn't breathe.

The door clicked shut behind her. She left without her sisters.

I pinched the bridge of my nose as my eyes burned, heart racing. I felt like I was dying. My world was unraveling. And I was pretty sure I was having a heart attack. I hurried to the door and shoved my feet into my boots before jogging after her. The cold air filled my lungs as I ran down the stairs.

Eve's hair flowed behind her as she trudged through the snow toward the hill.

"You can't go to Nashville," I yelled, catching up to her. My fingers slipped beneath her jacket and slid into the waist of her jeans.

She stopped, and I let go of her, but she didn't face me.

"You can't go to Nashville," I repeated softer.

She sniffled. "Why not?"

"Because it's not on the way to Colorado. And *we're* going to Colorado. If I have to pick you up in Nashville, it will throw off our whole trip. Josh will get unruly, asking when we're going to be there. I'll have to buy twice the amount of snacks. It's just not going to work. I'm sorry."

She didn't speak or move. And as much as I wanted her to look at me, I knew I needed to earn everything.

"It doesn't make sense for my heart to live in Nashville and yours to live in Colorado. They should just ... live together." I stepped in front of her.

She made no attempt to wipe her eyes or hide her tears.

"I'm scared that this won't work, but I'm terrified that it will work and I'm too damn stupid to take a chance on us. But I think"—I framed her face in my hands, and she blinked more tears—"if I'm doing the math correctly, and I let my heart love you as much as it's *dying* to love you, then you'll never want for more than me, my messy son, and that needy dog."

Her hands covered mine and she closed her eyes. I

leaned down to kiss her, stopping a breath from her lips. She opened her eyes, and I smiled.

But before I could kiss her, she said, "I'll think about it."

If I wasn't already frozen from the wind and flurries, her comment did it. Just as my heart began to sink into the bottom of my stomach, her lips twitched, and she rolled them between her teeth.

Was she hiding a grin?

I narrowed my eyes. "Are you—"

"Just kiss me like you do, so I can go home and pout before packing my things for Colorado."

"Evil," I whispered before kissing her.

I heard the door close in the distance, and I knew her sisters were watching us. It didn't matter. I still kissed her hard because I never wanted to hide my feelings for her again.

When I released her, I managed a straight face. "Go pack your bags and be pissed off that you fell in love with a nerd who had to do the math before he discovered that you in his life added up to infinity."

A triumphant smile hijacked her face. "You're so square, Mr. Collins."

"More like a cube, an ice cube." I turned and took several steps toward my house before glancing over my shoulder. "I love you, lady in red." I winked and continued to the porch just as Gabby and Sarah descended the stairs and Josh peeked through the partially ajar door.

"Ladies," I gave them a smile and polite nod as I passed them. "Merry Christmas."

Josh stepped back as I stomped my boots on the mat and stepped inside.

Behind me, I heard high-pitched squeals, and it made me smile.

"MERRY CHRISTMAS," my brother said after Josh answered the phone and talked his ear off for over ten minutes before handing it to me.

"Merry Christmas," I replied.

"Merry Christmas," my parents and Anne yelled in the background.

I sat in my recliner and chuckled.

"Are you packed?" he asked.

"Pretty much. We'll finish up a few things tomorrow and pick Adam up from the airport. Then we'll head out the following day."

"Have you made amends with Peter?"

I scratched my chin. "Define amends."

"Kyle, he's my best friend. I can't have my brother and my best friend at odds. It's going to take him a while to feel friendly toward you again, and that's understandable. But you need to extend a sincere apology."

"For falling in love with his daughter or for taking her to Colorado with me? Maybe both?"

Silence filled the line between us.

"I love her, Fred. So does Josh. And her age isn't enough of a reason not to be with her. So if I can push past all the crap I've been carrying around over Melinda abandoning us, then you and Peter and everyone else should be able to show a little support."

"Kyle, she's not just eighteen. She's a recovering alcoholic. What are you going to do when she falls off the wagon and steals a few cans of beer from your fridge while she's alone with Josh?"

"I'm not going to have beer in my fridge."

He laughed. "So you're done drinking?"

"Yes," I said without hesitation.

"What happens if she gets it someplace else?"

I sighed. "What happens if she gets desperate and drinks half a bottle of mouthwash or a whole bottle of vanilla extract? What happens if I fall out of another tree and break my back? What happens if Josh gets bit by a snake? We can what-if forever. And I won't have the answers for everything. But it doesn't mean I won't figure it out. I *love* her. And I will do whatever it takes to give her the best chance at maintaining sobriety. And *if* she falls off the wagon, I will pick her up and be the first to get her the help she needs. As soon as we get to Colorado, I'll find a place for her to attend meetings. We'll go to church every Sunday. What more can I possibly say or do?"

"You can let her go."

I shook my head. "No. I can't. I tried that, and it didn't work."

"Have you talked to Peter?"

"Not recently."

"Well, you need his permission before you run off with his daughter."

I rubbed the tension from the back of my neck. "I will ask for his *blessing*, but we'll live without it if he doesn't give it to us."

"Kyle—"

"Fred, I'm not asking for a dowry. This isn't an exchange of goods. Eve is an adult. And as sure as her father can refuse to give us his blessing, she can walk out that door without it and live her own life."

"Just steal the girl!" Anne yelled in the background.

"What is wrong with you," Fred said to her.

"They're in love, honey. Let them be," she said.

He grumbled.

"This is your fault. You told us to move here," I said.

"That is bullshit."

"Fred!" Anne scolded.

My brother cleared his throat. "That's nonsense."

I chuckled. "You're right. It's nobody's fault. Our love is not a fault at all. It's beautiful. She's beautiful and kind. Funny and irresistible. And I plan to spend the rest of my life loving her. So either you can get onboard or get out of the way."

Again, he grumbled.

"I love you too," I said. "See you soon."

Chapter Forty-Two

Loverboy, "Heaven in Your Eyes"

Eve

I STARED out my bedroom window a little before midnight. Lights were still on in the main level of Kyle's house. My family was asleep after hours of arguing over my decision. But my parents were outnumbered, so they eventually went to bed. I knew they'd pick things up in the morning after Sarah and Isaac left and Gabby headed to a friend's house. Grandma wouldn't be there. It would be two against one.

"Screw it," I mumbled to myself, jumping out of my window seat and throwing on my clothes.

I hopped through the snow, riding a wave of adrenaline, and tapped on Kyle's back door.

The lock clicked and he opened it, standing before me in jeans and a hoodie. "It's past your curfew." He stepped aside.

I toed off my boots and unzipped my coat. "After exhausting fights with my parents, I used to drink. But I don't drink anymore, so I need something to replace that bad habit. Something to help me relax. Got any ideas?"

Lines of concern spread across his forehead.

"Did you miss the part where I said I'm not going to drink?" I rubbed my finger along his worry creases, trying to erase them.

"What did you have in mind?" he asked, relaxing a bit.

I grinned, ghosting my fingers from his forehead down his nose and across his lips. "I'm sure it's just me because I've never lived on my own or with anyone except my parents, but I was wondering ..."

"What were you wondering?" He nipped at my fingers.

"I was wondering what it will be like when we're living together and we can have sex before Josh wakes up in the morning. And when he's at school, on days you're not substitute teaching, we can have sex. Like so much sex in every room. And after Josh is in bed at night, we can shower together. Sex against the bathroom vanity while looking at each other in the mirror. Sex in your truck when you take me fishing."

He smirked. "You're such a perv. You need to lay off the George Michael songs."

I started to speak, but he kissed me instead, snaking his good arm around me to hoist me up. I wrapped my legs around his waist, and he carried me upstairs.

As soon as his bedroom door was locked, we discarded our shirts. My bra landed on the floor a second before my back hit the bed. He unbuttoned my jeans while sucking my nipple into his mouth.

"Yesss ..." I arched my back and grabbed a fistful of his hair. His urgency fed my greed as he peeled off my jeans and underwear.

We skipped the slow seduction, and he had his jeans off and a condom on in the next breath. He entered me slowly at first but quickly moved into hard thrusts. It had been too long, and *need* became the theme that night.

He kissed me to muffle my moans and his own as I curled my fingers into his backside, gripping him harder while he drove into me faster. The best sensation unfurled in endless waves. Kyle hiked my leg closer to my chest and pistoned his hips faster until he came hard with an agonizing expression that settled into a huge grin when he opened his eyes and collapsed onto me.

I didn't want him to pull out or move or speak. Despite the suffocating feeling of his body draped over mine, I felt wholly loved and wanted.

Desired and accepted.

I felt like a woman and a lover.

He rolled to the side, taking me with him. His gaze swept along my face. "Let's take a shower," he said with a grin.

"I should get home," I murmured.

He slid his hand along my hip, up my side to my breast, thumb circling my nipple. "Baby," he leaned into me, brushing his lips over mine, "you've arrived. I'm your new home."

I closed my eyes as he peppered my face with light kisses. "Kyle, I love you," I whispered. "And I know you only came after me because some of Josh's favorite recipes are too complex for you to figure out."

"Shh ... let's not dwell on the reasons," he said.

I giggled.

THE FOLLOWING MORNING, I sat in the middle of Kyle's bed as he dressed.

"I'm scared," I said. "My dad is going to be so mad."

He threaded his arms into his long-sleeved T-shirt. "Josh will be with us. And I'll suggest we pray together before discussing anything."

"That's really smart."

"Thanks." He sat on the end of the bed and pulled on his socks. "I knew you'd eventually come around and acknowledge my superior intelligence."

I lifted onto my knees and pressed my chest to his back, arms around his neck. "You were going to let me go. That makes you stupid. I'm quite the catch."

"And humble. Don't forget how humble you are."

I laughed and he leaned back, forcing me onto my butt with his head on my leg. My fingers played in his hair.

"I can't make this right, Eve," he sighed.

"Make what right?"

"Us. There is nothing I can say to your father that will make him feel okay about us."

"That's because he's stubborn."

"No. He's your father. He's a man of God. And he's not entirely wrong to feel the way he does."

My fingers stilled, my whole body stiffened.

"Look at me, Eve." Kyle gazed up at me.

I clenched my teeth while looking at him.

"Think about it. Say it in your head. Imagine it's not us."

"Say what?" I questioned.

"You are eighteen. I am twenty-eight. That's ten years. When Josh was born, you were thirteen."

"What are you saying?" My voice felt tight, each word fighting for composure like the rest of me.

371

He sat up, rubbing his palms over his face. "I'm saying that what we have at our current ages is an outlier to social norms."

"I don't care about social norms. But clearly you do. And if our age is always going to be—"

"Eve!" He stood, stabbing his fingers into his hair and pacing the room a few times. "Take a step back. Can you do that?" He stopped, resting his hands on his hips. "If any other eighteen-year-old girl in this town were involved with a twenty-eight-year-old man, you and all of your friends would be talking about it because it's not normal. And I'm okay with us not fitting into the norm. It doesn't change how I feel about you. My ego screams 'fuck them' when I think about other people judging us. And that's why I ran after you yesterday. I don't care if anyone understands us. But it doesn't mean that I don't get it. I can take a step back and see it from their point of view. And that's called empathy. I think you—we—need to be empathetic to our families. Even if they don't understand us, we can give them space to change their minds over time as they see us thriving together."

I slowly nodded. "We can prove them wrong."

He shook his head. "Maybe take a bigger step back. It's not about proving anyone wrong. It's about giving them time to see us as two people in love. And eventually they won't see a ten-year age difference. They'll just see love."

Again, I nodded. "And then I can say I told you so."

Kyle laughed and I smirked.

"Yes, baby." He kneeled in front of the bed and pulled my legs, bringing me to the edge. "Then you can gloat." He wrapped his arms around me, resting his forehead on my chest.

Chapter Forty-Three

Percy Sledge, "When a Man Loves a Woman"

Kyle

I LEFT Eve with Josh while I trekked through the snow to ask Peter's permission to take his daughter to Colorado. I knew the answer, but I did it anyway.

"No." He shook his head as we talked in the living room.

Janet handed me a cup of coffee before sitting next to her husband. She offered me a sad smile as well.

"Well," I shrugged and took a sip of the coffee, "we're still leaving tomorrow."

"Then why on earth are you asking me if you don't care about my answer?" Peter asked.

"Because it's the right thing to do."

He scoffed. "The right thing to do is leave my daughter alone."

I nodded slowly. "I understand why you feel that way."

"You don't," he argued.

"I do. I see it from your side, but you can't see it from mine. And that's okay. But if you could step into my shoes, all you'd see and feel is love. I love Eve beyond words. Every day I will love her, protect her, and move heaven and earth to give her a beautiful life. When she stumbles, I will catch her. If she can't walk, I will carry her. I'm fully invested in her happiness. My son lights up like the sun when he sees her, and I can't put into words how that makes me feel."

I set my mug on the coffee table and folded my hands in front of me. "I don't see the young woman who hid alcohol by the creek or backed into a utility post or missed curfew. I don't see her job as a sign that she's lost without a dream. I see the person who dealt with a child vomiting on her and wetting his pants. I only see her patience and kindness. The meals she made for us, the laundry she folded. The costume she sewed. The times she gave up going out with friends to watch a five-year-old on a Friday night.

"Don't be angry that I love her. You should be shocked if I didn't fall deeply in love with her because she's amazing. You raised a wonderful, loving, compassionate woman. And I just want to spend the rest of my life proving to her and everyone else that I'm worthy of her heart."

Janet pressed a tissue to her cheek to dry her tears, and then she squeezed Peter's hand.

I gave it my all. And I knew from the look on his face that it wasn't enough, and that was okay. Had I been in his shoes, I wouldn't have given a twenty-eight-year-old single dad my blessing to take off with my eighteen-year-old daughter.

The front door creaked open, and a few seconds later, Eve and Josh poked their heads into the living room.

"Eve said I can help her pack," Josh said with excitement. "She's coming to Colorado with us." He beamed.

Peter bowed his head, rubbing the back of his neck while Janet smiled at Josh and stood, wiping a few more tears.

"I'll help too," she said, taking his hand and leading him up the stairs.

I grabbed my coffee and headed toward the kitchen, stopping to kiss Eve on the cheek as she stood at the threshold, staring at her father. As I stepped past her, she moved closer to him. I stopped just around the corner to listen.

"I love you," she said softly to him. "I'm going to make you proud, but not because I have to, just because I want to."

"Eve," he said her name, and his voice cracked with emotion.

She sniffled, and I continued to the kitchen.

It wasn't going to be easy, but it would be worth it.

Epilogue

Faith Hill & Tim McGraw, "It's Your Love"

10 years later ...
Eve

Colorado.

Alabama.

Washington.

"We're done moving," I said. "So you can take those flowers and shove them up your—"

"Tell Mommy to watch her mouth," Kyle said to our four-year-old twin girls, Bonnie and Louise, as he split the bouquet in half.

They walked behind the counter to give me the flowers in exchange for caramel apple cookies. I put the flowers in water while the girls sat at a café table by the window. My bakery opened in fifteen minutes.

"I got the call," Kyle said, wrapping his arms around me.

I refused to look at him. "The call" was code for *pack everything up, he got a new job, and it was time to move.*

"I'm not going. I *finally* opened my bakery. Josh graduates in three years. The girls love it here. Clifford has room to roam. My orchard is thriving. So no." I shook my head and refused to look at him even though his face was inches from mine. "It's my turn."

"You're sexy when you're mad," he said on a chuckle.

"I'm not mad. I'm matter-of-fact. And don't think of it as sexy because I'm not having sex with you ever again if we're moving. In fact, I'm not moving. I'll keep the kids and the dog, and you can leave. You're getting kind of old anyway. It might be time to trade you in for a younger model."

"Baby," he lowered his voice, brushing his lips along my ear, "I don't know where to start. First, we've already had sex twice today, and it's not even nine a.m. So your sex threats don't hold up."

I glanced over at the girls to see if they were listening to us.

"Second," he continued, "no other man could handle you. They'd try to tame you, and that would be a crime."

I frowned at his nonsense. "Whatever call you got, call them back and tell them no."

"I can't. I already said yes."

"Kyle," my voice cracked as I felt my dreams slipping away. I had only had my bakery for nine months.

We always moved for his job, chased his dreams. But he promised when we bought land with an apple orchard outside of Seattle, it would be the last time. He said he'd be content with coaching high school football and teaching math while supporting *my* dreams.

We'd painted rooms.

Made friends.

Found a church the girls liked.

He even built the girls and me a hut.

"I know," he kissed my forehead. "I could cry too."

I wasn't going to cry, but I was close.

"Because I never thought the Huskies would offer me the offensive coordinator position, but they did."

I blinked back my tears and reared my head to look at him. He grinned.

"What?"

He nodded.

"Oh my gosh! You got a job with the University of Washington?"

He nodded.

"In Seattle?"

Another nod.

"We're not moving?"

He shook his head.

I threw my arms around his neck and kissed him. It felt like we'd won the lottery.

He dragged his lips from my mouth to my ear. "And I only said yes because it didn't require us to move."

I released him and eyed him with distrust. "You mean to tell me that if the University of Iowa would have offered you the same position, you would have turned them down?"

"Correct."

"Liar."

He laughed. "I'm not lying. I told you years ago that when you were ready to spread those beautiful wings of yours, I would move heaven and earth to let you fly."

"You said that in the throes of passion."

"Baby, whenever we're in the same room, I'm in the

throes of passion. I said it because I meant it. I'm only happy when you're happy. Again, have you forgotten about this morning?"

I rolled my eyes.

"I have always said the world would be a better place if it were filled with more people like my wife. And *you* know that you'd never let me go because as much as you love this bakery and your orchard, you believe a job is an afterthought. When people think of you, you want them to say, 'Eve Collins loves to fish, stargaze, skip rocks along the water, pick apples and bake pies, dance to good music, go to the movies with friends, and make love in fields of wildflowers with her sexy husband who has a little gray in his beard.'"

I grinned because Kyle listened. He heard every word I said as a young woman ten years ago. And I grinned because he was right. It wasn't about selling cookies and pies, making money, or proving to anyone that I was a success. But it felt damn good that he knew that and still respected my desire to do it anyway.

"Thank you," I said with a face-splitting grin.

"For this morning?" He was a relentless flirt.

"I'm pretty sure it is you who should be thanking me for this morning, but I meant thank you for not leaving me behind ten years ago when I was newly sober, stupid as the day was long, and so stubborn because—"

"Because you were hot for teacher."

"Stop." I giggled, giving him a playful shove. "You're letting me spread my wings because you know the chances of finding someone who thinks you're irresistible *despite* your weird love for arithmetic is slim to none."

"Slim to none is not a real statistic, baby."

I shook my head, brushing past him. "You make my job

so easy by always proving my point." I retrieved my spatula and transferred the last batch of cookies from the baking sheet to the display tray.

When Kyle didn't say any more, I glanced over at him, and he had that smile, the one he always gave me before he kissed me.

"What?" I asked, blushing because he still had that effect on me.

"I love that you'll never stop taking my breath away. And when I'm old and on my deathbed, I'm going to give you this smile with my last breath, and doing so will be the greatest honor of my life."

The End

Also By
Jewel E. Ann

Sunday Morning Series

Sunday Morning

The Apple Tree

A Good Book

Wildfire Series

From Air

From Nowhere

The Fisherman Series

The Naked Fisherman

The Lost Fisherman

Jack & Jill Series

End of Day

Middle of Knight

Dawn of Forever

One (*standalone*)

Out of Love (*standalone*)

Because of Her (*standalone*)

Holding You Series

Holding You

Releasing Me

About The Author

Jewel E. Ann is a *Wall Street Journal* and *USA Today* bestselling author. She's written over thirty novels, including LOOK THE PART, a contemporary romance, the JACK & JILL TRILOGY, a romantic suspense series; and BEFORE US, an emotional women's fiction story. With 10 years of flossing lectures under her belt, she took early retirement from her dental hygiene career to write mind-bending love stories. She's living her best life in Iowa with her husband, three boys, and a Goldendoodle.

Receive special offers and stay informed of new releases, sales, and exclusive stories:
www.jeweleann.com

www.ingramcontent.com/pod-product-compliance
Ingram Content Group UK Ltd.
Pitfield, Milton Keynes, MK11 3LW, UK
UKHW040641270125
4300UKWH00004B/24